MW00470942

ARBITRATE OR DIE

ARBITRATE OR DIE

EXCEPTIONAL S. BEAUFONT™ BOOK 2

SARAH NOFFKE

MICHAEL ANDERLE

DISRUPTIVE IMAGINATION®

This book is a work of fiction. All of the characters, organizations, and events portrayed in this novel are either products of the author's imagination or are used fictitiously. Sometimes both.

Copyright © 2019 Sarah Noffke & Michael Anderle
Cover by Mihaela Voicu http://www.mihaelavoicu.com/
Cover copyright © LMBPN Publishing
A Michael Anderle Production

LMBPN Publishing supports the right to free expression and the value of copyright. The purpose of copyright is to encourage writers and artists to produce the creative works that enrich our culture.

The distribution of this book without permission is a theft of the author's intellectual property. If you would like permission to use material from the book (other than for review purposes), please contact support@lmbpn.com. Thank you for your support of the author's rights.

LMBPN Publishing
PMB 196, 2540 South Maryland Pkwy
Las Vegas, NV 89109

First US Edition, December 2019
Version 1.02, December 2019
eBook ISBN: 978-1-64202-626-9
Print ISBN: 978-1-64202-627-6

THE ARBITRATE OR DIE TEAM

Thanks to the Beta Team

Mary Morris, Nicole Emens, John Ashmore, Kelly O'Donnell, Larry Omans

Thanks to the JIT Readers

Angel LaVey
Dave Hicks
Deb Mader
Debi Sateren
Diane L. Smith
Dorothy Lloyd
Jackey Hankard-Brodie
Jeff Eaton
Jeff Goode
Kathleen Fettig
Larry Omans
Lori Hendricks
Micky Cocker
Misty Roa
Paul Westman
Peter Manis

If we've missed anyone, please let us know!

Editor
The Skyhunter Editing Team

Once again and a thousand times more, for Lydia.

— Sarah

*To Family, Friends and
Those Who Love
to Read.
May We All Enjoy Grace
to Live the Life We Are
Called.*

— Michael

CHAPTER ONE

Roughly four hundred years ago.

The blue sky was dotted with soaring dragons shooting fire at one another. The grass was covered with blood from riders and dragons. The air in Scotland was filled with vengeance as the war between the Dragon Elite and the Rogue Riders finally came to a head.

Hiker Wallace wasn't happy his men were about to take the advantage, winning the battle. He never wanted it to come to this, but Thad Reinhart had left him no choice.

"There are only two dragons left," Adam Rivalry said, landing on Kay-Rye beside Hiker on his own dragon, Bell. They stood on a bluff, overlooking the battlefield now littered with dead bodies.

"Leave Ember and Thad alive," Hiker ordered.

"But sir," Adam argued, his long white beard blowing over his shoulder from the wind. "Thad started this. You know as well as I do that he will never stop."

Hiker sighed as he watched two dragons collide in the air, wings tangling, teeth snapping at each other. Their riders fought from the dragon's backs, clanging swords.

The warrior for the Dragon Elite overpowered the other, knocking the Rogue Rider off his dragon, where he fell a lethal distance to the ground below, dying on impact. The dragon, severely injured, dove for his rider, speeding away from the dragon he'd been fighting.

The dragon had little time left, not just because his rider was dead, but because one of his wings was broken and his lung punctured. It wouldn't be long before he died, lying on the battlefield next to his rider.

"We have to give Thad a chance to surrender," Hiker said, running his blood-flecked hand over his short blond hair. For only being one-hundred years old, he'd seen his fair share of battles and death, but this was by far the worst.

Killing their own had never been what he wanted, but the Rogue Riders had broken the rules of adjudication, using their powers for their own gain instead of resolving conflict. People worldwide had grown fearful of dragons and riders, having witnessed them attack villages, pillage, and slaughter innocent mortals.

If left unchecked, the Rogue Riders would ruin everything that the Dragon Elite had worked for. They had to be stopped.

"It looks like you'll get your wish," Adam said, pointing to the orange dragon who soared overhead, Thad Reinhart upon her.

Ember was headed in their direction, completely unscathed from battle. Thad wore a full helmet that covered his face, but Hiker could sense his fury. He had lost, and there was nothing left to do but to surrender.

Hiker's men flew behind Thad, forming a barrier, should he think of escaping.

Ember landed on the edge of the bluff, her red eyes like hot coals in a fire, her long wings still spread.

Hiker's men crowded in behind him and Adam, providing protection should the last Rogue Rider try and fight.

It won't come to that, Hiker said to Bell, his dragon, in his head. *He won't fight.*

You want to believe that he's learned his lesson, she replied. *But rehabilitation isn't always an option for some.*

He made a mistake, Hiker said adamantly. *The power went to his head. Now he will see...now that he's lost almost everything.*

I don't know. You might consider listening to Adam on this, Bell stated.

He's not purely bad, Hiker argued.

He may not change, Bell warned. *The power might have gone to his head, or it might be who he is.*

Everyone can change, Hiker stated with conviction.

Not those that are born bad, Bell replied. *You know what I mean.*

I know what you think, he told her. *And on this, we disagree.*

Thad pulled off his helmet, his scarred face grimacing across the short distance at Hiker.

It had been a long time since he laid his eyes on the man before him. Much had changed about Thad Reinhart's appearance. He had always looked rough, but now he appeared soulless.

Hiker slid off of Bell, just as Thad did the same from Ember and strode over to him, his armor clanging as he walked.

"I bet you're happy now," Thad said, his eyes sliding to the dead bodies littering the moor behind Hiker.

"Not in the least," Hiker stated. "You know I never wanted it to come to this. You're the one who abused your power as a rider. We are meant to protect. To resolve. To keep the peace. And you've been doing the opposite."

"We are the most powerful magical creatures on this planet, and you want us to bow to mortals!" Thad yelled, his face blossoming to a bright shade of red.

"We serve the mortals," Hiker replied, keeping his temper under wraps. "That's how Mother Nature deemed it."

"She's wrong," Thad spat. "That old bat has been losing it for years, and you follow her blindly. I give her a century, maybe two before she's mad and throws this planet to shit. And you'll have gone with it unless you wise up."

"There's nothing to wise up to, Thad," Hiker reasoned. "We don't kill the innocent. We don't take what isn't ours. We serve. That's what the Dragon Elite are for."

Thad laughed. "That's just a daft organization you made up. We are dragonriders. We own the skies. We are in control of the most powerful beasts. We do as we damn well please. It's time you recognized that."

Hiker threw his arm to the battlefield behind him. "Your men are dead, defending you and your mission. What do I need to recognize? Your ways are wrong. They are polluting this Earth. They will get you killed. And you're ruining our name. People need to trust the dragonriders, but they can't as long as they fear us. Stop this nonsense, and I can allow you to live."

Thad looked at him with pure vengeance. "You're going to kill me?"

Hiker coughed out a long breath. "I'll do what it takes to keep the peace. There are some things I'm more bonded to than anything else, and that's one of them. Peace. It's what I was born to protect."

"You've got it all wrong," Thad spat.

"I don't," Hiker argued.

"So, you refuse to take the power that's rightfully ours?" Thad asked, his hands twitching at his side.

"I will always refuse anything that compromises Mother Nature's ultimate purpose," Hiker responded.

Thad shook his head. "She corrupted you long ago."

Hiker gritted his teeth together. "She's the very reason we are here."

"And sometimes you have to leave the shade of the family tree," Thad argued. "You should know that better than anyone."

"I do," Hiker stated. "But I'm not leaving her tree."

"Well," Thad said, and began backing for his dragon, "then we split ways here."

"No," Hiker stated. "You have to face the punishment for your crimes."

Thad held up his hands. "I believe I have. You've taken all my men."

"You made them fight us," Hiker spat.

"And we lost," Thad countered. "Now, I leave you."

"No," Hiker stated. "You have to face your crimes. You've killed. You've maimed. And none of it was necessary. I can't allow you to go without punishment."

Thad shot him a rebellious look. "Then you'll have to stop me, and we both know you won't do that."

Hiker froze. He didn't know how to respond.

The disobedient rider gave Hiker a challenging look. "That's what I thought," Thad added when Hiker didn't move.

Again, Hiker just stayed frozen.

"I guess I'll just be on my way," Thad said, turning for his dragon.

"He won't stop you," Adam yelled. "But I will." The dragonrider shot a powerful spell that was meant to incapacitate both rider and dragon, but it only hit the dragon, stopping Ember's heart and knocking her back several yards, where she free-fell over the side of the bluff, landing on the sharp rocks below.

It all happened so fast. Thad turned one way and then the other, confusion blanketing his face. Bewildered and then frantic, he ran to the edge of the bluff and looked down to where the earth met his dragon. It was hard to tell them apart, but it was certain that the dragon was dead.

"You!" Thad accused, turning and pointing his finger at Hiker.

"It was me," Adam argued. "You weren't going to change. You'll bring a curse upon us. Come after me, if you want to punish someone."

Hiker tried to quiet his friend, but it was useless.

"I'll take care of you, Adam, in time," Thad stated, fury in his red eyes. "But first, I'm going to make Hiker pay. If it's the last thing I do, I will ensure that the person who challenged me and killed my dragon dies painfully, while watching their precious Earth burn."

And before Hiker could respond, Thad rushed off, climbing down for his dragon far below, although it was useless to try and save her.

Hiker shook his head and turned to his men, knowing they deserved his praise for their efforts.

However, a new war had just started. Although Thad was alone, he was resourceful and wouldn't let this death go lightly. He would be more destructive than before.

He would be a true monster after Ember's death.

CHAPTER TWO

With a violent jerk, Hiker shot up in his bed, chest heaving as he tried to catch his breath. Sweat soaked the bed and he had the smell of fire and blood stuck in his nose. Like always before, the recurring dream felt so weird.

"It wasn't real," he said, looking around his dark room. The sun hadn't yet risen in the Gullington, but there would be no more sleep for Hiker Wallace.

The dream wasn't real, but the memory was. And for four-hundred years it had haunted him every day of his life.

Adam had continuously told him—when he was alive—that it wasn't his fault, what happened to Ember. His best friend had taken the blame, but Hiker knew better. Adam had done what he had to in order to protect. Thad had been out of control. He would have gone on to continue his rebellious wrath, unwilling to accept punishment for his crimes. Adam had only been trying to stop him.

Yes, Adam's spell had been miscalculated, killing Ember instead of incapacitating her and Thad. But it should have been Hiker who stopped the leader of the Rogue Riders, and he and Adam both knew it.

Hiker swung his legs over the side of his bed, enjoying the cold wood floors on his feet. It grounded him in the Castle when he still felt like he was in the dream on the moor, the recent battle thick in the air.

Shaking his head, he headed for the basin he kept on the side table. The Castle had had plumbing for a couple of centuries, but there were some things that Hiker couldn't get used to.

That was why he was skeptical that he'd ever get used to the Kindle where all his books were housed currently. Well, most of his books. He hadn't been able to find the *Complete History of Dragon Riders* on the device, but then, he didn't really know how to use it. Asking Sophia for help wasn't really an option. It was best if no one found that book and learned the secrets he'd worked hard to keep, especially now. But if he could find the book, then he thought that he might be able to discover solutions to other problems that didn't involve Thad Reinhart.

Pouring tepid water into the basin, Hiker shook his head.

Thad Reinhart was back. It was hard to believe.

Hiker was certain that he'd killed the man when his riders destroyed Thad's castle. But if Mama Jamba said that Thad was back, then he absolutely was.

Destroying Thad, after killing his dragon, hadn't been what Hiker wanted. Again, he'd hoped that the rider would reform. Killing the Rogue Riders was one thing, but destroying an ancient dragonrider when eggs were dwindling had never been one of Hiker's hopes. As an adjudicator, he wanted to preserve.

Ember's death made Thad more dangerous than ever. Before, the leader of the Rogue Riders had abused his powers, pillaging, and taking advantage of mortals. After Ember's death, Thad had had a personal vendetta toward the Dragon Elite.

Hiker had been naïve to think that Thad wouldn't be as powerful without his dragon since it was unlikely that he'd live long after his dragon's death. He was wrong. Thad didn't have anything left to lose, and those with nothing to lose were the most dangerous. He knew that now.

Pulling together all his resources, the leader of the Rogue Riders had recruited like never before, sending leagues of rebellious men after the Dragon Elite. Thad had always been compelling like that, getting the lost and lonely to follow him. Most of the men he recruited didn't survive, but what mattered more to Hiker was that most of his own men didn't either. The Rogue Riders nearly made the Dragon Elite extinct.

That's why Hiker gave the order to level Thad's castle, after trapping him in there. At least, Hiker thought he was in there. Turns out, he must not have been because he was living and breathing in this world, the very same one Hiker thought was safe from such villains.

Splashing water onto his face, he tried to wash away the sleep from his eyes and the memories from his mind. It had been four-hundred years and the vision of that day that Ember died hadn't faded for him. He had little hope that it would.

What was curious to him was how Thad had survived all these years without his dragon. If Hiker had the *Complete History of Dragon Riders*, he could look it up. He knew the information wasn't in *The Incomplete History*. He had that one memorized, and besides, the Castle had given that book to Sophia.

"I want my book back," Hiker grumbled to the Castle, knowing damn well that the stubborn old building heard his request. It had been hearing it and refusing to comply for weeks now.

He shook his head, shaking away the water on his face and beard.

It was time he faced the worst nightmare he could think of. Thad Reinhart was still alive. He was the greatest threat mortals and the planet Earth faced. It was so bad that Mama Jamba had come out of retirement. Worse was that she was close to giving up, thinking Thad was too powerful to beat.

Hiker always suspected that if unchecked, Thad would be a furious force that pillaged until the Earth was reduced to nothing. It appeared his greatest fears might come to fruition if he didn't do something to stop him.

CHAPTER THREE

Sophia had the strange desire to hum as she strode downstairs. She felt like she could feel the essence of the Castle striding next to her, encouraging her, singing with her. But she often felt that way and had started to realize how nuts she was going since talking to a building. Ironically, she thought Ainsley was crazy for the same thing, and now she was becoming just like the housekeeper.

In the magical community, few things were considered weird. Speaking to buildings was one of them, though. Seeing the future was the second. Otherwise, most things were fine, although subject to change depending on weather conditions.

"Where did I leave my earbuds?" she wondered as she walked around the Castle. She didn't want to go down to breakfast yet.

Evan was on the warpath and always showing up early, dictating different things. He'd taken it upon himself lately to have ownership of the bacon. Apparently, he was going after anything he could. Sophia figured it was because he felt useless, still recovering from electrocution. Bullying was ingrained in him and Quiet was, as always, one of his main targets.

"They are in your pocket," Mama Jamba said, lying on a settee, her face covered in thick white cream and cucumber slices covering her eyes.

Sophia was about to tell Mother Nature that this was impossible when she felt something press into her pocket. She halted and slipped her hand into her jeans, pulling out her earbuds.

"How did..." Sophia shook her head, marveling at the mystery of the Castle and the all-knowingness of Mama Jamba. Together they were a fun and mesmerizing force.

"What are you doing?" Sophia asked her, noticing the short woman was wearing a silver tracksuit, her toenails divided with cotton balls, having been freshly painted. Her silver hair was held back from the face mask with a headband and something glossy shimmered on her lips.

"I'm doing my weekly hydrating mask and beauty regimen," Mama Jamba informed her, pulling one cucumber off her eye and squinting like her vision was adjusting to the light. "I just did my nails and next is a deep conditioning treatment for my hair."

"That's nice," Sophia said, trying to keep the curiosity out of her voice.

"But..." Mama Jamba said.

"Well, I'm just wondering why you don't just magic yourself younger or more hydrated or whatever," Sophia admitted.

"I could certainly do that and have," Mama Jamba admitted. "I'm the most powerful magical entity in this world. However, that gives me the supreme intelligence to know that even when you magic your appearance, it doesn't affect the way you feel. The only thing that does that is pampering."

"Oh, well, that makes sense," Sophia said, remembering when she'd changed her appearance with magic. It changed the way she looked but not how she felt.

"When was the last time you had a massage or a pedicure or whatever, my dear?" Mama Jamba asked.

Sophia shrugged. "Never."

The woman sat up, the other cucumber falling off her face.

"Never? Well, that simply won't do. You must go and pamper yourself first thing today."

Sophia laughed. "Although that sounds nice, I have—"

Mama Jamba shook her head. "No arguments. You are going for a pedicure. I insist."

"Thank you, but Hiker will—"

"To hell with Hiker," Mama Jamba stated. "All missions can wait. You're going to see my lady. She's the best. I'll make you an appointment."

"That's really nice of you but—"

"It's not about being nice," Mama Jamba interrupted. "It's about taking care of my rider. You work for me, and I know that if you aren't feeling at your best, well, you won't be at your best."

"I work for you?" Sophia questioned. "I thought the angels had something to do with it."

"Well, you report to Hiker, technically," Mama Jamba stated. "But I'm his boss. The bit with the angels is a bit complicated. I technically work for them, but the managerial structure is sort of haywire at this point. Anyway, I say you're going to see Mae Ling straight after breakfast."

"Mae Ling?" Sophia questioned.

Mama Jamba held out her hand with a small slip of paper in it. "Yes, you can find her there. She will make you feel brand new. Taking care of your feet is almost as important as taking care of your heart."

Sophia took the piece of paper. "Okay, thank you."

"And," Mama Jamba said, a hint of mischief in her voice, "I daresay that there might be added benefits to seeing Mae."

"Like?" Sophia asked.

"You'll have to see that for yourself."

CHAPTER FOUR

The men fell silent when Sophia entered the dining hall for breakfast, not as late as she had expected. She swept her head around, looking over her shoulder when they all glanced up at her in unison, shocked expressions on their faces.

When she turned back, she shrugged. "So, there's not a demon following me through the Castle? Why are you all giving looks of horror?"

"Aside from the fact that you're wearing the most impractical color of armor in the world?" Evan asked, lounging back in his chair and putting his boots on the table.

"Oh good, you've recovered enough to have meals with us again," Sophia said dryly, taking her usual spot between Quiet and Mahkah. "Nice hair, Electric Boy."

Evan's grin dropped when he ran his hand over his shaved head, having lost his long black dreads to electrocution while trying to find the entrance to Mother Nature's temple. "This is just because I was ready for a change," he lied.

Wilder laughed. "Yeah, it was quite *shocking* to see the new hairstyle."

Unapologetically, Sophia glanced down at her pink outfit. "What's wrong with my armor?"

"Besides the fact that it is the exact opposite of camouflage and would get you easily spotted in combat?" Evan countered.

Sophia wasn't letting go of the advice that Rudolf had given her when they were in Tanzania. She was tired of downplaying the fact that she was a woman around these men. That meant she was going to stop wearing the boring colors and baggy clothes that hid her curves.

What she wasn't going to do was disclose to them where Mama Jamba was sending her later that morning. She was going to start being proud of her femininity, while also not coming off as prissy. It would be a fine balancing act, she had decided.

"Says the guy who has a purple dragon," Ainsley said, striding in from the kitchen carrying a pitcher of fresh-squeezed orange juice. She slapped Evan in the back of the head.

He ducked forward, giving her a look of offense. "What was that for?"

"Get your boots off my table, or you'll get another but harder this time," Ainsley warned, brandishing a fist at him.

"You don't want that, mate," Wilder stated. "You can't afford to fry any more brain cells."

Beside Sophia, Quiet muttered.

Ainsley laughed in response, nodding. "Quite right. Quite right."

Evan shook his head, pulling his boots off the table. "I don't know what the gnome said, but I'm sure it was an insult." He pointed at the groundskeeper. "Why don't you speak up, unless you're afraid of what will happen if I actually hear what you say?"

Quiet narrowed his eyes at Evan and mumbled again, his chin low.

Ainsley slapped her knee, laughing hard. "Oh, I couldn't have said it better myself."

Evan rolled his eyes. "The two of you are daft. Too many years in the Gullington have made you looney."

"Yes, Evan," Sophia said, spreading jam on her toast, "tell me all about your recent adventures out of the Gullington that didn't involve being electrified."

Evan flashed her an evil grin. "Hiker has cleared me to leave. I'll be out there doing all sorts of stuff now. And Coral blends into terrain with her coloring, unlike you, pretty little princess in pink."

"I'm not going out on a combat mission right now," Sophia fired back before taking a bite of her toast.

"Where are you going?" Hiker asked, standing in the entryway, his eyes on her.

She cleared her throat, her eyes drifting back to Evan. "And my armor isn't just pink. It's practical. I have pockets. So there."

He shook his hands in front of them. "Wow, look at you putting me in my place. You've shown me."

Ainsley smiled down at Sophia. "Pockets are a smart addition. Good going, S. Beaufont. You should go into fashion design."

"Yes, that's exactly what you should do while I'm off saving the world," Evan said proudly. "Make mine green, to match my eyes."

"It will match the boogers stuck in between his teeth," Ainsley said, hurrying for the kitchen with an empty tray.

Most everyone but Hiker and Evan howled with laughter, even Mahkah, who usually stayed neutral during such rip sessions.

"Good morning, Hiker," Wilder said cheerfully as their leader took a seat.

Hiker cut his eyes up to him and grunted, grabbing the container of eggs.

Wilder gave Sophia a curious expression, also reading the strange mood the Viking was in. She didn't expect him to be happy after learning that Thad Reinhart was back, an apparently monstrous villain. However, she did expect him to seem a bit more positive now that Mama Jamba was in the Castle.

"So, Mother Nature is here," Wilder said, leaning forward in a conspiratorial whisper. "Have any of you seen her?"

"S. Beaufont has," Ainsley sang loudly, coming back in carrying a plate of raw bacon. "She's the one who went and fetched her." The housekeeper leaned down low, her face next to Wilder's. "And whispering isn't really that effective since she can pretty much hear everything, always."

"I know that Sophia found her and brought her to the Castle," Wilder stated, glaring at the platter of uncooked bacon. "That's why we were all giving her stunned expressions when she entered."

"Not me," Evan replied. "I was looking at her ridiculous attire."

Ainsley laid the platter of meat next to Evan. "Do me a favor. The burners are all occupied. Can you warm this up for me, Sparky?"

He shoved the platter away as most of the table laughed at his expense again. "Would you get out of here, Ainsley? We have real business to attend to now that Mother Nature has returned."

The housekeeper slapped her hands to her face, her mouth falling open. "Of course, sir. Don't talk about your complex affairs until I leave the room. I wouldn't want my head to explode."

"Ha-ha," Evan said with no real humor. "You really wouldn't understand the things we have to battle."

"Nooooo." Ainsley drew out the one word. "I wouldn't. I just happen to be one of the few people who have met the villain that you'll have to face in your green uniform with lots of ruffles."

"Ainsley!" Hiker chided.

She cupped her hand to her ear. "What?" Turning her attention back to the table, the elf said, "Oh, I hear the Castle calling me. Apparently, it's afraid the stench from Evan's room will send Mother Nature away. I'm coming!" Ainsley hurried for the entryway.

"What's she talking about, sir?" Mahkah asked Hiker.

He sighed. "Mama Jamba has brought something of great concern to my attention."

"Mama who?" Evan asked.

"It's the name that Mother Nature prefers to go by," Sophia explained.

"Oh," Wilder exclaimed. "What's she like? I picture her like a tree with vines for hair and old soul eyes."

Sophia gave Hiker a hesitant expression. "She's not quite like that at all. Haven't any of you seen her around the Castle yet?"

They all shook their heads.

"Oh, but she's just up there on the first landing," Sophia said, pointing in the direction of the stairs. "You couldn't have missed her on your way down, and I'm certain she's been there for a while."

"Why are you certain of that?" Evan questioned skeptically.

Sophia didn't want to say it was because the face mask that Mother Nature had been wearing had looked about set, which meant she'd probably had it on for about half an hour. Instead, she shrugged. "I just am."

"So, Pocket Princess is the only one who has met Mother Nature," Evan grumbled, sitting back and crossing his arms over his chest.

"Well, she and Lunis are the ones who found her," Hiker replied.

"Will you tell us about this villain?" Mahkah asked, his face serious.

"Right." Hiker nodded and pushed his plate away, not having taken a single bite. "It appears that a treacherous man who I'd thought dead is still alive. I need to do more research before I go into detail, but his name is Thad Reinhart."

"Oh angels," Quiet said loud enough for everyone at the table to hear.

They all spun to look at the gnome, shock on their faces.

Hiker nodded. "Yes, of all the men to return from the dead, he's the worst, and I suspect he's behind much of the evil polluting the world. Mama Jamba has told me that much, but like I said, I've got to look into things myself."

"Tell us more about this Thad Reinhart," Wilder urged, leaning forward.

"Not right now," Hiker replied. "Tomorrow, I'll begin assigning you all cases. We need to systematically go after Thad, but it will take special planning."

"What kind of planning, sir?" Wilder asked. "Can we help?"

"No," Hiker said at once. "I've got to do this on my own."

Something seemed to be haunting the leader of the Dragon Elite. Last night as he had given Mama Jamba a speech about standing up to Thad, he'd had new confidence. It wasn't that it had entirely receded, but he seemed to have lost some of his spark, as if a new fear had taken seed in him during the night.

"He will come after us all," Ainsley said, shaking her head from the doorway.

Everyone turned their chins to look at her.

"Ainsley," Hiker warned.

She pursed her lips at him. "I know. You've got to do your research. And you don't want them knowing all the specifics until you're ready."

"What specifics?" Evan asked.

"I'll tell you tomorrow," Hiker retorted, his eyes narrowed on the housekeeper. "Today, you'll train. Prepare. We will meet first thing in the morning."

"Do we get to meet this Mama Jamba?" Evan asked.

"If you can find her," Ainsley stated. "I've still yet to encounter the woman. The Castle won't give me a clue about where she is."

"She's up there sitting on the settee," Sophia explained, pointing to the stairs.

Ainsley swung around. "Was that who was humming? I heard her just now, but I couldn't see anyone."

"That's because she doesn't want to be seen by you right now," Hiker related.

The shapeshifter morphed into almost an identical image of Sophia, if not for the scar on the side of her head. "What about now? Think this will work?"

Hiker's eyes fluttered with annoyance. "Mama Jamba can't be fooled. She'll show herself when she sees fit. In the meantime, I want you all out on the Expanse training. This may be the last time to hone and refresh skills before things get crazy. I don't know what to expect entirely yet, but I'm certain war is inevitable."

"Sir," Mahkah began. "Things are really going to happen? The Dragon Elite will come out as adjudicators once more? We will fight?" There was a new excitement building in the old rider who had been sequestered to the Gullington for so many centuries.

"Yes," Hiker answered simply.

Evan stretched. "Well, I'm ready. Pinky, would you like me to show you how to get on your dragon?"

Sophia scowled at him. "No, I'm good."

"You can spar with me this morning," Wilder offered.

"That's okay," Sophia replied, keeping her eyes off of Hiker who she sensed was giving her a piercing stare.

"I'm happy to run you and Lunis through some obstacle courses, if you like," Mahkah said to her.

"Thanks, but I actually can't train today," she answered, pretending to be inspecting a piece of ham on her plate.

"What's that now?" Hiker asked, leaning forward.

"Mama Jamba asked me to go do something," she said, keeping her eyes on the slab of meat.

"And what would that be?" Hiker questioned.

"It's nothing," Sophia answered, cutting her ham into little pieces like she was going to feed it to a kitten.

"It's not fair," Evan complained. "She's the only one of us who has gotten to meet Mother Nature, and now she gets to go on some secret mission for her."

"Indulge me about this nothing task Mama Jamba is sending you on," Hiker ordered.

Cutting her meat into even smaller pieces, Sophia mumbled, "I've-gotta-ge-ma-nails-done."

Wilder leaned in close. "I'm sorry, I couldn't quite make out what you said."

"Yeah," Evan added. "It's like she's impersonating Quiet all of a sudden."

The gnome's eyes flicked to Evan as he muttered something.

"I don't know what's wrong with your men's ears," Ainsley stated. "I heard her just fine." She patted Sophia on the shoulder. "And good for you. Well-deserved."

"What's well deserved?" Hiker asked, looking at the housekeeper and Sophia.

"Oh, really." Ainsley shook her head, making for the kitchen. "And they say you riders are supposed to have enhanced senses. Only thing most of you bunch have is an enhanced ego."

"Sophia," Hiker began, his chin down and a warning in his tone, "do tell me in a voice I can understand, what this mission is that Mama Jamba has sent you on."

With a sigh, Sophia resigned. "Fine. She wants me to get my nails done today."

"What?" Evan erupted. "We have to spend another day training at the Gullington, and she gets to go off and get pampered."

Hiker narrowed his eyes at him. "Do you want to go and get your nails done?"

"Well, no," Evan answered at once. "It's just that it seems a bit unfair that Mother Nature is sending her on missions and we have to stick around here." He gave her a snotty expression. "But I guess I understand. You can't get your hands too dirty. Be sure to paint them a pretty shade to match your outfit."

"I was thinking of red," Sophia fired. "That way, your blood won't show under my nails."

"Would you two stop it?" Hiker ordered.

"She started it," Evan said.

"I did not," Sophia argued. "You're the one who has been—"

"Enough," Hiker interrupted. "Sophia, go get your nails done. You men get to work. I want to see you in my office, first thing tomorrow morning. Get your rest. You'll need it."

CHAPTER FIVE

Sophia's appointment with Mae Ling wasn't for another half-hour. That wasn't enough time to get in any training, and honestly, she didn't really want to bicker with Evan anymore.

With the guys out of the Castle and Hiker shut up in his office, Sophia thought it would give her an opportunity to do some proper snooping.

She'd promised Trinity, the librarian for the Great Library in Zanzibar, that she'd search for *The Complete History of Dragon Riders*, which was apparently hidden somewhere in the Castle.

"The question is where," Sophia said, trying to clear her thoughts.

Quiet had once, in his own strange way, advised her to clear her mind to discover secrets in the Castle.

"How had Ainsley said to do it?" Sophia wondered aloud. "I can see the unseen and know the unknown, right?"

Thinking that sounded right, Sophia nodded, taking off down the dark corridor. "I can see the unseen and know the unknown, Castle," she repeated. "So just lead me to the room where you're hiding *The Complete History of Dragon Riders.*"

She half expected a door to appear in front of her, illuminating the path to the book. When it didn't, Sophia sighed.

"Okay, how about we make a deal?" Sophia offered to the Castle. "You probably want something, right? Like maybe some treasure that's outside the Gullington?"

The fire in the torches lining the walls dimmed before glowing brighter.

Sophia's heart skipped. "That's it! Isn't it? So, if I go on some adventure for you, then you'll give me the *Complete History of Dragon Riders?*"

"Or you'll go and get it what it wants, and then it won't deliver on its promise," Ainsley said at Sophia's back.

She spun to face the shapeshifter who was in the form of Mama Jamba. Sophia tilted her head at her in confusion. "Why are you impersonating Mother Nature?"

"Well, since I can't meet her face to face, I figured this would have to do," Ainsley said, turning to the wall where a mirror suddenly materialized, showing her full appearance. She bowed low to her image. "It's an ultimate honor to meet you, Mama Jamba." She rose. "Oh, please call me 'Mommy.' And the honor is all mine, Ainsley." The shapeshifter clasped her hands to her chest. "I don't even know what to say, Mommy."

"Ummm," Sophia interrupted. "Mommy? Really?"

Ainsley gave her an annoyed expression. "Excuse me, I'm talking to Mommy. And yes, that's what she wants me to call her. It's our little thing. Just between us."

"And that's not weird," Sophia muttered.

"Says the person who gets to chat with Mommy whenever she pleases," Ainsley fired.

Sophia softened. "I'm sure you'll meet her soon. She hasn't been here for long."

Ainsley resigned some of her frustration. "Yes, I'm sure you're right. And you're looking for the *Complete History of Dragon Riders.*"

Sophia nodded.

"I'd warn you about making a deal with the Castle," Ainsley stated, changing back to her normal appearance.

"You think the Castle will take whatever I agree to get for it and then not give me the book?" Sophia questioned.

The housekeeper shrugged. "Probably. The thing is, if the Castle wants you to have something, you will. If not, it can keep stuff hidden indefinitely. I've given up on trying to find Hiker's books."

"But what if it takes another nap?"

"It appears to be doing that when I sleep," Ainsley answered. "Which I haven't figured out how to avoid. Therefore, I'm a little skeptical that I'll be able to discover where the sneaky Castle is hiding the books or the pairs to all my socks or the lids to my leftover containers."

"Oh, socks and lids just sort of go missing," Sophia offered. "That's a common issue even in mortal homes, from what I've heard."

Ainsley shook her head. "No, that's the doing of Gully fairies. And guess where they originated?"

"The Gullington?" Sophia guessed.

"That's right," Ainsley affirmed. "Several centuries ago, there was a mass breakout of the Gully fairies. Apparently, some numbnuts left their cage open. They were an experimental magical creature by one of our dragonriders at the time. Anyway, a horde of them escaped and they spread all over the globe. The little buggers multiply fast and are impossible to spot."

"Wow," Sophia whispered. "So this person who let them out is the reason that most people don't have matching socks?"

"Yep."

"Well, they're a pretty hated individual worldwide," Sophia stated.

Ainsley huffed. "Good thing I wasn't planning on winning any popularity contests."

"Oh, it was *you*," Sophia said.

"Of course it was me," Ainsley replied as if this should have been obvious.

"Well, I told Trinity that I'd look for the *Complete History of Dragon Riders*," Sophia explained. "Do you have any idea what's in that book or why it can't be copied?"

The shapeshifter shook her head. "Honestly, Hiker guarded that book more than any others. It was locked up in a case in his office. But it disappeared with the others because if the Castle wants something, there's no stopping it."

Sophia tapped her chin, thinking. "Hmmm. Well, is there a way to make a deal with the Castle to ensure it delivers on its promise?"

"Beats me," Ainsley stated. "If you figure that out, let me know. So far, the little jerk goes back on any agreements I try and make."

Sophia sighed. Trinity had only asked that she look for *The Complete History of Dragon Riders*. She wasn't obligated to actually find the book, but Sophia wanted to know what was in it that would require Hiker to lock it up. And why was it that the Gullington made it so it couldn't be duplicated? There were a lot of unanswered questions, and finding that book was the only way to figure things out.

"Ains," Sophia said, shaking away the concerns about the book. "You told me you'd tell me more about Thad. Hiker doesn't really seem open to discussing him. What else can you tell me about this horrible man?"

"Oh, no, S. Beaufont," Ainsley said, backing down the corridor. "I know I said I would, but Hiker is already peeved at me for this morning. I better not push my luck with him right now. He's in the worst mood I've seen him in since…well, I can't say."

Sophia deflated. "Seriously? Hiker is going to be sour no matter what. At least if you give me some information on Thad then—"

"Maybe I will at some point," Ainsley cut in, "but for now, go get your nails done. Hiker needs to handle this his way. I see that much clearly. And if I'm honest, it's not my place to tell anyone about Thad Reinhart."

Something had shifted dramatically in the housekeeper since the night before when she seemed more open to sharing information.

"Ains, what's going on?" Sophia asked.

"He made me promise," Ainsley whispered. "And I might lie and steal and cheat, but I refuse to break a promise to anyone. Especially Hiker."

"Wait, Hiker made you promise not to tell me about Thad?" Sophia questioned.

"He made us promise not to tell anyone," she amended.

"Us?" Sophia asked. "You mean you and...Quiet?" The last part dawned on her. "You two know about this villain, right?"

"We don't know much," Ainsley stated. "I assure you of that."

"And did you just admit to lying, stealing, and cheating?" Sophia tilted her head, blinking at the elf.

"Did I?" Ainsley asked. "I really don't recall. Now hurry off, would you? It won't be good to miss your appointment."

Cautiously, Sophia nodded at her as she backed away, wondering what Hiker was hiding. And why was the Castle hiding the *Complete History of Dragon Riders*? She had so much to figure out, but it would have to wait since Mother Nature was making her go get a pedicure. Her life was indeed very bizarre.

CHAPTER SIX

The smell of chemicals was so strong that Sophia was forced to immediately cover her nose. She found it ironic that she could handle flying at high speeds on Lunis and fighting robots, but striding into a nail salon made her want to flee.

Maybe I'm not as girly as I believed, Sophia thought, realizing she'd never had a real pedicure.

The line to get into the busy shop was nearly out the door. Sophia was going to take it as a sign that she should return to the Gullington to train with the guys and was about to head back out the door when a small hand grabbed her arm.

"You're here for your appointment?" a small woman with short black hair in a small ponytail asked. "You're Sophia Beaufont?"

She nodded. "Yes, you're Mae Ling?"

Sophia, like most of the women in her family, was small in stature. Mae Ling was at least a head shorter, making her seem like a small child.

"I am," the woman said, tugging her through the crowded shop, surprisingly strong for her size. "I'll take you to my station. Are we doing the works? Mani? Pedi? Brows? Neck massage?"

"No, I'm thinking just a pedi, please," Sophia stated, thinking how strange it was for a dragonrider to get her nails done. She felt as though she should be at the Gullington preparing for the missions that Hiker was going to assign tomorrow. She should be sparring with Wilder, riding Lunis, or doing something that made her feel like a rider. Being in a crowded shop of women getting pampered didn't do that at all. It made her feel...normal.

"Everyone needs to get their nails done," Mae Ling said, pushing Sophia into a reclining chair with surprising force. The woman had Sophia seated before she was fully aware of what was going on.

There was a bowl under her feet, connected to the recliner, which was already vibrating under her back. Sophia realized it was an attempt to get her to relax, but it only made her tense from the strange sensation.

"What's that?" Sophia asked as Mae Ling began to fill the basin at her feet with warm water and bath salts.

"Don't worry about those boys and tomorrow," Mae Ling stated. "You need to be here."

"How did you know that I was worried about that?" she asked, wondering what had happened to her boots. Her pants were already rolled up to the knees, although she didn't remember doing it.

"Your friend told me," Mae Ling said, tapping the side of her head and winking.

"Do you mean Mama Jamba?" Sophia asked, pulling up her toes, nervous about dipping them into the water.

"Sure," she said, pushing Sophia's feet under the warm suds, submerging them completely.

"You are the one who Mama Jamba recommended, right?" Sophia asked.

The small woman nodded, pulling a small rolling chair over and taking a seat in front of Sophia's feet.

"How do you know each other?" Sophia asked.

"We go far back," Mae Ling said casually, drawing a cart over with a bit of magic.

"Back?" Sophia asked cautiously. "How far back?"

Mae Ling waved her off. "Not really that important." She pulled one of Sophia's feet out of the water and began trimming nails and pushing back cuticles. It wasn't as weird as Sophia would have expected, and before long, she found herself relaxing into the chair, allowing the slow vibrations to soothe her into a more relaxed experience.

"You're very tense," Mae Ling observed after a few moments of silence.

Sophia's eyes popped open. She hadn't realized that she'd closed them. "Huh? What?"

"You're very tense, aren't you?" Mae Ling repeated. "The pedicure will help, but you have other problems that a massage can't fix."

Sophia laughed, thinking of her problems with Thad Reinhart. "No, a massage can't fix my problems. But Mama Jamba thinks it might put me in a better frame of mind."

Mae Ling nodded, lathering a handful of lotion onto Sophia's feet and starting to push into various pressure points, pressing away tension. "Now, you know where to look for this Thad Reinhart, right?"

Again, Sophia's eyes popped open again. "What? I didn't mention his name. How did you know about him?"

"Well, of course, you did," Mae Ling said with a laugh. "We've been talking about him for half an hour and how you went to his facility, Chainley."

"We have?" Sophia asked and then straightened. "Chainley?"

"Yes," Mae Ling said, beginning to set Sophia's feet on the front of the basin, preparing them for nail polish. "That's where you freed those slaves. Where Adam was investigating and died."

"I told you about that?" Sophia asked, at a loss for what happened over the last half hour.

A bottle of nail polish that was Sophia's favorite shade of pink materialized in Mae Ling's hand. "Well, of course, you did. How else would I know about it?"

"Right," Sophia said, drawing out the word. "And that color..."

"You picked it when you came in, remember?" Mae Ling questioned again.

"Of course," Sophia said, wracking her brain for the memory but unable to find it.

"Anyway, I think you're absolutely right," Mae Ling began, painting Sophia's toenails. It was a nice, soft feeling that was both relaxing and sort of tickling. "You should go to one of Thad Reinhart's other small facilities. That one on that island off the coast of California seems like a good lead."

Sophia jerked, nearly making Mae Ling mess up. "The one off where?"

Mae glanced up at her. "Remember? You were just telling me about that facility on Catalina Island off the coast of your hometown of Los Angeles?"

"I was?" Sophia questioned. "I mean, I guess I was."

She really couldn't remember much since entering the shop, which was strangely empty now. *Hadn't it been full when I entered?* Sophia wondered, looking around and seeing she was the only customer there.

She glanced at the clock on the wall and couldn't believe the time. She'd been at Mae Ling's shop for hours, although she could have sworn it had only been twenty or thirty minutes.

"Well, you seemed to have needed this," Mae Ling stated, pushing back and beginning to clean up.

"Thank you," Sophia said, looking around, feeling disoriented. "I think you're right."

Mae Ling leaned forward. "And I think you're right about checking out the Nathaniel Facility in Catalina. That seems like a good lead."

"Nathaniel Facility in Catalina?" Sophia asked, swearing it was the first time she'd ever said those words together.

"Yes, you told me all about how that was where you supposed strange activity was going on that could be connected to Thad Reinhart," Mae Ling explained.

"I did?" Sophia asked and then shook her head. "I mean, of course, I did. But where did I get these leads?"

Mae Ling shrugged, trotting for the back. "Who knows? Maybe your fairy godmother?"

Sophia laughed, but then the lights started to dim. "Wait, are you closing up?"

"Yes, we're closed," Mae Ling called from the back. "Time for you to leave."

"But what do I owe you?" Sophia asked, peeling herself out of the chair, her back feeling more relaxed than...well, ever.

"Nothing," Mae Ling replied. "You'll pay me in time."

"But how?" Sophia asked, feeling compelled to walk toward the front exit.

"Oh, I don't know," Mae Ling answered. "We'll figure something out. Maybe we'll trade, or you'll have something I want, or you'll save the world."

"What did you say?" Sophia asked, suddenly her fingers on the handle for the door, although she didn't remember how it happened.

"I said goodnight and see you next time," Mae Ling sang.

Suddenly Sophia found herself outside the shop. All the lights on the streets had dimmed, and the shop behind her was completely dark.

She couldn't shake the strange feeling that she'd just gotten a lead and a pedicure from her fairy godmother.

Drawing a breath, she opened a portal right outside the Gullington, two words rolling around her mind: Nathaniel Facility.

CHAPTER SEVEN

Hiker Wallace worried that he was going to let everyone
down.

He picked up the stack of papers on his desk and threw them
across his office, where they slammed against the empty shelves on
the far wall and scattered over the wood floor. A deep groan of frustration ripped out of his mouth.

The records he'd been able to dig up on Thad Reinhart were
useless. Nothing gave him a lead on where he could find the man
presently.

As usual, Thad Reinhart had done his due diligence covering up
his tracks. His business dealings were hidden behind corporations,
making it even harder to determine what he was doing.

The Elite Globe remained unresponsive to Hiker's attempts to
show him where Thad was located. He couldn't find a single rider
outside the Dragon Elite. It had been his own fault. Frustrated that so
many riders didn't want to be a part of the Dragon Elite, Hiker had
erased anyone once they parted ways, making their location disappear

from the globe. Getting them to show back up on the Elite Globe was proving impossible.

Wrapping his hand around his forehead, Hiker felt the irritation well up in him, threatening to erupt.

"For heaven's sake," Mama Jamba said at Hiker's back. "The Castle is peeved at you, isn't it hun?"

Hiker glanced at her over his shoulder, letting out a hot breath. "The Castle and I aren't seeing eye to eye anymore. I'm considering moving out."

Mama Jamba laughed, striding around the office, peering at the empty bookshelf. "Oh, you know you can't do that. The Gullington was a gift to the Dragon Elite."

"Well, you should think of taking it back."

She ran her finger along the empty bookshelves as she walked. "And what are you going to do? Move into a condo in the city? Put Bell on an island in a nearby loch?"

He grunted in reply.

"Ainsley is doing an excellent job of caring for the Castle," Mama Jamba offered proudly.

"Don't tell her that," he stated. "It will go to her head, and then she'll be even more intolerable."

Mama Jamba halted next to Hiker, looking out the tiny window on his wall. The wall that used to have a long bank of glass that showed a breathtaking view of the Pond. "I wasn't sure if she'd be right for the job when you assigned her, but the Castle likes her." She glanced up at Hiker. He towered a couple of feet over the small, unassuming woman with large silver hair and long eyelashes. "Really, it seems that you're the only one who doesn't get along well with the Castle."

He scowled down at her. "It doesn't like Evan, either."

"Well, that should tell you all that you need to know," Mama Jamba said. "What happened to all your books?"

"The Castle," he answered plainly.

She giggled.

"It's not funny," he complained. "Ever since Sophia showed up, the Castle has been antagonizing me."

"That's because she's new blood," Mama Jamba explained. "You're old blood. It's trying to get you to evolve."

He threw up his hands. "What's the point? I can't even find Thad."

Mama Jamba nodded like she expected this.

"Tell me where to find him, Mama?"

"Oh, no," she answered at once. "Sometimes it's better if you figure out things on your own."

"That's what I have been doing for centuries," he nearly yelled.

"No, you've been sitting on your hands."

"And you have too!" he exclaimed, and immediately regretting yelling at her. "I'm sorry, but it's frustrating. I can't find anything on Thad. And the Elite Globe is rubbish."

"Well, maybe you should consider new resources," Mama Jamba offered, rocking forward on her toes and back again, a sneaky expression on her face. "It does appear that the Castle is trying to force you in that direction. But I bet you're glad that it took the *Complete History of Dragon Riders* at least."

He shook his head. "No, if I had that book, I might be able to find Thad. There's a lot that I'd know if I had it."

"And there's a lot that others would know as well," Mama Jamba offered.

"No," he argued. "I kept it locked up. No one will find out." He gave her a measured glare. "Unless you're talking?"

"Oh, no, darling," she said slyly. "Your secret is safe with me."

He sighed with relief. "Thank you. And you know, the others are curious to see you. Why are you avoiding them?"

She shrugged, taking a seat on the couch in front of the flickering fire. "I've been right out in the open for them to see. They just don't know how to look anymore."

He huffed. "Oh, you and your riddles. You're just like this bloody Castle."

"Well, it is a part of me," she explained. "Sophia sees me, though. How do you explain that?"

"She sees a lot," he stated.

"The riders have been conditioned to see what they expect," she continued. "You have made them complacent like that. But to survive, you're going to have to train them to have a fresh perspective. Otherwise, they will fix new world problems with old thinking, which we both know, or at least I hope we both do, would never work." She gave him a pursed expression.

"And that's why you sent Sophia here, isn't it? To give us that new world perspective?" he asked.

"That's not it entirely," she answered, something mischievous simmering under the surface.

A soft growl made his beard vibrate. "You and your ways, Mama."

She smiled, satisfied with herself. "Yes, me and my ways."

"Why can't you save things?" Hiker asked, immediately knowing the answer.

She answered, "You know that it has never been my job to save this planet. That has always been the job of the Dragon Elite. I can protect you only so much. Which is why I'm here."

Hiker had been telling himself lately that Mama Jamba wasn't doing enough, but he also knew that she worked through mysterious ways. And she was right, she looked after the planet, but it was the Dragon Elite's job to look after the mortals. And he'd obviously failed if Thad Reinhart was polluting, exploiting mortals, and taking advantage of everything he could.

"I'm glad you're here," he said after a moment.

"But you're madder than hell about that one thing, aren't you, hun?" she asked, a coy smile on her face.

There was no point hiding it from her. He nodded. "You promised me, after the last time, no more twins. Sophia is one. You know that, right?"

"Of course I do," she answered. "But her twin is dead."

"But why choose a twin?" Hiker questioned. "You know the result is never good. One is always pure goodness, and the other, well, you remember..."

Mama Jamba nodded. "I know. But I think we know what side Sophia lands on, and there's an important reason for me choosing her as a rider."

"Which I'm suspecting you won't be sharing with me?" Hiker asked.

She waved him off. "You know that you don't want spoilers, darling."

He growled again. "I wouldn't hate them."

"Hiker, why do you think I made her a rider?"

He thought for a moment. "She inherited her twin's power when he died, didn't she? That's one reason she's so powerful, isn't it?"

Mama Jamba nodded.

"You did it so that she would be powerful? Marking a new age of dragonriders?" he guessed.

"I did it to save you all, or at least I hope that's what it does, but you won't see that for quite some time, if at all."

Hiker wasn't sure how he could love someone so much and still want to strangle her.

Mama Jamba must have read his frustration with her, because she said, "Oh, Hiker Wallace, you know, despite your bad attitude, you're still my favorite."

"You're not supposed to have favorites," he said, trying to keep his tough attitude but softening despite himself. There was nothing quite like the affection of Mama Jamba. There never had been, and he'd forgotten how much he missed it.

She shrugged. "Well, sue me then because you're one of my favorites, hence the reason I appointed you as the leader of my Dragon Elite."

"I thought it was because you never wanted me to have a day off or a moment of peace."

Mama Jamba laughed. "We both know that you wouldn't know what to do with rest and relaxation."

Hiker strode over to his desk and looked at the papers strewn across it. "If I can't locate Thad, I'm not sure what we will do. Not much of a leader I turned out to be."

"If you don't find Thad Reinhart, this planet will perish from his evil deeds," Mama Jamba said matter-of-factly. "But that is the least of your problems."

He glanced up, irritation heavy in his eyes. "Strangely, it's not. I like this planet and would prefer not to lose it."

"Well, you still have a good century, maybe even two, until you have to worry about that," she said, lying back on the sofa and covering her forehead with her hand. "If you don't find Thad sooner, rather than later, then you won't see the destruction of this planet."

He gritted his teeth together, anticipating what she was about to say.

"I'm certain that Thad will make the dragonriders extinct well before he destroys my lovely Earth," she said, a rare sadness edging into her voice.

"Mama…"

She sniffed. "You know it's his ultimate mission. He won't rest until you're all dead."

"I know…"

"And I believe he'd rather this whole planet perish with him on it, than live in cooperation with mortals or magical creatures," Mama Jamba continued. "The thing about the soulless is, when they lose, they would rather bring everyone down with them than search for redemption."

"He's not soulless," Hiker attempted to argue, guilt prickling beneath the surface. He was the reason Thad had gone over the edge, the reason he couldn't be redeemed. At least, that's what Hiker believed.

Mama sat up, giving him a meaningful expression. "We both know that Thad is soulless. If he wasn't before, then he is now."

"Then why did you have him become a rider?" Hiker questioned.

She laid back down, covering her eyes with her forearm. "It was the angels' idea. I haven't a clue what they were thinking, but I know they are rarely wrong."

"I will never understand how you all operate," Hiker said, having never met an angel before. He knew they protected Mama Jamba's riders, but information other than that was murky at best.

The Complete History of Dragon Riders probably explained it well enough, but he had never taken the time to study it. Really, he had mostly kept that book locked away, afraid of what would happen otherwise. And now it was missing, and who knew what would happen if it fell into the wrong hands?

CHAPTER EIGHT

"Your nails look great," Mama Jamba said when Sophia entered Hiker's office.

Mother Nature was laid across the couch in front of the fire, her eyes obscured by her forearm lying over her head. Furthermore, Sophia was wearing boots.

Sophia glanced down, confusion making her brow wrinkle. "Ummm…thanks." Sophia assumed that Mama Jamba simply knew that she'd had her nails done as she was ordered to do and was being polite.

"And what a pretty shade of pink," Mama Jamba continued.

Sophia's eyes darted to Hiker, who had paused his nervous pacing and was studying her. He shook his head, rolled his eyes, and continued to stride back and forth behind his desk.

"Did you really have to miss an entire day of training to get your… whatever it was that you were doing?" Hiker asked her, disapproval heavy in his voice.

"Yes, she did," Mama Jamba answered for her.

"An entire day though, Mama?" he argued.

"Mae Ling has a process that can't be rushed," she explained, her

Southern accent making the words sound polite, although irritation was creeping into her tone.

"And really, if you're going to be around here, then I can't have you overstepping your bounds with my riders," Hiker said to Mama Jamba.

"You do know how a hierarchy works, my dear, don't you?" Mama Jamba asked him.

"Of course I do," he answered with a heavy breath.

"Oh good, because I was worried I was going to have to teach you about managerial structure," she stated.

"Mama…" he said, a warning in his tone.

"The angels protect my riders," she continued, undeterred. "And they protect my Earth through the rules of adjudication since disagreements, greed, and abuse between mortals and magical creatures are the greatest risks to the health of this planet. You oversee the Dragon Elite, and I do…well, whatever I damn well please."

"But if you expect me to do my job then you've got to—"

Wilder came to an abrupt halt upon entering the office, interrupting Hiker. The rider's eyes grew wide as he took in the sight of Mother Nature stretched across the couch. He pointed at her, mouthing to Sophia. "Is that her?"

"Yes, that's her," Mama Jamba replied, loud and clear. "And Wilder Thomson, is that really any way to greet me since I haven't seen you in a couple centuries?"

He dipped into a bow. "I'm sorry, Mother Nature. My sincere and deepest apologies. How may I earn back your favor?"

Mama Jamba giggled like a young schoolgirl as she sat up, blushing slightly. "Oh, dear, you've lost no favor with me, but you're as charming as ever. Do stand, so I can take a look at you."

Wilder rose to his full height, his shoulders back and chin held up proudly. "It's lovely to see you, Mother Nature."

"Oh, good," Hiker said dryly. "They can see you now."

"Well, Sophia is here and she sees me, so they are forced to," Mama Jamba explained before returning her attention to Wilder. "You walked right by me in the corridor this morning."

"I did?" Wilder asked. "I'm terribly sorry. If I would have known—"

"You would have stopped doing that cute little dance and singing that song, which was wonderful entertainment for me," Mama Jamba interrupted. "But yes, it appears the men will be able to see me after this, which is why Evander McIntosh is hanging out in the hallway, pretending that he hasn't arrived yet."

A loud cough erupted from the hallway.

"Get in here, Evan," Hiker scolded.

The young dragonrider slid into the room, gliding down to one knee, his hands extended to Mama Jamba. "Mother Nature, it is a true honor to make your acquaintance."

She smiled good-naturedly at him. "And you missed me this morning too." Mama Jamba nodded at Hiker. "But he was picking his nose." She glanced at Evan. "You did find what you were looking for, didn't you?"

He flushed as he stood. "Oh. Sorry you saw that. I…"

She waved him off. "I hope you all aren't going to start acting all stiff now that you can see me. That will make for a really boring time."

Mahkah entered the office, giving a polite nod to Mother Nature before taking his position beside Wilder.

"Good to see you again, Mahkah Tomahawk," Mama Jamba said.

"You as well, Mama Jamba," he said stoically.

"Of course, Mahkah saw her," Evan said with a sigh. "Why didn't you tell us?"

Mahkah didn't answer.

"Well, make yourself comfortable," Mama Jamba said, scooting down to the side of the couch, making room.

Hiker cleared his throat and directed a pointed look at Mother Nature.

She scrunched up her shoulders. "Oh, right. My apologies. Hiker, this is your office and your meeting."

He nodded, looking around at the riders. "Take a seat."

"But we shouldn't make ourselves comfortable?" Wilder dared to ask, a hint of mischief in his voice.

"This isn't your bedroom, so no," Hiker answered at once.

"Copy that," Wilder replied, not taking a seat but instead remaining rigid.

Sophia shook her head at his playful act and slid down on the sofa next to Mama Jamba, hoping to get the meeting started.

"I agree," Mama Jamba said to her. "Let's get down to business, Soph."

Hiker cut his eyes at the two women.

Mama Jamba shrugged, pulling out a nail file from the pocket of her velour suit and beginning to work on her long nails. "Again, my apologies, Hiker. Your meeting. Please run it how you see fit."

He nodded, resuming his pacing. "Yes, I will."

Hiker picked up a report on his desk and ran his eyes over it. "I think there are a few cases worldwide that we should start with to make our roles as adjudicators known more widely."

"I thought we were going after Thad Reinhart," Evan interrupted.

Hiker lowered his chin. "Well, we will, once I know where to look for him or his dealings."

"Doesn't she know?" Evan asked, pointing at Mama Jamba.

Sophia shook her head at him. "It's not polite to point."

"You tell him, Soph," Mama Jamba said, running her file across the tip of her nail.

"Oh, I forgot it's the runt's job to teach us all manners," Evan said with a sigh.

"As I was saying," Hiker began again, "I haven't been able to pinpoint where to start our search for Thad Reinhart. The facility north of here, which I believe was part of one of his operations, has since been deserted with no leads. I believe that by intervening in these cases around the world, it will draw Thad out. Once he gets wind that the Dragon Elite are back, he will come after us."

"How do you know?" Evan asked.

"I know," Hiker said with confidence. "Which is why it's more important than ever that we be ready. War is imminent."

"Which is why most of us have been training," Evan said, looking straight at Sophia. "While some of us have been getting pedicures."

She ignored him, waiting for her moment to reveal the information Mae Ling had told her.

"Sophia is well aware that she needs to finish her training," Hiker stated. "Which is why when the three of you go on these cases I've gathered, she will stay behind and train with Lunis."

"What?" Sophia bolted forward. "But I should—"

The murderous expression Hiker gave her made her halt.

"I should go to the House of Fourteen," she amended, sitting back again.

"Because?" he asked.

"Because they are the ones who asked us to find Mama Jamba when their seers saw events that would need her attention," Sophia argued.

"So?" Hiker continued to question.

"So, it might be helpful to give them a status update and see if there is any information they can offer us on Thad Reinhart, now that we know he's behind the evil they were seeing," she explained.

Hiker considered this for a moment.

"And working with the House of Fourteen, rather than on our own, will help us to maximize our resources," Sophia continued, persuasion laced into her tone.

"Smart thinking, little lady," Mama Jamba commended. "I like it when others work together, rather than trying to reinvent the wheel."

Hiker shot Mama Jamba an impatient glare. "I'm not sure that's the best use of your time, Sophia."

"Well, then can I go look into this?" Sophia asked, holding out her hand, a file on the Nathaniel facility on Catalina Island materializing. She'd gotten up early to research it. There was definitely something shady about the top-secret area that deserved their attention. She'd been able to find a few aerial shots that suggested weapons of mass destruction were being housed there.

Hiker yanked the file from her hand, a skeptical glare on his face. He opened the file, his eyes growing wider as he flipped through the folder's content. "How did you find this information?"

Sophia looked sideways at Mama Jamba. "I went and got my nails done."

An abrupt laugh fell out of the squirrel's mouth that was sitting on the empty bookshelf.

Everyone turned to look at the strange creature with its paws over its mouth as it continued to giggle. The squirrel turned and looked behind itself as if everyone in the room was looking at something behind it.

"Ainsley," Hiker said, his tone punishing.

The housekeeper morphed into her normal willowy appearance, sitting on the cabinet, her legs crossed. "Hello," she said to the room before looking directly at Mama Jamba. "It's a pleasure to make your acquaintance."

Mama Jamba winked at her. "And yours, Ainsley Carter."

"You know that you're not supposed to be in here during meetings," Hiker scolded Ainsley.

"Which is why I was in disguise," she said, scooting off the cabinet and striding for the door.

Hiker shook his head before returning his attention to Sophia. "In all seriousness, tell me where you got this information on this Nathaniel facility."

"She told you," Mama Jamba answered for her. "Nail salons are wonderful places to get information. People there talk, and if you listen, you can learn things. Should I schedule a pedicure for you, Hiker?"

He gave her an incredulous glare. "Of course not! I simply want to know where Sophia is getting this information. I want to talk to this person who told you about this place."

"Oh, no," Mama Jamba stated, shaking her head. "You see Mae to get your nails done, or you don't see her at all."

He scoffed, thoroughly offended. "I will not go to a nail salon!"

"Then you'll have to rely on Sophia to get this information," Mama Jamba stated, turning to face her. "And as a bonus, you'll get pampered. Maybe next time she can give you a new hairstyle."

Sophia grabbed at her blonde locks. "What's wrong with my hair?"

"Nothing, dear," Mama Jamba said. "But a little more poof might be fun for a change. Big Dallas hair is my new favorite thing."

"What are you two talking about?" Evan asked.

"Enough," Hiker cut in. "I'm going to this Nathaniel facility while you three—"

The look Mama Jamba gave him apparently cut Hiker off.

"Right," he said with a growl. "As your leader, it would be best for me to assign this to one of you."

Mama Jamba nodded proudly and continued to file her nails.

"And since I found the case," Sophia offered, a hint in her voice.

"Then you've done quite enough," Hiker stated right away.

"But I've already gone into one of Thad's facilities," Sophia argued. "I know about the magical tech that he uses. I'm familiar with—"

"But you haven't finished your training, and you went to that facility without my consent," Hiker cut in.

"Oh, burn," Evan whispered loudly.

"You had kicked me out of the Castle," Sophia argued.

"Regardless of how things happened, neither you nor I are going to this facility," Hiker stated. He turned his attention to Mahkah. "As our most seasoned rider, I trust you can do reconnaissance on this."

Mahkah nodded, taking the file from him. "Yes, sir. I'll report back to you with what I learn."

"And the rest of you will go on adjudication cases," Hiker said, looking back at the others.

"So I get to go—"

"Except for Sophia," Hiker amended, making her deflate.

"But sir—"

"I think," he began, interrupting her again, "that you're right about sharing information with the House of Fourteen. If you found this tip getting your nails done, then it might be good if we keep communications open with the House."

"And who said that an old dog can't change," Mama Jamba said under her breath, inspecting her polished nails.

"What was that?" Hiker barked.

"Nothing," she chirped in reply.

"But when you return, Sophia," he continued, "you will finish your training. There will be no cases for you until you're completely ready."

"Which only took me about a hundred years," Evan offered. "So good luck, girl."

"Thanks," Sophia said, hoping it didn't take her a hundred years to pass her training.

She needed to be out there, solving disputes, finding the bad guys, and making the world a better place. *But* she also needed to follow Hiker's orders, or he was going to kick her out again and set them back more. They may not see eye to eye on all things, and that was okay, but they needed to mostly get along, or finding solutions for mortals' disputes would be impossible.

How could they solve other's problems if they couldn't solve their own?

CHAPTER NINE

I
t was strange that although Sophia had been born and raised in
the House of Fourteen, it didn't feel like her home anymore.
Maybe it never had. Once she felt the comfort that the Gullington
gave her, she knew the difference.

In the entryway, she halted, staring at the golden passage dazzling
with the ancient language of the Founders. She couldn't understand
what it said even as she ran her hands over it, making the symbols
dance.

Liv could read the language because she was a Warrior for the
House of Fourteen, but to Sophia, it was gibberish.

"You've returned," Plato said, materializing beside her as she strode
down the corridor.

The lynx hardly spoke to anyone but Liv, but lately, he'd been a bit
more open to her. It was strange to find him there without Liv, but
popping up randomly was definitely his thing. It was like he wanted
to spook those he visited, but it hadn't worked on Sophia that time.

"Of course I've returned," she stated, turning back to the long
corridor and appreciating the elegant beauty of the entryway. It was
different every time she saw it, morphing to accommodate whatever

was going on in the House of Fourteen at the current time. "Why wouldn't I?"

He flicked his tail back and forth. "Someone worries that with your new position, you'll abandon the House altogether."

She sighed, having sensed this. "Well, you can tell her that I'd never do that."

The feline scoffed at her. "I was referring to Clark. I read his journal last night."

Sophia would have laughed but she knew he was being honest. "The Dragon Elite are used to existing separate from the rest of the magical organizations, but I'm trying to change that."

"Spoken like a true Beaufont," he said proudly.

Something occurred to Sophia and she halted, looking down at the black and white cat. "You knew my parents, right?"

He arched a skeptical eyebrow at her. "I've paid my debt in full. I'm no longer under obligation to—"

She waved him off. "No, I'm not sure what that's all about, but I have a different question."

He studied her for a moment. "Your mother's favorite color was gray-blue."

"The same as Liv's," she stated.

"Your father's favorite book was *The Great Gatsby*," he continued.

"Also the same as Liv's," she affirmed.

"And they both listened to way too much folk music."

Sophia laughed. "Thanks for the insights. But actually, that's not what I was wondering about."

Plato's mouth twitched. "Well, I'm not sure what else I can offer."

Sophia wasn't like Liv and Clark, deeply connected to the family she'd lost. Of course, she missed Ian and Reese, her older sister and brother, but that was because she remembered them. No matter how hard she tried, she couldn't remember her parents, and strangely she thought she was better off for that. She had witnessed the dull ache in Liv and Clark's eyes when they recounted memories of their parents. Sophia didn't have that. Instead, she had a void where her parent's memory should have been.

That wasn't even the problem for her. It was the sword at her side, Inexorabilis. It was her mother's sword, made by a very talented elf. It held the memories of her mother, and it had the benefit of years of battles. But unless Sophia bonded with the sword entirely, she wasn't going to be the best fighter she could be. She and Lunis had figured that out recently and concluded that to complete her combat training, she was going to have to bond to the sword. She wasn't entirely sure how to do that.

Before she could expand, Plato's eyes slid down to the sword, where her hand had fallen absentmindedly. "You need to bond to your mother's sword," he guessed.

She blew out a breath. "No wonder Liv keeps you around. You're good."

"She keeps me around mostly because she can't get rid of me," he answered.

Sophia laughed. "I doubt she'd want to ever do that."

"Ask her that tomorrow when she finds out what I did to her favorite sweater," he said coyly.

"What did you do to it?" Sophia asked.

"I made it into a bunch of different sweaters," he replied.

"Well, that sounds nice," she stated.

He tucked his chin, appearing guilty. "For mice..."

"Oh, well, thankfully, Liv is forgiving."

Plato gave her a curious expression. "We are talking about Liv, as in Olivia Beaufont, right?"

"I won't tell her that you called her that," she said.

"Thanks. That would be for the best." Plato continued to walk beside her. "Now, your mother's sword. What do you want to know so you can bond to it?"

"Well, what do I need to know?" Sophia asked.

He shrugged. "It depends on the sword. See, unlike Liv's sword, Bellator, which was created for her, yours was created for your mother Guinevere. That means it bonded to her and is keeping allegiance to her, maybe believing that she's coming back and it shouldn't lose its loyalty."

"But she's not," Sophia said, strange hope in her voice.

He shook his head. "I've seen a few return from the dead, and your mother is definitely not a candidate. I'm sorry."

She nodded.

"My point is," Plato continued, "that Inexorabilis won't bond to you until you convince it that your mother is gone and not coming back and that you are the rightful heir and should be trusted."

"How do I do that?" Sophia asked him.

"Well, it might seem a bit impossible," Plato said, disappointment in his voice.

"Why?" she asked, sharing his tone.

"Well, for starters, you're going to need an expert in weapons who can read the past experiences of your sword," Plato explained. "I would recommend you see the person who created your mother's sword, Hawaiki, but she's taken a long worldwide voyage with her dragon, Indikos, and I suspect she'll be hard to find since she's constantly on the move. Unfortunately, I'm pessimistic that you'll find a weapon's expert, as I've explained. They are extremely rare."

Sophia smiled, thinking of Wilder and his ability to see all the experiences a weapon has had. "I might actually know someone."

"Of course you do," he said with a sigh.

"So if I can somehow locate this person," she began slowly. "Then what do I do?"

"Then you murder them and extract all their blood so that you can start the ancient spell of unlocking."

Sophia rolled her eyes. "Seriously, what do I do?"

He huffed. "My jokes don't work on you either."

"Maybe Clark," she offered.

"Oh, he loathes my jokes. Always thinks I'm serious until I burst out laughing in his face."

Sophia rolled her hand forward. "Go on then. Tell me what you know about this."

"Fine," he said as they made it to the end of the long corridor. "Once you travel the globe and find this rare person, then they need to hold your mother's sword and find the moment when she bonded with Inexorabilis and do something quite impossible but necessary for you to proceed."

"What is it?" Sophia asked.

"They have to erase that moment when she bonded to the sword," he explained.

"What?" she said in shock.

"Inexorabilis can't bond with you as long as it is bonded to Guinevere, even if only in memory," he stated. "So in a way, you're setting it free. It will remember all their battles, but then once that bonding memory is erased, it will be open to bond with you."

Sophia nodded, taking in everything he said. "Okay. That doesn't sound that difficult."

Plato halted, shaking his head at her. "It's not that which is difficult, Sophia. It's that when you erase that moment from Inexorabilis, you erase it from the world. Whatever your mother did when she bonded to that sword will change. It will be undone."

"Which means…"

"It means your first act after bonding with Inexorabilis will be to fix whatever you undid," Plato offered.

"Is it possible that she simply cut a bunch of firewood when she bonded to the sword?" she asked, scrunching up her shoulders with uncertainty.

"Maybe," he stated. "But it's more likely that she freed hundreds or fought and slaughtered an ancient beast. So…"

"So I've got my work cut out for me, don't I?" she asked.

"If you want to bond to that sword, you have to do something that probably took your mother years to accomplish," he stated.

Sophia nodded. She needed to finish her training. There was no other option. And she didn't have years. Which meant she had to work fast, but more importantly, smart.

CHAPTER TEN

Even though Sophia had entered the Chamber of the Tree before, it still felt like trespassing. She wasn't a Warrior or a Councilor, and they were the only ones allowed inside the holy chamber. Her dragonrider blood changed all of that, giving her access to places most weren't allowed.

The House of Fourteen shouldn't have been expecting her since she hadn't made an appointment or anything. However, everyone was looking straight at Sophia when she entered the Chamber.

"You've returned," Haro Takahashi, a Councilor for the House of Fourteen said, staring down at her as she strode into the center of the round room.

There was an unfamiliar woman beside him. The newly appointed magician family who replaced the Sinclairs, Sophia guessed.

There were actually so many strange faces around the chamber that it was somewhat overwhelming. The House, which used to consist of seven Warriors and seven Councilors, had grown significantly since Liv had taken her role. Now the council included the Mortal Seven as well as delegates from the elves, giants, gnomes, and fae. It went to reason that there should be a delegate from the Dragon

Elite, Sophia supposed, sticking the thought to the back of her mind for later.

"Yes," Sophia answered, striding past the Warriors and offering a small smile to Liv, who stood in the center of the arc.

Stopping in the middle of the room with the Warriors at her back and Councilors staring down at her, Sophia drew in a breath. "I have an update that I thought you all would be interested in hearing."

"Please share," Hester DeVries stated, a pleasant expression on her face.

"We were able to locate Mother Nature, per your advice, based on the vision your oracle had seen."

A great bit of muttering began, silencing Sophia.

"Are you sure she's the real Mother Nature?" Lorenzo Rosario questioned, a skeptical expression making his brow wrinkle. "There have been many impersonators throughout the centuries."

"That's because Mother Nature planted them," Rory Laurens, the representative for the giants, stated.

"Why would she do that?" Bianca Mantovani questioned, her high-pitched voice matching the snotty expression on her pale face.

"Because she's Mother Nature," Rory stated. "Much like Father Time, when she was active on Earth, she was constantly inundated with requests. It's one reason that she went into hiding."

"Father Time and she actually made a deal to go into hiding at the same time," Sophia offered.

"But Father Time returned," Hester stated.

"And so has Mother Nature," Sophia said proudly. "She has agreed to offer some insights, guiding the Dragon Elite in finding and apprehending the offender your oracle saw who is abusing the planet."

"Is what our oracle saw accurate?" Haro asked.

"Unfortunately, it is," Sophia answered. "If left unchecked, this rising evil will destroy the planet within a century, possibly longer, but not by much."

Again the chamber filled with whispers, this time coated with fear.

When the council had quieted down, Clark leaned forward out of the shadows, staring down at his sister. Sophia found herself smiling at him. "Can you disclose to us what group is behind this evil?"

"It's not a group. It is a single man," Sophia answered.

Gasps echoed around the chamber, followed by rapid muttering.

"Oh my God," Liv said with a sigh at Sophia's back. "Will you let the girl talk?"

"Warrior Beaufont, you do not have the floor presently," Bianca said in a punishing tone.

"Yes, but I can relate because it's ever so difficult to get out a report with you all interrupting with your shock and awe," Liv stated.

"I think the shock is due to the fact that it's impossible for a single man to be behind the demise of our planet," Lorenzo said with confidence.

"Right," Liv chirped. "Because if we look back at history, a single man has never been able to do horrific acts. There are zero exceptions to that."

"What about Hitler?" Stefan Ludwig asked beside Liv, sounding amused.

Sophia turned to see Liv slap her forehead with her hand. "Oh, right. I forgot about Hitler. There's one exception. But there are no more."

"And then there's Stalin," Trudy DeVries, another Warrior, chimed in.

"Damn it," Liv said, pretending to be serious. "Okay, that's another exception. But there aren't anymore."

"Wasn't there that one guy who nearly destroyed mortals recently?" King Rudolf asked from the bench, snapping his fingers like trying to remember. "What was his name? Falon Tinclair, wasn't it?"

"Talon Sinclair," Rory corrected.

"Right!" Rudolf exclaimed. "Yeah, that guy made it so mortals couldn't see magic, almost erasing it from the globe, which would have sent us into a huge downward spiral, pretty much destroying the Earth."

Bianca narrowed her eyes. "I think you all have made your little point."

"I'd argue it's a big point," Liv stated proudly.

"Warrior Beaufont is correct," Haro stated. "If we underestimate what one man can do, then we are setting ourselves up to repeat history. Please continue, Sophia. Who is this man?"

"His name is Thad Reinhart," she said and paused, certain that she'd be cut off again, but the Councilor simply continued to blink down at her. "You haven't heard of him?"

The Councilors all looked around at each other. "I don't believe so," Haro answered for the group.

She nodded. "It has been difficult to find much information on him. We believe that he's hiding behind many different corporations which invariably are a part of the scandalous activity that's destroying the Earth, harming millions and who knows what else."

"And what do the Dragon Elite plan to do about this Thad Reinhart?" Bianca asked.

"We are going to stop him," Sophia said with conviction, resenting the fact that Bianca was putting her nose into their business. It wouldn't be okay for her to ask how the House of Fourteen was dealing with things.

"How?" Bianca questioned.

"I'm not at liberty to say," Sophia answered.

"This is a problem that affects us all," Lorenzo stated. "I believe it would be wise for the Dragon Elite to communicate with us."

"Actually," John Carraway began, the first Mortal Seven on the council, "Sophia is not a member of this council and therefore under no obligation to be transparent with us. She could very well be guarding secrets that we shouldn't be privy too."

"That's an excellent point," Raina Ludwig chimed in. "It's a good reason for us to consider offering a position on the council to the Dragon Elite, now that they have resurfaced after all these years."

Sophia's heart began to beat fast. Everything was coming together. All of her worlds colliding, as she had secretly hoped without realizing it.

"They can't afford to assign a delegate with the reports of their numbers," Lorenzo stated, immediately making Sophia deflate.

"Excuse me?" she interjected. "What does that mean?"

He sighed. "With all due respect, it is assumed by the council based on our projections that the Dragon Elite's numbers aren't what they once were."

"The Great War with mortals and the time when they couldn't see magic did affect us," Sophia argued. "However, we are taking back our roles as adjudicators. It won't be long before we're a force that all turn to for direction and justice."

Bianca snickered, looking pleased with herself. "She doesn't know," she said to those around her.

"But you apparently do," Liv cut in.

The Councilor narrowed her eyes at Liv before returning her gaze to Sophia. "If our reports are correct, then it would seem that the dragon population is on a sharp decline and at a rate that is unrecoverable. So it makes no sense for us to give a position on the council to the Dragon Elite, does it?"

The air felt like it had suddenly been sucked out of Sophia's lungs. She wanted to answer but didn't know what to say. She knew there had only ever been one-thousand dragon eggs. That's how many the angels created and spread throughout the Earth.

Some had hatched, but Sophia hadn't considered they all had and that dragons were going extinct.

The information on the subject in *The Incomplete History of Dragon Riders* was murky, but apparently, Mother Nature chose the riders who could magnetize to the eggs and those became candidates for the Elite, which served her, protecting the planet through adjudication.

"Where did you get this information?" Liv asked, stepping forward to stand even with Sophia.

It immediately made her feel better to have Liv there.

"We have our sources," Bianca stated primly.

"*The Forgotten Archives*," Clark answered, earning a scolding look from Bianca. "As well as a few other sources like oracles, and reports from the giants and elves."

"The point is," Lorenzo stated, "that not only is inviting the Dragon Elite to the House of Fourteen unrealistic with you facing extinction, but it also makes me wonder how you are going to fight and overwhelm an evil such as this Thad Reinhart."

Sophia wanted to argue, but she knew it was worthless. For one, she couldn't tell everyone the secrets that went on in the Gullington. And secondly, deep inside, she knew they were right. There were only a few riders in the Dragon Elite, apparently mostly due to Thad Reinhart's efforts. Maybe the council was right, and they didn't stand a chance.

"I think underestimating the Dragon Elite is what is unwise," Hester stated boldly, looking down the bench at her contemporaries. "Yes, their numbers have declined due to circumstance, but they are back now and taking their rightful roles. Mother Nature has returned. And as the magical creatures with the longest lifespan and strongest abilities, I have every confidence they can rally."

Sophia wanted to run up and hug the healer known as Hester. Instead, she simply smiled at her.

"Although that speech was nice, I think it's unrealistic to believe the Dragon Elite can take back their roles without dragons," Lorenzo stated. "If the rumors are true, there are no more eggs out there. No more dragons to magnetize too. You're limited to the dragonriders already in existence."

Sophia's eyes cut to Rory, who gave her a pointed expression. She immediately remembered something of great importance.

"I think," Haro said, contemplating, "that Councilor DeVries makes an excellent point. The time for recruitment is now. I've heard reports that there are riders scattered around the planet that aren't a part of the Dragon Elite." He offered Sophia a kind expression. "I'm not trying to interject my advice onto you, but it makes sense that finding those riders could help with fighting this Thad Reinhart."

Sophia nodded, trying to keep her expression neutral.

"I think," Raina began, "that whatever the Dragon Elite do, they should know that they have our full support. It is overdue that we all come together to support each other. We are no longer operating singularly as evidenced by the diverse makeup of our council."

"Yes," Clark stated. "The Dragon Elite have had to recover from what Talon Sinclair did to this world, just as the House of Fourteen had to do. Their journey will be different than ours, but if there is anything we can do to help, please don't hesitate to ask."

For a moment, Sophia pretended the man before her wasn't her biased brother who loved her unconditionally. She pictured him as a fellow magician who saw her as a competent Dragon Elite and believed in her because she deserved it.

CHAPTER ELEVEN

"I wouldn't go in there right now," Ainsley warned Sophia as she headed for Hiker's office.

She could hear banging echoing from the room at the top of the stairs. Sophia paused, giving the housekeeper a tentative expression. "Because Hiker is strangely in a bad mood, which is different from any other day?"

Ainsley laughed. "You know him well. But he's in a worse mood than usual."

"But we have a lead for Thad Reinhart, the other riders are off doing things to reinforce our roles as adjudicators, and Mother Nature is back."

"And the Castle did something to his office," Ainsley added on the heels of her statement.

"What?" Sophia questioned. "Because taking away most of his windows and all of his books wasn't enough?"

"Apparently," she answered.

"What's the Castle's deal with Hiker?" Sophia asked.

"Aside from the fact that he leaves his grubby hair in the bath drain and never says thank you after a good meal?" Ainsley questioned.

"That's why the Castle is mad at Hiker?"

Ainsley shook her head. "Well, those are my complaints, actually. The Castle won't reveal much to me about its grievances, but I suspect it doesn't like how Hiker is tackling his job."

"He's doing the best that he knows how based on all the flux of activity." Sophia found it strange that she was defending the Viking, but there it was.

"He's hiding something, S. Beaufont," Ainsley said in a conspiratorial whisper. "At least, that's the hint I've been given by the Castle."

"How is that?"

"Well, every time I'm going off about Hiker, the Castle hides something of mine," Ainsley explained. "I mean, it hides my stuff all the time, but I get the feeling that this is personally tied to Hiker."

"Hmmm," Sophia said, continuing to climb the stairs to Hiker's office.

"Didn't you hear what I said about Hiker's mood?" Ainsley asked.

"Yes, but he doesn't scare me," she replied.

"And that's why you're the best of us, S. Beaufont."

Upon entering Hiker's office, Sophia figured out what the banging sound was from. The Viking was thumping his head on the surface of his desk, which looked a bit crowded in an office about half the size that it had been, all the furniture scooted in closer to the center of the room.

"Sir?" Sophia asked, knocking on the door frame.

He stopped banging his head and looked at her, his eyes filled with a sober expression. "I'm busy."

She nodded. "I can see that. But maybe if you can take a minute?"

He laid his head on his hands. "Go on, then."

Striding into the office, she tried to negotiate around the crowded furniture, feeling claustrophobic without the windows or space. "So the Castle...why do you think it's—"

"Your reason for coming here," he ordered.

She swallowed, thinking of taking a seat but deciding against it.

"Yeah, sorry. It's just that I went to the House of Fourteen and gave them a status update."

"And they said we are a bunch of dimwits who have no idea what we're doing, and we're going to fail," he said in a muffled voice.

"Actually, I think their concerns were more about our dwindling numbers," Sophia said, scrunching up her shoulders and waiting for Hiker's outburst.

He covered his head with both his large hands. "So they know."

"I think they suspect," she admitted.

"How many of them are there in the House of Fourteen?" Hiker asked.

Before she could answer, he added, "Can we kill them all?"

"My sister and brother are in the House of Fourteen, sir," she said, insulted.

"So you're opposed to the idea then?" he asked, hope in his voice.

"Vehemently," she stated, hands on her hips. *"Familia est Sempiternum."*

"Is that a spell?" he asked, appearing almost drunk with emotion.

"It's a family motto," she stated. "There's nothing more important to me than family. Which got me thinking after I left the House of Fourteen."

"You're leaving to go and join them?" he guessed.

"No," she said, offense in her voice. "I love it here. The Gullington is my home. The Dragon Elite is where I belong, whether you want me or not. *Familia est Sempiternum.*"

He gulped. Opened his mouth like he was going to respond. But he didn't.

When Hiker didn't say anything, Sophia decided to charge on. "Anyway, the House is concerned about our ability to challenge Thad Reinhart based on our numbers. And they mentioned something that I wasn't that aware of, but I guess it makes sense. Sir, are we as dragonriders facing extinction?"

He slammed his mouth shut, looking around his desk like he misplaced something.

"I mean," she continued. "There have to be enough dragons first for there to be riders. And I know there are a finite number of eggs. So is it possible, after everything Thad did, and whatever else that we are—"

"Yes," he answered at once, cutting her off. "Our numbers have been dwindling for a while. Thad saw to that. And then after him, no one wanted to join us. And now...well, you were the first dragonrider in a century."

"And not at all what you were expecting," Sophia said, looking down at her colored armor.

"That's not relevant," he stated at once. "You can do the math on this."

Sophia decided to gloss over this. "Have you thought about going out to find more of the riders who didn't at first want anything to do with the Dragon Elite? They are probably still out there, and now that our mission has been renewed, it might be worth approaching them again?"

He shook his head. "I'm not sure it's worth our time. I have a very strict way of qualifying new riders."

"You treat them like you don't want them and kick them out, and only if they return do you let them stay?" she asked.

He gave her a look of annoyance. "Strangely, that sounds about right."

"Well, although that is a good strategy," Sophia began, "the world has changed. And we are in a different position. Maybe it's a good idea to put on your diplomatic recruiting hat and entice lone riders to come back and join our forces?"

He shook his head. "We don't need them."

"I think we do, sir," Sophia dared to argue. "How are we going to face Thad and win if we don't have the numbers? We already know that he has jets and robots and technology and who knows what else. What do you think will happen if we try and fight him?"

"We'll all die," he said simply.

"That's one option, but I was considering the one where we lived."

Hiker nodded. "I know. I get it. It's just that I disqualified those other riders because they didn't have what it took to be a Dragon

Elite. You have to have heart. You have to care more about others than yourself. And they left because the job wasn't glamorous enough. The payoff wasn't worth the sacrifice. How can I allow them back when my instinct tells me they don't have what it takes?"

"Maybe they've changed?" Sophia offered. "It's been a long time. And they are out there on their own. We know how lonely that is."

"Maybe," he said, resignation edging into his voice.

"Well, I could go out and find them," she suggested.

"No," Hiker said at once. "You need to finish your training, and if I'm sending anyone to recruit dragonriders, it will be—"

"A man," she interrupted, making him shut his mouth.

"It's not that," Hiker argued. "It's just that the others have experience and age on their side, and that would be more compelling for recruitment efforts."

"Right," Sophia said. "And if I showed up all young and female, they might think that the Dragon Elite had gone to hell."

"It's not that," he stated but didn't have anything to add.

"Okay, well, what if I told you I knew where there were other dragon eggs that hadn't hatched yet, at least according to my recent knowledge?"

Now she had Hiker's attention. He tilted his head, remaining quiet and waiting for her to continue.

"When I magnetized to Lunis' egg, there were a few other eggs," Sophia explained. "I know where the shop is. You won't allow me to recruit riders, but will you let me go after those eggs if I can return them to you?"

Hiker seemed to think about this. "Are you sure you know where they are?"

"Yes," she answered.

"But you need to be training," he argued.

"Which I will continue to do," she stated.

"And if I allow you to go on this mission and you bring back the eggs, what do you want?" Hiker asked, a sly expression twinkling in his eyes.

Sophia had to give him credit. He was wising up to her ways.

"Well, I think if I give you what could be the last of the remaining unhatched dragon eggs on Earth, then you should allow me to go after the riders out there."

He considered it. "Any other offers?"

"Well, I can keep the location of the eggs to myself and do nothing," she suggested.

Hiker shook his head. "Fine, but you have to train at the same time. I'm not allowing you to go after other riders unless you're progressing. But first, you have to recover those eggs. Do we understand each other?"

Sophia straightened. "Yes, sir. Thank you."

CHAPTER TWELVE

S ophia was up early, waiting for the guys to return from the missions. Evan merely grunted at her when she greeted him on the steps of the Castle, not even looking directly at her. However, Wilder gave her a wide smile.

"What are those?" he asked, eyeing the donuts she offered him on a plate she'd grabbed from the kitchen. Ainsley had acted like she was cutting off one of her limbs by allowing Sophia to borrow it.

"They are donuts," Sophia explained. "They come from a place called Krispy Kreme."

"Oh," Wilder said, sounding intrigued. "Simi has actually called me that a time or two when I collided with her fire."

"That's perfect, actually," Sophia said with a laugh, watching as he took a donut.

Wilder halted when the sugary treat was close to his mouth. "You want something, don't you?"

"No," she lied. "Just wanted to welcome you back." She slumped. "Okay, yes, but it can wait until you've eaten and rested."

He chomped into the donut. "You know what, I haven't been greeted with rewards even when someone wanted something. So you can..." His face transformed with pure delight. "Never mind. Keep giving me those donuts, and you can have whatever you want. Can you teach Ainsley how to make those?"

Sophia laughed. "I really just wanted to train with you, but I can wait until later."

He shook his head. "No, I've decided that this kind of behavior of giving me donuts must be rewarded. Get on the Expanse and start warming up. I'll be down there in five minutes."

"Are you sure?" Sophia asked, still holding the platter of donuts.

Wilder grabbed another and stuck it in his mouth. "I'm absolutely positive."

"What did the cat tell you?" Wilder asked, finishing off another donut.

"He said that I have to find out what bonded my mother to Inexorabilis and then go back and undo that moment," Sophia asked, swinging her sword at a straw dummy. She turned to face him. "Does that sound right to you at all?"

He swallowed and nodded. "Unfortunately, it makes perfect sense. I mean, every sword is different. Each has different ways of wanting to bond with a new person. But this isn't uncharacteristic based on what I've learned over time."

"So, do you think you can help me?" Sophia asked, rolling out her shoulder.

"The question is," Wilder said, wiping his mouth, "if your mother did something grand with that sword to bond with it, can you, firstly, do that again? And will you feel okay with erasing her act to do it your own way?"

Sophia gulped, not having realized the full implications. "I mean, it's already been done, right?"

"But we're going to undo it using very powerful magic," he stated. "That means you have to fix things twice."

"Just tell me this," she said, sticking her sword into a bale of hay. "Can I progress in my combat training, and pass if I don't bond with that sword?"

"Not a chance," Wilder said, shaking his head without hesitation.

"Then the answer is easy," she stated.

"I could," he began, a speculative glare in his eyes, "consider picking out a different weapon for you that won't be as hard to bond with. For instance, a new sword will bond with you on your own adventure. You won't have to rewrite history."

Sophia shook her head at once. "No, I have to have my mother's sword."

"But this was created for her," Wilder argued.

"And wouldn't you say it's a good weapon?" she asked.

"Soph, it's the best," he stated with confidence. "I can't improve upon it. Inexorabilis was made with a craftmanship I could study all my life and not master."

"And that's not even why I want it with me," Sophia stated. "It belonged to one of the greatest Warriors for the House of Fourteen. I'm a part of that. My sister recovered that sword. My brother, Ian, continued my mother's fight. I will too. But that means doing things the hard way. That means I have to bond to this weapon even if it means facing something dangerous."

Wilder lowered his chin, giving her a serious expression. "I'm glad. Because I'm afraid it will probably mean facing something incredibly difficult. But I have faith you'll do it with the right help."

"What does that mean?" she asked.

He held out her sword, offering it back to her. "It means I'll be there. But first, let's figure out what I'll be there for."

CHAPTER THIRTEEN

"Did I say I'd be there?" Wilder said, laying down Inexorabilis and quickly striding away.

"What did you see?" Sophia asked.

"Our deaths," he said at once.

"You're a dragonrider," she argued. "How bad can it be?"

"What's the worst you can imagine?"

She thought for a moment, but before she could answer, he interrupted.

"It's twice as bad as that," he stated.

"But you're in, right?" Sophia asked.

Wilder drew in a breath. "Soph, I want to help. And—"

"And you will because you're amazing and want donuts?" Sophia posed.

He considered her. "Yes, I love your donuts. But seriously. Even with our dragons, this is beyond our powers and you with an untested sword—"

"How else can I bond with it?" she argued.

Wilder's shoulders slumped. "You simply can't. If you don't face this, you won't win Inexorabilis."

"Then tell me how to do it," she stated. "You don't even have to go with me."

"Oh no," he stated. "I'm all in. I've already committed. Donuts or no donuts."

"Okay, well, tell me what I have to undo and then redo," Sophia said.

Wilder's jaw flexed. "Have you heard of the Phantom?"

She shook her head.

"No, no, you haven't," he stated with a sigh. "Because your mom killed the Phantom, ending its brutal reign, which I can't believe one person was able to do. But now you've got to bring it back, which is going to be hard enough. Then you're going to have to kill it again and hope that this bonds you to Inexorabilis."

"All of your optimism is really making it hard to understand your message," she joked.

He leveled his gaze at her. "This might be impossible. I'll start making you a new sword this afternoon."

"No," Sophia argued. "Firstly, you have missions and things you need to be doing. And secondly, I'm doing whatever it takes to bond to Inexorabilis."

"What if it's not worth it," he argued, strangely serious.

"It has to be," she stated. "But is there really a chance that I could go through all of this and the same act that bonded the sword to my mother, doesn't bond it to me?"

He shrugged. "It's a gamble. There are no guarantees with things like this."

"Okay, well, first start by telling me about this Phantom."

"You'll want to do some research on your own," Wilder began to explain. "But from what I remember and saw in the vision given by the sword, the Phantom is an evil unicorn."

Sophia couldn't help but laugh. "Unicorns aren't evil."

"They aren't any more, thanks to Guinevere Beaufont," he stated.

"The Phantom made other unicorns evil?" Sophia asked.

"No," Wilder said, shaking his head. "It made everything evil.

People, plants, animals, places, whatever you can think of. It was like a disease, spreading negativity like the plague."

A smile flicked to her mouth. "And my mom rid the world of that."

"Yes, and you're going to have to bring back that giant, black unicorn, which is the first impossible part of this mission."

She sighed. "That does seem really difficult. I don't know any spells that reverse events, but I can start looking into it."

"What you need is a time travel spell, but I can only think of one person who can give you one of those," Wilder imparted.

"Father Time," Sophia guessed.

"Yes, and finding him is damn near impossible."

"Oh, but Liv works for him," Sophia rejoiced.

"That's right. I forgot your family is royalty who knows everyone," Wilder said with a laugh.

"You didn't forget that," she argued. "You just saw a vision of my mother as a Warrior, slaughtering the Phantom." Her eyes lit up with hope. "But if you saw that vision, then you know how she did it and you can tell me, making my job that much easier."

"Yes, I can," he stated.

"How did she do it?"

"With a sword," he said dryly and pointed to Inexorabilis. "That one, specifically."

Sophia rolled her eyes at him. "I was hoping for something a bit more specific regarding technique and strategy."

"We can get to that later. First, you have to get the spell from Father Time, then we can talk about strategy."

She nodded undeterred, although Wilder appeared less than hopeful about the situation. "I'll get the spell. Then you can help me. But you really don't have to go with me to do this. I can do it on my own, just like my mother did."

A smile made Wilder appear younger suddenly. "Why do you think she did it alone?"

Sophia blinked at him in surprise. "Oh, didn't she? Was another Warrior with her?"

"I don't think so," Wilder answered. "It was a man, and I think it was your father."

"My father? Really? Why do you think he was with her?" Sophia asked.

His gaze ran over her face. "Because he had your eyes."

A shiver ran down Sophia's spine. "So my parents ended the Phantom together. That's amazing."

"Yes, your father used magic to subdue the beast while your mother used her sword to end him," Wilder explained. "I think it will require two people."

"Are you sure you want to do this with me?" Sophia asked. "I could ask Liv to help me."

"You could, and if you'd prefer to do this with your sister, then I understand," Wilder said. "However, we are dragonriders, which means we don't back down from a challenge and we help each other without question. So if you want my help, then you have it fully."

Sophia smiled at him. "Thank you. I think I'd prefer to have your help."

"Because I have a dragon?" he asked with a wink.

"Well, that and also, Liv will kill me if I tell her what I'm going to do," Sophia related with a laugh.

"Don't you think that her boss will divulge that information when you ask him for the spell?"

Sophia sighed heavily. "And now I've got to figure out a way to bribe Papa Creola."

Wilder pointed to the empty plate sitting on a nearby hay bale. "May I suggest that you bring donuts?"

CHAPTER FOURTEEN

Although it had been days since Sophia had seen Lunis, she felt like no time had passed. That was mostly because he was always in her head, listening to her thoughts. Sometimes commenting. His affection for her was like a silent song that played in her head and surrounded her heart.

"Papa Creola will give me the spell, right?" she asked him, checking the reins on his saddle.

"I think you'll have to make a stronger case for yourself," he answered. "Stating that you simply want to undo things so you can redo them to bond to a sword won't work. Maybe there is a benefit to bringing back the Phantom momentarily."

"I don't know," Sophia said speculatively. "Wilder says that he's pure evil. What benefit can there be to resurrecting him?"

"Nothing is pure evil," Lunis imparted, stretching his wings. "We are all made up of both good and bad. Some are closer on the spectrum to Hiker evil than others, though."

"Good point," Sophia said, her head still spinning, trying to find a good reason to bring back an evil unicorn.

"While we think on it, do you want to try that take off again?" Lunis asked.

SARAH NOFFKE & MICHAEL ANDERLE

Mahkah hadn't returned from his mission to investigate the Nathaniel Facility, which meant that she had to train with Lunis on their own. A dozen times she'd tried to do the running-jump-mount, as she had taken to calling it. So far, she'd landed on her face a dozen times, with zero progress.

Evan had made it look so easy when he demonstrated the move. He'd simply run beside Coral, and when she launched into the air, he jumped onto her back, swinging his leg around and sliding effortlessly into the saddle.

Sophia, conversely, had been knocked in the face by Lunis' wing so many times that she was going to need a healing spell to fix the bruises.

"Okay, yeah, let's try it again." She pulled in a breath, preparing herself.

"I won't run as fast," Lunis stated, reading the nervousness in her.

"No, you need to, or you can't take off," Sophia argued. "Just do everything as you normally would. I'm the one who has to adapt."

"I don't actually have to run to take off," Lunis stated. "I could just jump."

Sophia shook her head. "Yeah, then I'll definitely eat dirt. Let's try the running start again."

She crouched, pulling in a quick breath.

Lunis burst forward, beside her, his wings still tucked into his body.

Sophia took off, sprinting as fast as she could but already losing him. In her peripheral, she caught the sight of his backend.

No! Not again, Sophia thought, furiously.

She continued to push forward, waiting for when Lunis telegraphed that he was about to spring into the air. She'd learned to spot the way his clawed feet shifted before takeoff, followed by his wings expanding. That was usually when she dove for the saddle and got knocked out by his wings.

She knew he was too far in front of her for it to work on this attempt. But she didn't want to give up.

When Lunis was just about to launch into the air, Sophia dove, grabbing for the dragon.

To her surprise, she caught something. At first, she thought she'd grabbed one of his back feet, but there were no claws.

The dragon soared into the air, lifting her off the ground.

"I'm on Lunis," she exclaimed and instantly deflated.

In fact, she wasn't hanging onto one of his feet or the side of him or even part of his wing where she could climb up to her saddle.

No, Sophia was holding onto the dragon's tail, dangling over the Expanse as he climbed higher. She held on for dear life, the idea of what she looked like making her cringe with embarrassment.

She couldn't wait for Lunis to land, but disembarking had to be done just right, or she was going to eat dirt again.

Are you ready for me to land? Lunis asked in her head.

Of course, she stated.

How about now? he asked, turning to the side and giving her a view of who was standing on the Expanse, watching the entire thing and laughing uncontrollably.

Evan looked like he was ready to fall over from his fit of laughter.

On second thought, go drop me in the Pond, Sophia said, sliding a bit on the tail, the wind whipping her around in a truly ungraceful manner.

CHAPTER FIFTEEN

According to Wilder, Evan had ridden on Coral's tail a time or two trying to get that move right. That made Sophia feel marginally better, but she still ducked out of the Castle as soon as she could, tired of Evan's constant teasing.

He had taken to calling her Dragon Tail and making jokes about how she didn't know she was supposed to actually ride on Lunis' back.

She sought to shake off the embarrassment as she stepped through the portal into Los Angeles.

The bright colors of Santee Alley were a stark contrast to the rolling green hills of the Gullington, where Sophia had been minutes prior.

The noise of people jostling through the streets and cars passing at her back was deafening at first. Sophia's heightened senses often took a beating when she entered new places. She was learning to dial down her senses when in overwhelming places, such as the fashion district in downtown Los Angeles.

Covering her nose, Sophia tried to breathe through her mouth. The scents of fried food, people, and pollution mixed together for a disgusting combination.

She focused on minimizing her senses like she was narrowing the range on a telescope. Sophia knew she was successful when she could hear, smell, and see only that which was in the immediate vicinity.

Good work blocking out, Lunis said in her head.

Thank you, she replied.

Sophia might have failed at her attempts to jump onto Lunis while running, but she hadn't been deterred from their training. She figured that returning to the shop where she got the dragon's egg was a perfect opportunity to work on their scrying.

It was harder for Lunis to see, hear, and experience her environment the farther apart they were. However, that was even more reason to practice it. Lunis wouldn't be able to join Sophia in places like Santee Alley for practical reasons. A dragon simply couldn't fit in the crowded lane. As they got better at scrying, he could offer insights on her experiences as long as they maintained the connection.

Sophia spun around, trying to get her bearings. It felt like a million years since she'd been to this place where she met her soul mate.

Head north, Lunis stated.

She scrunched up her brow. *That's not right,* Sophia replied. *The shop is east.*

Shop? Lunis questioned. *No, I want you to grab one of those tamales from that street vendor.*

Lunis had been playing with the idea that they could also share tastes during scrying. It made sense because he could experience everything else that Sophia did.

No, you're not getting tamales, she stated. *You know that Mexican food gives you heartburn.*

Worth it, her dragon replied.

Sophia shook her head. *You're the weirdest.*

You are, he retorted.

Okay, I've got to focus on finding this shop, so shush it.

Why did you have to say that? Lunis questioned. *Now you've thrown down the gauntlet.*

Don't, she warned, knowing what was coming next.

I have to, he stated.

You don't...

This is... Lunis began.

Stop, she urged, used to this little game that he loved to play lately.

The song that never ends, he continued singing.

You're the worst, she stated, sliding through the crowd.

It goes on and on, my friend, the dragon sang in her head.

I will sever our connection, she joked.

Some people started singing it not knowing—

Fine, Sophia stated. *I'll get a tamale. Just stop.*

Thank you, Lunis said proudly.

But first, I'm going to Zuma Zat, she told him.

I vote tamales first. You know you work better on a full stomach.

No, I don't, she argued. *That makes me sluggish and sleepy.*

Oh, right, he corrected. *That's me I'm thinking of.*

Shop first, then tamales. Don't threaten me with that song again.

I don't have to, he teased. *It's already stuck in your head.*

Yes, it is, she admitted with a sigh.

Mission accomplished.

The shop where Sophia had magnetized to Lunis' egg was at the back of a seemingly normal place that sold hair extensions. Zuma Zat specialized in strange and unique magical items that couldn't be sold in normal shops. The giant Rory had vouched for Sophia, getting her into Zuma Zat.

She was hoping that she'd be able to get in again since she had been the one to magnetize to a dragon, shocking the store owner. However, that was the least of her concerns when she came to the hair extension shop.

Santee Alley was filled with people, but the area around the hair extension store was deserted like it was a quarantined area, closed off to the public with invisible tape.

"What the..." Sophia said aloud, looking around.

Something is wrong, Lunis observed.

Sophia nodded, carefully approaching the store. It was closed down, all the windows covered up, preventing her from seeing what was going on inside.

Do you think they moved Zuma Zat? Lunis asked.

There is only one way to find out, Sophia responded, sticking her finger up to the lock on the door and muttering a single incantation. The door clicked, opening an inch.

Looking over her shoulder first, Sophia slipped into the closed shop and pulled the door shut behind her.

The smell of dust was thick. She remembered being overwhelmed by the array of strange and interesting objects displayed all over the first time she entered. Although it was dark, Sophia could easily make out the details of the bogus storefront. It had been cleared out, all of the shelves bare.

Sophia didn't sense anyone in the shop as she approached the back.

The rear of the shop didn't appear much different than before, but everything was covered in a fine layer of dust, distracting from the colors she'd remembered.

Weird flowers full of corkscrews and spikes sat in vases on the far wall. Music that made Sophia both sleepy and alert came from a flute hovering in the air like it was being played by an invisible elf. Gems and crystals hung from the ceiling, making it look like a starry sky overhead, and sparkling objects seemed to call for attention from all over.

Many strange magical objects were displayed all over the abandoned shop. Chusetors, bulsters, depours, and other exotic items that if Sophia had the opportunity, she would buy. However, there wasn't anyone to buy anything from, which was the major concern.

The shop owner brought the case of dragon eggs in from the back, Sophia said to Lunis, indicating a doorway in the back.

He isn't back there, Lunis stated with confidence.

I don't think anyone has been here for a while, Sophia stated.

Which doesn't mean the place is safe, Lunis offered.

Yes, because if they abandoned their shop, it was for a good reason, Sophia told him.

Exactly.

Whereas the front two parts of the shop had been abandoned or untouched, the back room told a different story. It had been ransacked.

Broken glass and debris littered the floor.

Someone was looking for something, Lunis stated.

Sophia's eyes searched until she found the case where she'd first seen the dragon eggs. She strode over to it, noticing that it was slightly ajar. Cautiously she lifted the lid, confirming what she had suspected since entering the abandoned shop.

And it looks like they found it, she told Lunis, knowing he could see what she did.

The chest was empty. Someone had taken the five remaining dragon eggs.

CHAPTER SIXTEEN

*I*s it possible that the shop owner took the eggs and fled? Sophia asked Lunis.

Maybe, he mused. *But why does it look like there was a struggle?*

It did appear that way, Sophia observed, noting the many broken objects strewn across the floor.

And if the shop owner took the eggs, why didn't he keep them in the case? she wondered, looking around for more clues.

So either he fled with the eggs, Lunis stated, *or someone fought him and took the dragon eggs.*

Sophia noticed a heap of fabric in the corner. Tentatively, she pushed the material to the side, stepping back at once. Lying under the curtains was Shin, the man Sophia remembered showing her the dragon eggs.

His eyes were wide and his mouth was open like he had just seen something horrific. He was, without a doubt, dead.

I think we know what happened now, Sophia told Lunis.

The dragon eggs were stolen, he said.

She glanced around. *But by who and where can they be now?* Sophia suspected that the shop was full of clues that would paint a story, hopefully telling her where to look for the eggs. She just needed a chance to look around.

It will take more investigation, Lunis stated.

Do you think that Thad Reinhart is behind this? Sophia asked him.

He didn't have a chance to respond because a moment later, she got a text message. Normally Sophia would have ignored it, but something told her to check the message. For one, her phone had been on silent mode, but it buzzed loudly from the alert. That was always cause for alarm. Only certain people like Liv knew how to override silent mode, making the phone ring.

Pulling up her phone, Sophia read the text message. It was perplexing. For starters, the message simply read, **Hey, you!**

But even stranger was that it was from someone she didn't know: Leeve R. Naw.

That wasn't too weird since magical tech made it possible to have anyone's number. However, the name seemed awfully odd.

What do you make of this, Sophia asked Lunis.

I don't think the actual message is what's important, he stated.

You think it's the person it's from?

"Leeve R. Naw," she said out loud, trying to think if she'd heard that name before.

Say that again, but faster, Lunis ordered, his voice urgent.

"Leeve R. Naw," Sophia repeated.

Her eyes widened. "Angels above!"

Leave right now! Lunis exclaimed in her head.

Sophia didn't need any more encouragement. She tried to make a portal, but the area was protected. Darting for the exit, she ran through the shop, nearly tripping on furniture and having to swerve around crowded displays.

Go, Sophia, Lunis ordered. *Faster.*

She didn't know what she was running from, and she didn't look back, but she noticed a few brownies disappearing when she tore through the hair extension shop. She burst through the shop door, continuing to sprint.

When she was only a few feet from the threshold, Zuma Zat exploded at her back, erupting with fire.

Sophia dove behind the nearest building and shielded her face with her arm, protecting herself from the magical blaze. The entire shop had been destroyed, all evidence gone.

CHAPTER SEVENTEEN

Not wanting to risk her luck, Sophia portaled away as soon as she could, stepping through to a safe location.

She pressed her back up against the brick wall behind her and tried to catch her breath.

You're okay, Lunis said more out of confirmation, rather than as a question.

Thanks to that strange message, Sophia related, glancing at her phone.

The brownies, Lunis stated.

She nodded. *Yes, I think they are the ones who warned me. They must have known the shop was rigged to blow if someone tried to investigate.*

It wasn't that big a shock to Sophia that the little house fairies who usually secretly cleaned mortals' homes had come to her rescue. They were everywhere, always spying for the good of others. Actually, the brownies were Liv's main source of information when she was on a search. It appeared they were looking out for Sophia now too.

And although she was eternally grateful for the help, Sophia had her own source of insider knowledge, which was where she was headed.

She shook off the adrenaline and turned her attention to the nail salon, preparing herself to see Mae Ling yet again.

When Sophia entered the shop, Mae Ling was seated at a nail station. She pointed to the seat across from her. "I'm all ready for you. Come join me, Sophia."

"Hi." Sophia greeted the small woman with a smile. The shop was deserted, unlike the first time she'd been there.

"Let me see your hands," Mae Ling ordered when Sophia took a seat across from her.

"Actually, I'm not here to get anything done," Sophia said politely. "I've just come—"

"From near death," Mae Ling stated matter-of-factly, waving her off. "Yes, I'm aware. But you need information, and you only get that if you have a service."

"Right," Sophia said, offering the woman her hands, which were covered in blisters and callouses from sparring and riding.

Mae Ling studied them with great interest. "Yes, you're a Cancer. That explains a lot about you."

"What?" Sophia questioned. "You can tell my zodiac by looking at my hands?"

"Well, of course," she answered.

"And you miraculously knew that I'd just come from a near-death experience?" Sophia asked.

"You have ash in your hair," Mae Ling stated, pointing a file at Sophia's head.

She ran her hands through her strands. "Oh, well, I guess that makes sense."

"I don't know everything," Mae Ling explained, taking Sophia's right hand and inspecting her nails. "I mean, I like to think I'm a know-it-all, but my knowledge is somewhat limited. But let's start with why you are here."

"Well, there are some dragon eggs that have gone missing, and I was hoping you could tell me where to look," Sophia said as Mae Ling began clipping her nails.

"Yes, someone who works for Thad Reinhart," the nail technician said in a conspiratorial whisper, although there was no one else in the shop.

"Really?" Sophia said, nearly jerking her hand from Mae Ling's. "Are you sure?"

The old woman pursed her lips at her, cinching onto her fingers. "Of course, I'm sure and if you can't stay still, you can't get a manicure."

"Sorry," Sophia stated. "So you know that someone stole the dragon eggs, and that someone works for Thad Reinhart? Do you know where I can find them?"

Mae Ling simply nodded.

"Will you tell me?"

The woman shook her head.

Sighing, Sophia twitched her mouth. "Do you need me to do you a favor?"

Mae Ling shook her head again.

"Well, what can I do to get you to tell me?"

"There is nothing you need to do," Mae Ling informed her, moving on to the other hand, the right one strangely already trimmed, filed, and polished, although Sophia didn't remember her doing it.

"Well, then I'm confused," Sophia said, keeping her eyes on the left hand, wanting to see the process herself this time.

"Sometimes being confused is acceptable," Mae Ling stated. "But for now, I can't tell you where the eggs are. They are in transport, and it is unsafe for you to pursue them. If you did it now, the fight would result in the loss of the eggs."

"Oh," Sophia said, looking up at the woman. "It's incredible that you know that. When can I go after them? It's very important."

"Of course it is, or you wouldn't be here, and I wouldn't be helping you," Mae Ling said, pushing back in her seat.

To Sophia's surprise, she'd finished with the left hand too, and she'd missed it entirely.

"I'll send you a message when it's safe to go after the eggs," Mae Ling informed her, cleaning up her station.

"On my phone?" Sophia asked.

Mae Ling chuckled. "Oh, heavens, no. I don't use that fandangled technology. I'll send you a message through basic means."

"Like the mail?" Sophia questioned again, wanting to know exactly what to look for. She didn't even know how to receive regular mail at the Gullington or if she could.

"Again, I'm not into modern communications," Mae Ling stated. "But don't worry. You won't miss my message. I promise that."

"Okay, well, thank you," Sophia said, standing from the chair, again feeling strange about asking the nail technician for advice. "Are you sure there isn't anything I can do to pay you for the service or information?"

"Would you pay your fairy godmother?" Mae Ling asked, her expression pursed.

"No…" Sophia guessed, unsure what the answer actually was.

"No," Mae Ling said adamantly. She withdrew a sealed envelope from the apron fastened around her hips. "Now, after you find the eggs, and only afterward, I want you to read this. If you look at it beforehand, I won't be able to help you anymore."

"I won't peek," Sophia stated, taking the envelope. "Is it the location of other dragon eggs around the globe?"

Mae shook her head. "I can say no more right now. And it's time you left."

"Oh, sorry," Sophia said, looking around. "I guess you were closed, weren't you? Sorry."

"No, I'm never closed," Mae Ling stated. "But there is someone at the Gullington who needs your attention, and if you don't hurry, you'll miss it."

"Miss what?" Sophia asked, leaning forward.

"Miss what they are doing," Mae Ling answered, sweeping her hand forward, ushering Sophia from her shop.

CHAPTER EIGHTEEN

"Lunis!" Sophia exclaimed in her head and out loud when she stepped through the portal, just a bit outside the Barrier to the Gullington. "Are you okay?"

Yes, why? he asked in her mind.

She took a calming breath. *Mae Ling said someone at the Gullington needs my help. I was worried it was you.*

I believe that what the mysterious woman said was "someone needs your attention" and if you didn't hurry back, "you'd miss it."

Right, Sophia stated, looking around. *Does she have to talk in riddles?*

I'm certain that it goes with the job description, he replied.

Sophia stepped through the Barrier, used to the strange feeling that always accompanied reentering the Gullington. A weight seemed to fall off her chest as she took in the Castle in the distance across the Expanse. She loved this place unlike any other, ever before. And it was unfathomable that she could ever love another place more.

She was fondly taking in the many curves of the Expanse, having memorized the gentle slopes of the hills over the last several weeks, when something in the distance caught her eyes.

The sun was starting to set over the Pond, making her think that the shadows were playing with her eyes. However, the more she focused, the more she made out the figure of the groundskeeper hurrying across the Expanse. She would have dismissed the sight entirely, thinking he was simply doing one of his many jobs, but he kept looking over his shoulder like he was worried someone was following him.

"Is that what Mae Ling was referring to?" Sophia asked aloud, mostly to herself.

Follow him, and you'll find out, Lunis instructed.

You're excellent at spying from the sky, she suggested. *Why don't you come out and watch?*

Because every time I do, he notices me, Lunis explained. *He holds the dragons in great revere.*

As he should, Sophia stated.

But my point is that my presence won't go unnoticed by the gnome, Lunis said. *However, you can practice your stealth and follow him.*

Okay, Sophia confirmed, hurrying across the Expanse in the direction of the groundskeeper.

There were few trees between Sophia and Quiet, so every time he turned around, she had to drop to the ground, hoping he didn't notice her following him. She was absolutely tired of eating dirt lately, but she guessed that it was for a good reason in this case.

Quiet seemed to be up to something, which was curious. The gnome was very mysterious in the first place, always seeing what went on but never talking. Sophia could only wonder what he could be doing in secret. She trusted everyone at the Gullington, even if she didn't understand them, but she wondered if this blind faith would get her in trouble. She shook off the doubt seeking to edge into her mind and hurried after the gnome as he made his way down closer to the water's edge.

Her enhanced speed brought her across the grounds soundlessly. It was only when Sophia was almost to the cliffs that she realized the gnome had turned to face her directly, his eyes narrowed in her direction. For some reason, the scolding expression on his face immediately filled her with regret, as if she'd disappointed a parent figure.

He'd caught her, and his face stated he wasn't happy about her spying.

The groundskeeper mumbled something that Sophia couldn't hear, even with her enhanced senses.

Then he snapped his fingers and she disappeared, to find herself lying in her bed in the Castle.

CHAPTER NINETEEN

Bolting upright, Sophia looked around frantically, trying to understand how the gnome had transported her. She didn't think that was allowed within the grounds of the Gullington.

Running her hands over the covers to her bed to ground herself, Sophia confirmed she was actually in the Castle. She breathed in the comforting smell of the place, realizing that she missed it, even though it hadn't been that long. Still, the scents from Los Angeles had been in her nose, congesting her. She thought what she needed most was a nice hot shower so she could wash the ash out of her hair and the strangeness of events from her mind. Maybe then she could reassemble everything she had learned so she could make sense of it.

Sophia might have boiled herself in the hot shower, but for some reason, she felt like she needed to have it really hot. There were so many things bouncing around in her head that she was hoping something would simmer to the surface in her mind.

What had happened to the dragon eggs? Thad Reinhart was behind it, but who was working for him? And what were they doing with the eggs? Sophia worried that they were going to be destroyed, but hopefully not before she found them. They couldn't stand to lose a single dragon.

Then there was the explosion that she narrowly missed being a part of. Just a few more seconds and she would have gone up with the shop. She definitely had someone to thank for saving her, but who, she wasn't sure.

And she knew that she owed Mae Ling some gratitude, but the woman didn't work through normal means, even in the magical world.

More curious than almost any of that was the groundskeeper. He was up to something. Maybe he was covering something up. It was unclear what, but he definitely didn't want Sophia to know about it, which was why he'd been able to transport her when she didn't think that was an option in the Gullington.

Stepping out of the shower, Sophia could hardly see a thing. She had fogged up the bathroom so badly that it was hard to make out where the sink was.

Drying off, she made her way to the sink, wishing there was a vent fan. A moment later, the Castle had installed one in the bathroom, and it was sucking up the steam.

Sophia smiled, loving how magically beautiful the Castle was. Well, for her anyway. All she had to do was wish for something and the Castle read her thoughts, making it happen. For Hiker, it wasn't so easy.

She wanted to wish for Hiker to get a break, but Sophia knew that the Viking and the Castle had to work things out on their own. She couldn't fix his problems for him.

Lost in thoughts about Hiker and the Castle, Sophia went to brush her teeth when she noticed something on the mirror in front of her.

Written in the condensation on the glass was a message. It read, Go to Chimerick's Bar and Grill on Roya Lane. Love, Mae Ling.

Sophia read the message twice through.

The crazy nail technician was correct. There was no way that she would have missed that message, but still, its delivery was strange.

Like, did she actually want to take a hot, hot shower, or was that something she was spelled to do to make the bathroom steamy? All the mystery crowded her mind.

Sophia shrugged it off and began to get ready. She needed to put on her clothes and get to Roya Lane. Apparently, she'd find a lead for the dragon eggs at Chimerick's Bar and Grill.

Maybe she'd start getting a lot more answers and fewer questions.

CHAPTER TWENTY

Roya Lane was a hidden street in London that was home to many magical shops, headquarters, and lots of other strange activity. Liv spent a lot of time on Roya Lane, hunting down leads or chasing bad guys.

Sophia hadn't been out of the House of Fourteen a lot, thanks to her protective big brother Clark who was afraid someone would notice that she had her magic at a young age. Therefore, this was Sophia's first time on the magical street.

She tried to cover her awe as she strode through the portal and witnessed the multitude of strange sights around her. There was a woman on the corner who was turning chickens into strange sweaters that laid eggs. Down the block from her was an elf pushing a cart that appeared to sell light bulbs that gave their owners "bright ideas." All down the lane there were many other sights that called for Sophia's attention.

However, she worked hard to keep herself focused, searching for Chimerick's Bar and Grill.

"You look lost," a voice said at her shoulder.

Sophia was about to tell whoever it was that she was fine when she turned to find a person she simultaneously adored and loathed, if such a combination could exist.

"Oh good, it's you," she said, trying to inject pleasure into her voice.

"At your service, Lady Sophia," Rudolf said, dropping into a low bow.

"How are the triplets?" she asked.

"They are really quiet," he offered. "I can't understand a word they say."

"Is that because they are still in your wife's stomach?"

He shrugged. "How am I supposed to know how science works? So, where are you headed?"

"I'm looking for..." Sophia was about to ask for directions to Chimerick's Bar and Grill but remembered something. "Actually, I need to talk to Papa Creola. Doesn't he have a shop on Roya Lane?"

"He does," the fae answered, stroking his blond hair out of his face. "But why wouldn't you just ask your sister where to find him? She is best buds with Father Time."

Sophia shook her head. "Actually, I was hoping Liv wouldn't find out about this. It's sort of a surprise."

"Oh, I'm awful at keeping surprises," Rudolf admitted. "Don't tell me any more or I'll ruin it. It's like that one time that Liv told me she was getting you a summer beach house for your birthday, and I accidentally told you."

"She hasn't gotten me a beach house for any of my birthdays," Sophia said.

He covered his face. "Oops. Wait, it's for your next birthday. My bad. There, I did it again."

"Okay, well, how about you just forget about this conversation after we're done," Sophia suggested. "For now, will you simply tell me where to find Papa Creola? I need to ask him something."

Rudolf plugged his ears. "Say no more. I don't want any information I can divulge." He indicated with his chin toward the end of the Lane. "Look for the Fantastical Armory. That's Subner's shop, his assistant. If Papa Creola can be found, it will be there."

"Thank you," Sophia said, finding that interaction with Rudolf strangely helpful and surprisingly painless.

"By the way, I don't think you've abandoned your family at all for the Dragon Elite, despite what jerks on the council for the House of Fourteen say," Rudolf called from down the lane.

Sophia narrowed her eyes. "Who has said that?"

"Oh, no one. Just those who miss seeing you around and think that you've joined a dying group of crusty old men when the House of Fourteen is fighting the real fight." He covered his mouth, his eyes bulging. "I've said too much again, haven't I?"

She let out a measured breath. "Just a smidge."

"Forget it all," he said, zipping his mouth with his fingers. He murmured a goodbye as he waved.

Sophia shook her head at him as she waved back, heading in the direction of the Fantastical Armory. "Thank the angels that man is pretty and sweet, or otherwise he might be completely useless."

CHAPTER TWENTY-ONE

Sophia knew that Father Time had regenerated recently, changing his appearance. Whereas before he took on the look of a gnome, he currently was in the form of an elf.

She entered the Fantastical Armory, thinking her attention would be on finding Papa Creola. However, she was immediately overwhelmed by the incredible collection of weapons on display in the shop.

"What can I help—" the elf who had greeted her appeared to be cut off by pure amazement. He had long stringy brown hair and was wearing cut off shorts and a T-shirt that said, "If the climate can change, then so can you."

"Subner?" Sophia asked, squinting at the tall figure.

"Little Sophia?" he asked, shaking his head at her. "Is that you?"

She smiled, not really recognizing Papa Creola's assistant, but seeing a familiarity in his eyes. "I'm not that little anymore, am I?"

He shook his head. "Not at all. What brings you this way? Looking for Liv? I think she's gone up to heaven."

"What?" Sophia asked, her heart suddenly racing.

He shook his head. "Sorry. I mean on a field trip. She got a special pass from Papa Creola. He needed her to negotiate with the angels on some deal they have been going back on." He tilted his head to the side, cupping his mouth. "Between you and me, never make business dealings with angels. They will bat their eyelashes, and you'll be too enamored to negotiate over the good stuff."

"I thought it was angels who made the dragonriders," Sophia said.

"They did," he stated, shaking his head. "And sorry if that's offensive to you. The angels are all right for the most part, but I just wouldn't go into business with one, if you know what I mean."

"Thanks for the advice," Sophia stated. "And I'm not looking for Liv, but I'm glad she's only in heaven visiting. Is that even allowed?"

"Perk of working for Papa Creola," Subner stated. "She had to sign a ten-thousand-page non-disclosure agreement. Believe me, we heard about that for ages."

Sophia giggled, picturing Liv complaining about such things. "Well, I was actually hoping to talk to Papa Creola if he's here."

Subner studied her. "You want to ask him a favor, don't you?"

She didn't know if she should fess up or not.

His eyes flicked to Inexorabilis on her hip. "Oh, I get it. Yeah, he's totally not going to do that."

Sophia's eyes bulged. Her sister's friends were the strangest, most awesome people, and also infuriating. "You already know what I want?"

"Well, I can guess," he stated. "I mean, you haven't bonded to the elfin-made sword that once belonged to Guinevere Beaufont, but you really want to. And the only way to do that is to undo the act it did to bond with her, which is why you're here because only Father Time can reverse such a large act."

"How do you know all that?" Sophia asked with disbelief.

He held out his arm to the shop. "I own and operate the best armory in the world. It's my business to know weapons. And without even touching that sword, I know that you have to reverse the act that banished the Phantom from this world. Papa Creola won't do it."

Sophia deflated. "Well, then maybe you can help me find a new sword because I can't progress in my training without bonding to my own."

"Don't lose hope yet, young dragonrider," Subner stated thoughtfully. "I said that Papa Creola wasn't going to bring back the Phantom under those circumstances. However, when your mother killed him, she didn't know something of great importance."

"Which is?" Sophia asked.

"Well, she simply slew him, which was understandable," Subner explained. "He was creating havoc in the world and needed to be stopped. It was only after he was gone that we learned his horn was a supreme source of power that could erase evil in certain places of the world. Yet, once he was slain, his horn died. If we had known, Guinevere would have been instructed to harvest the horn first and then slay the beast."

Sophia's heart leapt with hope. "So if I tell Papa Creola that I want to bring the Phantom back so I can get the horn and then kill him, you think he'll go for it?"

"It's worth a shot," Subner stated.

Sophia smiled broadly at him. "Thank you. That's so helpful."

She had remembered Liv saying that Subner was cold and unhelpful for the most part to her. But that hadn't been her experience. Maybe it was being a dragonrider that put things in her favor.

"Now…" Subner said, leaning forward. "Now that I've helped you, I'm hoping that maybe you can help locate a weapon for me that's housed at the Gullington."

Sophia sighed. And there it was, she thought.

Of course, he had been nice to her. Subner wanted something. It was fine, though, she realized. As long as she was making progress.

"Tell me what the weapon looks like, and I'll keep an eye out," Sophia offered.

He pointed at her pocket. "I've gone ahead and sent a description to your phone. Thanks so much." The elf walked for the back just as the door behind the counter opened.

A man she didn't recognize strode out of the back, his long ponytail swishing as he placed buds in his ears.

"Papa, you have company," Subner stated, pointing in Sophia's direction.

Father Time looked up at her, blinking. "Oh, well, if it isn't the new version of Sophia Beaufont. I was getting tired of seeing you in that little girl form."

"Ummm, what?" she asked, confused.

He stretched his neck back and forth, looking like he was getting ready for a run in his shorts and jogging shoes. "Well, it's just that I see you in this form in most of the visions, so it was always weird when you were little. Kind of like seeing a person as a fetus. You're just like, hurry up and get on with it."

"Right," Sophia said, drawing out the word, not used to this version of Papa Creola. Subner was enough of a change, but the hippie, athletic version of Father Time was going to take some getting used to.

"What can I do for you?" Papa Creola asked, stretching his calves.

"I've come to make a request of you," Sophia began, injecting hope into her voice.

CHAPTER TWENTY-TWO

After Sophia made her case to Papa Creola, he remained quiet, giving her a studious expression. She wanted to keep talking, coming up with more reasons that he should do what she asked, but she'd learned the art of negotiation from Liv and knew that silence was a golden commodity when it came to discussions.

Past the point of uncomfortable silence, Papa Creola remained quiet. Sophia desperately wanted to interject one more point or argument, but instead, she simply continued to gaze at the oldest entity on Earth, besides Mother Nature, of course.

"Okay," Papa Creola finally said. "I'll make you a deal."

Sophia finally drew in a breath. "I'm listening." She tried not to appear anxious or excited.

"I, of course, will want the Phantom's horn," he began.

"Of course," she said, nodding.

"But that kind of spell to reverse events is very costly for the spectrum of time," he stated. "Which means, I'll need some extra power to fuel it."

"I can stop by the coffee shop and get you a double espresso before you hand off the spell," Sophia joked.

He scowled at her. "You have your sister's humor."

"Thank you," Sophia said, realizing that he didn't intend this as a compliment.

"In order to help you, I'm going to need Mother Nature to give me a bottle of her essence," he stated.

Sophia's eyes shifted back and forth. "Is it appropriate for me to ask her for that? Maybe you should do that? It seems personal. Like I'm asking for an organ or something."

He shook his head. "I'm very busy. If I'm going to do it, then I need some of her power. And you'll have to ask her."

"But why will she do it?" Sophia asked. "She's not getting anything. She's merely giving up something."

He gave her a skeptical glare. "If you think for a second that I believe you're undoing Phantom's death so I can have his horn, you must have been born yesterday, Sophia Beaufont. I know that you have something to gain from this, but I commend you on positioning it in a way that benefits me immensely. Smart thinking. And what benefits you in this equation will help Mother Nature, who you work for. So it behooves Mama Jamba to do this. However, she might have her own hesitations, so you'll have to take those up with her. If I get her essence, then I'll hand over the spell. Otherwise, no deal."

"Okay," Sophia said, drawing out the one word. "I guess this seems fair."

"And to help the situation," Papa Creola began, "I don't tell Liv about this."

"You won't?" she asked, hope in her voice.

"Well, there's no point," he reasoned. "She worries enough as it is, and when she does, she's not as productive. So we will keep it between us."

"Thanks, Papa Creola," Sophia said, feeling more hopeful as she headed out into Roya Lane.

CHAPTER TWENTY-THREE

R oya Lane was even more crowded when Sophia exited the Fantastical Armory. She wished she would have asked for directions from Papa Creola, but asking the Father of Time for such things seemed like a bad use of his.

Thankfully, after weaving her way through gnomes gambling at cardboard boxes made into tables and fae who she could have sworn were offering themselves in return for money, she found the greasy bar. Chimerick's Bar and Grill was lackluster to say the least, many of the neon letters in the sign having burned out. It read: him rick Ba an G i l. Still, she was able to find the place, which she was grateful for.

When she entered the dirty place, she was certain it wasn't somewhere that young magicians didn't frequent. Many of the patrons turned to gawk at her with their good eyes. She could say that since at least three of the people had eye patches or glass eyes. That seemed like a large number since there were only about six people inside. For a moment, she wondered if she'd walked into a strange optometrist office by accident.

"What brings you here, sweetheart," the bartender said, throwing a dirty coaster in her direction on the bar.

Now that Sophia had finally made it to Chimerick's Bar and Grill, she didn't know what to do. She hadn't really thought that far ahead. Mae Ling's message had simply told her to come here. She did know that she was looking for someone.

"I'm looking for someone," she began in a whisper, aware that everyone in the bar was watching her.

The bartender, a burly guy with a smudged nametag that read Clive or Clyde—it was hard to tell, banged his arm on the countertop, making the jukebox in the corner start playing music, drowning out their conversation.

"Go on, then darling," he said cordially. "They can't hear you over the music. Their ears are worse than their eyesight."

Sophia nodded. "I'm looking for someone who I think has some…"

"You're going to just have to spit it out, or I can't help you," Clive or Clyde stated.

This was tough for Sophia. She didn't know if she should just be honest and get help or if that would endanger her entire mission.

I think he's okay, Lunis said in her head.

Never before had she been so grateful to share her mind with a dragon.

Really? she asked.

Yeah, but if he pulls out the magical revolver under the bar, you better hightail it, Lunis stated.

How do you even know that he has that? she asked.

Maybe because of all the bullet holes in the walls, he answered.

Good point, she said, noticing them now and wishing that she hadn't.

"I'm looking for someone who might have some dragon eggs," she finally said to the bartender.

He considered her for a long moment. She was grateful that she had the practice of playing the quiet game with Papa Creola because otherwise, she might have broken first.

"Okay, well, since you seem like a good kid," the bartender said, leaning forward, his hot breath smelling sour. "There's this guy, Griff, who has been coming around lately. Usually around closing time. He drinks all my whiskey and usually scares off a few patrons, but he tips well, so I don't throw him out."

"And he's been talking about dragon eggs?" Sophia asked.

He nodded. "Loudly, when he drinks too much. The other day he was asking about how to shield eggs, but none of us paid much attention since there's no way the fellow can actually have dragon eggs. I mean, they are extinct, right?" He laughed.

Sophia joined in with him, shaking her head like the idea of dragon eggs was crazy. It made sense to her that the dragon eggs were shielded, though, because that would keep the dragons from finding them if they set their senses to do so. It wasn't foolproof, but sometimes dragons could find their eggs, and none of the dragons in the Cave had sensed anything of the sort, according to Lunis.

"So, did someone tell him how to shield the dragon eggs he thought he had?" Sophia asked.

"Beats me," he answered. "You might be able to ask him yourself, but he won't talk to a pretty thing such as yourself. The guy is a chauvinist pig. Always harassing the ladies in the bar."

"So he would talk to a man?" Sophia asked.

Clive or Clyde shrugged. "If he's ugly and fat. The guy has a true complex and really doesn't talk to anyone who doesn't intimidate him. He insults them. Throws beer bottles at their head, but he doesn't talk to them."

"Okay, so I need to be an ugly, fat man," Sophia said, mostly to herself.

The bartender laughed. "Yeah, good luck with that, sweetheart. Is there anything I can get for you?"

Sophia shook her head. "No, thanks. This has been quite helpful."

"What would be helpful is if people like you would hang around my establishment instead of this lot." He threw his head in the direction of the regulars.

She backed for the door. "Well, maybe I'll be back."

"Please do," he said, winking at her.

Sophia had every intention of coming back, but the owner wouldn't recognize her when she did.

CHAPTER TWENTY-FOUR

The banging from Hiker's office sounded about the same as the last time Sophia visited the Viking. She was grateful that she didn't have to see him right then, although she was sorry that his troubles didn't seem to have subsided.

She wanted to make his worries less, but something told her it was going to get worse before it got better.

"I'm grateful to see you're pampering yourself," Mama Jamba said to Sophia, passing her in the entryway, reading a magazine and chewing on a celery stick.

"Oh, you noticed my nails," Sophia said, holding up Mae Ling's handy work.

"No, I noticed your glow," Mama Jamba stated, holding up the frayed celery stick. "You know, you need to contact whoever made these things and tell them they are not good, no matter what you put on them. Simply awful rubbish."

Sophia gave her a sideways expression. "Ummm, wouldn't that be you? Aren't you responsible for celery?"

Mama Jamba winked at her. "Why do you think I went into hiding the first few times?" She laughed loudly. "But I keep trying celery, thinking I had good intentions. Turns out I think I was drunk on plum wine. It was a strange Tuesday when I created celery. Don't even get me started on what happened on the Wednesday I created potatoes."

"What happened?" Sophia asked.

"Only good things, hun," she said proudly. "Only good things. Potatoes are still one of my favorite creations. Well, that and oceans, but whatever."

It was simply breathtaking to Sophia that she was standing there having a conversation with the entity who created the Earth. Even stranger was that she was about to ask her for something for Father Time. Sophia's life had gotten really strange, really fast.

"Mama Jamba, I wanted to ask you something," Sophia began.

She turned and faced her. "No, I don't think that powder works for your complexion."

"What?" Sophia asked. "I'm not wearing powder."

"Oh, well, then let's back up," Mama Jamba said. "Firstly, there are some great options in the realm of powder. Maybe I should send you to my esthetician."

"That would be great," Sophia said, trying to get the conversation back on track. "But first, I need to ask you a favor from Papa Creola."

She lowered her chin. "What does that man want?"

"Well, you see, I need to undo the death of the Phantom so he can have his horn and I can bond to my mother's sword, but in order to do it I'm supposed to get the essence of your magic or something like that so that Papa Creola can create the spell." She said the entire explanation in one long sentence, not taking a breath until she was done. Then she offered Mama Jamba a smile. "So, will you give me that so I can continue on my way?"

"No," Mama Jamba said, not even deliberating on the question. She turned for the dining hall, returning her attention to the magazine.

"But Mama!" Sophia complained, trudging after her, strangely feeling like a teenager about to have a tantrum.

"That man has been asking for the essence of my magic forever," Mama said, dog-earring one of the pages of the magazine like she wanted to make that face mask recipe later. "He thinks he's figured out a way to get it by having one of my riders ask for it, but it's not going to work."

"But I need to raise the Phantom and take his horn and kill him again to bond to my mother's sword," Sophia said, trailing behind Mama Jamba, who kept her eyes on the magazine.

"I totally get that, dear, but I'm simply not giving Papa my magic," she said, licking her fingers and turning a page. "He says he needs it for one thing, but I guarantee he's going to use it for something else."

"So?" Sophia argued. "In the end, it will help me complete my training, and that will benefit you."

Mama Jamba faced Sophia. She reached out her hand and held up Sophia's chin. "I know you're disappointed. I'm sorry. I never, ever want to hurt one of my own. But who do you think invented tough love?"

"You?" Sophia guessed.

Mama Jamba shook her head. "Oh, no. That term was coined in the 1980s by some pop psychologist. But you'll just have to find another way. I'm not in a position where I want to go giving my magic away."

"But it's for Papa Creola," Sophia argued, not willing to give up her cause.

"I know," Mama Jamba said, nodding. "And I trust him like no one else. He and I are tight. Well, we're pretty much married except I live in my own house and don't have to clean up his dirty laundry, so it's the best marriage ever. But the answer is still no, my dear. I'm not changing my mind on it."

Sophia slumped slightly. "Okay, well, thanks for listening."

"Oh, perk up, love," Mama Jamba said. "You look so much more beautiful when you don't slouch. Well, you'd look beautiful with cheese on your head, but that's just the way it is with my riders. You are all a gorgeous bunch. Even Hiker would be attractive if he shaved that beard."

"I heard that!" Hiker barked all the way from his office.

"And I said it," Mama Jamba called back up to him.

She shook her head at Sophia. "I'd head through the kitchen and as far from that man as possible. He's as grumpy as I was on the day I created durian fruit."

Sophia laughed, heading for the kitchen and leaving Mama Jamba in the dining hall.

CHAPTER TWENTY-FIVE

The kitchen was filled with an assortment of strange smells. Ainsley was leaning over the stove, churning a pot, her brow sweating.

"I don't understand how to replicate those quesadillas you got for us from Uber Eats," Ainsley said, catching sight of Sophia when she entered the kitchen.

Sophia strode over and peered into the pot of gray liquid. "Well, for one, they aren't usually made in a single pot," Sophia offered sympathetically.

Ainsley threw up her hands. "Are you serious? What sort of magic creates this Mexican food you feed to us?"

Sophia shook her head. "None. It's just recipes. You know, take some tortillas, cheese, and whatever else and put them together."

"Hold up," Ainsley said, rushing over to a pad and pen. "You're going to need to slow down. I don't understand this business you speak of."

"Ainsley, you know what I think would help your culinary endeavors?" Sophia asked.

"A lobotomy, S. Beaufont?" she answered, a slightly serious expression on her face.

"No," Sophia said, trying to sound positive. "How about a field trip out of the Gullington?"

"Oh, I went into town this morning to get groceries," Ainsley replied.

"Actually," Sophia began. "I'm thinking something a bit more exotic and farther from home."

"Oh," Ainsley said, giving her a scandalous expression. "But my next century birthday isn't for another forty years."

Sophia couldn't help but laugh. "Do you really have to wait that long to leave here?"

"Well… I mean, the Castle likes me here or close," Ainsley stated. "And what if Hiker needs someone to yell at? Or what if Evan *can* find his cape? Someone has to hide it for him so that he has a bad morning."

Sophia laughed again. "You all are my favorite people, and that's saying a lot."

"Anyway, let's plan an outing to a few towns over in forty years," Ainsley said, turning her attention back to the pot of sludge. "I think I can fix this dish. Maybe if I add some kale."

Sophia shook her head. "No! Kale never fixed anything, ever. Ever!"

Ainsley's eyes widened. "Wow, I've never seen you so passionate."

"Well, I just had a conversation with the inventor of all vegetables, so I guess it rubbed off on me," Sophia explained.

"Oh, was Mama Jamba going through her list of regrets again?" Ainsley asked. "Yeah, we had a long heart to heart last night about rutabaga." She shook her head, looking remorseful. "That fruit really had so much possibility, but it just didn't work out."

"I think it's a vegetable," Sophia corrected.

"Well, tell that woman that," Ainsley said, pointing in the direction of the dining room. "Currently, she's classifying it as trash, but I think she's just going through a thing, you know with returning to the surface of Earth and having to take ownership over her riders again. It's a time of reflection for us all. Hiker has a bump on his forehead the size of a golf ball."

"From ramming his head against his desk?" Sophia asked.

Ainsley nodded. "Yes, I think he's working on a song."

"I think he's working on a headache," Sophia said, thinking she could hear the constant drumming even then. "Anyway, Ainsley," Sophia continued, "I have a mission, and I need your help."

"Me!" Ainsley said. "I can help. Do you want me to make you some stew? Get you dressed? Clean your boots?"

Sophia shook her head. "No, I need you to go incognito to meet someone."

"What?" Ainsley said, clapping her hands to her face. "Oh, no. S. Beaufont, you've lost your mind. What did you eat? I knew all that modern stuff would go to your head."

Sophia waved the housekeeper off. "No, I haven't lost my mind. It's just that I need someone to meet with this guy who has the locations of a few dragon eggs. It's important that I find them. He won't talk to you or me. He'll only talk to someone who is a man, old, fat, and ugly."

"Why don't you send—"

"It's probably better if you don't finish that sentence," Sophia cut her off.

Ainsley nodded. "You're right. The Castle has ears and repeats things. Anyway, I know you're good at changing your appearance. You have the best outfits. Why don't you do it?"

"Because my disguises aren't fool-proof," Sophia explained. "I can't keep them up for long periods of time, especially when I need to be on guard. And I don't trust this guy at all because he probably works for Thad Reinhart, so I want to be there to defend. But you can change your appearance easily, and if you talked to him, you could find out what he knows and I could be there to listen. And as a bonus, you'd leave the Gullington and see the world. Imagine all the inspiration you'd get. We could even go for gelato or something afterward."

Ainsley considered this. "Gelato is a type of coffee, right?"

"Ice cream," Sophia corrected.

"And I could wear a crazy hat, right? The Castle hates my hats."

"Sure," Sophia said, making a note about the Castle's preferences. "Will you please do it?"

"This will help the Dragon Elite?" Ainsley asked.

"Yes," Sophia answered.

"And it will help me in my role?" the housekeeper asked.

"There's no better way to improve than to get out and get some perspective," Sophia stated. "How long has it been since you've seen the modern world?"

Ainsley leaned forward, looking around like someone was listening. "Never, S. Beaufont."

"What?" Sophia asked. "You leave the Gullington, though."

"Yes, but I don't go far," she argued. "I was born not far from here, and I'm new to pretty much everything. So it's like taking a baby out. Do you think you can handle that?"

Sophia only realized right then what kind of challenge she'd signed on for. She smiled, accepting it proudly. "Yes, we are going to find out where those eggs are and get you a fresh new perspective to bring back to the Gullington."

"Great!" Ainsley said excitedly. "What do I need to do first?"

"Get rid of that pot of sludge and make yourself fat and ugly."

CHAPTER TWENTY-SIX

"Are you sure that I'm ugly enough?" Ainsley asked as they strode for the Barrier on the edge of the Gullington.

Sophia gave her a slight smile. "I never thought I'd be saying this to you Ains, but you're so ugly, I don't want to look at you."

The shapeshifter had made herself into a short, round man with patches of gray hair on his boxed-shaped head. There were multiple large moles on his face, all of them sprouting wiry gray hair. And his teeth were crooked and yellow when he attempted to smile, which looked more like a devious scowl.

"Thank you, S. Beaufont. I know you wouldn't say that unless it was true."

When they were at the Barrier, the housekeeper turned and looked at the Castle with quiet longing.

"Hey, the Castle will be fine without you for a bit," Sophia consoled, sensing that Ainsley didn't want to leave her home, even for a couple of hours. Strangely, Sophia thought she was more worried about leaving the Gullington than she was nervous about seeing the modern world.

A truly melancholy expression took over Ainsley's face. "You think it will be okay?"

"No," Sophia said at once, realizing her mistake. "The Castle is probably going to fall into a full-on depression, decorating the inside and outside with black and gothic décor."

Ainsley perked up. "Oh, you think so? I hope. I wouldn't want to think that this place wouldn't fall apart without me, although I did ask Quiet to look after things in my absence."

Sophia paused. "Hey, about Quiet…"

"Yes?" Ainsley asked. "Is this about his real name?"

Now that Sophia was thinking about it, Quiet had mentioned on the one occasion she understood him that his real name wasn't Quiet, and he'd tell her what it was if she stuck around. "You can tell me what it is, can you?"

Ainsley shook her head. "No, it wouldn't be right."

"Well, that's actually not what I wanted to ask about," Sophia began. "Have you noticed that he's been acting suspicious lately?"

Ainsley lifted a curious eyebrow. "You do realize that the groundskeeper for the Gullington is the quintessential definition of suspicious, right? I can't find him half the time, and neither can the Castle, which is bizarre. If anything goes on in the Expanse, he absolutely knows about it. And I'm certain that he's been hoarding snacks in his room, which I haven't been able to enter in over four centuries."

"Oh," Sophia said, surprised. "And he teleported me through the Gullington, which I didn't think could happen."

"It can't," Ainsley affirmed. "But some rules don't apply to the gnome."

"I wonder why," Sophia mused as they crossed the Barrier to where she could create a portal to Roya Lane.

"I wouldn't wonder too much on it, S. Beaufont. There are some mysteries that aren't worth your time."

"Okay, well, after you," Sophia said, holding out her hand to Ainsley.

The housekeeper simply regarded her with a tentative expression.

"It's fine," Sophia stated. "I'll come through right after you. Since I opened the portal, it's better if I go through after you."

Ainsley shook her head. "It's not that. It's just been so long since I've stepped through a portal."

"Oh, you're nervous then?" Sophia questioned.

The ugly man nodded.

"Well, it's a bit of a strange feeling when you enter a portal," Sophia reminded her. "But just try to acclimate as soon as you step through. Take in as many of the things around you as possible: smells, sounds, and sights. If you do that, then you should be okay, although being slightly nauseous is common."

"We could just take a train there," Ainsley offered. "Roya Lane is in London, right?"

"Yes, but you can only get there using portal magic since only magical creatures are allowed to enter."

"Fiddlesticks," she complained. "Fine. I'll do it, but any words of wisdom on what I'll see?"

"Roya Lane is sort of hard to explain," Sophia stated. "It changes often, and at night, I'm certain it's probably more chaotic."

"Why don't you draw me a picture really quickly?" Ainsley summoned a pad and pen.

Sophia shook her head at the housekeeper. "You know, tough love is sometimes for the best." Using her quick reflexes, she reached out and pushed the squat man through the portal before he could react.

CHAPTER TWENTY-SEVEN

"That was a rotten thing to do!" Ainsley yelled at Sophia when she stepped through the portal.

She offered her a sympathetic expression. "I apologize, but you were stalling, and sometimes the best thing to do is just take the plunge."

Ainsley looked around, her eyes roaming over the various shops and strange creatures striding through the cobbled street. "Yes, and going through the portal wasn't so bad. But being here is…well, making me think I should have brought my heart medicine."

Sophia whipped around. "Are you okay? You have heart medicine? Do you want me to go back and get it?"

"Oh, no. I don't have any. If I did, I would have brought it," Ainsley answered.

Sophia sighed with relief. "Well, if the gnomes try and talk to you, ignore them. They just want to get you to gamble, and no one ever wins. Don't take any food samples. And if you see a gorgeous fae, ignore him unless you want to lose a few hundred brain cells."

Ainsley turned in a circle, her droopy eyes wide. "I've never seen so many amazing things at once. This place is incredible!"

Many of the magical creatures on the street turned to look at the pair, giving them curious expressions like they were wondering what Sophia would be doing accompanying such a homely man.

"Ains, it might be better if you didn't draw so much attention to us," Sophia said, pulling the hood from her cloak up over her head. "We are supposed to be incognito."

"I know, but S., this place is bursting with smells and sights and sounds!" Ainsley rejoiced. "It makes me want to kick up my heels and do a dance!"

"Don't!" a group of gnomes yelled at Ainsley. "No one wants to see you dance."

"No one wants to see you," an elf woman replied. "But I can sell you a face cream that will take care of those warts."

"He's fine," Sophia said, ushering Ainsley down the lane toward Chimerick's Bar and Grill. "Now, you remember what you're supposed to do?"

Ainsley nodded, staring wide-eyed at every shop they passed, her knobby hands dragging longingly against the glass, leaving behind fingerprints. "I'm supposed to go into the bar, chat up the loudmouth at the bar, buy him a drink, and get him talking."

"That's right," Sophia said. "I'll be in the corner if anything goes wrong."

Ainsley halted. "What is going to go wrong? Do they put out spider poison in this bar? Oh, please tell me there are spiders in there."

"What?" Sophia asked. "Why would you want that?"

Giving her an expression of disbelief, she said, "You do know that spiders are crucial for the well-being of a place, right? People who kill the spiders who grace their residence open themselves for all sorts of problems."

"So, you don't do anything about the spiders in the Gullington?" Sophia asked.

"I try to make them feel as comfortable as possible," Ainsley stated. "The nest under your bed gets a lot of my attention."

"Oh, angels," Sophia said, suddenly lightheaded. "We might need to move that nest when we return."

Ainsley shrugged. "Suit yourself. I thought I was doing you a favor by putting them in your room."

"Move them to Evan's, please," Sophia requested.

"Fine, fine."

"Okay, here we go," Sophia said, giving Ainsley one last look over her shoulder before slipping into Chimerick's Bar and Grill and disappearing into the shadows, unnoticed by the patrons, thanks to a shielding spell.

She was seated at a table in the corner by the time Ainsley entered after her. Hobbling up to the bar, the shapeshifter glanced around.

Sophia had given Ainsley the description of their target. She'd told her to ignore those with eye patches but was worried the housekeeper wouldn't be able to find the character. Her fears were relieved at once when a drunk at the bar began hollering loudly at Ainsley.

"Wow, you should come sit next to me, fella!" the man yelled. "People like you make me look good." He was medium height and build, with thinning hair and a face full of wrinkles.

Sophia had turned on her heightened senses so she could overhear the conversation and immediately regretted her enhanced ability to smell. Even from across the bar, she could smell the man's rancid breath and felt bad for Ainsley, who had to sit next to him.

The shapeshifter made several attempts to try and get onto the tall bar stool, nearly falling as she jumped. Her large butt didn't fit really well on the narrow surface when she got up there, but Sophia was proud of Ainsley's determination to stay on the seat by bracing herself on the bar.

"What can I get for you?" the bartender who had helped Sophia asked, throwing a napkin in front of Ainsley on the bar.

"Something strong," she said, her voice deep and gruff as if she spent too many years in the coal mines. "And make it a double for my new friend."

The man beside her smiled thoughtfully. "That's mighty nice of you. I knew I liked you from the moment you walked through that door."

"That's because no one else in here wants to talk to you, Griff," Clive or Clyde stated, pouring two double shots of whiskey.

So we have the right guy, Sophia thought, grateful for their good luck.

"To our good health," Ainsley said, raising her glass to cheers with Griff.

"To mine," Griff replied. "I'm not sure about you, buddy. You might want to get checked out soon. That yellowish tone to your skin can't be good."

"Well then, to putting in a hard week of work," Ainsley said, not missing a beat.

"I can cheer to that," Griff said, clinking his glass against the other one before knocking back the entire drink. "I tell you, this was the week from hell."

"How is that?" Ainsley asked him, leaning forward and keeping her voice down.

Sophia felt miserable that Ains had to inhale Griff's nasty scent, but not having too many overhear their conversation was for the best.

Griff leaned down, matching Ainsley's volume. That technique always worked, it seemed. "Well, I had the displeasure of doing a job for probably the most despicable human being on this planet. But he overpaid on a somewhat easy job, so I was good with it."

"Oh?" Ainsley asked. "I'm looking for work. Who is this guy?"

Griff shook his head. "He wouldn't give me his name. I didn't even get to meet him. But his communications were downright insulting. Micromanaged every aspect of the job. I just don't work like that."

"This job?" Ainsley inquired.

"You wouldn't believe me even if I told you," Griff answered.

"Well, what if I bought you another drink?" Ainsley offered, still not having touched her whiskey.

"I can't object to that," Griff stated cheerfully.

"Make it two more," Ainsley said to the bartender.

He nodded, pouring another couple of doubles and sliding them in front of the men.

Griff threw back his drink, pulling his arm across his mouth as he shook his head. "Oh, that stuff burns, but in a good way."

Ainsley slid her other drink over to him. "Here, have mine?"

At this, Griff gave her a questioning expression. "Why? You trying to get me drunk?"

Sophia stiffened.

Griff tensed, his eyes narrowing at Ainsley.

The shapeshifter looked momentarily thrown off, making Sophia's pulse beat loudly in her head.

"Yeah, because I'm trying to get you to take me home," Ainsley said with a laugh.

To Sophia's relief, Griff erupted in laughter, slapping the bar. "There isn't enough whiskey in this world, old buddy." He picked up the drink and threw it back.

When Ainsley slid the other drink she still hadn't touched, Griff didn't object this time, taking the glass, but not drinking it this time. Instead, he began to sway, pointing a finger at Ainsley.

"You won't believe what this son-of-a-so-and-so had me do," Griff began, his speech slurring. He leaned in closer to Ainsley. "Dragon eggs."

"No?" Ainsley replied. "I didn't think there were any more out there."

"Me too," the guy said, raising the glass of whiskey to his mouth and sniffing it, but deciding not to take a drink just yet. He appeared close to falling off his barstool. Sophia worried that Ainsley had gotten him too drunk. There was a fine line between getting people to open up with booze and them passing out from too much.

"Anyway, this man told me to go and get these dragon eggs, so I did what I was told," Griff went on. "But after I had them in my possession, he tells me that they need to be shielded. I start worrying that assassins or the Dragon Elite were going to come after me. But we all know that those guys are all gone, am I right?"

Ainsley nodded. "As far as I know. But assassins. I'd worry about them."

"Well, and also poachers," the man related. "Wouldn't you know, as soon as I got those eggs away from their location, I had all sorts of people on my ass. And that guy, whoever it was who hired me, didn't give a damn. He just wanted me to transport them to a safe location. I nearly lost a body part getting away from those ruthless poachers. Then I would have looked like all the deformed people in this bar!"

Sophia remembered when Lunis was in his egg and they had to transport him, it did bring out a bunch of poachers. They were apparently clued in to the energy a dragon egg gave off and came out in full force as soon as they sensed it. Rory and a few other giants helped to shield Lunis' egg once they got it to his place, where it was safe. She realized now that there must have been something about the case at Zuma Zat's that protected the eggs, but Griff hadn't been smart enough to keep them in that chest, probably thinking there was a tracking device on it.

"So, what happened?" Ainsley asked him.

"Well, thanks to nobody in this dump," Griff continued, "I was able to get the eggs to safety, but no one could tell me how to shield them. Thankfully, they are off my hands now and not my problem. I'm tired of looking over my shoulder and getting shot at."

"I imagine, buddy," Ainsley related. "But I wonder what kind of place you took them to? It must be shielded to keep the eggs protected from those poachers who were after you."

"Oh, it is, and a genius location for eggs," Griff said, taking a sip of the whiskey and swaying so much that Ainsley had to reach out and grab him to keep him from tumbling back.

"You've got my attention now," Ainsley said with a laugh. "You're quite the storyteller. I'm on the edge of my chair with curiosity."

The man looked at her proudly before leaning in closer, his eyes shifting back and forth like he didn't want to be overheard. "It's in an underwater facility in the South Pacific, if you can believe. Some place they called the Institute."

"That's genius," Ainsley said in a hushed voice.

It was brilliant, Sophia realized. The water would shield the energy of the dragon eggs, keeping them off the radar of poachers, dragons, and anyone else on the hunt, namely the Dragon Elite.

"Yeah, this place was abandoned," Griff stated. "Apparently it used to be this fancy headquarters for a strange population of people. Real vigilante types. The guy who hired me took it over. It's full of all sorts of magical tech."

"How did you get in there?" Ainsley asked.

"Oh, I had to take a submarine," Griff stated. "That was nerve-wracking since I'm totally claustrophobic. Not until I got there did they tell me there's this single room where you can portal to but the wards have to be taken down. Another tiny room that was too cramped was called the GAD-C. I don't know. But thankfully, I was able to portal out of there and didn't have to take the submarine back. I was happy to be out of the Institute. That place was like a tin box."

"This place, the Institute," Ainsley began, "you said it was full of magical tech? That's nuts. Lots of people too, I'm guessing."

"Oh, no," the guy stated. "That's the thing, this billionaire or whatever he is, doesn't like employing people. He told me that much but apparently had to resort to having me go after the eggs. He relies on robots mostly."

That made sense based on what Sophia had seen when she went to the facility north of the Gullington. She guessed the jet pilots were human, but maybe not. They could be cyborgs. But the guards around the facility were definitely robots, powered by magical tech.

"That's nuts," Ainsley said as Griff finished the rest of the whiskey.

"You want to know what's crazy?" he asked.

"What's that?" Ainsley asked.

"The way the room is spinning," he stated, swaying before he toppled over backward, passing out.

CHAPTER TWENTY-EIGHT

Sophia had her phone pinned up to her ear when she entered Hiker's office. He gazed up at her, a less than happy expression on his face.

"Oh, good," he said, "you're one of those people."

She covered the receiver. "One of what people?"

"One of those people who can't do anything without a phone attached to your face," he stated.

"How would you know about those people, Viking?" she asked, wondering if she was pushing her luck with him. They had bantered, but she sensed she could cross the line fast.

"I've been in the modern world, remember? When I tried to get the Presidents and world leaders to recognize us as adjudicators," he explained. "And half of them had devices attached to their faces during our meetings as if being in the present moment would kill them."

"Oh, hold up a second," Sophia said, cutting him off.

Hiker growled with frustration.

"Yes, I can hear you," she said into the phone, replying to Liv. "Yeah, the phone in the Gullington works perfectly, thanks to the upgrades you did to it."

"And it's also giving us all radiation," Hiker complained loudly.

"I'm not going to tell him that," Sophia said to Liv on the phone.

"Tell me what?" he asked, narrowing his eyes.

She smiled, batting her eyelashes at him. "That you are a handsome and formidable leader."

"That's not what your sister said," he argued.

"Not in so many words, but that was the gist," Sophia said before holding up her finger to pause him from saying anything more. "Okay, yeah. That's great news. And you can send it over to me? With a map and coordinates?"

"Map of what?" Hiker asked, his forehead wrinkling.

Sophia held up her finger again, trying to get him to shush. "Sounds great. Thanks so much for your help with this. Hiker is also super grateful for the House of Fourteen's help."

"I didn't say that," he argued, but Liv didn't hear him because Sophia switched off the phone. "What was that all about?"

"I found the dragon eggs," Sophia stated.

He stood suddenly, anticipation making his face bright. "They are here? Where?"

She tilted her head back and forth. "They aren't actually here, per se."

"What do you mean, per se?" he asked. "Are they in the Cave?"

She shook her head. "No, I should be more specific. They aren't here at all."

"Where are they?"

"In a hidden, underwater facility that's guarded by lots of Thad Reinhart's magical tech," Sophia said in a rush. "But the good news is that Liv helped me to find the actual coordinates for the facility."

He lowered his chin. "So Thad has the eggs?"

"Yes, but I think we can get them back," Sophia stated. "I know where the facility is, and Liv has offered to give me a bunch of magical tech that will help in fighting Thad's guards, which are all robots like those I encountered at the place north of here."

"We don't need the House of Fourteen's help," he argued.

"But we do," Sophia stated. "Without Liv's help, I wouldn't have been able to find the location for this place. She was able to do some radar stuff, and now I know roughly where to look."

"And how are you going to get into this underwater facility?" Hiker asked.

"Well, I'm still working that out," Sophia stated. "The guy we got drunk to find out this information—"

"This just keeps getting better and better," Hiker said, not meaning it. "Who is this 'we.'"

"Well, I took Ainsley to Roya Lane in disguise so that we could question this guy who moved the eggs."

He shook his head. "You took my housekeeper to Roya Lane? You really know no bounds do you?"

Sophia narrowed her eyes at him. "Yes, I let her leave the Gullington for more than to just go to the market in the town over. I'm such a rebel."

"Sophia, Ainsley belongs here at the Gullington," Hiker stated. "It's her job to look after the Castle and us. She's not used to the modern world and I'm tired of you filling her head with—"

"Potential?" Sophia interrupted. "Are you afraid if she sees the world outside of here that she'll leave you?"

"No!" he yelled and then softened. "Well, maybe. But you have to understand, we aren't used to all the strange things in the world like you. And you're always filling her head with glamorous ideas. I need her here, not dreaming of...well, whatever you have her dreaming of."

"If you took a moment to understand Ainsley, you'd see that she loves this place so much that leaving here only makes her more committed to it," Sophia explained. "She nearly kissed the stairs of the Castle when we returned. But you're so afraid of things changing that you don't give her a chance to see anything."

"You will mind your place," he said sternly.

Sophia let out a breath, realizing she was definitely pushing it. "Yes, sir."

"Continue about this guy you got drunk on Roya Lane," Hiker stated.

"Well, he was the one Thad hired to transport the eggs," Sophia explained. "He took a submarine, so I was thinking I could do that. But there is also a room in this facility that will allow portaling if someone flips a switch or something. I'm not absolutely sure. So if I need backup, then I could have Wilder portal there, and we can get the dragon eggs and then return."

"You think that you're going to this facility on the rescue mission, do you?" he asked, tapping his foot.

"Well, Mahkah is off on the Nathaniel mission still," Sophia reasoned. "And you will need someone who understands magical tech, which is me. So I just figured that Wilder and I—"

"You figured wrong," Hiker cut her off.

"What?" Sophia exclaimed. "But the others don't know about magical tech. You send them in there without their dragons, and they will be powerless to take down the security systems. Liv coached me on the best techniques. I have devices that can take robots offline. I'm the best choice."

"I don't disagree," Hiker said to her surprise.

"You don't?" she asked, astonished.

He shook his head. "But Wilder isn't right for the job."

Sophia deflated. "No, please don't say it…"

"Look," Hiker began, "You and Evan may not always get along, but Coral is aligned with the water element. She's the only dragon we have that can swim great distances underwater. Actually, her ability makes it so that when connected to her, Evan can breathe underwater. He's the natural choice for a mission of this sort."

Sophia wanted to argue, but she knew he was right. "Okay, so then he's the one who gets in there then?"

"Yes, and once in there, you'll get him to this portal room and then you can join him," Hiker ordered.

"So, you're really going to allow me to go, even though I'm not done with my training?"

He considered her for a moment. "I still want you progressing, but yes. You're the right man for the job…person."

"Thank you, sir," she said, excitement in her voice. "I'll get the dragon eggs and return them to the Gullington."

"Just don't get yourself killed in the process," Hiker said. "A few dragon eggs aren't more valuable than an actual rider and dragon."

She smiled at him. "I think you sort of just said you value me."

"You hear what you want," he said with a grunt, dismissing her from his office.

CHAPTER TWENTY-NINE

The shimmering moonlight reflected off the two dragons waiting on the Expanse. Lunis' eyes shone red as he watched Sophia and Evan approach from the Castle.

The moon, as his element, made his eyes flash red when it was full. It also would make Lunis stronger, faster, and enhanced in almost every possible way. It was lucky then that tonight was when they'd go to the Institute. Unlucky was that Lunis couldn't enter the facility. Still, he would be stationed close in case Sophia needed anything. And his connection to her in her mind was a comfort that she knew kept her sane when losing her mind was a total possibility.

Coral stood majestically next to Lunis, slightly larger than him. He was still growing, and it was highly suspected that one day, he would be much bigger than her—much bigger than any dragon in history.

Dragons didn't grow consistently. They might stop growing for several years and then go through an unexpected growth spurt, doubling in size in a few short days. Mahkah had explained that it was unknown what would spark a dragon's growth and therefore antici-pating it was unwise. Instead, Sophia simply expected to see Lunis the same every day until one day, he was different. There was something in that sentiment that she thought worked for the people in her life.

So often, people don't allow those around them to change, worried about how their evolution would affect them. And that stagnation inevitably resulted in corruption. She tucked away that idea so she could focus on the approaching mission.

Handing over two earpieces to Evan, she gave him a sturdy expression. "This is how we will stay in communication. Put those in your ears."

"What are these? Walkie-Talkies of sorts?" he asked.

"Yes, the modern version of them," she explained. "They are waterproof, and I should be able to hear everything that you do from at least ten miles away."

"Groovy," he said, putting the magical tech into his ears.

Sophia shook her head. "'Groovy' is out."

"Out?" he asked. "I thought that was a hip word?"

"Yeah, like a few decades ago," she explained.

"Okay, well, what are the kids saying these days then?" he asked.

Sophia wanted to laugh. As irritating as Evan was, at his core, he was a good person, and it shone in his green eyes. But he also appeared quite immature, even though he was over a hundred years old. What her sister had told her was true: girls matured faster than boys.

"They say things like, 'Man, that's h-e double toothpicks i-s-h,'" Sophia lied, realizing she still had her own immature streak as she messed with Evan. She reasoned that he deserved it.

"Why would they say that?" he asked, skepticism written on his face. "Why not just say, 'Man, that's hellish'?"

She shook her head. "It's cooler to spell it out."

He puffed out his chest. "Well, I'm the model for cool."

"Then you'll want to say what's hip," she reasoned.

"Or what's h-e double toothpicks i-s-h," he fired back.

"Exactly," Sophia said, pulling up her phone and looking at the schematics that Liv had sent her for the facility. "According to my sources—"

"Your sister," he interrupted.

"A Warrior for the House of Fourteen and assistant to Father Time," Sophia corrected.

"Who happens to be your big sister," he said.

"Your mom goes to college," she fired back, at a loss for a better comeback and just having watched the movie the night before with Ainsley. Now the housekeeper was wearing a Vote for Pedro t-shirt compliments of the Castle, and Hiker was wearing an irritated expression in response.

He didn't get the reference and said he absolutely didn't want to. No one was surprised when the Castle replaced all his traditional Viking clothes with retro suits and t-shirts like what Napoleon Dynamite would wear. The joke was apparently on all them, though, because the leader of the Dragon Elite refused to wear any of those clothes and came down to the dining hall topless, with his bed sheet tied around his waist. Ainsley immediately went and changed back into her plain brown dress and began fervently begging the Castle to give Hiker back his old clothes.

"One swift breeze, S. Beaufont, and my eyes will be burned forever," Ainsley had said when Sophia tried to cover her laughter.

"I'm sure the Castle can't keep his clothes for long," Sophia argued.

"Oh, you'd be surprised," Ainsley stated. "And all my efforts to make him clothes are worthless. They disappear as soon as I take my eyes off them."

"Well, then our rigid leader might just have to adapt," Sophia reasoned.

"That will happen when he allows Mama Jamba to give him an afro to match his graphic t-shirt collection."

Sophia was still giggling about the experience as she and Evan made their way to the dragons. "Anyway, as I was saying," she continued, reading the map on her phone, "I was able to get rough plans for the facility we're entering. It apparently used to belong to a group called the Lucidites, who had some pretty advanced technology."

"But Thad Reinhart came in and annihilated them before taking over their headquarters," Evan cut in.

Sophia shook her head. "No, no one knows what happened to them or really much about them in general."

"They sound like the Dragon Elite," Evan offered.

"Yeah, my thoughts exactly. Maybe they are laying low and practicing their archery techniques for a few centuries, waiting to be needed again," Sophia mused. "Anyway, as I was saying, it appears Thad Reinhart moved into their space. It just goes to show that he's pretty much everywhere, and not much is closed off to him. He had the facility north of here, the one on Catalina Island that Mahkah is investigating, and this one, which is bizarrely underwater."

"Which is where we come in," Evan said proudly, fondly petting Coral when they were near enough to the dragons.

Sophia nodded to Lunis before returning her attention to the map. "According to Griff, there is a dry dock for submarines to enter the Institute. And according to what we were able to dig up, that should be on the upper level of the building. You'll need to enter through there and then remain in contact. I'll be able to help you navigate from there until you find this GAD-C room."

"Yeah, yeah," Evan said. "You know, we might save ourselves the time and just have me grab the eggs while I'm down there. That's probably a better use of my efforts than finding this portal room so you can join me."

Sophia lowered her chin, giving him a stern look. She'd expected Evan to say something like this. "Look, you might think you can waltz in there and find the eggs on your own, but you don't know what you're up against."

"And you do?" he questioned.

The dragon's heads rose up as they watched the two riders square off to each other.

"What do you do if you encounter a guardian robot?" Sophia questioned.

Evan patted the axe on his hip. "I turn it into scrap metal."

"Yeah, not if it sears you with its laser eyes," Sophia countered.

Evan laughed. "You watch too many fi-sci movies."

"Sci-fi movies," she corrected. "And no, I don't. I watch just enough of them. Anyway, fighting magical tech with brute force is a surefire way to get yourself killed. Magic should be fought with magic. And in many cases, technology needs to be fought with itself."

"I get it, pink princess," Evan said, rolling his eyes and looking bored by the conversation. "I wasn't born yesterday, though."

"No, you were born one-hundred and twenty-five years ago before the dawn of technology," Sophia argued. "Do you know how to spot surveillance cameras, laser beam security systems, or how to bypass computerized locks?"

"I don't even know what half that stuff is," Evan admitted.

"Well, I do," Sophia said proudly. "And more importantly, I know how to disable magical tech on the fly." She pulled a key card out of her pocket and pressed it into his chest. "Use this to unlock the main door in the dry dock. The GAD-C room should be right off there. Get in there and tell me what you see so I can portal in and save your ass before the robots show up and give you another haircut."

A sly smile lit up Evan's face. "You know what, for a young lady, you're all right."

"You know what? For a human, you're barely passable," she fired back.

Evan shook his head as he went to get on his dragon. "Yeah, whatever, Princess. We're going to have fun together, and I think it scares you."

Sophia easily climbed onto Lunis. "I'm afraid you're going to get me killed, and that is what scares me."

CHAPTER THIRTY

Both dragons took off in unison, springing into the night's air filled with radiant moonlight. The rush of cold through Sophia's hair immediately spiked her adrenaline, making her feel alive.

Lunis moved the way he always did, an incredible force of muscles and power, effortlessly coasting over the winds and gliding through the sky. On that night, there was something different about him. His strength was dynamic, his movements sharper, his connection to Sophia somehow deeper.

Maybe in another century or two, the dragon and rider would understand better how the moon affected him. However, they were still new to themselves and each other, learning about this connection to the moon.

Beside them, Coral and Evan flew, both camouflaged by the night due to their dark appearances. The Gullington receded into the background as the dragons made quick progress over the hills of Scotland.

"Portaling in ten," Sophia said, knowing Evan could hear her over the comm. Otherwise, it would have been impossible over the beating of wings and rush of air.

"I'm ready, Pink Princess," he fired back.

Sophia ignored the unpleasant nickname and projected a portal several hundred yards in front of the dragon. It opened, expanding wide enough for both riders and dragons just as they passed through it, arriving over the south Pacific.

The air was warmer in their new location, and the moon hadn't risen over the ocean waters yet. The sun was making its final descent, soon to be replaced by the white orb in the sky. Something shifted in Lunis, and Sophia only just sensed it before she spotted the small abandoned island where they would land.

"I'll be down there," Sophia said to Evan over the comm, pointing to the island mostly full of vegetation and birds.

"And I'll be down there," he replied, pointing to the sparkling water in the distance.

"You know the directions," she said. "Stay in communication once you get there."

"Copy that, Pink Princess," he fired back, kneeling down low on Coral as she dove for the water.

Lunis paused in mid-air, holding them up on the winds as they watched a spectacular sight that both had only heard about.

Dragons could swim, but it obviously wasn't their strong suit. Mostly they could employ an effective diving technique with their flying. It had actually been Bell taking a bath in a lake that started the rumors regarding the Loch Ness Monster. It was during a brief period in time when mortals could see magic. Something wore off, allowing them to see magic for about an hour before the curse was reinstated, blinding mortals to dragons and all other magical creatures. But a few brief sightings of Bell swimming in the lake were enough to start a myth that inspired millions to search for the famous Loch Ness Monster.

Coral wasn't just a good swimmer. Her connection to the water made her excellent at navigating, too. She could dive deep, swim fast, and both she and her rider could breathe underwater for long periods of time. Sophia only hoped all that was enough to help them find the entrance to this facility.

She held onto that hope and her breath as Evan and Coral raced toward the surface of the water, plunging into it and diving deep, disappearing at once.

CHAPTER THIRTY-ONE

During their plunge through the waters of the South Pacific, Evan wouldn't be able to communicate with Sophia. That meant she was forced to wait in silence, hoping that he found the entrance without issue.

Lunis landed on the beach of the small island, the tide greeting his feet. He kicked around in the water, splashing Sophia. She ducked, laughing, muting her side of the comm so she didn't distract Evan.

"I thought you might feel left out that Evan gets to have all the water fun," Lunis told her.

She shook her head, sliding off his back and sinking her boots into the soft sand. "If your elemental power was water, then that would be fine, but I'm glad that you are connected to the moon."

"Doesn't do us much good here, living in the past," he stated, looking to the horizon where the moon would rise soon.

"Yes, but who knows what the night will bring," Sophia said, not fully prepared for whatever they would face at the Institute.

"Just remember that magicians can't portal with the eggs," Lunis reminded her. "You can only do that atop a dragon."

"Right," she muttered, hiking up farther on the beach so that she could create a portal to the Institute when the time was right. "I'll have to trust Evan to get them out of there on Coral. Then once they are outside of the Institute and back in the air, we will all portal back."

"Which they can do, but you are going to have to start believing in him," Lunis stated.

She cut her eyes at him. "I believe in him."

"To steal all the pastries and earn a contemptuous glare from Hiker regularly," Lunis added.

"And to chew with his mouth open and talk with his mouth full," she said.

"But you're going to have to believe in him to do his part here," Lunis lectured. "He has a lot to learn and is arrogant, but he wouldn't be a rider if he didn't have extraordinary abilities. In battle is the time that we must offer our support to our comrades the most. Sometimes it is precisely that encouragement that gets someone through."

Sophia nodded reluctantly. "Okay. I know you're right. I guess if he manages to get into the Institute, then I'll have a bit more confidence in him."

CHAPTER THIRTY-TWO

Bubbles raced over Coral and Evan as they dove deeper into the cold waters of the Pacific. The two were nearly melded together, moving as one as the waters darkened.

Coral could see well underwater, lending that ability to her rider. Although Sophia had given Evan specifics on what he was looking for, he still worried that he wouldn't be able to find this entrance.

They might only have a limited amount of time to find the dry dock since surveillance was most likely happening, and a dragon swimming in the area wouldn't go unnoticed for long. Evan planned to cloak them once they were through the entrance, but doing so now would pull from their magical reserves, potentially drowning them. Coral needed all of their power to navigate the ocean waters as they searched.

Evan played a tough act, but silently inside, he wasn't at all confident about this mission. Only Coral knew that he was worried he'd fail. He had already gotten himself nearly electrocuted to death and Sophia had to save him. What if he screwed up again?

You hadn't screwed up, Coral argued in his head. *You simply didn't know what you were getting yourself into.*

Hearing her voice as they swam deeper was a comfort that he needed.

No, but that's exactly why I do need Sophia, he related. *She knows about magical tech, which I never anticipated.*

And she needs our help getting into this place, Coral offered. *You two are a team. Remember that, and you'll be successful.*

A good reminder, he said to her, continuing to search but only seeing marine life and nothing that looked like an underwater facility.

They could only stay submerged for another couple of minutes, and that might be the time they needed to race back up to the surface. Evan was considering whether they should head up before making another attempt. There were so many problems with that scenario that he didn't even want to consider it.

For Coral, it would be best if she dove from a flight position, which meant more risk of them being spotted. And with each attempt, they were losing precious reserves. This was harder than Evan anticipated and he felt their energy depleting fast.

He was just about to make the hard call to go back up to the surface when he spotted something. It was shiny, reflecting light from an unknown source.

Get closer, he urged Coral.

She complied, her wings pushing them deeper toward the strange sight.

Evan was about to quit again, thinking they'd simply stumbled upon ship wreckage at the bottom of the ocean. However, if this was a ship, it was unlike any he'd seen before.

As they swam closer, he realized it was large enough to be a huge freighter, but it was sleek, covered in brushed steel. And whereas a ship would have curves, this structure was like a box.

Evan had never seen anything like the massive structure that stood not far from them. Sitting on the bottom of the ocean floor was a five-story building that looked like it had just popped out of one of those strange movies Sophia watched. It was mysterious in the way it glowed in the water, and a strange pulse of energy radiated off the place, sending a chill through dragon and rider.

Nothing about this place is natural, Coral related.

No, which is why we're getting our dragon eggs from it and getting the hell out of here, Evan stated, steering her toward an opening that had to lead to the dry dock. He hoped so, anyway, because if it didn't then they might drown down there, too far from the surface and lacking the reserves to make it back in time.

CHAPTER THIRTY-THREE

"I'm in," Evan said over the comm.

Sophia let out a giant breath of air. "Oh, fantastic."

She heard a beep from the other side of the comm. "It that the key card?"

"Yes," Evan answered in a whisper. "So far, this is too easy."

"Don't get ahead of yourself," she stated. "You need to find the GAD-C room. I'm not sure what it will look like, so just tell me what you see."

"Well, I see a door beside the one I just came through that's labeled 'GAD-C,'" Evan informed her. "Do you think that's a coincidence or what?"

Sophia rolled her eyes. "Get in there!"

"Hold your dragons," he complained. "I'm trying to ensure that there's no one around."

"Are you cloaked?" Sophia asked, pacing the beach

"Yes, as we discussed," he answered, "And so is Coral. But I can't maintain that on both of us for long. The swim took a lot more out of us than I expected."

"Well, get me in there, and you can drop the cloaks once I knock out the surveillance."

"And therein lies the problem," Evan stated over the comm.

Sophia tensed. "Why? I thought you found the GAD-C room where I can portal to."

"Yes, but you need me to do something to open the portaling capabilities, right?"

"Yes," she answered.

"I haven't got a clue how to even begin describing this room to you."

Sophia sighed. "Seriously, all of you guys need to get phones."

"Hiker doesn't want us to," Evan confessed.

"And I'm apparently the only one who does things that man doesn't like."

"Right, like take the housekeeper to Roya Lane," Evan said with a laugh. "He's still mad about that, which has gotten him off my back. Thanks, Pink Princess."

"Okay, Sparky, get to describing the room to me."

"Sparky, huh?" Evan asked. "I don't like it."

"Well, you chose my handle, and I chose yours. It's only fair."

"Mmmm, let me try giving this a shot," Evan said, speculatively. "There's a bunch of buttons on one wall. And then there's this raised platform that has this telescope looking thing hovering over it."

"That sounds like equipment," Sophia mused, mostly to herself. "Look for a computer. Do you see one of those? You know what those look like, right?"

Evan scoffed. "Of course I do. But just to be on the safe side, tell me what your version of a computer looks like."

"Man, I'm sending you all to tech school," Sophia said.

"Your mom goes to school," Evan replied.

She laughed. "That's not how that phrase goes."

"Well, I didn't understand it the first time, and my invite to watch the movie was apparently lost in the mail," Evan complained.

"That's because you talked all the way through the Doctor Who episode I showed you."

"How could I not?" Evan countered. "That sci-fi business makes zero sense. None of that stuff could really happen. And really, traveling through time in a police box. Like the authorities wouldn't figure that out."

"Science fiction is completely lost on you," Sophia grumbled. "I need you to look for something with a television screen and a keyboard in front of it. Do you see anything like that?"

"Oh, that's a computer?" Evan asked, relief in his voice. "Yeah, there's one of those here."

"What's on the screen?"

"Not much," Evan said. "It says 'error 584958: resolve to enable portaling.'"

"Hmmmm," Sophia murmured.

"What's that error?" Evan asked.

"I have no clue," she answered. "Look on the rectangular box next to the computer for a power button."

"How did you know there was a box next to the television?" he asked.

"Experience," she stated. "And it's called a monitor."

"I thought it was called a computer," Evan said, confused.

"No, the computer is the box. The monitor is the screen," she explained.

"That's weird."

"You're weird," she replied. "Now, did you find the power button?"

"I think so. Is it the thingy that has a circle with a line halfway through it?" he asked.

"Yes!" Sophia exclaimed.

"Great, do I destroy it?"

"No," Sophia stated at once. "You need to do exactly what I say. It's really important."

"Okay, I'm ready. What is it?"

"You're going to turn the computer off and then back on," she answered.

Evan laughed. "That's it? That's your bloody plan to fix the error?"

"Don't doubt this technique," Sophia stated. "It's pretty much the answer to all technical errors."

"Whatever," Evan said. "I'm turning it off."

"All right, then wait a few seconds and tell me what happens when you power it back up."

"Are you sure I shouldn't just destroy the computer?" Evan asked. "It's what's keeping you from portaling in here, right?"

"Yes and no," Sophia answered. She'd already tried to portal into the Institute, but no luck. "I think based on what Griff said and didn't understand was that the room is free to portaling most of the time, but the computer got the error, preventing it."

"But then anyone could enter the Institute at any time," Evan argued.

"No, they'd need to know that they could only enter through the GAD-C room," Sophia said. "Trying to portal anywhere else in the Institute wouldn't work."

"Well, your voodoo worked," Evan said. "The computer fixed the monitor."

"That's not really how it works, but tell me what it says."

"It now says 'Portal allowed.'"

"Okay, let's see if that's in fact correct." Sophia gave Lunis a look of hope before attempting to open a portal into the GAD-C room in the Institute. Unlike before, the shimmering bright door through space and time opened. "Looks like I'm on my way," she said, stepping through the portal and entering Thad Reinhart's territory.

CHAPTER THIRTY-FOUR

The GAD-C room was dark when Sophia entered. And cramped. She collided straight into Evan, or she thought it must be him since he was cloaked. He dropped his cloak, smiling down at her.

"I got you in here."

"Great. Now can you scoot?" Sophia asked, looking around at the strange room. The contraption in the room looked like an MRI machine. The buttons on the wall appeared to be what operated it. Sophia didn't know what it did, but she'd been able to portal in there, so that was all that mattered.

She hunched over the computer, accessing the files. Sophia thought if she could get an idea from there about the security, she might be able to take it down from one spot. However, that computer appeared to only control the portaling wards. She'd prepared for this.

"What's that?" Evan asked, pointing to the small device she pulled from her cloak. "Is it candy?"

Sophia tilted her head to the side, giving him a petulant expression. "Yes, I decided it was the perfect opportunity to take a snack break."

He rubbed his stomach. "Yeah, that's a great idea. I'm starving after that swim."

"This," she said, holding up the small device, "isn't a candy bar. It's a high-frequency adjuster that jams security systems, bringing them down for short periods of time."

Evan shook his head. "I don't think it's too late for you to learn how to speak English, but currently, I can't understand a word you're saying."

"I'm going to bring down the Institute's drawbridge so we can storm the castle," she explained. "Does that make sense?"

"Why didn't you just say that?"

"Well, it hasn't worked yet," Sophia said, turning on the device. "It's brand-new magic tech, so hopefully Thad doesn't have a patch for it. Once this is out for a month or so, every hack in the magical world will be aware of it, having firewalls that prevent it from doing what it's supposed to."

The red light on the device blinked, making Sophia hold her breath.

"We are back to me not understanding a word you're saying," Evan stated.

The light flashed red several times before turning green. "It worked. That's all you need to know."

"Which means?" Evan asked.

"Which means that although I have been able to take down surveillance, most security measures should be disabled, but not for long."

"Which means?" he asked.

"We get to have fun storming the castle," Sophia said, sliding up to the door, preparing to enter the actual Institute.

CHAPTER THIRTY-FIVE

"How was I supposed to know that's a movie reference?" Evan asked.

Sophia stood squarely in the long corridor, having already knocked out a security camera on the ceiling. The hallway was sort of dizzying. The walls and ceiling were all brushed stainless steel, the carpet a shimmering blue that resembled water. This place felt like something straight out of a science fiction novel.

"Everyone on the planet would get that reference," Sophia stated and then amended. "Everyone but the guys in the Dragon Elite."

"Well, here's an idea," Evan offered. "Stop making popular culture references since you know we've been living in a bubble and won't get them."

She shook her head, carefully starting forward. "I can't do that. Half the stuff I say is references to pop culture. You're just going to have to get with the times."

There were a few doors in the corridor. Sophia halted in front of the first one they came to.

"There's no handle," Evan observed. "How do you think you open it? Magic maybe?"

"Well, magic is relative," Sophia said, pressing the button beside the door, making it recede into the wall.

"Man, that's h-e double toothpicks i-s-h," Evan said in awe.

Sophia stuck her head into the room, finding it crammed with boxes. It appeared to be a supply closet.

She shut the door and continued down the hallway.

"So, the eggs weren't in there?" Evan asked.

"They were totally in there," she answered sarcastically. "I destroyed them with my laser eyes."

"No, you didn't. You don't have laser eyes," Evan argued.

She turned to him, rolling her eyes. "Yes, that's the takeaway. And why would I destroy the eggs we are here to recover?"

The sounds of a hydraulic made Sophia freeze. The next door was up ahead several yards. And whatever was approaching was on the other side of a bend. She pulled Evan even with the wall.

"What is it?" he mouthed.

"Something with actual laser eyes," she said, remembering the powerful robots she encountered at the first facility.

"That's an actual thing?" Evan asked. "I thought it was science fiction."

The robot was getting closer. Sophia knew it was a risk using the device to take the security systems offline, and blowing out the camera had also probably been a trigger to send the guards down to this corridor.

"Do you have ice magic?" she asked Evan, hearing the robot get closer.

He huffed. "I'm a dragonrider for the Elite. What do you want? Snowballs? Icicles?"

"We're not creating a winter wonderland," Sophia said. "Something that freezes large objects."

"How large?" Evan asked, fear springing to his eyes as he looked between her and the corner where the noise was coming from.

A second later and a robot whose head nearly reached the ceiling materialized. It looked like a skeleton, covered in chrome, its red eyes scanning.

"Whoa," Evan said, backing up.

This was exactly like the robots she'd faced before, which meant she knew how to take them down. Thinking it was probably better if she saved her reserves for taking down unfamiliar magical tech, she said, "Blast it with cold."

Evan held up his hand just as the robot went to do the same, a gun protruding from where its hand should have been.

"Hurry!" Sophia urged, about to step in, but remembering what Lunis had said about encouraging Evan. "You can do this. Freeze it!"

Snow and ice blasted from Evan's hand, soaring through the air and hitting the robot. The machine held its ground as snow covered it quickly. Still, the effort seemed to immobilize the beast. Within several seconds, the entire robot was covered from head to toe in snow. Sophia didn't know if that was enough to subdue it, but then its red eyes flickered and dimmed as a sound like it was shorting out sparked from the head.

Evan relaxed, having also assumed that the robot was down. "Pretty awesome job on my part, huh?"

Sophia let out a sigh. "Yeah, but next time, just freeze it. You don't have to make it into a snowman."

"I like to do things with a bit of flair," Evan argued. "So that was a robot, huh? What was that thing on its arm?"

"A gun," Sophia answered, listening for other robots.

"Oh, so we nearly got blasted?"

"Yes, so next time pass up the flair for efficiency," she advised.

"I didn't see you stepping up with your magic to help," he stated.

"Yes, because if I deplete my reserves and we need them to battle unfamiliar magical tech, we're screwed."

"Fine," Evan said. "But then we should cut it to the eggs. Where do you think they are?"

She nodded, knowing the device wouldn't keep the security down for much longer.

Lunis, are you getting any readings on the eggs? she asked in her mind.

I've narrowed it down to the fifth level, Lunis stated. *Take the elevators there. Then Coral will have a better radar through Evan since she's actually there.*

Okay, thank you. Sophia strode forward, waving Evan along.

"Coral can help us find the location of the eggs," Sophia informed him. "But we have to go up to the fifth level."

"Where do you suspect the stairs are?" Evan asked, looking around when they came to the intersection of the hallway.

"Today, you get to ride an elevator," Sophia said, pointing to a set of doors.

"Dude, I'm old, but I've been around since elevators," Evan stated.

Sophia touched the button for the elevator, making it ding too loudly in the seemingly deserted facility. It was strange how quiet the place was. Could its express purpose be to hide the dragon eggs? And why? What was Thad Reinhart's grievance with the dragonriders? She knew from Hiker that he'd wiped out a huge amount of their numbers, but no one had filled her in on why, which suddenly seemed like a question she should have asked.

The doors opened with a "shushing" sound, showing a small metal box.

"Wait, we're supposed to get in here?" Evan asked, hesitation heavy in his voice. "Doesn't that seem like a trap?"

Sophia strode forward. "And here I thought you'd experienced elevators."

CHAPTER THIRTY-SIX

"I said that I knew about them," Evan stated. "I didn't say I rode around on them a lot."

Sophia pressed the button for level five. "Firstly, elevators don't go round and round. Usually just up and down. And secondly, you need to see if Coral can sense where the eggs are. Inside the Institute, they shouldn't be shielded since the water was doing that."

He nodded, his eyes drifting to the right. Sophia suspected that was what she looked like when talking to Lunis, as if she was deep in thought.

"She says they are in a large lab," he stated after a moment.

The doors to the elevator sprang open, and immediately bullets whizzed by the compartment, making Sophia spring for the corner closest to the front. She indicated to Evan to take the other side.

The sound of hydraulics was heavy in the corridor. There were at least a few magical tech robots on this level, probably guarding the lab where the eggs were held.

Sophia gave Evan a sturdy look, holding up her hand beside her face like it was a gun and she was about to swing around the corner, barrel blazing. "You take the right, I'll take the left. Send a fast, deadly blast straight at their heads."

He nodded. "You got it, Pink Princess."

"Ready, set..." She waited for the gunfire in the corridor to pause, maybe when the robots reloaded...hoping that they did. To her relief, the robot stopped firing, maybe wondering if it was a false alarm and there was no one in the elevator.

"Go," she mouthed, swinging around and sending a bolt of electricity from her palm. That seemed like the best bet. It hit the robot standing in the hallway and knocked it back several feet, making its head come off. The electricity wrapped around its body, sending it into convulsions.

She whipped around to find Evan with both his hands extended and two frozen to the core robots lying flat on the floor.

Lifting his pointer fingers up like guns, he blew on them. "That was a piece of cake."

Right then, something shook the floor under their feet as a loud sound thundered from the opposite side of the far corridor.

His eyes swept to her. "What was that?"

"I think it is the whole cake," she said, hearing the hydraulics but making note that whatever was using them to move was much larger than the giant robots they'd taken down.

CHAPTER THIRTY-SEVEN

The robots they had just disabled seemed like skinny guys compared to the mech warrior that stepped around the corner. Huge cannons were attached to its thick arms, and its legs were the size of barrels.

Simply shooting it with ice and electricity wasn't going to do.

Evan lifted his hand like he was going to attempt the same strategy.

"No," Sophia said quickly, noticing something different about the robot besides the fact that it was huge.

"No, like, let's call this our final resting place?" he asked.

"No, like, look at the protective field encircling that thing," she stated, pointing.

He narrowed his eyes before they widened with recognition. Pulsing around the robot was an almost invisible armor, but the sparks shimmering every so often gave it away. And explained why the robot hadn't fired at them yet. It wanted them to take the first shot, which would invariably ricochet and hit them. Why use unnecessary power when you could use your enemies' attacks against them? Which gave Sophia an idea.

"What are we going to do if we can't attack it?" Evan asked.
Sophia grabbed his hand and pulled hard. "Run!"

CHAPTER THIRTY-EIGHT

"You get that as courageous dragonriders, we don't run, right?" he asked, still hightailing it beside Sophia.

"No, we don't," she answered, listening to the tell-tale signs of the weapons charging up behind them—a high-pitched threatening sound. Whatever that robot shot, it was powerful, not just some bullets. "However, we do run if we need to secure an advantage."

"Which is?" Evan asked.

"Distance," Sophia stated, rounding the bend of the hallway.

"That strangely still sounds like a coward's way," Evan complained, looking over his shoulder. "What is that thing? A robot or a magician on steroids?"

Sophia thought the latter was a more accurate description. This was just more proof that Thad Reinhart invested in offensive magical tech meant to protect and destroy like the robots that had guarded the slaves at the facility. Liv had questioned all of them, not learning much about how they were taken or by whom. It was cloaked in mystery and forgotten memories.

"I'm certain that it's more magical than tech," Sophia related, turning to face the hallway where the mech demon would be coming from. "Help me create a thin sheet of ice. Something that is so transparent, it almost goes unnoticed, like glass."

Evan shot her a confused expression. "I don't get it."

"Reinforce it so that it has a reflective quality," Sophia went on, working fast to create the barrier between them and the approaching robot.

Evan might have been confused, but he was still doing as he was instructed. "Reflective...I don't...oh, wait. You want the..."

"Exactly," Sophia said in a hushed voice as the sheet of ice materialized. Sitting in the stainless-steel hallway, it went almost completely unnoticed, like a cobweb stretched across a path. One wouldn't even know they were about to pass through it until it knocked them in the face. And Sophia hoped that the mech wouldn't notice it until it was too late.

"How's that?" Evan asked, adding a touch of something using his magic that reinforced the barrier, adding double protection between them and the robot.

"Good thinking," Sophia said, looking over her shoulder. They had come to a dead end. There was only one door at their back, which meant that this better work or they were trapped.

"Now what do we do?" Evan asked, recognizing the situation they'd gotten themselves into.

"We wait," Sophia said, hearing the mech magician approaching. It wasn't as fast as the other robots, but she didn't think it needed to be. It was meant for one purpose—to protect and destroy—and it was about to try and fulfill that.

"You know, with you, this dragonrider business is a whole lot less glamorous," Evan whispered tensely. "It's all strategy and not a lot of fistfights and swordplay."

"Why get your hands dirty if you don't have to?" Sophia asked, stiffening as the mech charged around the corner, its eyes red and weapons glowing hot.

"So, we just stand here and do what?" Evan asked.

"Don't shoot at it," she warned.

He gave her a pursed expression. "Thanks, I sort of got that, Sherlock."

"I don't know." Sophia shrugged. "We want it to shoot at us, so taunt it."

"But doesn't it want us to shoot at it?" Evan asked from the corner of his mouth.

Sophia nodded. "It's sort of a standoff."

"I'm supposed to resist my very nature and just wait for it to make the first move?"

"Yes, let's hope that between you and it, the robot has more testosterone," Sophia joked, scowling at the machine.

Unlike many of the magical tech robots she'd encountered in Liv's shop, this one appeared empty, like a soulless piece of technology. That was the thing about electronics when they were paired with magic. They were supposed to take on a new life with personality and a unique flair that was often uncontrollable to a degree.

But Thad Reinhart's magical tech was different. It was almost as if it had been manufactured to have all the reliability of technology with the added power of magic but none of the personality that went along with it.

"Hey metal brains," Evan said to the robot that seemed to be studying them as it halted just feet from the barrier both magicians were working to reinforce. "You look like you have a screw loose."

"What are you doing?" Sophia asked from the corner of her mouth.

"I'm taunting it," Evan said with satisfaction.

"It's a robot," she argued. "I don't think it can be offended."

"Everything can be. You just have to find the right button," Evan stated.

Sophia rolled her eyes so hard it nearly hurt her head. "That was the worst pun ever, and I've heard some bad ones."

"Why thank you," he whispered, throwing his arms out wide to the mech. "Oh, look at you with your big guns and armor, but you're still afraid to shoot."

"This isn't going to work," Sophia said.

"It will," Evan whispered to her, puffing his chest out wide to the robot. "Come on, Pink Princess. We should go. This hunk of metal doesn't know what to do. Just goes to show you can give a robot a weapon, but that doesn't make it a man."

"Really?" Sophia questioned in a terse whisper. "Male jokes?"

"It will work," he replied in a hushed voice. "Now, follow my lead." Evan turned around, pulling Sophia. "Let's go and do what we came here for since nothing is going to stop us."

The charge of the weapon grew suddenly louder. Sophia spun to see the radiant blast just as the mech shot it. At first, she worried their shield wouldn't hold, and they were about to be hit at close range by an attack they wouldn't survive. But then it ricocheted off the barrier, going straight back at the mech warrior. Its protective field reflected the attack, which bounced off the shield again, like a pinball in a machine. This happened several times until the protective field around the robot failed—thankfully before their barrier. If Sophia had made it alone, it wouldn't have withstood the force.

The blast hit the shield once more before rebounding at the robot, sending it back with a furious force and exploding it against the far wall. The barrier broke a second later, sending shards of ice every-where and a gust of wind that was both cold and hot over Sophia and Evan.

She shielded her face with her arm as another explosion came from the mech robot, sending flames into the air. For a moment, she worried that the robot would rally as it tried to lift its cannon arm, aiming it at then.

She grabbed Evan's arm, preparing to drag him to the nearest door, their only escape. The weapon glowed faintly.

If they made it through the door, the blast would hit the dead-end behind them, and again, the robot would be blasted by its own attack. She was just about to tug Evan for the door when he stepped forward, out of her grasp.

The cannon shifted to a red glow as if the robot had unlocked a set of reserves, bringing it back.

Evan lifted his hand and sent a blinding attack at the robot that froze it on the spot. It was such an intense blast that the robot cracked all over at once before exploding into a thousand pieces of frozen bits, sending debris all over them.

Sophia and Evan both ducked, covering themselves as metal ripped past them, scratching at them but doing no real damage.

When the chaos had settled, Sophia rose alongside Evan and looked at the mech's guts strewn all up and down the hallway. The only part of it that still seemed alive was a section of its face with half of a glowing eye, looking up from the floor.

Evan stepped forward and crushed the piece with his boot until the light was extinguished. "Not today, Satan. Not today."

CHAPTER THIRTY-NINE

"I was going to let it destroy itself," Sophia said, having explained her idea to Evan.

He shook his head. "I can play your strategy game only so much. Sometimes I just need to blow some shit up."

She looked around at the hallway full of destroyed magical tech. "And so you did."

"And hopefully that won't be all of it," Evan said, striding back the way they came. "Coral said to look for a lab. Maybe it's this way."

Sophia glanced over her shoulder at the one door standing at the end of the hallway. "Actually, I think I've found it."

"Why is that?" Evan asked, doubling back.

Sophia nodded at the sign next to the door. "Because it says, 'Aiden's Lab.'"

"Who is Aiden?" Evan asked.

"Beats me," Sophia answered, hovering her hand just over the button for the door. "Let's hope he's not another robot."

To her relief, the security device was still working, disabling most of the locking mechanisms around the Institute. The door slid back at once, making a shushing sound.

The lab was dark, save for the light illuminating a glass case similar to an aquarium in the center of the large room. The five dragon eggs appeared quite strange, hovering in midair behind the glass of the case.

CHAPTER FORTY

The various colored eggs were exactly as Sophia remembered them. They were all about the size of a small cantaloupe, their shimmering surfaces reflecting the light.

Evan rushed over at once.

"No," Sophia warned, stopping him from touching the case. "It's got to be protected."

Evan searched the area. "By what?"

"I don't know," Sophia said. "But there has to be some sort of protective field keeping them suspended like that. I bet if we try and grab one, they all drop."

"Aren't dragon eggs pretty tough?" Evan reasoned. "Maybe they won't break."

"I don't think we can risk it." Sophia used her magic to reach out to the eggs in the case, trying to grab them. Strangely she could get to them, pulling all five up a few inches.

"Whoa, that's you?" Evan asked, looking between her and the eggs.

"Yes, but I can't get them out of the case." Sophia gritted her teeth, trying to get around whatever security measure was blocking her. "There's something preventing them from being released."

"Is this when I get to smash stuff?" Evan patted the axe at his side.

"Not yet," Sophia stated, nodding in the direction of the main workstation. "That key card I gave you also acts as a hack. If you can slip it into one of the drives of that computer, we might be able to find a back door through the security protocol which will release these eggs from whatever is holding them."

"Why me?" Evan asked.

"Because I'm still holding the eggs and don't want to release them," Sophia explained. "And when you bring down the security, they would drop. So I need to keep a hold of them."

"Clever system," Evan said, striding over to the computer. "Someone tries to hack the security, and they risk losing what they came for."

"Yeah," Sophia mused. "Which makes me think that Thad Reinhart doesn't really care if the dragon eggs stay alive."

"Well, he did apparently kill a lot of dragonriders, so I'm guessing he's more about our demise than anything else," Evan related, continuing to search the computer for the drive.

"Seems like a lovely fellow," Sophia joked.

A blast from the corner nearly made her drop her hold on the eggs. Sophia jerked her head up, watching as a security camera exploded from the ceiling.

She gave Evan a look of surprise.

He was wearing a proud expression. "I can knock down security systems and cameras too."

"Good idea," Sophia said. "But I think it's too late to worry about surveillance. I'm certain we've missed some, and they already know we are here. Thankfully, I think that 'they' are a bunch of tin men, who we have proved we can handle."

"Let's just hope they don't know how to call Daddy," Evan said, returning his attention to the computer.

"Well, now that you've mentioned that idea, that's all I'll be thinking about. Hurry," Sophia encouraged. "There's a prong on the side of the key card. You're going to stick that into a jump drive that's probably on the side of that computer."

"Jump drive…" Evan drummed his lips together, searching. "And that looks like?"

Sophia really wanted to rush over and help, but she already had her lock on the eggs and felt protective of them, not wanting to ever let them go. It was a strange feeling.

"Look on the side for a small rectangular opening," Sophia said.

"When you say side, you mean on the screen thingy or the computer thingy?"

She sighed. "Computer thingy."

"Right, just checking."

"Seriously, how have you all survived so long with such ignorance in the Gullington?" she asked.

"It's an art form," he said proudly. "I think I found it. So I just stick this thing into the other thing. That's not so complicated."

"Well, you aren't the genius who created the magical tech in that override device," Sophia stated.

"And you aren't either." A small clicking sound echoed from the computer as he slid the device into place.

"No, but I know geniuses, which makes me a genius."

The screen came to life. "I think it is working."

Sophia glanced over. There was a progress bar streaking across the screen. "What does it say?"

"It wants me to enter a confirmation code," he said, reading. "It says something about proving I'm not a bot?"

Sophia laughed. "Clever. Yeah, just type out the code on the screen."

"No problem," Evan said, peeking at the keyboard. "The code is Y4ZM789$."

"Great, put it in." Sophia held onto the eggs, her hands extended, and adrenaline pumping in her veins.

"Y…where is the Y?" Evan said, searching the keyboard. "Oh, there you are, little buddy." He punched the key. "Now 4…where is that 4?"

"Oh, for the love of the angels," Sophia groaned. "You have to be kidding me."

"Wait, I messed up. Where's the erase key? You have those, right?"

He looked up suddenly. "Wait, if you don't have erase keys, I'm totally inventing those. Then I'll be rich."

"I hate to ruin this brand new and unrealistic dream for you, but they've already been invented. It's called the backspace key and should be on the top right-hand side."

"'Backspace key?'" Evan said, not sounding impressed. "What a horrible name for it. Mine was going to be called the erase key."

"Right...next time, Einstein."

"Oh, there it is," Evan rejoiced. "It's a bigger key. People must make lots of typing mistakes. Now where is that Z..."

"I know someone who is getting typing lessons for Christmas," Sophia muttered.

Evan glanced up. "Oh, we don't exchange gifts at the Gullington. Hiker thinks it's wasteful and doesn't like the decorations."

"Of course he doesn't," Sophia said. "And those lessons are a gift for me. Will you hurry up already? My arms are starting to shake."

"I'm almost there. How do I make the dollar sign?"

"Shift plus 4," Sophia stated in a rush.

"Shift..."

She looked up to the ceiling. "Angels, if you're listening, will you kill me now? I don't have what it takes to be a dragonrider if it involves teaching this man about technology."

"Found the shift key!" Evan exclaimed.

"Congrats. Now hold it down and press 4," she ordered.

"Both? At the same time?" Evan looked like his fingers were playing a strange game of Twister. "This is an odd feeling."

"You can ride a freaking dragon," Sophia complained. "I think you can handle some elementary level typing."

"There!" Evan said, having finally finished putting in the code. "Now what?"

"Hit the enter key!"

"Finally, I get to hit something." He pulled back his fist, looking the keyboard over. "So, where do I punch?"

Again, Sophia glared up at the ceiling. "You all are laughing at me right now, aren't you?" Returning her gaze to Evan, she said. "Just tap the big button under the backspace key. No axe-throwing with the keyboard."

"Oh," he said, deflating a bit. A small tap on the keyboard was followed by a loud beeping noise.

Everything happened in quick succession. The buzzing of the security field faded. The only light in the room from the case extinguished. And the eggs were released, dropping down several inches before Sophia regained her hold on them.

Standing in the dark of the lab, magically holding onto the five eggs, Sophia realized that they'd done it.

And then the sirens blared overhead, sending a strobe of red light through the room.

CHAPTER FORTY-ONE

"I think we tripped a security alarm!" Evan yelled over the commotion.

"You think?" Sophia fired back, sarcastically. "Get over here and grab the eggs."

"I'm already on it." Evan rushed over, pulling the bag that Ainsley had made just for this task from his traveling cloak. Thankfully the strobing red lights provided just enough light for them to see what they were doing.

Expertly, Evan slipped the small satchel over the first egg without touching it, which wasn't necessary but did benefit the dragon inside. The less others had contact with its shell, the better. He pulled the bag over, swallowing up another of the eggs, releasing its weight from Sophia.

When he had all five eggs in the bag, she dropped her hands, taking a breath. The sack wasn't any larger than when he started, although it should have looked like Santa Claus' toy bag by that point. Another perk of magic.

"Okay, so what's our exit strategy?" Evan asked her as they headed for the door.

"I'll get you back to the drydock," Sophia said, opening the door and peering into the hallway. It was thankfully empty. "Then I'll portal to Lunis and meet you."

"So, your concern isn't with getting out of this actual building?" Evan asked as they rounded the corner, meeting one of the smaller, less assuming robots.

Sophia shot it with a blast of electricity that knocked it clear back to the far side of the hallway, past the elevators and into the wall where it sank in a heap of metal, shocks still running over it. "Yeah, no. I think I've got these guys numbers. But something tells me reinforcements might be on the way."

"Why is that?" Evan asked as they loaded into the elevator.

Something rocked the compartment, making the lights dim.

"Just a hunch," she said, bursting from the elevator, hands at the ready as two more robots turned in their direction. Since Evan had his hands full carrying the eggs, Sophia used her magic to attack both of the robots, sending a giant wind at them both, knocking them into each other where they tangled together before being sent down the long corridor.

They weren't disabled, though, since Sophia was running low on magic. She didn't want to use it all here in case she needed it to escape. The robots sent laser attacks in their directions that made loud buzzing sounds and scorched the carpet under their feet as they sprinted for the drydock.

"Those guys don't mess around," Evan said, ducking from an attack that nearly severed his head.

Sophia sent another blast of wind over her shoulder, knocking the robots off-balance and disturbing their aim. A laser seared the ceiling, splitting it in two.

"That attack was meant for my head, wasn't it?" Evan asked.

"Oh, yeah." Sophia slid into the GAD-C room, tapping the button for the drydock.

A quick glance out there told her it was still empty, but who knew how long it would stay that way.

"Get out of here," Sophia ordered. "I'll portal now and meet you over the water."

"Sounds good," Evan chirped, speeding out the door with the eggs in tow.

CHAPTER FORTY-TWO

The look of relief on Lunis' face when Sophia stepped through the portal was palpable. She ran for her dragon, jumping onto the wing he had extended and sliding into the saddle in one swift movement.

"You made it," he said, relief in his voice as he sprung into the air, the full moon out once more. "Good work on the eggs."

Sophia grabbed the reins, feeling them as an extension of herself. The minutest movement from her transferred through the reins and straight into Lunis, making him shift directions.

"Now all we have to do is get the eggs back," Sophia related. "I'm going to open the portal now so that Evan can go right through it once he surfaces."

"Although I appreciate that you're being proactive, you might want to wait on that," Lunis said, a warning in his voice.

She was going to ask what he meant, but at that exact moment, she saw it and groaned. If she never again saw another of those magical tech jets that brought down Adam and chased her at the facility, it would be fine with her. But that wasn't how things were going to go, she realized as she saw two jets rapidly approaching.

CHAPTER FORTY-THREE

Navigating out of the drydock with five dragon eggs wasn't as hard as Evan would have thought. Coral had rested while they were in the Institute and now sped through the tunnels like a shark, but with wings...and totally more majestically.

The blaring of the sirens from the facility was muffled in the dark waters and started to sound like strange music to Evan's ears.

He was already dreaming of the feast that they'd have to celebrate his major victory when he returned to the Gullington. He would even throw up a glass to toast Sophia for being the best darn assistant a dragonrider could hope for.

Incoming, Coral said in his mind, her voice urgent.

Evan shook off his fantasy of roasted duck and buttery rolls, sitting up to see what his dragon was referring to. Ahead the tunnel out of the Institute ended, and it appeared that there was something waiting for them.

What is that? he asked her.

I do not know, Coral answered. *Sophia would. It's manmade.*

The vessel that appeared to be close to blocking their exit was smooth and shaped like a large capsule. It wasn't far from the Institute and the tunnel.

We need to speed up, or we won't make it out, Evan urged.

I can't go any faster, Coral stated, her wings moving like fins in the water, propelling them forward.

We're going to have to use a compartment spell, Evan stated.

It will weaken us greatly, Coral argued. *It will slow us down.*

But it won't matter if we can't get out of here, Evan countered.

The large vessel was nearly to the tunnel, turning its broad side to block them in. Only a small gap remaining that was about the size of a cow.

Evan hunched down on his dragon. *We can do it, Coral. Come on.*

Under him, he felt his dragon shrink. They'd practiced this a hundred times but never had a chance to do it in battle, especially while submerged. His dragon could only maintain it for a brief time, but if they got it right, it would be the difference between life and death.

Evan nearly clenched his eyes shut as they sped toward the opening. It was going to be a tight fit. And Coral was moving too fast for them to avoid a collision.

He felt Coral suck in as if she was trying to make herself as small as possible by any means. He did the same, cementing himself to her, the eggs also melding into his back. The pair slipped through the opening, Coral's wings nearly colliding with the tunnel.

She burst out to the other side, doubling in size at once and returning to her normal form. The compartment spell had drained them significantly, and she moved at half her usual speed as they made for the surface of the water.

Evan turned to take in the form of the thing that had tried to block them in. It appeared almost like a whale with its long body and the strange fin on its top. Thankfully it didn't seem to be able to move as fast as them, although he could tell it was going to pursue, having changed direction to follow them.

We can outpace it, Evan said with relief. *Just keep going.*

His ears picked up a strange noise from behind him. With a curious glance, he watched as the metal whale shot out a baby of sorts.

It was long and shaped like the bigger thing. And it was racing much faster than its mom, barreling in their direction.

CHAPTER FORTY-FOUR

*T*wo jets, powered by magic—no problem, Sophia said to Lunis.

Usually they would be a major problem, Lunis answered. *But not on this night.*

The blue dragon sped up, moving unlike Sophia had ever felt him. The surface of the water blurred as they raced straight toward the two jets headed in their direction.

Usually I prefer to go away from enemies, Sophia said, wondering what he was planning.

Yes, but Coral and Evan will be coming from this direction, Lunis argued. *And I have a plan.*

I like plans, Sophia said, the wind beating against her face so hard it felt like she was falling through space to the Earth, about to burn up entering the atmosphere. *Are you going to share?*

I usually would, but I'm too excited to surprise you with this one, Lunis said.

She knew there was something incredibly special about him that night. The moon enhanced him, but they'd never had the opportunity to experience it like this before. Lunis was more mature, his powers building. And he was rested, having waited to step into battle.

The jets sped straight at them, flying in formation.

Sophia worried they were going to fly straight into them. She thought the pilots had to be thinking the same thing. It seemed like a game of chicken. Much like with the mech robot, it appeared that they were facing off, seeing who was going to divert first.

Not us, Lunis said in her mind, having read her thoughts.

I don't think it will be them either, Sophia stated, noticing the jets charging forward on their path, seemingly undeterred.

I'm counting on them not backing down, Lunis stated.

I thought self-preservation was a thing, though, Sophia said, bracing herself.

Yes, but what if your sole mission is to attack and destroy, Lunis posed. *What if those pilots aren't real with lives of their own?*

That made perfect sense based on what she was learning about Thad Reinhart. The pilot that had attacked Adam had been human, but maybe since then, the evil tycoon had decided to stop employing them altogether since they were prone to fear and mistakes.

So they are going to hit us, destroying themselves just to take us down, Sophia guessed.

That's what they think they are going to do, Lunis stated just as they closed the distance.

Lunis changed directions suddenly, moving at rapid speed, too fast for the human eye to register. He moved into a vertical position, his wings extended flat as they slid between the two jets.

Everything slowed down for Sophia as she witnessed the incredible power and strategy of her dragon.

When they were between the two passing jets, perfectly arranged in the space that shouldn't have been large enough for such a passage, Lunis grabbed the plane below him with his talons and slung it around, twisting in the air.

Sophia hadn't realized he was that big until she realized he dwarfed the jet, holding onto it like it was a toy plane. He then rolled to the side and threw the jet straight at the other one beside them, making the two collide in a fiery assault.

The blast sent Lunis and Sophia back, but he flew unaffected, gliding away as the two jets fell into the ocean, tangled together, explosions lighting up the dark sky.

Lunis, Sophia said, feeling suddenly tiny on the monster-size dragon. He was simply huge, and it had happened in the blink of an eye. Her dragon, who was usually twenty feet long, not including his neck and tail, was now easily five times that length, making her feel like she was riding on top of a plane.

The moon is good to me tonight, he said proudly.

She pushed her face close to him, hugging the dragon. *Wow, I can't believe how big you can grow*, she said.

Well, size can sometimes be to my disadvantage, Lunis stated, pointing ahead.

Sophia lifted her face up, her heart dropping as she saw what he was referring to. Racing out of the water and headed in their direction was a torpedo fueled by magical tech.

CHAPTER FORTY-FIVE

*W*e're a huge target, Sophia declared to Lunis.

Yes, and we're headed in the wrong direction, Lunis said, shrinking down and turning like a tiny car on a dime.

She looked back, realizing that they could outrace the torpedo easily. The problem wasn't that. It was that Coral and Evan had just sprung from the water and couldn't move as fast.

We have to go back for them, she told Lunis.

I'm already on it, he said, diving forward and flying upside down, swiveling out of the trajectory of the torpedo. It turned around, but in a wide arc, not moving as nimbly. The magical tech did give the torpedo many advantages though, namely allowing it to fly above the water.

"We're being pursued," Evan said over the comm.

"I see that," Sophia stated.

"I already got away from one of those things using magic, but it cost us greatly," Evan said, his voice indeed sounding tired.

"We need to portal back," Sophia said.

"Yes, but it will follow us through," Evan argued.

"Which means we either get a head start or we take it out," Sophia offered.

"I'm not sure I can manage either," Evan stated.

Sophia cut her eyes at the other dragonrider as they approached. He was hurt. She could plainly see that.

"What happened?"

"I made the first thing racing after us explode," he stated.

"On you?"

"Sort of," he answered. "We are fine, though. Just need to get home."

He doesn't look fine, Sophia said to Lunis.

Nor is Coral, he agreed. *She can't fly much longer.*

And if I create a portal, the torpedo will just follow us through it, Sophia reasoned.

Which we wouldn't want if we were portaling to the Gullington, Lunis stated.

But that gave Sophia an idea.

"Sparky, can you and Coral stay put where you are?" Sophia asked Evan over the comm.

"What and leave you to deal with that thing?" Evan stated.

Sophia had already given Lunis the idea and he was quickly speeding away from the others, drawing the torpedo targeted on them away.

"Yes, we're going to deal with this thing. It's called a torpedo. And then we're getting you two back."

"Copy that, Pink Princess," Evan said through heavy breaths.

Lunis easily outpaced the torpedo. He could outrun it all night. But that wouldn't help them to get their friends to safety, so they were going to do what they did best and use strategy to defeat their opponents.

When they were a good distance from the torpedo, Sophia threw out a portal in front of them.

Without her having to even make the command, Lunis slowed, as if he'd suddenly lost power.

The torpedo caught up with them, zooming dangerously close, seconds from hitting them.

Again, everything slowed down as Lunis sped toward the portal, the torpedo quick on his tail. Just before he slipped through the portal, he nose-dived, heading for the surface of the ocean. The torpedo couldn't change direction as fast and flew straight through the portal that led to space, a place Sophia would never go, knowing she wouldn't survive.

She closed the portal immediately. The torpedo would soon explode on the other side, a safe distance from them.

Lunis flew above the surface of the water, the moist breeze a welcome feeling as they slowed, catching up to Evan and Coral hovering in midair.

"That was quick thinking," Evan said, pointing to where the portal had been that trapped the torpedo. His face was bloody in places and there were quite a few lacerations on Coral, but otherwise, their eyes were bright with determination.

"Thank you," Sophia said. "And the dragon eggs?"

Evan patted the bag across his back. "They are ready to return to where they rightfully belong."

Sophia smiled, opening a portal to the place she hoped to always return to at the end of every battle—the Gullington.

CHAPTER FORTY-SIX

Hiker was speechless as Sophia slid the bag away from the dragon eggs to reveal the five large objects.

Evan and Coral were being looked after by Ainsley and Quiet, who had greeted them at the Barrier, their faces covered in worry like they knew a dragon and rider had been injured. Sophia had lugged the dragon eggs to the Castle, after being told by the housekeeper that Evan and his dragon would be in good hands.

She stepped back from the desk, waiting for the leader of the Dragon Elite to say the first word after the big reveal. He was wearing a sheet still wrapped oddly around his barrel chest.

"In all my life..." he said, shaking his head. "I've never seen one in person."

That seemed so strange to Sophia, but she had to remember that she was maybe the first to ever magnetize to a dragon while they were still in the egg. Most dragons hatched and lived several hundred years before magnetizing to a rider.

"This marks a great achievement for the Dragon Elite," Mama Jamba stated.

"Yes," Hiker agreed. "Our numbers could recover. If we can

recover these, imagine what else we can find out there. We can protect the dragons from Thad. We can build ourselves up and fight him."

"I'm afraid that regardless of whether you build back the Dragon Elite," Mama Jamba began, "you're going to have to fight Thad Reinhart. He will know that you're back more than ever. This incident won't be lost on him."

Hiker nodded solemnly. "Yes, I expect the attacks to start soon. He will target us." A rare smile made his beard twitch. "But we have five dragon eggs. It's a new beginning."

Mama shook her head, ironically her usual smile falling away. "Actually, I'm afraid what you're witnessing is more of an end."

He looked up at her suddenly. "What do you mean?"

She pointed at Sophia. "She has to be the one to tell you."

"Me?" Sophia questioned, indicating to herself. "I don't know what you mean. Tell him what?"

Mama Jamba's finger dropped, pointing at the pocket of Sophia's cloak. "Oh, but you do, darling. You were given a message to pass along when the time was right."

Sophia glanced down at the cloak, not having remembered putting the sealed envelope from Mae Ling there. It was sitting inside her pocket, unharmed from the adventures she'd just been on.

Mae Ling had told her that she could only open the envelope once she'd recovered the five dragon eggs. Sophia had nearly forgotten about that. However, Mama Jamba apparently hadn't.

Holding her breath, Sophia pulled out the envelope.

"What's that?" Hiker asked gruffly.

"It is something you must know now," Mama Jamba stated, nodding to Sophia. "Go on, darling."

She broke the seal, opening the envelope. The paper was thick, and the handwriting on it flowery. Sophia sucked in a breath when she read the note.

Seven short words.

How could seven short words break Sophia's heart? And yet, they did.

"What does it say?" Hiker asked.

Sophia wanted to answer him, but instead, she looked at Mama Jamba. "Is this true?"

"I'm afraid so, hun," she answered sympathetically.

"What is it?" Hiker asked, his voice shaking.

Sophia turned the note around so he could read it with his own eyes, in case he didn't believe what she told him. "These are all the dragon eggs left."

CHAPTER FORTY-SEVEN

Learning that out of a thousand dragon eggs only five remained didn't defeat Hiker the way Sophia had thought.

He went silent, his light-colored eyes marked by stress, but his gaze was soon filled with a new determination. That's when he made the decision Sophia had been hoping for. He agreed it was time they go out and find the lost riders, recruiting them back to the Dragon Elite.

It was unclear how long it would be until any of the eggs hatched. It might be tomorrow, or not in any of their lifetimes. But it was certain that now that Thad Reinhart knew the Dragon Elite were back, he would come after them. Any plans he had would be accelerated. And after having his facility stormed and eggs stolen, he'd be madder than hell.

Although Sophia had felt heavy after learning there would only ever be five dragons left to hatch in the world and then they'd be an extinct race, Hiker was strangely optimistic. When she went to leave his office, feeling heavy and exhausted from battle, he stopped her.

"At least we know," Hiker had said to her, a strange hope in his voice. "Now we can prepare. Now we know what we have to work with. We can let go of the hope that we'll reign with massive numbers and focus on using strategy. I hear it's how some of the best operate."

She forced a smile. "Yeah, it's just that I never knew the world when dragons dominated it, and now I never will."

"That's because you were born for a different time," Hiker said.

She knew she should be grateful to have been successful, but right then, it just felt like a blow to learn how close dragons were to extinction.

"You and Lunis did well to recover these," Hiker said when she finished debriefing him on everything that happened at the Institute. "And you worked well with Evan, which proves even more about your character and capacity for patience."

"He isn't so bad," she said and then added, "but you all are taking computer classes."

He blinked at her rapidly. "I think I've dealt well enough with all these changes. I draw the line at computer classes."

"Fine," Sophia said, smelling smoke in her hair and looking forward to a shower. "Well, maybe the Castle will give you back your clothes, and then you can consider some other changes, like letting the riders have phones."

He shook his head. "It's not necessary."

"What about Christmas?" Sophia asked.

Again another head shake. "You really know how to threaten my patience."

"Okay, but I get to go on missions to recruit lone riders, so I guess I've won one battle," she said, proudly.

"Sophia, I hope that you and I get to a point where we don't think of it as battling each other," Hiker stated thoughtfully. "But for now, I think that it's a part of our dynamic."

"Because you're a crusty old Viking who is resistant to change?" she asked.

"Yes, and you're a young, know-it-all who insists on being a pain in my ass," he answered.

She nodded. "I think we play out our roles rather well."

Hiker actually winked. "I would agree."

CHAPTER FORTY-EIGHT

All Sophia wanted to do was lay down in her bed and sleep after the long adventure. That's why she was sorely disappointed after getting out of the shower to find her bed missing from her room.

She crossed her arms in front of her chest. "So, Castle, you don't want me to sleep then?"

In reply, the door to her room opened with a creak, inviting her out into the hallway.

"Fine," she said, trudging forward, realizing she was being forced to play the game of the Castle.

When she got to the stairs that led to the entryway, she heard a strange sound.

"Is that music?" she asked aloud.

"It is, indeed," Wilder said, joining her on the landing to the stairs. "And I hope you're ready to experience more strangeness because bringing those dragon eggs into the Castle has put some people in weird moods."

"How so?" she asked, hurrying down the stairs while trying to recognize the music.

"It's better if you see for yourself," he answered.

"Is that Elvis?" Sophia asked, recognizing the song Blue Suede Shoes.

"Is it?" Wilder questioned. "Beats me. I don't know much about music, but I used to play the fiddle."

"And then what…"

"I magnetized to a dragon and have since had less time to spend with my band," he answered.

"Oh, the life of a dragonrider. It will invariably break up a band," she related. "I'll give you some tunes to listen to. I've got some great lists on my Spotify account."

"And I've got some awesome nibs on my Bubble-Bear account," he said.

"What? What are you talking about?"

He shrugged. "I haven't got a clue. I just wanted you to experience what it's like to have no idea what I'm referring to."

She nodded. "Well-played."

Sophia was so amused by Wilder's antics that she did a double-take upon entering the dining hall.

Wilder laughed. "Told you that you had to see it for yourself."

"Is this real?" she asked, rubbing her eyes.

"I assure you that it is," he answered.

Sitting at the dining room table having his hair braided by Mama Jamba was none other than Hiker Wallace, the leader of the Dragon Elite. But that wasn't even the strangest part. It was that the Viking had abandoned his sheet and was wearing a retro-seventies suit complete with a thick tie and bell-bottom pants. The collar of the shirt was too large and made him look like he was about to go to a disco bar.

"Did Ainsley spike the food again?" Sophia asked.

"No, I didn't," she said, hobbling in from the kitchen carrying a couple of bottles of whiskey. "I didn't have to. Hiker asked that I bring out the good stuff tonight."

"I was also hoping for some food to go along with it," Hiker said, moving his head as Mama Jamba tied up his braid.

"Oh, you are the indulgent type," Ainsley said, slamming the bottles down bitterly. "Fine, I'll go and fix you something to eat, but nothing lavish."

He nodded, grimacing as Mama Jamba fidgeted with his braid.

"Don't move, Hiker, or I won't be able to get it just right, and then I'll have to start over."

He nodded, to Sophia's shock.

She turned to Wilder. "Did I return to the right Gullington, or is this the one in the parallel universe where everyone is insane?"

Mama Jamba sang along to *Blue Suede Shoes* as Ainsley brought in a large tray full of roasted duck and vegetables.

"I just whipped this up," Ainsley said, sticking it on the table. "That's all you're getting."

"How about some bread?" Hiker asked.

"Okay, but it won't be fresh," the housekeeper said, disappearing into the kitchen again.

"Ummmm, silly question," Sophia began. "What the hell is going on?"

Hiker reached out, pulling a leg from the duck. "I decided that since I can't beat the Castle, I should join it."

"Smart thinking, doll," Mama Jamba said, coming around to admire Hiker from the front.

"Did it fix your office?" Sophia asked.

He shook his head, taking a bite. "No, and it probably won't. But for tonight, I'll indulge it by wearing this awful outfit and allow Mama to fix my hair."

"But tomorrow, you're back to your grumpy self, right?" Ainsley said, dumping a basket of fresh-baked rolls on the table.

"Would you get me some jam to go with these?" Hiker asked, holding up one of the steaming hot rolls.

"Ainsley," she corrected, drawing out the name.

"Sorry, what?" he asked.

"My name is Ainsley," she stated. "I get that after all these centuries it's hard to remember, but I actually don't go by 'Would you.' That was my mum."

"Very funny," he said, taking a bite of the roll, crumbs landing in his beard.

"I bet you're starving after all those adventures," Wilder said, pulling out a chair at the table for Sophia.

"Actually, I'm not. I wanted to check on Evan and Coral," she answered.

"Oh, they are resting up, dear," Mama Jamba said, holding out her arm. "I'll take you up there to see Evan, though. While he's asleep, we can put perfume on him so he doesn't smell so manly. That scent really does permeate this whole place."

"I wonder why?" Hiker said through a mouthful of meat.

Mama Jamba led Sophia back toward the staircase, looking over her shoulder at the leader of the Dragon Elite. "You look very smart, Hiker."

"Thanks, Mama," he said, raising a glass to her as they left.

Once in the entryway, Mama Jamba halted beside the staircase. "I think you can find your way up to Evan on your own. He's fine, though. And I know you really just want to sleep."

"Oh, yeah, I am tired. But the Castle took my bed."

"Because it wanted you to come down here and see the festivities, which are mostly due to you."

"Oh, well, recovering the final dragon eggs in existence is pretty exciting. I wish Evan was here to join in."

"No," Mama Jamba argued. "It was because of you that this place is taking on a new life, regardless of the dragon eggs. Hiker is changing. The men are growing. And even the staff is going through their own evolution. I knew my Sophia would shake up the dragonrider world, I just never knew how much."

She smiled proudly. "That's the thing about being a mother. Your children surprise you all the time. I never think I can love them more, but somehow I do."

"Well..."

Mama Jamba waved her off. "You're tired, as you should be. Words are hard, and I don't need to hear any more from you tonight. The Castle has returned your bed, so go rest up."

"Okay," Sophia said, wishing she could stay to enjoy the strangeness happening in the dining hall, but knowing she was too tired for it.

"Is Mahkah okay?" she asked Mama Jamba.

"Oh, I suspect so," she answered. "Still on the mission on Catalina Island."

Sophia nodded, sensing there was something else Mother Nature wanted to say to her. "Is everything else okay? Like my sister and brother? You seem like you have something on your mind."

Mama Jamba's eyes sparkled. "Always the intuitive one. And yes, I'm on the brink of making a decision that I've been reluctant to. You know how those go? You want to do it because you feel suddenly compelled, maybe because you're drunk on old whiskey or a grumpy goose let you braid his hair or because Elvis music just puts you in a good mood. You know what I mean?"

"I'm not sure I do," Sophia related.

"What I'm trying to say, and I hope I don't regret it, is that I've agreed to help you, Sophia. I'm going to give Papa Creola the essence of my magic."

"What!" Sophia exclaimed, completely surprised. "You are?"

"Well, I've had good reasons not to in the past, but now they don't seem that big of a deal," Mama Jamba stated. "And you've proven a lot in a little bit of time, so I see no better reason. You get to recover the horn, Papa gets something he wants, and you bond with your mother's sword—completing your training. It really makes sense, but maybe that's the whiskey and music talking."

"Wow, thank you so much, Mama Jamba!" Sophia gushed. "I'm very grateful."

Mama Jamba smiled at her sweetly. "Oh, I know you are honey. But many hardships will come out of this. Reversing acts is mentally and emotionally tough for everyone on this timeline. And slaying the Phantom, well, that will be horribly difficult. But the biggest thing is this must, it absolutely must, set you on a course to finish your dragon-rider training."

"Why is that?" Sophia asked.

Mother Nature gave her a look full of love and wisdom. "Because it's essential that you're ready for what's coming."

"You mean the war with Thad Reinhart?"

"Yes, there is that," Mama Jamba said, hiding a sneaky grin. "But there's more to it. If and when you complete your training, it will spark something that could change everything."

"Why?" Sophia asked, wondering how her training could have such far-reaching effects.

The oldest entity alive gave her an expression of pure fondness. "Because, darling, that's the way I set it up."

"Oh," she said, feeling confused. "And all I have to do is complete my training?"

Mama Jamba laughed. "Yes, but that's like saying, 'All I have to do is eat a dinosaur for dinner.' There will be no greater challenge in your life than the trials you must pass to earn your wings as a dragonrider. It pains me that you will have to overcome such obstacles, and yet there is no other way."

Sophia nodded, her head full and her body tired. "Okay, well, I'll give it all I have. Thank you again for helping me."

"Don't mention it," Mama Jamba said, backing toward the dining hall, which was growing louder with music and laughter. "Seriously, don't ever mention it, or I'll have requests coming out of my nose."

Sophia nodded, turning for the stairs, her head buzzing from all the strange new events. She was going to be able to go after other lone riders and recruit them. They would hopefully build back up the numbers of the Dragon Elite, but not to what it once was. It would never be that. But hopefully, they could be a formidable enough force to take down Thad Reinhart. And Sophia was going to be given the chance to bond to her mother's sword, completing her training with the Dragon Elite.

But first, all of that would have to wait. Even young dragonriders needed their rest, for there would be many more adventures tomorrow.

CHAPTER FORTY-NINE

The beast's clawed feet stomped on the stone floor, shaking the walls of the castle. The chained dragon tried again to break through the muzzle that kept its jaws together and the fire it breathed from shooting on its captors.

Thad Reinhart sighed impatiently. "Sedate it," he said to his head scientist, Alexander Drake.

"But, sir," the round man with a long white beard argued, "I need him to be conscious for these tests."

Thad backed away from the cell that held the green dragon. The creature wasn't large, but it had proven to be powerful for its size. "Fine, he will wear himself out. Then do what you have to."

"He might also hurt himself, like the others," Drake explained. "And then his parts will be useless to you."

"Then sedate him," Thad growled, his Scottish accent thicker when he was angry, although he'd worked to refine his speech and tried to erase all parts of his past.

"That's the thing, sir. I'm wrestling with the two projects you would have me do. I can't do both using the same dragon." Drake held his hand up and pointed to the other cells where dragons lay half alive, suffering from the many experiments done on them. "And these other ones, well, they won't do."

Thad shook his head. "No, they won't. But keep them alive. We never know when we could use them."

"Will there be more dragons that you'll be bringing in?" Drake asked, striding beside Thad as he made his way down the long corridor of the dungeon.

"I would hope so," Thad answered. "But I've had trouble finding them."

"Well, if you manage to find more, I would devote one to the new project and use this one for the other." Drake swept his arm back, indicating the green dragon still trying to free itself from the magically enhanced chains, the only things that could restrain it so effectively.

Thad spun around, his eyes narrow as he stared at Drake. "There is nothing more important than the 'other project,' as you call it."

The scientist cleared his throat. "I get that, sir. Which has me thinking that maybe I should abandon the new project. It won't destroy a dragon and its rider, which I know is your end goal. And—"

"No, this project won't kill them. What it will do is worse." Thad balled his fist at his side and felt his temper rising. It would be best if he kept himself in check. He didn't want to replace another scientist due to one of his outbursts. "Death is easy," he continued. "It is nothing. But to be alive and have the very thing you love destroyed…that's punishment. It kills you slowly from the inside, which is what I want for the Dragon Elite. It's what Hiker Wallace deserves."

"Okay, so you want me to continue with both projects?" Drake asked and swallowed, the familiar fear Thad induced heavy in his eyes.

"Of course I do," Thad stated. "And yes, I'm working on finding you more dragons, but as you know, that's difficult."

"There aren't many lone dragons left, are there?" Drake's tone was careful.

Thad shook his head. "No, and there are even fewer dragons with riders. I've seen to that."

"Which is what I could use for the new project," Drake explained. "To learn how to sever their connection, I would need both. And although this dragon does help, it isn't really the same without a rider. Those dragons are different. They are more complex."

"I know that," Thad said in a hushed voice, his breath hot and his pulse rapid. "Go ahead and use this one for parts. I will find you a dragon and rider. I think even without the Dragon Elite globe, I can track down the few that remain outside the Gullington. I just need to do it before Hiker Wallace gets to them, trying to recruit."

"So, you know Hiker is back?" Drake asked, his cracked lips twitching with nervousness. "The Dragon Elite are active once more?"

"Yes," Thad answered. "I'm certain of it. His dragonriders have trespassed in two of my facilities and stolen the last remaining dragon eggs."

"How do you know they are the last?" Drake asked.

"Because it's my job to know these things," Thad stated, stomping toward the exit at the end of the hallway, tired of smelling the putrid rot.

"How do you know Hiker Wallace will go after the other dragons and riders out there?" Drake questioned. "You said he had written them off."

Thad turned. "I simply know. I know how that man thinks."

CHAPTER FIFTY

Sophia Beaufont had never been in the Cave at the Gullington where the dragons resided. No human had. It was a sacred place for the dragons that even their riders weren't allowed to enter—no matter what.

Scrying changed those rules for Sophia.

Wow, it's dark in there, Sophia commented to Lunis telepathically, seeing the inside of the Cave for the first time by looking through his eyes. Even in the dark, she could make out his surroundings.

And there are no couches to lie on, he stated, displeasure in his tone. *We're supposed to lie on the cold ground like savages.*

Or rather, like prehistoric dragons. I'd lodge a complaint with management if I were you, Sophia joked.

I would, but it would do me no favors. The others already think I'm strange and spoiled. They aren't wrong, Lunis imparted objectively. *It's just weird not to have any furniture in the Cave.*

Or a television, she added, searching the Cave as Lunis revolved his head around the large room.

I'm actually working on fixing that. I can deal with no furniture, but miss entertainment? The others are a bit resistant to the idea, though, he explained.

Give them one show of The Umbrella Academy *and they'll be hooked,* Sophia suggested.

I don't think they'll do well with fantasy, Lunis argued.

Dragons, really? she questioned. *You don't think fire-breathing dragons with magic will take to fantasy? Well, how about The* Good Place, *or The* Office, *or* Parks and Recreation?

I don't think so. They don't have the same sense of humor as me, Lunis commented.

I didn't think they had any sense of humor at all, actually, Sophia said.

They do, but it's drier.

Okay, then something British, Sophia stated. Father Ted, Vicar of Dibley, Black Books. *You think any of those will work?*

You've had a very strange upbringing that you even know those shows. Have you ever watched something normal for an American girl?

Like The Little Mermaid *or* Beauty and the Beast? Sophia asked

Exactly, Lunis answered. He already knew the answer but enjoyed teasing Sophia about how different she was from the modern youth of America. *And I don't think those British comedies would go over well with the other dragons. Maybe something with action would be better for them.*

Braveheart, Sophia offered.

Don't even go there, Lunis said, sounding offended.

Sophia giggled. *Oh, I thought that depiction of the Scottish was spot on.*

It's like your impression of the Scottish accent, Lunis declared.

Which is amazing, Sophia joked. "What are pants?" she asked aloud, doing her best Scottish accent and impression of Hiker Wallace, which she knew was offensively atrocious.

Lunis shook his head, changing her view. *Stop. You must stop doing that.*

I can try, but I have little hope it will work. It's an incurable affliction, Sophia said, looking around at the cave through Lunis' eyes.

Bones of animals littered the cave floor. The ceiling was high, uneven, and covered in bright green moss. The light that did stream in through the large opening provided enough to see that there were no amenities to the space. Just cold rock and claw-marked cave walls.

But there was something of extraordinary value that was newly hidden in the Cave.

There they are, Sophia said when Lunis looked directly at the five dragon eggs nestled in the corner.

They hadn't grown, although that had been one assumption. The other dragonriders had speculated that the eggs would change and grow after coming to the Gullington. They still might, but presently they shimmered with the same effervescence as when Sophia laid eyes on them when she was nine-years-old in the shop in Los Angeles.

That had only been a year or so ago, but for Sophia, it had been over a decade. The passing of time was different for her because of the chi of the dragon. Apparently, Father Time also had a hand in accelerating her age.

Sophia wasn't a child in an adult body. She was every bit an adult, matured both mentally and emotionally.

Do you think they are happier now? Sophia asked Lunis, referring to the dragon eggs.

I believe so, he answered. *It's hard to know, though. As dragons, we are all connected, but not like you and I are. We can't feel what each other does, or know what the others think. We simply have always known one another, but only on a surface level.*

That's confusing, Sophia said.

Tell me about it, he said with a huff. *Imagine having a thousand of your relatives cataloged in your head. We know each other, and then we don't.*

So you don't know who will come out of those eggs? she asked. *Like what their names are or what their personalities will be like?*

He indicated an emerald-colored egg. *I know that one will be green.*

Okay, you're ruining the wise dragon thing for me right now, Sophia said, seeing a different part of the Cave as Lunis glanced around. It was more of the same—cold walls and dark corners.

Where do you keep your blanket and mini-piano? Sophia joked, knowing he particularly loathed that one.

Lunis, he corrected. *My name is Lunis, not Linus. And I'm not a cartoon character either.*

Of course not, Sophia stated. *You're a majestic dragon. By the way, do you want to see what you look like with the new Snapchat filters I got? There's one that switches our faces. I want to see what I look like with horns.*

Heck, yes, I do, Lunis said, walking toward the opening of the Cave. *When do you leave to recruit dragonriders?*

How did you know about that? Sophia asked.

You're in my head right now, he answered.

Oh, and you're in mine most all the time, she said, realizing he must have witnessed her conversation with Hiker about her next mission. *I'm not sure when I'll leave. The Viking is still trying to locate the lone riders out there, and I don't believe he's giving it his full effort yet. I realize he knows what the Dragon Elite must do, but progress is hard for him. There is something holding him back, I think, besides his old-world thinking. It's always one step forward, two back with Mr. Kilts.*

I'm not sure I'd call him that to his face, Lunis advised.

Sophia laughed. *So, you don't think I should run my Scottish accent by him either? I think he'd love it.*

That's a negative, he answered.

"What's a fork?" Sophia asked aloud in her worst Scottish accent. "What does sunlight feel like?"

I'm begging you to stop this, Lunis said, his tone pained.

Okay, fine, she agreed. *But only for you. Actually, anything for you.*

She felt him smile.

Same here, Sophia.

CHAPTER FIFTY-ONE

It was definitely not the day to attempt to tease Hiker, Sophia realized as soon as she walked down the grand staircase of the Castle and into the dining hall.

The Viking was sitting in his normal chair, buttering his toast as if the bread had done something to offend him. He broke it in half with the next stroke of his knife, both pieces falling onto the plate. The Castle had apparently decided to give him back his regular clothes, so he wasn't wearing the retro suit anymore, but rather his traditional kilt and a sullen expression. His blond hair was back to hanging loosely around his face, although the creases from the braid Mama Jamba had given him were still noticeable.

Conversely, Mama Jamba sat beside him, not one of her gray hairs out of place. She was wearing a fresh pink tracksuit and a joyous smile. In front of her was a plate drenched in maple syrup and sprinkled with pancake crumbs.

"Ainsley," Mama Jamba called to the kitchen. "Another short stack of pancakes, please, my dear."

Sophia cut her eyes to Wilder, who was giving her a curious expression that seemed to say, "Take a seat and just watch. Don't say a word."

227

Silently, she took a seat, took a sip of water to cover her roaming eyes, and studied the obvious tension between Hiker and Mama Jamba.

Ainsley trotted through the kitchen door, holding two plates. She set a fresh stack of pancakes in front of Mama Jamba, then fluidly swapped out Hiker's plate of broken toast for a fresh one, unscathed by the Dragon Elite leader's knife.

"Do you want me to butter it for you?" the housekeeper asked, the empty plates hitched on her hip and a cunning grin in her green eyes.

He growled, his beard vibrating. "I'm perfectly capable of buttering my own toast, Ainsley. Thank you very much."

"He's just mad. He'll get over it," Mama Jamba said before taking a bite of buttery pancakes dripping in syrup.

Ainsley clapped her free hand to her cheek and pretended to appear shocked. "What? Hiker Wallace is angry? Well, I never. What has happened to make our placid leader quake?"

Hiker's eyes fluttered with annoyance as his knife cut into the butter. "I think there's something burning in the kitchen, Ainsley. Would you run along and check on it?"

She shook her head. "That's impossible. I'm not cooking anything."

He glanced up at her. "What do you mean? There is no bacon out here yet. And where are the eggs?"

"Mama Jamba asked for pancakes," she answered. "And the kids seem fine just watching the show." She indicated Sophia and Wilder, who still had empty plates and keen expressions. They immediately shuffled for the various plates of fruits and pastries as Hiker cut his eyes at them.

"Would you get us eggs and bacon?" Hiker said tersely. "They will need protein for today's training."

"Ainsley is my name," she replied. "Not 'Would You.'"

He shook his head at her. "And you cooked those pancakes for Mama, so stop fibbing and make some eggs and bacon."

"Fine, fine," she answered, striding toward the kitchen. The swinging door was hardly shut before she buzzed back with two trays, one with steaming eggs and the other with bacon, still sizzling.

Hiker paused, his knife an inch from his toast. "I thought you weren't cooking anything?"

"I wasn't," Ainsley stated. "There's this thing called magic. It's sort of hard to explain. But you see, the Castle, where you're currently sitting, is full of this magic. And sometimes when I need something, the Castle—"

"Ainsley, you're fired," Hiker said plainly, dropping the knife with the pat of butter and sticking the dry toast in his mouth.

"Very well, sir," she said, curtsying. "I did need a day off. It's been about four hundred years, so I'm a little overdue."

"It's not a day off," Hiker argued. "You're fired. For good. We no longer need your help."

"Of course, sir," Ainsley replied, taking off her apron, wadding it up, and throwing it on the table. "I'll appreciate references when I start looking for work, of course."

"We are a secret society of dragonriders," Hiker stated. "I can't give you references."

Mama Jamba didn't seem to notice the conversation going on as she polished off yet another plate of pancakes.

"I understand, sir." Ainsley looked around the dining hall fondly. "Well, if you all need anything, I'll be staying at the Inn in town," she said before striding toward the exit.

"We won't need anything," Hiker said, a fire burning in his eyes.

"I could use more pancakes," Mama Jamba chirped, looking up suddenly.

"And I can't find my sword," Wilder added.

Ainsley paused in the doorway and gave Hiker a challenging expression.

He glanced at Mama Jamba. "You've had enough pancakes." His gaze drifted to Wilder. "Your sword will turn up. It always does."

Evan strode into the dining hall, swerving around Ainsley. "Hey, why is your office chained shut, sir?" he asked Hiker.

The Viking dropped his toast and pinned both his hands on the table. "Because I'm firing a nuisance who is in cahoots with this bloody Castle."

"You said cahoots," Evan quipped with a snicker, grabbing several strips of bacon with his bare hands.

Sophia gave him a punishing look.

He coughed. "Oh, I get that my lack of manners is once again an issue for you. In my defense, I'm still injured. Give me a break, Soph."

She shook her head. He was looking recovered after the mission to the Lucidite's Institute to get the dragon eggs. She might actually like and respect him after their assignment together, but she wasn't going to tell him that, ever. No, Evan was like the little brother that she never had…who was actually older than her by one-hundred years.

Ainsley glanced up the stairs that leveled out next to Hiker's study. "Oh, that's a large lock. Good luck with that one, sir. Well, if there isn't anything else, I'll just be off."

"Pancakes, please," Mama Jamba said again, sliding her empty plate away and looking pleasantly around the table.

Hiker huffed. "Fine. You're not fired. But no more sass today. I'm not in the mood."

"Which is different from—" Ainsley straightened. "Never mind, sir. Of course, sir. I'll be on my best behavior. And I'll just buzz off and get those pancakes, Mama Jamba."

There was a loud noise outside the dining hall. Ainsley glanced up before giving Hiker a smile. "Looks like you can get back in your office again, sir. Cheers."

He growled. "And when will it put it back the way it was with my books and all?"

No one said anything. Mama Jamba simply looked around at the others, smiling sweetly.

Ainsley returned with another plate of pancakes, setting them down in front of Mother Nature. "The Castle says that it will fix your office soon."

"When?" Hiker asked.

Ainsley lifted her chin, listening. "Within the century."

He picked up his toast and tore a bite off, chewing angrily. "How can you eat like that with everything going on?" he asked Mama Jamba.

The picture of poise, she wiped the corners of her mouth with her napkin before smiling at him. "These are simply delicious pancakes. That's how."

"Those eggs in the Cave are the last of the dragons," he argued. "We'll soon be extinct. And you're over there having a pancake party."

Mama Jamba laughed. "Oh, no. You must have more than one person eating pancakes for that. And I'm the only one since you've dictated that your riders eat protein."

Sophia looked down at her untouched plate.

"Hiker, I see you've sobered up if you're back to worrying about the eggs," Ainsley said, returning with another plate of pancakes. "These are for anyone who wants to join Mama Jamba's pancake party."

Evan stuck a fork in the top two pancakes before the plate had even touched the surface of the table. "That would be me! Yonk!"

"I was sober last night," Hiker argued. "And what did I say about the sass?"

"Oh, you were sober last night? That's why you allowed me to braid your hair while you were wearing a suit from the 1970s?" Mama Jamba asked.

"That was me giving up, but it didn't last for long, and thankfully, the Castle gave me back my clothes," Hiker said.

"Because we were all tired of seeing your bare chest in those sheet robes," Ainsley said, shaking her head.

"And," Hiker continued, "now our present reality is setting in. We've got to take action or risk losing it all."

"I agree," Mama Jamba said, licking her lips before taking another bite.

"Why aren't you taking this more seriously? We are about to be erased!" he questioned.

She shrugged. "I have no idea what it's like to have something you love more than anything waste away until it's close to dying."

"Oh, fine, you're talking about the Earth," Hiker replied. "I get it."

Mama Jamba pushed her plate away. "I know that this isn't easy for you, Hiker. You are going back and forth between acceptance and denial. Frustration and perseverance. Optimism and pessimism. That's normal. But the fact of the matter is, the Earth is endangered and along with that, the dragonriders. This can't be a surprise to you. The two have always been intimately intertwined."

"So it's over then?" he asked her.

She shook her head. "No, it never is. Not until the curtain closes, and we're not even to the final act yet."

Hiker's eyes fell to his piece of toast.

"Look, my dear," Mama Jamba continued. "Recruit the lone dragonriders. Have your newest rider finish her training." She indicated Sophia. "And have the world accept you as adjudicators. Then you'll go after Thad Reinhart. That's the right plan. I just know it."

"And if I do all that then the Dragon Elite will be saved?" he asked, hope in his voice. "And we will save the Earth?"

Mama Jamba pushed away from the table, stretching to a standing position. "Oh, heavens. I have no clue. But if you fail, at least you'll know you did everything you could."

The woman who was both unassuming and all-powerful waved to the others before heading for the entryway, whistling *Blue Suede Shoes*.

CHAPTER FIFTY-TWO

Sophia and Wilder had been on the Expanse for less than a minute, about to start sparring practice, when Quiet rushed over wildly waving his arms.

"What is it?" Sophia asked, meeting him halfway, the gnome's short legs making his progress slow, even though he was running as she'd never seen him do before.

His mouth was moving fast, but she couldn't make out any of his words.

Sophia spun to face Wilder, a frantic look on her face that said, "Do you know what he's saying?"

He seemed to understand her expression and shook his head before sliding to a kneeling position in front of the gnome. "Talk to us, Quiet. What's going on?"

Again, the groundskeeper spoke rapidly, but none of his words were audible.

Sophia leaned close to his mouth with her ear, straining to understand the rushed whispers. She made out only one word, and it was enough to make her pulse quicken.

Straightening, she turned to Wilder, her look making his eyes widen with horror.

"What did you hear?" he asked her.

"Mahkah," she answered just as something at the front of the Castle caught her attention.

Hiker had bolted out the front door but halted immediately. His eyes flicked to the three on the Expanse and then to the sky overhead.

Sophia followed his gaze, and only then did she see it. Tumbling through the Barrier end over end were Mahkah and Tala. Mahkah was attached to his dragon, but it appeared that they would crash into the ground, both seemingly unconscious.

Lunis, Sophia called telepathically to her dragon.

Yes, he replied instantly.

Get out here, she said, sending him the visual.

Lunis exploded a second later from the Cave, Bell and Simi behind him. They were too far away, though, and Mahkah and Tala were tumbling fast.

And then they froze in midair like they were suspended from invisible ropes.

Sophia spun to face Hiker, but he wasn't the one responsible for the incredible display of magic holding the dragon and rider in the air. The leader of the Dragon Elite was hurrying in their direction, his eyes screwed up in confusion.

Her gaze swiveled, and Sophia knew exactly who was responsible for saving the two from crashing to the earth.

Quiet had his squatty hand in the air. His mouth was still moving fast, but this time, he was whispering a spell. Sophia recognized the focus. It was different from when he'd been trying to frantically communicate a message. Now he was gathering his power, sending it to keep the dragon and rider from falling. The effort was costing him greatly. Sweat poured from his brow, and his hand was beginning to shake.

"You can do it," Wilder encouraged, noticing the same thing as Sophia.

The dragon and rider dropped several yards rapidly before freezing in the sky once more. The gnome couldn't keep this up for long, and if Sophia tried to help, she could undo his spell entirely. She wasn't even sure if she could achieve what he was doing. Holding two magical creatures in the air was a feat that she hadn't ever attempted.

"Steady now," Hiker stated firmly, arriving beside the gnome. "Hold them there."

Sophia didn't know why Quiet didn't simply use his magic to lower them safely to the ground. She guessed that would be too risky, possibly making them crash.

"Only another few seconds," Hiker said, his tone carrying great strength.

It was only a few more seconds before the dragons arrived around the unconscious pair, their wings beating to keep them in place as they disentangled the two. Bell picked up Mahkah with her front legs, grasping him by the shoulders. Lunis and Simi each took hold of Tala on either side and carried the unconscious dragon to the Cave as Bell descended with Mahkah. It wasn't until she'd laid him on the ground at their feet that Sophia considered he might be dead. That hadn't occurred to her before because of Hiker's demeanor. He was worried, yet not frantic. He'd had a quiet knowing about him.

The dragonrider appeared surprisingly unscathed, with no marks on his body. This observation seemed to perplex Hiker as well.

"Take him to the Castle," he ordered Bell.

She picked him up again and flew low, speeding for the Castle.

"Sir?" Sophia asked, hurrying after Hiker, who was rushing for the Castle.

"Stay here," he ordered.

She halted, confused. "But…"

He turned and gave her a stern expression. "Stay here. We don't know what is wrong with him or whether it can spread. You two train. I will give you an update when I have it."

Slowly Sophia nodded, which seemed to make Hiker relax.

He let out a tense breath and sped for the Castle, Quiet scurrying to keep up.

CHAPTER FIFTY-THREE

"He will be okay," Wilder offered thoughtfully.

Sophia shook her head. "We don't know that. We don't even know what's wrong with him. Or Tala."

Wilder nodded. "They went to investigate that facility of Thad Reinhart's. The Castle will know what to do. Mahkah did the right thing, returning here. It's the only option when a dragonrider is on their last legs."

"So, the Castle can always save us?" Sophia asked.

He let out a breath, tilting his head back and forth. "I don't want to say that, but it is our best bet in the worst-case scenario."

"Because it is our home," Sophia guessed.

Wilder smiled. "There is a strange magic to the place we seek refuge. To a home."

"What do you think Hiker meant when he said he didn't want it to spread?" Sophia asked. "Like Mahkah had been infected by a contagious disease."

"I don't know," Wilder answered. "I think he's just being cautious. He knows more about Thad Reinhart than anyone else. Maybe he knows how the man works, something like putting a curse on Makah that's infectious. Or, more likely, he's just being Hiker. He doesn't take chances. He never has."

"That's true," Sophia said, picking up Inexorabilis. She was doubtful that she could focus long enough to actually train.

"So, your sword," Wilder said, a hint of curiosity in his voice.

He knew that she had to reverse the act that her mother had done to bond with Inexorabilis, which involved bringing back the Phantom, an evil unicorn who infected the world with evil.

"Yeah, I have what I need from Papa Creola to do it," she admitted.

His eyes bulged. "You do? That was fast."

"Well, Mama Jamba helped me," Sophia said, remembering waking up the morning after Mother Nature said that she'd give Papa Creola the essence of her magic in return for him reversing the death of the Phantom. That morning, Sophia found a small hourglass on her bedside table with instructions on what to do and where to go to re-kill the Phantom.

"So now we just have to go and slay that impossible beast," Wilder said, tension in his voice.

"You don't have to go," she argued.

"I promised you," he said at once. "And of course, I'm going."

"But it's more complicated than I thought originally."

He actually smiled. "I would have it no other way."

"Papa Creola requires that we harvest the Phantom's horn," Sophia explained.

"Which is like trying to give a raging bull a pedicure," Wilder said with a laugh.

"Yeah, it should prove to be quite difficult," Sophia agreed.

"But it will be worth it," Wilder said, enthusiasm in his voice.

Sophia remembered what Subner had asked her to do, perking up. "Hey, do you think you can help me to find a weapon that's some-where in the Gullington?"

"You mean the Castle?" he asked.

She shrugged. "I don't know. I was told it's somewhere in the Gullington, so it could be in the Castle."

"I've met most weapons in the Castle," Wilder stated. "What is this weapon?"

She pulled out her phone and scrolled until she found the description that Subner had sent her. "Here, take a look at this and see if it sounds familiar."

She handed him her phone.

He narrowed his eyes at the screen. "How do you manage to read on this?"

"You get used to it," she explained.

"What's wrong with paper?" he asked.

She shook her head. "It's for old men."

He bowed slightly. "I pride myself on being one, but not looking like one."

"And sometimes you still act like a teenager," she teased.

"Watch it, Soph," he mock-threatened. "You want my help, don't you?"

"Take a look and tell me if you're familiar with this weapon," she said, indicating the phone.

He glanced back at it, reading. After a moment, he asked, "How do you even get these types of missions? Oh, just go and reverse events that slaughtered an evil unicorn and harvest its horn. Then kill it again. Easy-peasy. And then go find a weapon I've never seen in the Castle because if I had, it would be on my back right now."

"Sooooo…you can help?" she asked.

He sighed. "Really, you're supposed to find Devon's bow?"

"Yeah," she answered. "Was he a dragonrider?"

"Yes, Sophia, he was a dragonrider," he said, humoring her. "He also created the very first bow and arrows."

"Oh…"

"Yeah, so this bow you're looking for, it's the first one ever," Wilder stated.

"Well, I need to find it," Sophia said, thinking.

"Yeah, now that I know it's in the Gullington, I need to find it too."

She shook her head. "No, I have to give it to Subner, Papa Creola's assistant. He helped me so that Father Time would agree to help me if

Mother Nature helped him. And so far, everyone has complied. I need to make good on my promise to Subner."

Wilder gave her an amused expression. "You get that you're ridiculous, right?"

"I'm just different than you and have a tad bit more going on," she argued.

He laughed. "Fine. So you want my help tracking down Devon's bow?"

"Well, if you can spare the time," she said meekly.

"You mean before I go off to my death to re-kill the Phantom?" he asked.

"Don't you want to go out with a bang?" she asked.

"Actually, I wanted to die in my sleep when I was a thousand years old," he answered.

"What if I let you use the bow when we face the Phantom?" she offered.

He considered. "I thought you had to give it to Subner?"

"I do," she answered. "But I also have to give Father Time the horn. We might as well do it at the same time. And if that's the case, someone might as well use the bow beforehand."

"You know, Sophia, I have rarely been so intrigued to go on what might be an endless mission, followed by an impossible mission, followed by my death."

"So you'll do it?" she asked.

"I'll probably regret it, but yes. If you want help, then I'm your man."

CHAPTER FIFTY-FOUR

After not eating lunch and waiting for word about Mahkah, Sophia found herself back on the Expanse. Hiker wasn't at lunch, and his office door was shut. No one seemed to know what was going on with Mahkah, although Ainsley said she thought he'd be okay.

Too consumed with thoughts about what hurt the rider and his dragon, Sophia couldn't eat any of her cock-a-leekie soup. Her mind was also reeling with how she'd find Devon's bow. She had zero leads and a large territory full of possibilities.

The bow could be in the Cave or in any of the nooks and crannies of the Expanse. It could be buried at the bottom of the Pond. And more terrifying than any of those possibilities was that it could be hidden in the Castle—where she'd never find it unless the Castle wanted it found.

"Did you try asking the Castle if it had the bow?" Wilder asked, striding over to her. His question came on the heels of her thoughts like he was reading them.

She turned, feeling a blast of cold on her cheeks. Winter was coming, and the autumn air was hinting at how unrelenting the season would be. "Yeah, I asked the Castle."

"And it didn't offer up Devon's bow?" he questioned, his chin high and green eyes narrowed on the hills in front of them.

"It totally gave me the bow, which is why I asked for your help," she replied.

He glared at her through his long eyelashes, a smile tucked at the corner of his mouth. "Oh, you and your sarcasm. A true mark of a modern girl."

"I thought it was my phone and snazzy clothes with zippers," she stated.

"What's a zipper?" he asked.

"One day, I'll teach you all about the magic of hoodies and zippers and Velcro," she said with a smile.

"And my head will explode, but I'll have finally entered the modern era."

"So, I don't think the Castle has the bow," Sophia responded, returning to the subject at hand. "Which means we have to search the Expanse. Any clue where to start?"

"We could try a finding spell," Wilder offered.

"Already tried that."

He nodded. "Of course you did. You know, I didn't know how to do a finding spell until I was over a hundred years old."

"But boys mature slower than girls," she said. "I think we are both too optimistic to think Devon's bow can be found with a simple spell. It's hidden for a reason, so finding it won't be easy."

"It's hidden because it's probably the most powerful bow in the world," Wilder pointed out.

"How?" Sophia asked.

"Only one way to tell," he answered.

"Okay, well, let's set off," Sophia said, holding out her hand. "You know this place better than me, so lead the way."

"I don't think even after two hundred years I know the Gullington all that well," Wilder admitted. "That's part of the magic of this place. It shifts and changes based on who is inside of it and what's going on outside in the world."

"That sounds a lot like the House where I grew up," Sophia related.

"You mean the location for the House of Fourteen?" he asked.

She nodded. "Whoever named the House and Castle was lacking in imagination. Why couldn't they be called something as extraordinary as they are? Why just call them House and Castle?"

"Because that's what they are," Wilder said. "Sometimes, the most complex things in the world need to be called by the simplest names, like the elements or love or joy."

"Yeah, I guess so," Sophia replied, marveling at how awesome and mysterious the Castle and House were. They shared similarities that often made her wonder if they could somehow be connected. Maybe it was just because both were enhanced with magic that they seemed alike. The Castle was much more mischievous than the House, though. Actually, the House was very reactive to the people in it, whereas the Castle was more proactive, seeming to be constantly scheming. There was no doubt that the Castle inside the Gullington was more powerful than the House, but that shouldn't surprise her since it belonged to the dragonriders, which predated the House of Fourteen.

For over an hour, Sophia and Wilder hiked over the Expanse, finding nothing of particular interest. The whole mission seemed futile, and Sophia was the first to admit what they were both thinking.

"This is ridiculous," she said, pausing on the top of a hill that overlooked the Pond.

Wilder seemed happy for the break and nodded. "What if we can't find Devon's bow?"

She shrugged. "I mean, I don't know. Subner asked me to."

"But you don't need it to complete your training, right?"

"No," she answered. "I need to bond to my sword for that. But I feel like the bow has to be a part of that."

"Why?" he questioned.

"Just a gut thing."

He fired a finger at her. "Trust that, then."

"Okay, but we still don't know where to look," she grumbled. "We could be out here for the rest of our lives and not uncover the bow."

"Which is why we need to employ the help of someone who will know exactly where Devon's bow is." Wilder flashed her a sly smile.

Sophia arched a curious brow at him and knew exactly who he was referring to. Striding up over the hill bordering the Pond was the groundskeeper. Quiet appeared cautious as he glanced over his shoulder, again like he was afraid he was being followed.

"Do you think he will tell us anything?" Sophia asked and then realized how dumb the question was.

"I think that he might tell you, in his own weird way," Wilder answered, combing his hand through his hair.

"Why me? You haven't antagonized him like Evan."

"Yes, but Quiet likes you more than the rest of us," Wilder explained.

"Only because I'm new and haven't gotten on his last nerve like the rest of you."

"True," Wilder chirped. "But let's go test my theory."

He took off in front of her, hurrying in the direction of the gnome. Quiet always seemed to be working, but never doing anything. It was perplexing. His hands were usually dirty and his brow covered in sweat, but Sophia never saw him actually doing anything.

"Quiet!" Wilder called after the gnome. "Quiet! I need your help!"

The groundskeeper pivoted at once, putting his back toward Wilder and hurrying in the opposite direction.

"Quiet!" Wilder continued. "I have an important question for you!"

The gnome held up his hand, shaking it like he was busy and running in the direction of the Pond.

Wilder gave Sophia a challenging expression. "Okay, your turn, Miss."

She rolled his eyes at him. "Fine."

Speeding after the gnome, she yelled, "Quiet! Hey, there! I need your help."

The groundskeeper spun at once, his eyes bright and attentive. He muttered something, his chin out like he was waiting for her to say more.

Wilder sidled up next to Sophia, a satisfied expression on his face. "Next time, we're betting something."

She narrowed her eyes at him before turning her attention to Quiet. "Why is it that you'll help me but not Wilder?"

Sophia wasn't sure what she expected, but his response was typical. He pointed at Wilder, muttering wildly. Making a wide movement around his head, he pointed at his own head covered in a cap.

"Are you saying that Wilder doesn't have a brain?" Sophia asked.

"No," Wilder interrupted. "He's saying how my hair is too amazing and intimidates him."

Sophia glanced at the gnome, who now had his arms crossed over his chest. He shook his head radically. "Well, regardless, I'm grateful for your help, Quiet. I'm...we're looking for something we believe to be in the Gullington. It's a bow."

The gnome's eyes widened before he covered his reaction.

"Have you heard of Devon's bow?" Sophia asked.

To her surprise, Quiet nodded.

"Do you know if it's in the Gullington?" she questioned.

Another nod.

Sophia grinned at Wilder, feeling like she was finally making some progress. Turning back to Quiet, she asked, "Can you tell us where it is?"

He shook his head.

"And there you go," Wilder said, throwing his hands up and spinning like he was headed back for the Castle.

Quiet held up a short finger, a twinkle in his eyes.

Sophia wasn't sure why, but words fell out of her mouth she hadn't expected to say. "You won't tell me, but you can show me, right?"

The gnome nodded.

Wilder whipped back around. "What?"

Sophia waved him off. "Go on then," she encouraged the groundskeeper. "Where is Devon's bow?"

Quiet lifted his hand, and gold dust sparkled from his fingertips. It twirled over his head before flying off, creating a trail across the

Expanse and the Pond from where he stood until it disappeared from view.

"That leads to the bow?" Sophia asked.

He nodded.

"And all we have to do is follow it to find Devon's bow?" she questioned.

Quiet tilted his head to the side, giving her a challenging expression.

"Yeah, it probably leads to a maze, a pit of hell and a deadly beast," Wilder said with a laugh. "But yeah, if we get past all that, I'm sure the bow is ours."

Sophia shook her head at the other rider and smiled at the gnome. "Thanks so much for helping. I'm always here to return the favor."

Quiet muttered in reply. Although Sophia couldn't make out exactly what he said, she could have sworn it sounded like, "Oh, you definitely will."

CHAPTER FIFTY-FIVE

"Well, that all worked out," Sophia said proudly as they followed the trail of gold dust.

Wilder sighed beside her. "Your optimism that this will be so simple is amusing."

She leveled her gaze at him. "Oh, and your cynicism is annoying."

"Do you think that this trail is just going to lead us to the most powerful bow in the world without any challenges?" Wilder asked.

"Now I know why Quiet doesn't want to help you," she remarked.

"Yes, because I've got great hair, and I'm devilishly handsome," he replied.

"And a bad attitude."

"I'm just saying," he began, "that nothing in this place comes without a challenge. That's the way it works. Nothing is handed to the dragonriders. We fight for it."

"You all fight," Sophia argued. "I strategize."

They climbed down the steep hill that led to the placid waters of the Pond. Sophia had never been this close to the shore and wondered why. There was an instant calm that came over her as she neared the water.

"How are you going to strategize that?" Wilder pointed to the trail of gold dust streaked out over the shore and across the water, disappearing into what appeared to be the middle of the Pond, although it was hard to tell since the body of water was so large.

"Easy," she replied proudly. "I'll just call Lunis."

Wilder pursed his lips, a smile in his eyes. "Go for it, hotshot."

She gave him a defiant expression before reaching out to her dragon.

Lunis, I need your help.

I can't right now, he answered at once. *We are attending to Tala.*

Oh, is she...

She will be okay, but it is taking our collective energy to heal her, he explained.

Okay, well, let me know if I can help, Sophia said, feeling slightly less pumped.

Find that bow, Lunis stated. *And bond to your sword.*

Working on it, she said, realizing an expression of defeat was showing on her face.

"So you realize the dragons can't help right now," Wilder stated, a cocky tone in his voice.

"Yeah," Sophia admitted. "We just need a way across the Pond so we can follow the trail."

"Summon a boat," Wilder suggested.

"I don't own a boat," Sophia stated, slightly annoyed. "I can only summon that which I own or have access to."

"Looks like someone should have been saving her gold instead of spending it on shiny devices," Wilder teased.

"Our currency isn't gold, and what use do I have for a boat?"

He held up his hand at the trail. "Well, if you had one right now, we'd be cruising across the water."

Sophia searched the area around the Pond. "How is there no boat around here?"

"You really haven't been paying attention, have you?" Wilder asked. "There's not much in the Gullington, just a Castle, a Cave, and a Pond. The Expanse is just hills and the flock. We don't have anything extra. No vehicles or equipment or barns."

Sophia grunted with frustration. "Well, it seems that between the two of us, we should be able to figure out how to get across the Pond."

"We should," he replied, a hint of mischief in his voice.

"I mean, the answer has to be obvious," she went on, keeping her face neutral.

"So obvious," he sang.

"I just wish I could figure it out," she stated, continuing to play the game he had no idea she was playing.

Wilder pulled off his boots, shaking his head. "Yes, and sometimes the obvious is the answer."

"What are you doing?" Sophia asked, watching him take off his belt and sword.

He pointed at himself, putting a spell on his body. "I'm going to follow the trail."

"But you'll freeze," Sophia stated.

"No, because I just put a warming spell on myself," he answered, wading into the water.

"You're going after the bow?" she asked, trying to keep the cheer out of her voice.

"Yes, Soph. Because some of us find solutions while others sit on the shore, all dry." Wilder dove into the water, disappearing under its surface.

She grinned. "And some of us strategize, knowing that ego-driven ones will get wet for us."

CHAPTER FIFTY-SIX

It wasn't Wilder Thomson's first time to swim in the Pond. His first summer in the Gullington as a dragonrider, he'd stripped off his clothes and dove in to escape the boredom, tired of having nothing to do.

Hiker had sped out of the Castle like an angry parent, commanding Wilder to get out immediately. He, of course, did as he was told. Still new to the Viking and afraid of him, he'd stood on the shore dripping wet and shivering as Hiker tore into him. He was told that under no circumstances was he ever to enter the Pond. It was for the dragons. It was part of Quiet's domain. It wasn't a place that any of the riders were allowed to enter.

As Wilder swam through the green water, he finally knew why Hiker had made the Pond off-limits. It was where Devon's bow was hidden.

Clever approach, Hiker, Wilder thought.

He started to wonder how many other things Hiker had made off-limits that were actually guarding some sort of treasure. Wilder trusted the leader of the Dragon Elite like no one else. He knew that in Hiker's weird way, he had their interests at heart. Never before had he ever wanted to challenge his trusted leader...but then Sophia Beaufont had come along.

She didn't necessarily defy Hiker as much as bend rules and attempt things that had never even occurred to the rest of them. Sophia was a unique brand of dragonrider who would either save them from their dark plight or get them all killed. Strangely, Wilder smiled at the notion as he came up for air.

He waved to Sophia on the shore, amazed by how much progress he'd made. Swimming on top of the water, he continued to follow the golden trail made by Quiet.

After several yards, the trail seemed to disappear. A cursory glance down told Wilder where it went. The bow was buried at the bottom of the Pond.

Maybe Sophia was right, and this isn't going to be so difficult, Wilder thought.

Of course, without Quiet's help, finding the bow would have been impossible. But with the gnome's help, it only took a bit of ingenuity.

Taking a deep breath, Wilder kicked under the water and followed the shimmering trail. It, unsurprisingly, led down.

Sunken treasure, he mused, swimming hard so that he didn't run out of air. The bottom wasn't far.

When the trail ran out, Wilder noticed something shiny only a few yards away on the floor of the Pond.

It was a large chest.

Nice, he thought, kicking harder.

His magic didn't work well underwater, usually due to lack of oxygen and movement, so he was grateful to find there wasn't a lock on the chest. That was a relief since it was too big for him to carry up to the surface.

The top of the chest was held shut with a single latch.

This was turning out to be a straightforward mission. *It must be the way of Sophia Beaufont,* he thought, pushing on the latch.

It was stuck, rusted in place. *That seems about right.*

Bubbles spilled from Wilder's mouth as he struggled with the latch. He held onto the side of the chest and kicked at it, trying to make it budge. Launching his heel, he kicked as hard as he could.

The latch shot back, making the lid open. Wilder helped to pull it back, finding it resistant due to age. Inside he found what he'd only read about but never thought he'd lay his eyes on. He had thought it was the stuff of legends and didn't really exist. But Wilder's gift with weapons told him immediately that this was Devon's bow. As soon as he laid his hands on it, the battles it had been in through the ages poured through his body.

He saw its construction during the dawning of the ages. He saw the bow in the first battles the Dragon Elite had ever fought. He saw centuries of fights, all from the vantage point of the arrows launched from the bowstring.

Wilder had no idea what Devon's bow's special power was, but in his hands, he knew he held one of the most incredible weapons on the planet.

And all I had to do was swim for it, he thought, putting the bow over his back and preparing to kick up to the surface. He closed the chest and only then saw it.

Staring at him in the distance was a sea creature with green eyes that glowed through the water and several rows of teeth. And though Wilder didn't know what the beast was, he knew with absolute certainty it was hungry.

CHAPTER FIFTY-SEVEN

Wilder was taking forever, Sophia mused, deciding to take a seat on the beach, and began to doodle in the sand.

For some reason, she couldn't shake the restless feeling in her chest. She felt like she should be doing something, but what she didn't know. Wilder had followed the trail. The dragons were attending to Tala. The Castle was taking care of Mahkah. There didn't seem to be anything for Sophia to do. So she simply sat on the beach, making pictures in the sand.

The beast opened its mouth, showing a chasm of black that could easily swallow Wilder whole.

He kicked off the treasure chest and shot up for the surface. A piercing echo shot through the water that had to be from the sea creature.

Wilder didn't look back, knowing he didn't have a second to spare. Not only did he need to get up to the surface, but he had to get across the Pond, and the chances of making that with a hungry monster pursuing him weren't good.

It was ironic to him that he had the most powerful bow in the world but couldn't use it on the enemy chasing him. He was full of combat magic, but it did him no good as he swam in the murky waters of the Pond.

When he was almost to the surface, Wilder dared to look over his shoulder. The monster had strangely paused. He did too. Their eyes met. With the light overhead illuminating the beast, he noticed that it looked like a giant eel. Its long body wiggled behind it, telegraphing its next move.

The monster wasn't standing down, as Wilder had hoped. It was gearing up to launch itself at him.

CHAPTER FIFTY-EIGHT

Something seemed to scream in Sophia's mind, making her bolt to a standing position. She didn't know what it was and couldn't hear anything. It was a feeling, an emotion that had sound in her body. Color in her vision. It made her heart pound.

Searching the surface of the water, she looked for Wilder. The placid waters of the Pond seemed to stare back at her rebelliously, hiding what lay beneath.

Wilder had been under for a minute or more. She'd lost track, and somehow, deep in her spirit, she knew something was wrong...no, not wrong...but about to be.

Then a splash stole her attention as Wilder broke the surface. Unlike before, his arms were waving wildly, and even from a distance, she could read the panic in his eyes. Furiously, he swam in her direction.

There was nothing that she could see pursuing him. She assumed that his warming spell had worn off and he was freezing.

Sophia rubbed her hands together, preparing to create a warming spell to dry him off once he got to shore. He'd be shivering.

She pressed her hands together and felt the warmth pooling.

Behind Wilder a monster shot straight into the air, shrieking so loud that it shook the ground under Sophia's feet.

When it was twenty feet in the air, the monster curved and dove back for the surface. It was then that Sophia realized the sheer size of the long creature. It reminded her of a giant eel, its black body sleek and covered in long fins.

When its head went under, the creature's body rippled behind it like a ribbon being whipped on the ground.

Wilder continued to swim fast, but there was no way he could outrace the monster. Sophia saw then that it was messing with Wilder. Taunting him until it decided to seal the deal and take a bite.

Standing on the shore of the Pond, Sophia felt helpless.

She thought about reaching out to Lunis again but she didn't want to be the reason anything happened to Tala. She needed the dragons, and Sophia needed to help Wilder. She had gotten him into this mess, after all, taunting him to dive into the Pond.

"Come on, Wilder!" she called, knowing that when she had been at her lowest, small words of encouragement had helped her to move faster, harder. "Come on!"

Her words were drowned out by the giant splash behind Wilder as the sea creature shot up again, shrieking once more—a noise that sounded like a victory cry.

"That's a bit premature!" Sophia yelled and threw her hand in the air, muttering an incantation she'd never tried but knew by heart. The blast shot off her hand and flew toward the monster but missed it by inches.

Undeterred, Sophia shot three more blasts at the beast. The first two missed their target, but the third hit it as it dove for the water again, about to disappear. When the blast connected with the creature, a net shot out in all directions, encapsulating it. It stretched and contorted, making huge splashes as the magical net worked to corral it.

Wilder finally made progress away from the monster as it thrashed, throwing itself into the air and wiggling to free itself. Everything it did made Sophia's net tighten around its body.

With a shriek that sounded more like a defeated groan, the monster finally sank below the surface of the Pond, its glowing green eyes the last thing Sophia saw before it was gone. She was certain she'd made a permanent enemy of the thing, but hopefully, it would realize she'd spared it later on.

CHAPTER FIFTY-NINE

Sophia had burned out her magic by the time Wilder dragged himself out of the water. She couldn't warm him up as she'd wanted, having been depleted by attempting not one but four spells she'd never done before. The net spell was something she thought of using on the fly. There had to be more efficient ways to do it, but at that moment, she hadn't known how. She was now depleted, and Wilder was shivering.

"Do you want my cloak?" she asked, rushing over to him.

"No," he said breathlessly. "I'm fine. My warming spell, remember?"

She nodded. It had simply been the sea creature that had scared him, not that that wasn't enough.

"Are you okay?" she asked, looking him over, thinking back to when Evan had nearly lost it in the water, escaping a modern-day sea creature known as a submarine.

He nodded, gulping. "Yeah, thanks for saving me."

Sophia made to smile but found herself too shaken.

"Interesting approach with the nets," Wilder said, turning to regard the Pond, which had magically gone completely placid like there hadn't just been a battle on its surface.

"Yeah…"

"Tell me," he said, wiping his hands through his wet hair, "why not just blast the monster and kill it? That would have cost significantly less magic."

Sophia thought for a moment. "I'm not sure, actually. It was just a feeling that I had, like I shouldn't harm the beast."

"Well, it's currently pinned in a net at the bottom of the Pond," he argued.

"It will get out," Sophia stated.

"Believe me, I know," he said with wide eyes. "I saw that thing's teeth. It will be out in no time."

"And unharmed," she added.

He shook his head. "You're a strange beast, Sophia Beaufont."

Her eyes connected with the bow strung across Wilder's back. The excitement of the moment had made her forget the mission. "You got it! Devon's bow!"

He smiled and pulled the bow off. "I did indeed. It nearly cost me my toes, but hopefully, it was worth it."

Sophia reached for the bow but paused when her fingers were only inches away. She pulled back.

"What?" Wilder asked, sensing the hesitation in her eyes.

"Is it the real thing?"

The smile that lit Wilder's face gave her the answer. "It absolutely is. I've never experienced a weapon like this. I've held every one in the Gullington, and they are all full of history, and things most shouldn't see. However, this one, well, it's more than a weapon. It was the beginning of a new experience. Before the bow was made, battles were different. Hunting was harder. Bows changed everything. I saw the moment of its conception, and it was a beautiful thing. Thanks for allowing me to be a part of this, Soph."

He held out the bow for her. She shook her head, stepping back. "You're welcome, but a promise is a promise. You hold onto that until after we defeat the Phantom. You deserve to wield that weapon in at least one battle before it goes to Subner, where I believe it will be safe."

Wilder winked at her. "Thanks. You're honorable. And I can't imagine how it can be safer than at the bottom of the Pond guarded by a sea creature, but I'm not arguing."

"I actually don't know what Subner will do with it, but I trust the assistant to Father Time," she stated.

"If we can't trust that man, then we are all doomed," he said, holding out his hand. "Shall we head up to the Castle and prepare for our next adventure?"

Sophia nodded and let out a deep breath, grateful that her friend had helped her and she him. That was what the dragonriders were all about at the end of the day. They saved one another so that they could save the world.

CHAPTER SIXTY

"Oh, you two are in so much trouble," Ainsley said to Sophia and Wilder when they entered the Castle.

Halting in the entryway, Wilder gave the housekeeper an apologetic look. "Oh. I'm sorry for dripping water on the floor."

Ainsley waved her hand, drying up the water instantly. "That's not it. Although I appreciate that S. Beaufont is wearing off on you. Before you wouldn't have even noticed that you dirtied the Castle."

"What is it?" Sophia asked Ainsley. "Why are we in trouble?"

Ainsley lowered her chin. "That's cute. You're pretending like you don't know. Hamish was loud enough to wake the dead, and since I'd thought he was for the longest time, maybe he was loud enough to wake himself. You can be confident that Hiker knows about this."

Sophia and Wilder exchanged curious expressions.

"Hamish?" Sophia asked.

"Who is that?" Wilder questioned.

Ainsley waved them off. "Oh, well, that's just what I call him. I'm not sure what his real name is. You see, we've never met."

Sophia scratched her head. "Sorry, but I'm not following."

"I've made it as clear as I can," Ainsley said with a sigh.

"Can you try again?" Wilder asked.

"Fine." Ainsley sighed. "Hamish is the sea monster that lives in the Pond. I call him that, anyway. I'm sure he has a better name, something like Montgomery or Seymore."

"Those are better names?" Wilder asked.

Sophia slapped him on the arm. "You heard Hamish...or whatever he is?"

"Oh, yes, S. Beaufont." Ainsley pointed up to the stairs, where Hiker's office door was wide open. "More importantly, Mr. Grumpy Kilts heard him. He asked to see you straight away."

"Thanks," Sophia said, trudging forward, bent on facing the wrath of Hiker.

Wilder yawned loudly. "Man, I'm beat from that swim. Think I'm going to tuck in before—"

"I don't think so," Sophia interrupted, grabbing him by the arm and hauling him up the stairs.

To Sophia's relief, Hiker didn't start yelling at them as soon as they entered his study. Maybe it was because Mama Jamba was lounging on the sofa, her feet tucked up under her and an amused expression twinkling in her bright blue eyes.

"Explain yourself," Hiker said, stationed behind his desk, his chin tucked and eyes hooded.

Before Sophia could say anything, Wilder launched into a speech. "Sir, I just want to say that if you're going to be mad at anyone, if there's anyone that you should direct your anger at, if someone should be punished, it should totally be Sophia." He pointed at her.

She whipped around to face him, her hands fisted. "Seriously? *Friend?*"

Wilder cracked a smile, winking at her again. "Just kidding." He lifted his gaze, looking at their leader. "Sir, I know you told me to never go into the Pond."

"But you don't listen anymore," Hiker boomed. "You do what you want because the Gullington is changing and because the world is changing all of a sudden. You think that means the rules are changing."

"Well, that wasn't my exact reasoning, but okay," Wilder said, taking a step back. "Your turn, Soph."

She tried smiling at Hiker, which made him angrier. "How is Mahkah?"

Hiker shook his head. "He's fine. So is Tala. Don't change the subject."

"But I want to know," Sophia argued.

"As you should," Mama Jamba chimed in, earning a seething glare from Hiker.

He sighed. "We still don't know what happened to him. We won't until he wakes up and can talk. But he will make a full recovery. There's no reason for us to think any differently."

Sophia nodded. "Okay, well, I didn't know that we weren't allowed to go into the Pond."

Wilder tapped her on the shoulder. "Hey, Soph. We're not allowed in the Pond for unknown reasons."

"Thanks," she said.

"I suspect you know those reasons now, don't you?" Hiker asked, his eyes narrowed.

"Yeah, Hamish," Wilder said.

"Who?" Hiker asked.

"That's Ainsley's nickname for the sea creature," Sophia explained.

He rolled his eyes. "Of course, it is." Suddenly, Hiker stood and began to pace behind his desk. "Now there will be a huge mess for Quiet to clean up, not to mention the balance this will upset, you two killing the sea creature who guards the Pond."

"We didn't kill it," Sophia cut in.

"What?" Hiker asked.

"She zapped it with this impressive net spell that pinned the creature until I could get away," Wilder explained. "I would have just killed the thing, but she is a gentle soul."

Sophia glared at Wilder and wondered if slapping him again would make her feel better. She guessed it wouldn't.

"Why didn't you kill it?" Hiker asked. "It was coming after you, right?"

"Wilder, actually," Sophia answered. "And I don't know. I just didn't think that was the right approach. I think you have to make a deliberate choice when you kill something. I knew I needed to subdue it, but killing it felt wrong."

"She listens," Mama Jamba said simply.

"Listens to what?" Sophia questioned.

"To what's important," Mama Jamba stated.

Hiker shook his head. "She makes strange decisions that somehow by a stroke of luck appear to be right."

"So you're glad that I didn't kill Hamish...or whatever he or she is called?" Sophia asked.

"Hamish is a she," Mama Jamba supplied. "Her name is more a series of notes." She began humming.

Hiker let out a long breath. "Yes, I'm glad you didn't kill the sea creature in the Pond. It's a part of the Gullington. I don't even understand everything about it. If you want those answers, ask this one here, but fat chance of learning anything." He pointed at Mama Jamba, who smiled wide and waved at them.

"And why in the world did you go into the Pond when I expressly told you never to do so under any circumstances?" Hiker asked.

"Old man, would you open your eyes?" Mama Jamba asked with a laugh.

"What are you talking about?" he questioned, running his gaze over Sophia and then Wilder. When he saw the bow strung over Wilder's shoulder, he leaned forward. "What is that?"

Wilder pulled the bow off his back. "It's what I went to retrieve. Devon's bow. I guess you knew it was down there."

Hiker gave him a startled expression. "Devon's bow? That was down there?"

"I don't think he knew," Mama Jamba sang.

"Of course, I didn't," Hiker stated. "How... Why... What..."

"Well, you see, sir," Sophia began, "Father Time's assistant asked me to recover the bow and give it to him. In exchange, he helped me to convince Papa Creola to reverse events so I could bring back the Phantom and kill him again and therefore bond to my sword, bringing me one step closer to completing my training." She took a deep breath, having rushed through the explanation. "I apologize for all the trouble I've created, but I was merely trying to do what you asked and finish my training."

Hiker pressed his fingertips into his forehead. "Did anyone else hear the absurdity that I just heard, or am I hallucinating?"

"I heard it all. Oh, and she left out a great bit," Mama Jamba stated. "Like, that I'm involved, having loaned a bit of my essence to get Papa Creola's compliance. And Sophia has to harvest the horn this time or the deal's off with Papa. And she's also recruited Wilder to help her and told him he can use the bow, but that's only until the job is done, and then it goes to Subner."

Hiker stuck both of his hands to his head like it might help it from exploding. "Sophia, is it incredibly difficult for you to just train like a normal dragonrider, practicing on your dragon and doing combat exercises on the Expanse?"

"Well, sir, I'm not a normal dragonrider, if such a thing actually exists," Sophia began. "And I'm merely doing what I was told I needed to do to complete training. Mama Jamba told me that was of supreme importance."

"It is," Mother Nature chirped.

"It's just that I've had many a rider, and none seem to get into the same shenanigans as you in such a short period of time," Hiker said.

"That's kind of what I said," Wilder stated with a snicker.

Sophia cast him an evil glare.

"And you," Hiker fumed, looking at Wilder. "You agreed to go on this impossible mission? The Phantom? Really?"

"Well, it seemed like a good idea at the time, but I won't go if you don't approve, sir," Wilder stated, straightening.

"Her training," Mama Jamba said, subtly, although her voice carried great power.

"I'm aware," Hiker barked. "And Devon's bow, that belongs here. You were just going to take it off to Father Time's assistant?"

"He has a lot to do with weapons," Mama Jamba reasoned. "He can ensure that it goes to good use. It was quite useless sitting on the bottom of the Pond for the last several centuries."

"I didn't even know it was there!" Hiker yelled.

"But now you do," Wilder said, holding out the bow. "Do you want to hold it?"

Hiker's face was beet red. "No. I'm good. And fine, you can take it to Subner. But as far as this mission to slaughter the Phantom—"

"Re-slaughter," Mama Jamba corrected. "They have to bring it back to life, take its horn and kill it again."

"Right," Hiker growled. "As far as that goes, well, there are other matters that demand your attention, so you can't go."

"Oh, do you know where the lone riders are that you want me to go after?" Sophia asked, hopeful.

He shook his head. "No, this business with Mahkah has interrupted my research."

"Oh, do you have adjudicator missions for us?" Wilder asked.

Again, Hiker shook his head. "I sent Evan on one, but I'm still combing through finding other ones that will give us the right profile. Image is everything right now, especially as we gear up to face Thad."

"So, why can't they go on this mission which will bond Sophia to her sword, helping her to get that much closer to finishing training?" Mama Jamba asked innocently.

Hiker's eyes fluttered with annoyance. "There isn't a reason. I guess you can go, but you can't take your dragons. They need to stay with Tala until she's recovered."

"Thank you, sir," Sophia said, bowing slightly.

"Don't thank me," he replied. "I might have just sent you to your death. I wouldn't want to face the Phantom with the assistance of a league of dragons, and you two don't have any."

Wilder gave Sophia a nervous expression. "You sure you still want to do this?"

Sophia glanced back at Mama Jamba, who gave her a look that rocked her insides. "Absolutely," she answered with confidence.

CHAPTER SIXTY-ONE

Ainsley set a plate of perfectly poached eggs nestled on top of English muffins and covered in hollandaise sauce in front of Sophia the next morning at breakfast.

"Your favorite, Eggs Benedict, S. Beaufont," the housekeeper said, before returning to the kitchen.

Sophia smiled as she cut into an egg, watching the yolk ooze out.

A moment later, Ainsley returned, laying a plate in front of Wilder. "And cinnamon French toast for you, my dear."

"My favorite!" he exclaimed wide-eyed.

"I know," Ainsley said, heading for the kitchen.

"Oh, man." Evan rubbed his hands together. "That means I'm getting chocolate chip pancakes."

He had returned from his adjudicator mission but would be headed out again later that morning, according to him.

Ainsley came through the swinging door just as Quiet entered the dining hall, covered in dirt as usual.

"And porridge for you, Evan," she said, setting a bowl of steaming sludge in front of him.

"What?" Evan argued. "Porridge isn't my favorite."

"Right," Ainsley said. "It's your least favorite. I'm well aware. You've only told me that every morning I've served it for one hundred bloody years. But I'm not counting or anything."

"What gives?" Evan asked, pointing at Sophia and Wilder, who were making quick work of their dishes. "Why do they get their favorite breakfast meals and I get my least favorite?"

"There are many reasons," Ainsley began. "For one, I don't like you. Secondly, we were running low on supplies. I'll have to pop off to the village soon." She glanced down at Quiet. "Porridge okay with you?"

The gnome nodded, tucking his napkin into his shirt.

The housekeeper snapped her fingers, and another bowl of steaming porridge materialized in front of Quiet.

"What are these other reasons?" Evan asked. "You had supplies enough to make them their favorite meals." He looked at Wilder's French toast longingly.

Ainsley tucked a strand of her red hair behind her pointy ears. "Oh, well, it's probably their last meal, so I wanted to make it memorable."

In unison, Sophia and Wilder set down their forks.

"Say what?" Wilder asked.

She smiled at him. "Well, the Castle and I are taking bets on whether you'll return from facing the Phantom. It seems to think you will."

"You bet against us?" Sophia asked, insulted.

Ainsley shrugged. "I mean, it's a numbers game really. Most who face the Phantom are either corrupted or killed."

"Not my mother," Sophia argued.

"Oh, yes, your mother," Ainsley said fondly. "She skewed the results slightly, but my money is still on you two dying or turning evil."

Wilder pushed his plate of half-eaten french toast away. "Thanks for the vote of confidence."

Evan took it upon himself to grab Wilder's plate, digging into his leftovers. "At least the Castle is on your side, mate."

"We aren't dying or falling victim to the Phantom's evil persuasions," Sophia said adamantly, a bite of ham and egg on her fork, but suddenly not hungry.

Quiet muttered, dumping a huge spoonful of sugar onto his porridge.

"I agree," Ainsley said to the groundskeeper. "If they do that, then they will definitely be successful and slay that beast."

Sophia leaned forward. "What? What did Quiet just say?"

Ainsley rolled her eyes. "Oh, it was plain as day. I'm not repeating, but he can if he wants."

Quiet didn't seem to be paying attention as he sprinkled another spoonful of sugar onto his porridge.

"Quiet, what did you say?" Sophia asked. "What can we do to be successful facing the Phantom?"

The gnome's lips moved as he stirred his bowl, now more sugar than porridge, but no sound came out of his mouth.

"That was very kind of you to repeat it," Ainsley said, clapping him on the shoulder before returning to the kitchen.

Sophia gave Wilder a wide-eyed expression, which he returned.

Evan grabbed for Sophia's plate, having already finished off Wilder's. "Man, you two are screwed."

"Again, thanks to everyone who has been so helpful and encouraging," Sophia said dryly. She glanced at Wilder. "Ready to go die?"

He gulped and rubbed his stomach. "Yeah, I think I might throw up on the Phantom."

"I don't think that will work, mate," Evan said, shoving a large bite into his mouth. "You have to kill him, not disgust him."

"Thanks, Ev," Sophia said, pushing up from the table, feeling queasy too.

"You're welcome," he sang through a mouthful of food. "If you die, can I have your television?"

"If I die," Sophia began, "then I'm going to haunt you for the rest of your life."

"Get in line," Evan said with a laugh. "Most of the ghosts in the Castle haunt me. They think I'm a bit obnoxious and I think Ainsley puts them up to it."

"I absolutely do," Ainsley chimed in as she reentered like she'd been a part of the conversation all along. "And if S. Beaufont dies, I want her bean bag chair."

Sophia gave Wilder a tired expression. "Are you ready to head out?"

"Yes, but I think we should go burn all your stuff first," he replied. "That way, these scoundrels don't benefit from your death."

She nodded. "Good call. Let's burn my stuff and then head to our death."

CHAPTER SIXTY-TWO

The marshlands that stretched out in front of Sophia looked like a painting. It wasn't until the smell of mossy water hit her nose that she knew she'd stepped through the portal into the right place.

"Why was the Phantom in Florida?" Wilder asked, beside her.

She scoffed. "Because obviously, that's where all evil originates and spreads out."

He nodded. "Yeah, that makes sense."

Sophia pulled out the hourglass that had materialized on her bedside table with instructions on how to bring back the Phantom.

"So, what are we supposed to do?" Wilder asked, Devon's bow clenched in his hand as he scanned the marshland.

"Once I activate the hourglass, the Phantom should materialize somewhere around here because this was where it was killed by my mother and father," she explained.

"And I'm supposed to hold it with magic while you do your thing?" Wilder questioned.

"Yes, but we have to be incredibly careful," Sophia stated. "I have to harvest the horn and kill it, but that's not the biggest concern."

Wilder lifted his foot, which made a squelching sound as it was sucked out of the mud. "Is it what Ainsley will do to us when we track mud into the Castle later?"

Sophia laughed, liking that he was breaking up the tension with humor. They both felt the daunting task before them, and thinking of returning to the Castle gave her hope. "The most important thing is that you don't look the Phantom in the eyes. If you do, you'll be infected by its evil."

"Okay, don't look the beast in the eyes," Wilder said like this was an easy task. "I'll just pretend he's Ainsley when she's questioning me about who ate the rest of the mince pies."

"Whatever works for you," Sophia stated, not sure what her strategy was going to be.

"All right," Wilder said, bolstering his confidence by lifting his chest. The wind tangled his dark hair, adding to his already rugged appearance.

"Hey, don't listen to what the others were saying," Sophia encouraged. "We are going to do this."

"I know," he stated. "And I'm glad I'm doing it alongside you, but…"

She tilted her head to the side. "But…"

"Well, I mean, I get that I've been training for almost two centuries, but…"

It dawned on Sophia at that moment, and the realization was odd. "You haven't been in any real battles since…"

"Since magnetizing to Simi," he finished her sentence. "The curse had fallen over the mortals by that point, and I never had a mission."

"Just year after year in the Gullington," Sophia said, the idea still confounding her.

"Hiker has sent us out on adjudicator missions, but they didn't require any combat," he explained. "Just smooth-talking and a wink."

She shook her head. "You know you can't coast on your looks forever, right?"

"No, but I will while I can," he joked. "Someone taught me, 'Why get your hands dirty when you can strategize?'"

"Sounds like a smart person," she chuckled.

"Clever for sure, but she's a real pain in the ass some say," he fired back.

"Don't listen to those dummies."

"Anyway, I know you went with Evan to recover the eggs," Wilder stated.

"Yes, and we faced magical tech robots and submarines," Sophia stated.

"I don't know what either of those things are, but you can explain later."

She nodded.

"And before that, you went to that facility north of the Gullington, having your other combat experience," he went on. "Oh, and then there was when you went to recover Evan and Mother Nature."

"Is it odd that I've been a dragonrider for about a minute and a half and been in more combat than you?" she asked, thinking that was where he was going with this.

"Well, it definitely speaks to your rebellious nature," he said. "I don't think Hiker authorized most of those missions."

She offered him an encouraging smile. "You've been preparing for this all this time. Before you magnetized to Simi, you had your fair share of battles, right?"

"For sure," he said with confidence.

"And you've experienced every single battle that every weapon you've ever touched had," Sophia added.

"Right," he said, seeming to grow more secure.

"So it's in you, even if you haven't been in action in a while," Sophia stated. "As soon as you need to, you're going to fall right back into it without issue because, at the end of the day, you were born for this. You're Dragon Elite."

Wilder smiled, a dimple surfacing on his left cheek. "You know, you're a lot better at this motivational thing than Hiker."

"Yeah, but for as much trouble as I give him, I recognize that he's a good leader," Sophia said.

Wilder nodded. "That he is. I'm glad you see it. I wouldn't have stuck around during centuries of mundane if I didn't believe in the man."

"Okay, are you ready for this?" Sophia asked, holding up the hourglass.

"Yes. I admit I might have been stalling a bit."

"Me too," Sophia agreed and then remembered something. She pointed to the bow in his hand. "Did you figure out what its special power is?"

He nodded. "It can find a target, no matter what. And it always shoots to kill."

Sophia's eyes widened. "That sounds incredibly useful and also dangerous if in the wrong hands."

"I agree," Wilder stated. "Thankfully, it's my hands, and I don't plan on using it."

"Oh, yeah," Sophia said, realizing that she promised him he could use the bow on this mission. But if he did, then she couldn't do her job, using her sword to kill the Phantom and bonding with Inexorabilis.

"You're going to apologize, but don't," Wilder declared. "I got to recover the first and most powerful bow in the world. I don't need to use it to experience it."

Sophia smiled subtly. "And you're probably one of the few in the world that's true for."

He shouldered the bow and held out his hands. "I'm ready to do my part with magic and watch you slay the beast."

"Okay, then," Sophia said, holding up the hourglass. "Without further ado."

CHAPTER SIXTY-THREE

There was nothing that could accurately prepare Sophia for what she was going to do next. Not only was she about to face a beast responsible for spreading hate and negativity all over the world, but she was going to battle one of the first monsters her mother had slain. Killing the Phantom had been how Guinevere Beaufont had bonded to Inexorabilis, creating a partnership that lasted a lifetime, making her a stronger Warrior for the House of Fourteen, and therefore making the magical world a safer place.

For a woman who didn't remember her mother, Sophia still felt intimately bonded to her. Guinevere's ghost seemed to walk beside Sophia so many times in her life. Maybe it was her imagination, but she often heard a voice in her head, echoing in her heart that didn't sound like her own. She always wanted to believe it was her mother, looking after her from wherever she might be.

The fact that Sophia's father had also been a part of banishing the Phantom made this more symbolic. All her life, Sophia had been told by her siblings about their parent's unyielding love for each other.

Theodore and Guinevere Beaufont had a romance that inspired novels. It was the stuff of legends. Clark, her brother, the least romantic type Sophia knew, had once told her, "One could live a thousand lives and not find a love like what our parents had. They weren't just partners like most married couples. They had a love that others felt when in the room with them. Their feelings for each other were infectious. I'm certain that they unknowingly inspired love all around the world."

Sophia closed her eyes and pictured her parent's ghosts swirling around her, encouraging her. I want to make you proud, she said, directing the words to them.

She pulled Inexorabilis from its sheath as she opened her eyes. "*Familia Est Sempiternum,*" Sophia said aloud, feeling the sword pulse in her hand, ready for the battle to come.

"Is that the spell to unlock the hourglass?" Wilder asked, tense beside her.

She shook her head. "No, those are the words that bond my family together no matter what."

"Oh, I'm not familiar with that spell," he stated.

She lifted the hourglass. "It's not really a spell. It's love, but I guess that's the most powerful spell there ever was."

"I can't argue with that, Soph," Wilder said, flashing her a smile.

She wrapped her fingers around the hourglass, muttering the spell that Father Time had included with the item. As soon as she spoke the words, the object warmed in her hand. She opened her palm and held it up to see a strange sight.

CHAPTER SIXTY-FOUR

Most hourglasses dropped the granules of sand from top to bottom. This one was definitely not ordinary. At the conclusion of the spell, the sand on the bottom of the hourglass began to trickle upwards, gliding into the top.

"It's reversing time," Wilder observed.

"Actually," Sophia corrected, "it's reversing one event in time."

Wilder looked out at the marsh, his eyes narrowed on the long grass as it swayed in the wind. "When will it be here?"

Sophia drew in a breath. "As soon as the last granule slips into the top," she said, recalling the instructions.

He cut his gaze to the hourglass, nervousness covering his face. "Not long now."

"Just remember," she warned, "don't look into his eyes. Anywhere else."

The last granule rose up, landing at the top with the rest. Sophia's heart sped up. She lowered her hand, slipping the hourglass into her pocket. It had done its job, or at least she hoped.

The minute that ticked by was the longest sixty seconds of her life. The rustling of the wind made her jump. The rolling of the puffy clouds in the blue sky seemed to hold a sinister edge like they might turn into storms at any moment. And when the marsh fell completely silent, Sophia knew the moment of reckoning was upon them.

She stepped forward, holding Inexorabilis in both hands. *It's time we bond,* she said to the sword, feeling a small twinge run up her arm.

A thundering like a hundred horses streaking across the ground echoed in Sophia's ears. She didn't look back at Wilder. Instead, she kept her eyes peeled on the landscape in front of them.

Waiting.

It was one of the hardest things she'd ever done, to keep her eyes wide, knowing she couldn't look at the gaze of the monster about to arrive. She could look at his horn, his hooves, his body, but one glance into the Phantom's eyes would end her. Or at least it would end who she was currently. She'd be worse than a demon. Sophia would roam the Earth, spreading the legacy of the Phantom, sending hate everywhere she went. And that would kill her.

The thundering was almost overwhelming when it disappeared, leaving the marsh silent once more. For a second, she thought that it hadn't worked. Or maybe the Phantom had taken its chance to escape, and she'd have to track it.

But then from the trees, something both incredibly beautiful and full of a sinister evil unlike any Sophia had ever known materialized.

The Phantom had arrived.

CHAPTER SIXTY-FIVE

Careful to keep her eyes on its body, Sophia did her best to study the beast that galloped out onto the marsh, splashing up water. The evil unicorn was all black, its coat shimmering in the sunlight. Its long black mane flowed behind it as it ran, and the horn on its head was more like that of a rhinoceros than a unicorn's. It curved up and was iridescent, strangely reminding Sophia of the weird sheen that covers meat that's going bad.

The Phantom's tail swished when it halted only fifteen yards away. Sophia allowed her eyes to trail over its body—its muscles rippled. The Phantom was back, and it was like it had never been gone as it assaulted the earth with its hooves, kicking up water and grass.

All at once, Sophia felt so many negative emotions spill through her. She saw war in her mind and wanted it. She felt pain in her heart, and it made her satisfied. Hunger, poverty, hate—all these feelings spiraled through her, the product of being close to the Phantom. But it hadn't infected her yet, and she was damned if it ever would.

Stepping forward, Sophia held up Inexorabilis. "It's time for you to die," she said, standing in front of the Phantom. "Again."

It huffed, steam spilling from its nostrils as though it breathed fire like a dragon. Sophia kept her eyes on the horn, her intention set.

The beast slammed its hoof into the marsh, throwing up water and grass once more.

Sophia turned her body to the side, her boots partially submerged.

When the Phantom charged, she was ready. She spun Inexorabilis in an arc to the side and caught the horn like it was another blade.

The sheer strength of the evil unicorn was overwhelming, nearly pushing her off her feet. Sophia kept her footing as the beast lowered its head, willing her to look into its eyes. She realized then why it hadn't thrown her down, although she knew it could since its strength was easily more than hers. It was trying to corrupt her, not defeat her. There was an important distinction there.

She kept her chin up, staring at the horn, pressing her sword into the beast.

Sophia was just about to use her strength to push back when the Phantom rose on its back legs, front legs in the air, hooves about to come down on her.

She had seconds to react and fell to the ground, rolling in the water and mud just as the monster dropped back down, shaking its head.

It looked at Wilder and seemed strangely uninterested in him as he held Devon's bow at the ready.

Sophia knew it would take Wilder several minutes to home in on the Phantom, finding the best way to hold the monster with magic. Only then could they harvest the horn. Her job was to stall the beast until he was ready. She waited for the cue.

Instantly, the Phantom turned, putting its attention back on Sophia. She closed her eyes as she brought her chin up, finding the horn once more.

That will belong to me, she told herself, leveling her sword as she waited for the monster to charge.

This time when the Phantom approached, it swerved to the side at the last moment, giving her full access to its body. Right then she could have killed it, but that wasn't what she was there for.

Did the Phantom know they were going for the horn? she wondered.

And just as the thought streaked through her head, the back

hooves of the beast kicked Sophia's shoulder, knocking her back like she'd been hit by a bus. She flew several yards and landed on her back.

Sophia drank marsh water as she sank into the mud. She didn't have a chance to get up before the horse charged her, stopping only a few feet away. Driven by instinct, Sophia covered her eyes with her arm, looking to the side and hoping not to be trampled. She held her breath, feeling the earth under her shake.

"It's done," Wilder said, just when Sophia thought her death imminent.

She couldn't believe it. Turning her head to the side, away from where she knew the evil unicorn to be, she blinked to clear the mud from her eyes.

"It's subdued?" she asked.

"Yes, but I can't hold it for long," Wilder said, his voice strained.

Sophia pushed to her feet, careful to keep her eyes low. When she turned, her chin was pointed at the sky. Carefully she lowered her gaze until she connected with the horn. There it was, sitting on the top of the frozen beast's head. In her peripheral vision, she could see the muscles of the monster twitch, but Wilder had the Phantom paralyzed.

Sophia tightened her grip on Inexorabilis. Just two things to do, then the sword would really be hers. She'd be that much closer to gaining her wings as a dragonrider.

First thing, she thought, holding the sword at the ready.

A roar ripped out of her mouth as she brought the sword up and across. This time it didn't meet the horn like it was a steel wall. Instead, Inexorabilis sliced through cleanly, completely severing it from the beast.

The horn dropped into the water of the marsh, disappearing.

Sophia's gaze fell with it, searching.

She thought she knew where the horn had gone and knelt, reaching into the water and feeling around for the horn.

A shadow fell across her and a hot stream of air rustled her hair. Wilder had lost his hold on the Phantom. It was bearing down on her, ready to attack and madder than hell.

She quit searching and tightened her grip on her sword. Carefully, she brought her eyes to the ground between them, noticing that its legs were only a few feet away.

Too close. Right in front of her face, she could see the thumping of the monster's chest. It lowered its head, and Sophia knew she had few options. She would have to be fast, and she'd also need a miracle.

Still crouched, Sophia brought her other hand to Inexorabilis, ready for the second part of this mission, but her hand never connected with the hilt. The Phantom charged her, the jagged stump of its horn slamming into her side, sending her through the air like a football being kicked.

Again, Sophia landed on her back, breathless and in pain everywhere, but that wasn't the worst part. The toss had made her lose her sword. She glanced around, keeping her eyes low. Inexorabilis was buried under the waters of the marsh, and finding it would take time she didn't have the luxury of.

Sophia was about to try to summon it when the dark shadow fell on her again. She didn't dare look up at the beast that was bearing down overhead.

She was out of options.

Unlike her mother, she wouldn't kill the Phantom. She had failed just as everyone feared, and the worst part was, she'd freed a monster who, left unchecked, would spread evil.

Hot breath sent her hair away from her face. The Phantom dared to lower its head until it was even with her face. It was willing her to look into its eyes, and what was the point in resisting? Either way, she'd lost. It would either trample her or turn her at this point.

Wilder, she knew, was working to paralyze the monster again, but she had little hope he could do it in time. Still, she held onto that tiny hope in her heart.

She felt the smooth black nose of the monster press into her cheek and shivered, although she wasn't cold. She could feel the heat radiate from the hellish beast. It lifted one leg and held it right in front of her. She was certain he would bring it down hard next, crushing her body.

Sophia prepared to roll out of the beast's way, but she knew that the chances of being fast enough were slim.

And then she felt the Phantom's head sway next to her. It tensed, rocked to the side, and fell back, landing with a giant splash.

Sophia took the opportunity to roll in the opposite direction. Ironically, she rolled over her sword and picked it up in one fluid movement as she jumped to her feet, staring low and finding a sight that at first didn't register.

Lying lifeless in the marsh was the Phantom, an arrow protruding from its midsection. Strange magic radiated like electricity, wrapping the unicorn's body.

In the distance, on the other side of the marsh, was Wilder, Devon's bow in his hands and a look of total regret on his face.

"I'm sorry, Soph," he said. "I had no choice. I had to save you."

Sophia nodded and dared to look at the face of the monster. Its eyes were closed, its body lifeless.

The Phantom was dead once more, but she hadn't been the one to kill it. Wilder had—in order to save her.

And although she was grateful, her chance to bond to Inexorabilis was gone.

CHAPTER SIXTY-SIX

It took Sophia and Wilder an hour to find the Phantom's horn in the mud of the marsh. The entire time, Wilder kept flashing her apologetic looks.

"It's fine," she said for the billionth time, trying to console him, even as her heart was aching increasingly by the minute.

"It's not, though," he argued on his hands and knees, partially submerged in water filled with slippery creatures and plants. "You faced the Phantom, even though it's probably the biggest danger any of us have seen in centuries, so you could bond with your mother's sword. Now there's no way."

"You saved my life," Sophia argued. "There are always risks in battle. We don't go into it with certainties. I was never guaranteed to get the horn, kill the Phantom, or even survive. We did two out of three, and that's how it is."

He looked at her for a long moment with a strange expression on his face. "How are you not at least a hundred years old, saying things like that? Wisdom like that takes almost a lifetime to understand."

Sophia shrugged, feeling through the mud, and finding something sharp that felt like war and wrongness and evil. It was the horn, and it shot away from her fingers like it was trying to escape her grasp. Even severed, it had power. "I don't know," she finally answered. "My mother named me Sophia and told my father, according to my siblings, that I was born already grown up."

Wilder smiled as he continued to feel around in the marsh waters. "Oh, yes, 'Sophia.' It means wisdom, skillful, and clever. You were appropriately named."

She felt something pulse a few inches from her finger. It was a strange sensation. Without hesitating, she darted forward, throwing her body weight down and clasping what she believed to be the Phantom's horn. Her face and body submerged fully in the water, she held onto the horn as it tried to escape her attempts to remove it.

"Pull it up!" Wilder urged, standing beside her and opening a small bag. It was the one they'd used to hold the dragon eggs and had assorted characteristics.

As if holding a small bull, Sophia yanked the horn out of the water, trying to keep it in her grasp. The tip of the horn was aimed at her chest. It tried to stab her, but she was able to keep her arms stick-straight.

Wilder scooped the bag over the horn and she released it just as he tied it up. Instantly the bag went still, making them both relax.

Covered in mud from head to toe, Sophia shook her head and let out a breath. "How is it that something full of so much evil might be used to erase just that in the world?"

Wilder handed her the bag, shaking his head. "I don't know, but apparently Father Time does. Things are mysterious like that. Maybe it takes evil to erase evil. Like in the morning after too much whiskey, the only cure is more whiskey."

Sophia considered this as she tried to wipe the mud off her face, which only made things worse since every part of her was covered. "Yeah, I guess so. Certain diseases can be vaccinated against by using blood samples from those infected."

"Well, there you go," Wilder said. "But you've done your job and gotten the horn. You've done well even if you didn't do what you set out for."

"Thanks for accompanying me and…you know, saving my life and all."

He flashed her an irresistible smile. "Any time."

"I better portal us to Roya Lane," Sophia said, realizing that Wilder had probably never been there. That would be a treat to see his face when they entered the magical street.

"Oh, but first, Soph…"

She gave him a questioning look. "What?"

He pointed at his cheek. "You have something just right there and pretty much everywhere else."

She narrowed her eyes at him. "Thanks. It's my new look."

With a laugh, he said, "Well, the muddy warrior look suits you." He fidgeted with his clothes. "I'm not sure about me, though. I think I have a tadpole in my pants."

CHAPTER SIXTY-SEVEN

The smells and sounds of Roya Lane were a stark contrast to those of a marsh in Florida. Wilder was like a child in a large toy store, looking around at the sights with his eyes wide and his mouth agape.

"I don't get it," Sophia said, trying to encourage him forward. "You have been locked in the Gullington for about two centuries, but you also went out."

"Mostly only to go to Tanzania," he mentioned, watching as an elf shaved a pig, showing a group how well his hair growth formula worked. He pointed at the animal. "Isn't that animal testing and sort of bordering on abuse?"

Sophia smiled at him. "You are a true adjudicator. However, that's Phineas, and the pig is his wife Krysta. She changes into the pig for the demonstrations. Don't worry, the animal is consenting."

He gave her a perplexed expression. "Why doesn't he just do the hair growth thing on her as a human?"

"Would you have stopped if he was demonstrating on a person?" she asked.

It dawned on him. "Clever Phineas."

"Anyway, as I was saying," Sophia continued. "You've been out of the Gullington, although sparingly."

"And I was born outside of the Gullington," he admitted.

"Where?" she questioned.

"Scotland," he answered.

"Right, so not really then," Sophia said. "And you've been out recently on adjudicator missions. So why is it that this world and the rest of it is so strange for you?"

"Because usually when I've left, it's to go on diplomatic missions where I meet with leaders, have chats, and then ride off on Simi. It's not like I take a detour to see the sights."

Sophia nodded. "Yeah, that makes sense. But man, you and the rest of the men are like newborn babies."

"Well, even when I see things, if I'm not with you, I don't even know what they are," Wilder explained. "We need you to explain things to us. Like when you showed me that video of a dinosaur—"

"Guy in a dinosaur costume," Sophia corrected.

"Exactly, but how would I have known that?"

"Because dinosaurs are extinct," she argued.

"No, they aren't," a familiar voice said over Sophia's shoulders. She rolled her eyes, preparing for the ridiculous. "I saw one walking down the Las Vegas Strip the other day."

King Rudolf Sweetwater came around, a wide smile on the fae's face.

"No, again. That's a guy or a gal in a suit," Sophia stated, already feeling impatient.

Rudolf crossed his arms in front of his chest. "I thought so too, but this one was a T-Rex and had tiny arms. Where would they find a human who had tiny arms for that costume?"

"King Sweetwater, I'm not sure if it's worth taking the time to explain this to you," Sophia said with a groan.

"Hello, I'm Wilder." The dragonrider extended his hand.

"Wilder than what?" Rudolf asked, not taking his hand.

"That's my name," he explained.

"That's a weird name," Rudolf said.

"And what are you naming your triplets?" Sophia asked.

"Captain," he answered.

"Oh, what are you naming the other two?" Wilder asked.

Rudolf shot him a look of offense. "I just told you."

"You're naming all three of your triplets Captain?" Wilder questioned.

Sophia looked up at him. "And he thinks your name is strange. Just drop the whole thing."

Wilder lowered his hand. "So, you're a king?"

Rudolf suddenly looked like he'd swallowed something without chewing. "I was, but not anymore. That's what my wife told me."

Sophia blinked at the fae impassively. "What exactly did Serena say?"

"Well," Rudolf said, drawing out his word. "She said, 'Rudolf, if you don't get out of here right now, I'm going to break your crown.'"

"And then what happened?" Sophia asked in a bored voice.

"Well, I couldn't get out of there because my muffin still had a few minutes left in the Easy-Bake Oven," he explained.

"Then what happened?" Sophia continued her line of questioning.

"Well, so my dear, sweet, very pregnant wife threw my diamond-encrusted crown at the oven. Needless to say, the meeting of the two was bad for both." Rudolf frowned. "I think it was going to be the best chocolate chip muffin I'd made so far."

"Serena still has that sweet disposition, I see," Sophia stated.

"Yeah, I'm so glad I brought her back from the dead," he said fondly of his wife.

"Okay, but you get that her breaking the fae's treasured crown doesn't actually take away your title as king, right?" Sophia asked.

Rudolf gave her a sideways expression. "Are you certain?"

"Yes."

"What about the fact that she said I'm dead to her?" Rudolf questioned.

"Again, that doesn't affect your status as king."

"So, I'm not, in fact, dead to her?"

Sophia was having trouble keeping her patience. "Serena is just pregnant. In a few months, the babies will be here and…well, things will probably get a lot worse."

"Oh, you think so?" Rudolf said, hope in his twinkling eyes. "I hope you're not just trying to make me feel better. And she will only be pregnant for like, another few days."

"Wait…what?" Sophia asked. "I thought she was only a few months pregnant."

"Yeah, but fae don't have to be pregnant as long," he explained.

Sophia nodded. "So that's why you all act the way you do."

"Exactly!" Rudolf chirped and then looked confused. "Wait, what does that mean?"

"Nothing," Sophia said, turning her attention to Wilder, who appeared far too amused by this exchange. "Wilder, this is King Rudolf Sweetwater. He is the king of the fae, and also a member of the Council for the House of Fourteen."

"Well, actually…" Rudolf said, looking around. "They told me I had the day off. Apparently, the matters they were discussing don't involve me."

"Again, what exactly did they say?" Sophia questioned.

"They said, 'Rudolf, go play in the street. Today we don't need your nonsense.'"

"Okay," Sophia said. "I think you interpreted that one correctly."

"So, I decided to come here and hand out invitations to our babies' shower," he said, holding up his hand. A card materialized. "You're invited." He looked at Wilder. "Not you, though, because your name makes me feel inadequate."

Wilder laughed. "Great reasoning."

Sophia looked at the invitation, her brow furrowing. "Why does it say to wear a swimsuit?"

Rudolf rolled his eyes. "Duh. Because otherwise your clothes will get all wet. It's a shower."

"You get that—"

Wilder nudged Sophia's shoulder, interrupting her. "I'd just let it go."

She nodded. "Yeah, I'll wear my two-piece if I can make it."

"But you must make it," Rudolf begged. "I know for a fact that Serena demands yours and Liv's presence."

Sophia lowered her chin. "One more time, what did your wife say?"

"Well, she said, 'The Beaufont sisters will be there over my dead body,'" Rudolf stated. "And as you know, my wife was dead, so technically her body is dead, but also not really. It's confusing. I don't get the whole 'over my body' part, but I think that means she demands your presence. Many of those expressions escape me."

"Shocking." Sophia gave Wilder an annoyed expression.

"So you'll be there?" Rudolf asked, hope in his eyes.

"Well, I'm sort of busy with this whole dragon extinction problem the Council brought to my attention," Sophia argued.

Rudolf leaned in closer. "But maybe they are like dinosaurs…"

"And extinct?" Sophia asked.

"No, that's just what everyone thinks," Rudolf answered. "But then you're strolling down the Strip and bam, you run into one."

"She'll be there," Wilder cut in. "Sophia wouldn't miss it."

She cast him an evil glare. "Wild—"

"I'll cover your shift at the Gullington," he cut her off.

"We don't have shifts at the Gullington," she argued.

"Of course, we do," he said, trying to keep his laughter at bay. "I take the first one and you the second, so the aliens don't enter the planet's orbit."

"Wow, you two are doing good work," Rudolf said, shaking his head. "I'm glad you're on the job. But who is taking your shift right now if you two are here?"

"Evan," Wilder answered at once. "We've got all the shifts covered. Don't you worry, king."

"Okay, well then it's settled." Rudolf hugged Sophia without asking. "I'll see you at the shower. Buy us something really expensive. And remember we are having triplets, so that's not one present. It's four."

Sophia's head jerked to the side. "You get that…never mind. And yeah, I guess I'll be there since my friend has so thoughtfully offered to take my shift to protect the Earth from aliens."

"You are welcome," Wilder said with a wink.

Rudolf offered a hand to the dragonrider. "Despite the fact that you have better hair than me, I think I might grow to like you, Wild… yeah, I'm sorry, I can't say that name. It makes me feel like less than a man."

Wilder nodded, shaking King Rudolf's hand. "I'm glad to make your acquaintance. And the next time we meet, I'll wear a hat."

Rudolf beamed. "You're a good man."

CHAPTER SIXTY-EIGHT

"Why the hell did you tell Rudolf that I'd go to the baby shower?" Sophia nearly slapped Wilder as they walked to the Fantastical Armory at the end of Roya Lane.

He laughed *because he obviously wanted to die,* she thought. "How could I not? That was too perfect. I've never met anyone like King Rudolf."

"No one has until they do, and then you'll find him to be the most irritating and strangely helpful person you've ever met," Sophia related.

"I mean, how could you not want to go to a baby shower for four triplets all named Captain?" Wilder asked seriously. "I can only imagine the antics. I want to go."

"Well, you can't because you're covering my shift at the Gullington, guarding the Earth from aliens," Sophia seethed.

"Again, you're very welcome," he replied.

She shook her head. "You're the worst."

"That's so true," he said proudly as they entered the Fantastical Armory.

The easy grin on Wilder's face dropped as soon as they entered the shop with thousands of weapons on display. "Whoa..." He halted just over the threshold, a look of pure panic on his face.

Sophia, remembering his gift with weapons, gave him a careful expression. "Are you okay? Do you want to wait outside?"

He seemed to be trying to swallow. After a moment, he shook his head. "No, I just wasn't prepared. I have my shield up now."

Wilder, whether he touched or was simply in the presence of a weapon, could feel the battles they'd been in. He could see the maker's mark. The dragonrider understood a weapon better than most, and it was both a gift and a curse.

"Right on schedule," Subner said, looking like a hippie wearing mom jeans that rode up to the middle of his waist and suspenders over a tucked-in T-shirt that read, "You are my spirit animal."

Sophia didn't mean to, but she sighed, remembering how she'd failed to bond to her mother's sword. "Yeah, but I wasn't successful."

The elf with stringy brown hair waved her off, nearly pushing her to the side as he came to stand in front of Wilder. "We will get to you later, Sophia Beaufont. I was referring to Wilder. You are right on schedule."

The dragonrider tucked his head back on his neck, appearing confused. "You were expecting me? Today?"

"Yes," Subner replied. "I've been expecting you for..." He glanced at the iWatch on his wrist. "Well, since your birth."

Wilder gave Sophia a look of surprise. "Now, that's a way to be greeted. Take note."

"Noted," she said, looking around the shop.

Wilder extended a hand. "I'm Wilder, but I guess you know that."

Subner, in a rare show of respect, bowed low to the dragonrider. "And I am Subner, the assistant to Father Time and Protector of Weapons."

"You are the Protector?" Wilder asked, his surprise now morphing into shock. He glanced up at Sophia. "Why didn't you tell me that Subner was *the* Protector of Weapons?"

She shrugged, still looking for a way to get back at him for the baby shower business. "Hey, Wild, Subner is the *Protector* of Weapons."

"Thanks. You're a gem," he stated matter-of-factly.

"And honestly," Sophia began. "I really didn't know him as Protector of Weapons, but I guess that makes sense now." She studied the shop, which was unlike any she'd ever seen, every square inch of the walls covered in swords, shields, and other artifacts. The cases were filled with knives and various other weapons.

"Most only know me as Father Time's assistant, if they know me at all," Subner said, his eyes still intent on Wilder.

"You've been waiting to meet me, though?" Wilder asked, pointing at himself. "Why?"

"Because, you're one of mine," Subner explained, a certain secretive quality to his voice.

"Yours?" Wilder asked.

"Yes, but I can't really explain it in a way you'll fully understand," Subner stated, strolling for the door at the back. "I'll fetch Papa for you, Sophia, then we can get down to business."

The elf disappeared through the door, leaving Sophia and Wilder alone.

He scratched his head. "What did any of that mean?"

"Welcome to the riddle world of Papa Creola," she stated. "Nothing those two say will make sense, and yet, you'll believe everything they say."

"Wow, and here I thought Mama Jamba was eccentric," Wilder stated, looking overwhelmed.

"Oh, just you wait," Sophia said with a laugh.

"What does he mean, that I'm his?" Wilder asked, staring at his shoes like the answer might be written on the top of his boot.

"Maybe you're distantly related," she supplied. "Or he put a spark of his magic in you when you were born. Or he owns you, and now you must do his bidding for the rest of time—which apparently could be really short or long, depending on if Liv is successful on whatever mission she's working on."

"Really? The balance of time hangs on Liv's head?" Wilder asked.

"Usually," Sophia said casually. "She works for Papa Creola and does all his bidding. We all work for someone."

Subner returned a moment later carrying a cup of tea. He blew on the hot liquid as he strode over to Wilder. "Here, this is for you."

"Thanks," Wilder said, taking the mug that appeared to be handmade.

"I'll take coffee," Sophia said, feeling ignored.

Subner waved her off. "There's a coffee shop down the lane. But don't drink the peppermint lattes. It will give you hives."

"Thanks," she said.

"What's this?" Wilder asked, speculatively looking at the mug.

"It's tea with CBD oil and collagen," Subner answered.

"What will it do?" Wilder asked.

"Probably nothing, but in my new incarnation, I'm forced to do things consistent with hippie elf behavior." Subner gave Sophia a tired expression. "I miss being a gnome. Their demeanor suited me marginally better."

"This is so weird," Sophia said, shaking her head at him.

"Well, thanks," Wilder said, taking a sip. "What did you mean that I'm yours?"

"Maybe he meant you were his betrothed," Sophia joked. "I'll be at your bridal shower."

Wilder shook his head at her. "You're the worst."

"Takes one to know one," she fired back.

"Actually, Sophia was most correct with the explanation that she gave you while I was out of the room," Subner explained.

"Which part?" Sophia asked. "About you two being distantly related? Or that you put a spark of your magic in him? Or that you own him, and from now on, he'll do your bidding?" She laughed, thinking of the absurdity of the last statement.

Quite seriously, Subner stated, "All three, in fact."

Wilder set the mug down. "Wait, I'm related to Father Time's assistant?"

"Well, I was the Protector of Weapons before I took that position," Subner answered.

"I have no idea who is in charge of Human Resources for this planet, but I think we need some alignment in the organizational structure," Sophia said, striding over to a case and studying its contents.

"You put the spark in me that makes it so I can read weapons?" Wilder asked.

"Naturally," Subner stated.

"And now I work for you?" Wilder questioned. "What about the Dragon Elite?"

"Similar to Warrior Liv Beaufont, you'll work for both," Subner answered. "She works for both the House of Fourteen and Papa Creola."

"You're never getting a day off now," Sophia said.

"You're one to talk," Subner said, glancing at her over his shoulder. "You work for both the Dragon Elite and Mama Jamba."

"What's the difference?" she asked. "She's pretty much Hiker's boss."

"Yes, but Mama always has a side agenda," Subner stated. "You'll see."

"Can't wait," Sophia said.

"What will it include for me to work for you?" Wilder asked.

"You'll see," Subner replied.

Sophia giggled. "Don't you love that answer?"

"Now, I'll be taking Devon's bow." Subner held out his hands.

"Oh, right," Wilder said, having forgotten the bow was strapped to his back. "Here you are."

Subner ran his eyes appreciatively over the bow, his fingers fondly grazing its craftsmanship. "Simply incredible. And now in the right hands."

"It is quite an extraordinary weapon," Wilder stated. "And I can't believe—"

Subner grabbed the bow with both hands and snapped it in two.

"What the—why did you do that?" Wilder asked in shock.

Subner dropped the two halves on the floor, where they dissolved into ash. "It was too powerful of a weapon. The bow never misses its target and always kills. That is too many absolutes. Wilder, what is the most important factor that makes a weapon incredible?"

"The one who wields it," Wilder answered at once.

"Exactly," Subner said proudly. "And when it doesn't matter who wields it, it is of no use to this world. It is more trouble than good."

"Is that the reason there are no guns here?" Sophia asked.

"Partly, although marksmanship does count with guns," Subner stated. "But those are not weapons I condone. They are the product of a tyrannical energy that went unchecked when the Dragon Elite were made useless."

"Damn." Sophia shook her head, overwhelmed by the new information.

"So you wanted Devon's bow given to you so that you could destroy it?" Wilder questioned. "Why not just leave it at the bottom of the Pond?"

"Because it was time for us to meet," Subner stated, turning his attention to Sophia. "And this was the force that would finally bring us together."

She smiled. "I have a way. I also introduced him to King Rudolf."

"Which is why the fae is currently getting a haircut," Subner supplied. "Now, Sophia, you have the horn of the Phantom."

She pulled the bag with the evil horn off her shoulder. "Yeah, does Papa Creola want it?"

"Yes, but I'll take it. He's busy fixing a rift in the space-time continuum."

Wilder sighed dramatically. "That sounds like a typical Tuesday."

"So, you already know that I was unsuccessful at bonding to Inexorabilis." The regret began to pool in Sophia again.

"In fact, I do," Subner stated.

"Maybe you want the sword, then?" she offered, pulling the elf-made sword from her belt.

Subner ran his eyes over the blade. "I would be most honored, but I can't take it from you."

"But it does me no good if I'm not bonded to it," Sophia stated. "And I ruined that chance. I can't go back and kill the Phantom again."

"No, and in all simulations of that event, you never kill the Phantom," Subner offered. "It is always Wilder who does."

Sophia shook her head. "You have simulations of events? That's so odd."

"That's how time works and how we know what we do, which is relatively very little."

Her eyes cut to Wilder. "I told you. It's riddle world."

"That it is," he sang.

"So you sent me to kill, or re-kill, the Phantom, knowing that I'd be unsuccessful?" Sophia asked, growing frustrated.

"That I did," Subner answered simply.

"But why? Just so Papa Creola could have the horn?"

"Partly," Subner chirped.

"And so I could introduce you to Wilder, right?" Sophia couldn't help but feel like a pawn.

The elf looked at Wilder. "What did Sophia say when you told her the horror she'd face to bond with her sword?"

"She didn't back down from the challenge," he answered at once.

"Well, I couldn't," Sophia argued.

Subner gave her a look. "You absolutely could have. I have an assortment of weapons I could have given you. Wilder offered to make you a weapon, which would have been of the finest quality."

"It's weird that you know I offered that," Wilder said.

Sophia shook her head, still holding Inexorabilis. "No. I didn't want a weapon from you, but thank you. And I didn't want Wilder to make me one. I wanted to use my mother's sword. I don't have any memories of her. Liv has her ring, and Clark has her eyes. All I have is her sword, and I was going to be damned if I didn't do everything I could to bond with the last thing she left on this Earth before she died."

To Sophia's surprise, Subner smiled. "And therein lies the key."

In Sophia's hands, Inexorabilis warmed. She didn't drop the weapon even as it began to burn her palms. Her eyes simply widened as the blade glowed brightly, so much so that she had to look away. She felt the strangest energy wrap around her core, encircling her body and melting into her heart. When she brought her eyes back up, the blade was still glowing, but not as brightly. Instead, gold dust was radiating off the blade, trickling up her arms, and covering her chest.

"Am I…" she asked, tensely watching as the gold dust covered her body.

"You're bonding to the sword," Wilder supplied.

"Because all along, it wasn't the sword that needed to bond to you, but the other way around." Subner looked at her proudly.

The gold dust disappeared as the sword returned to its normal appearance. "What?" Sophia asked, her heart beating fast. "So why did Plato tell me that I needed to undo and redo the act that bonded my mother to the sword?"

"Because the lynx works in mysterious ways," Subner answered.

"You're one to talk," Wilder quipped.

"But it was a good call on his part," Subner continued. "I could think of no better way to prove your loyalty to Inexorabilis. And look, you've done it." He held his hand out to the sword, which suddenly felt like an old friend in Sophia's hands. She never wanted to let it go, and strangely, like Lunis, she knew it would be by her side for the rest of her life.

"So I didn't have to slay the Phantom with the sword to bond to it," Sophia said, mostly to herself.

"It is rarely the act that we must do that changes things, but rather our intention behind them," Subner stated sagely. "The sword knows what's in your heart now and how far you'll go for that. I dare say, you're more bonded to this weapon than most I've seen. It will be a beautiful partnership."

Wilder smiled wide on the other side of her. "I think I like the riddle world."

She couldn't help but return his grin. "You would. You're the worst."

He winked at her. "That I am, Soph. That I am."

CHAPTER SIXTY-NINE

Hiker was bent over the Elite Globe when Sophia and Wilder entered his office.

"So you didn't die after all," the Viking said, not pulling his eyes off the globe.

"I think you knew that sir," Wilder stated, standing at attention respectfully as he tended to do when addressing the leader of the Dragon Elite.

Sophia in contrast, slouched onto the sofa, exhausted after bonding with Inexorabilis. Subner had told her that this was typical, and she'd need to eat a lot of carbohydrates to replenish her strength. Ainsley was evidently already working on something. "Yeah, your magic globe would have told you if we were dead, but thanks for the sentiment. I can tell you were wrecked worrying about us."

Hiker gave her an annoyed glare over his shoulder. "The magical globe isn't working like it should. And you dying is a mixed bag for me."

"Thanks," Sophia said, flashing him a rebellious expression. "I'm going to take that as another sign that you love me, but I challenge you in ways that scare you. You obviously have avoidance commitment issues. There's a quiz in one of my *Cosmopolitan* magazines you should take to confirm that."

Hiker glanced at Wilder. "Why is it that I can't understand anything she says?"

"She hangs out with fae who gave all their brain cells away for good looks," Wilder answered.

"That seems about right." Hiker shook his head at Sophia. "We are the company we keep."

"Which doesn't bode well for me at all hanging around this place," Sophia fired back.

Wilder laughed. "You two have beautiful chemistry."

Hiker growled in reply.

"So, the globe is broken?" Sophia asked. "Did you try turning it off and back on?"

The scowl on Hiker's face deepened. "What does that even mean?"

"Pop culture reference," she answered.

"Oh good, you know how much I love those," Hiker said dryly. "The globe isn't showing me the lone riders out there."

"Isn't that because you erased them when you kicked them out of the Gullington for having opinions and free will?" Sophia asked.

"Even when I erased them, I was able to make them show back up when I wanted," Hiker stated, continuing to study the globe. "But something isn't right now."

"What can that mean, sir?" Wilder asked, his casual nature dropping.

"Well, it could mean a few things," he said speculatively. "I suspect that Thad is behind it somehow. He obviously never quit."

"Can you be more specific?" Sophia asked.

Hiker moved away from the globe and let out a deep breath. "Thad's mission was always to get rid of the dragonriders. He might have succeeded, with the exception of the Dragon Elite." He leveled his gaze at Wilder. "Which was one reason I was adamant about you lot staying inside the Gullington."

"Do you really think he could have killed all the rest of the lone riders?" Sophia questioned, sitting up.

Hiker nodded. "There weren't many...not after...well, it isn't important."

"Sounds important," she fired back.

"It's history. Boring stuff," he replied.

Sophia shook her head. "Let's agree to disagree on this one."

"So, there might not be any other dragonriders out there in the world?" Wilder asked, his voice tense.

"Maybe," Hiker answered. "Or it's possible that Thad has spelled the Elite Globe so that I can't find them, knowing that I'd come after them to recruit when I learned about his presence."

"Are you sure he can do that?" Sophia questioned.

"I know he can." Hiker combed his hands through his hair.

"How do you know that?"

"I just do," he said authoritatively.

"Spoken like a parent," Sophia grumbled.

"It's not important how I know," Hiker argued. "The point is that I can't find the dragonriders who are out there. I can't even confirm that they are out there, but I'll continue to work on it."

"And in the meantime?" Sophia asked. "What should we do?"

"Well, you're done reversing events and killing Phantoms?" Hiker questioned.

"Yes, and Sophia bonded to her sword," Wilder said proudly.

The Viking nodded. "Good."

"And Wilder found out that he works for the Protector of Weapons," Sophia informed.

Hiker's expression morphed into one of frustration. "You what?"

"Well, apparently, he's the reason I have such a connection with weapons," Wilder explained.

"What does this mean?" Hiker asked.

"I'm not sure yet, sir," Wilder answered. "I guess I might have to go on side-missions for him."

Hiker looked up to the ceiling. "For the love of the angels. Is it too much to ask to have a single dragonrider who works for me and isn't at someone else's behest?"

"Probably," Sophia answered.

He shot her a glare. "Well, before you two are pulled off on some other side quest, I have adjudicator missions for you."

Hiker snapped his fingers, and scrolls of parchment materialized in both Sophia's and Wilder's hands.

She unrolled hers. "Did you write this by hand?"

He rolled his eyes. "Yes, a bit of penmanship wouldn't hurt you. I've seen the way you scratch out your name."

"Why write when you can type," she joked, enjoying getting under his skin.

"When you return, Sophia, I hope to have information on where to find any lone riders, if you still want the challenge of finding them."

Sophia blinked at him, trying to decide if he was serious. "Is this because you think they will try to kill me?"

"Maybe," he answered. "But also because I suspect if there are any out there, you might be the only one who can recruit them."

"Why is that, sir?" Wilder questioned.

"Because they are a different breed of rider," Hiker answered. "They will probably be enthralled by her rebellious spirit."

Sophia smiled. "I'll take that as a compliment."

He shook his head. "Do what you will."

CHAPTER SEVENTY

Sophia couldn't help herself from wrapping her arms around Lunis when she saw him the next morning, refreshed from her adventures of bonding to Inexorabilis. She'd missed him in a way that was hard to explain. It was like a part of her had been severed, and she'd only just been reunited with it. Although Lunis was always in her head and heart, distance to their physical proximity had an effect on her spirit, she'd come to realize.

He pressed into her, although he said, "You know most riders don't hug their dragons."

Sophia pulled away, feeling tears aching to the surface. "Those other riders are missing out. There is nothing like a good dragon hug."

"I think that's the first time that's ever been said," Lunis stated, wrapping his neck around Sophia, pulling her in tighter. "We aren't considered really cuddly creatures."

After a long moment, Sophia pulled away. "Are you ready for a mission? How is Tala?"

He nodded. "Yes, getting out of the Cave and spreading my wings will be good. He is okay. Still disoriented, and I'm not certain either he or Mahkah knows what hit them."

"But it was definitely something at the Nathaniel Facility on Catalina Island?"

"I believe so, but I'm not sure it worked the way it was supposed to, or that they got away before it did the full extent of damage it was intended to do," Lunis explained. "We will find out more when they recover. Right now they need rest, but hopefully, in time, the events will become clearer, and we will know what we're up against."

Sophia shook her head. "Thad Reinhart is something else. Hiker thinks he might have taken out the lone dragonriders. And now this."

"I think there's a lot we don't know about Thad Reinhart, and that puts us at a serious disadvantage."

"Well, I'm hoping that when we return, Hiker will know where the lone riders are," Sophia informed him. "Then we can go recruit them and be that much closer to taking down that evil man and his treacherous companies that pollute the Earth and promote war."

"Until then..." Lunis extended one of his wings.

Sophia stepped onto it, swinging her leg around the other side of Lunis, taking a seat in the saddle. "Until then, we get to hopefully create peace."

With a grace Sophia had sorely missed, the dragon started forward, his wings flapping as he crossed the Expanse. It wasn't really the way she held the reins or leaned that steered the dragon up into the air. Mostly it was the connection between them that made for a brilliant take off as he launched into the air, flying toward the rising sun over the Expanse.

Once they were through the Barrier, Sophia opened a portal into the place that held their next mission.

I just don't see why that's important, Sophia replied telepathically to her dragon as they flew over the crystal blue waters of the ocean, warm winds racing through her hair.

It's part of your training, Lunis argued. *Without mastering air combat, you can't pass your training.*

But dragonriders don't fight other dragonriders, she countered. *There may not even be any more dragons.*

In the past, the dragonriders did battle one another.

What? Sophia asked, surprised. *That's not in the* Incomplete History of Dragonriders.

Because it's incomplete, he stated.

Tell me more about these battles, she urged as they neared land.

I don't know specifics, Lunis related. *I know the Dragon Elite were involved, quelling disputes that involved other dragonriders.*

Doesn't your collective consciousness give you details about the history of these disputes?

It doesn't really work that way, Lunis explained. *I know facts. That's what we pass along to one another. Wars aren't based on facts but rather emotions, therefore I don't know why dragonriders fought each other, but I can postulate that it was for power.*

It always is, Sophia said with a sigh.

The fact remains that you must work with the others to practice air combat, Lunis stated, not dropping this point. Since Sophia had told him that she'd bonded to her sword, which he was aware of from the moment it occurred, he'd been nagging her to complete other parts of her training.

To officially complete it and earn her wings, she'd have to get better at scrying and survive alone for an extended period of time with Lunis off the grid. She'd also have to master all the riding techniques, which involved a running mount, dismounting while in flight, sword fighting while flying, creating multiple portals in a row in quick succession, and many other skills.

Bonding with her sword was only the beginning of the training, she now realized. Sophia needed to master sword fighting, hand to hand combat, increase her stealth and agility as well as double her physical strength and speed.

Once she'd completed all of that, then she had to do the one thing that seemed nearly impossible. Sophia had to meditate for as long as it took to master her mind. Only then would she connect with the ancient power of the dragons, learning an ancient wisdom that would keep her tied to the chi of the dragon for all of time.

You're telling me that Evan completed this meditation challenge? Sophia asked Lunis as they scanned the ground for their destination.

Yes, all of the riders at the Gullington have.

But Evan can't even be quiet long enough to chew a piece of sausage. I'm so tired of seeing that dude's food while he's eating.

Evan might appear to be a goof, but when it comes to dragon-riding, he's an Elite for a reason.

And what is this surviving off the grid business? Sophia asked, having learned this new information from Lunis. *That sounds like a walkabout.*

It's important that we know how to survive in the worst conditions, away from the Gullington, which currently provides all our necessities.

You can hunt, though, she argued.

But can you?

No, but that's why I have you, she joked. *You'll share your sheep with me.*

Will I?

Won't you?

Do you want me to answer that?

Sophia groaned. *Fine. I'll learn how to hunt and make a fire.*

Without using magic, he added.

Man, this is just getting ridiculous, she complained. Sophia realized she'd been naïve to think that she'd master dragon training so quickly. She guessed that it might have taken Evan and the others many years, but they were born at a different time when the Dragon Elite was dead to the rest of the world.

Now there were adjudication missions and villains and riders to recruit. Sophia didn't want to slow down from all that to also train, although that was the deal she'd made with Hiker. And Mama Jamba was adamant about her finishing her training for some strange reason.

Every time she saw the southern belle, she was asked how training was going, as if she couldn't just dip into Sophia's mind and know for herself.

So the other dragonriders out there, the lone ones, Sophia began. *Do you think they finished training?*

No, Lunis answered simply.

I wonder how that makes them different, she pondered.

We will find out, Lunis said. *But for as much as you and Hiker butt heads, please note that his rigid adherence to protocol will be what keeps us alive in the most dangerous situations. He is giving you missions, but I believe he won't knowingly put you in any situation until he knows you're ready.*

Like when he sent me to recover Mama Jamba, nearly killing us both?

If you remember, he didn't think that you'd actually do it, Lunis stated.

Yeah, yet another Hiker test, Sophia thought with a laugh.

Well, I think he gave you this current mission because he believes your strategic mind will decrease the chance of violence and hopefully settle the dispute easily, Lunis said, landing on a busy street, earning the attention of everyone around them.

Yeah, let's hope you're right, Sophia said, steering her dragon toward the capital for the nation of Reerca. Soon their neighbors would be joining them, having unknowingly been summoned by Lunis and Sophia for this meeting as they flew over it on their way to this spot. Dragonriders had many tricks in their bags.

Calling meetings between disputing parties, whether they wanted to meet or not, was one of them.

CHAPTER SEVENTY-ONE

The country of Reerca was poor and disadvantaged in that its citizens suffered from lack of jobs, underdeveloped water systems, poor social systems, and many other issues that stemmed from a lack of economy.

Conversely, their neighbors to the north in Thleath prospered from a robust economy driven by a healthy export of fruits and vegetables. The stark difference in living conditions had sparked an immigration movement from Reerca to Thleath, resulting in a border dispute between the two nations.

That's where Sophia and Lunis came in. Currently, the tension had only caused small skirmishes, but the stress was building, and it was only a matter of time before war broke out.

There had been talks of a high-security fence being placed between the countries. Thleath's citizens complained about the immigrants from Reerca trespassing into their country, taking their resources.

Sophia studied Reerca's capitol building. It had seen better days.

As she decided where discussions should take place, Sophia was aware that those passing them on the streets were studying her and Lunis.

I think we have their attention, Lunis said, swishing his tail.

Good, Sophia answered.

Two guards rushed forward, holding automatic weapons.

I don't think you'll fit inside the building, Sophia observed, indicating the large stone building with a crumbling exterior

I most certainly won't, he replied.

I think the open courtyard suits us better anyway, Sophia said, undeterred by the menacing glares of the soldiers holding weapons.

She held up her hands and used a freezing spell on them, sensing their tension.

"We are not here to create problems. We are here to resolve them."

The men's eyes shifted with alarm as they realized they couldn't move.

Lunis strode beside her, giving those on the streets curious glances, earning whispers. This was an appearance that would get them worthy attention worldwide. Hiker had chosen the case well. She might even tell him that.

"I've only frozen you so you don't do something rash," Sophia explained, seeing the caution in the men's eyes grow.

"What do you want?" the first guard asked. Sophia knew he wasn't speaking a language she would normally understand, but the chi of the dragon translated it effortlessly for her.

Sophia shook her head. "You don't need to do anything but relax. Your leader has already been summoned."

The other man shook his head. "That's impossible. He's in meetings. He can't be disturbed. They are very important."

"Yeah," Sophia said casually. "I think he's going to want to change his mind on that."

It would take more training to hone the skills of a dragonrider, and summoning disputing parties was part of them. In the current situation, it was requiring the most energy Sophia and Lunis had used thus far for the special spell.

Apparently, according to what Sophia had learned from the *Incomplete History of Dragonriders,* when disputing parties were summoned, if the spell worked, they simply decided that whatever they were doing was not important. They would then go in the direction of the dragon and rider and meet them in the decided location.

This only worked once on disputing parties, forcing them to face each other, talk, and give the dragon and rider an idea of what they were up against for a resolution. After that, nothing short of threats could bring two parties together when they chose to stay separate. That was the reason the first meeting was extremely important.

A horde of politicians in much shinier suits than the guards exited a vehicle, an entourage surrounding them at once. Sophia didn't have a chance to greet the leaders from Thleath because at that same moment, the very busy President of Reerca materialized, hurrying down the stairs of the capitol building.

The guards turned, confused by the sight around them.

"Open the gates," Lunis said, and if there had been any doubts about the two outsiders, it wasn't questioned at that moment.

A third guard, having heard the command, started the process of opening the two large gates.

"What is going on?" the frontman for Thleath asked, marching forward, intimidating figures flanking him.

Sophia held her arm wide to the courtyard. "The Dragon Elite is here to resolve your disputes with Reerca."

The man's eyes swept to Lunis and he softened slightly, another gift of the dragons when in negotiations. They calmed. They intimidated. And they urged resolutions.

"Fine," the man said. "We will talk. But I believe there's little to talk about."

Sophia nodded. "We shall see."

CHAPTER SEVENTY-TWO

After an hour of discussions, Sophia was reluctant to admit that the leader from Thleath might be right. There was little to discuss. No matter how she and Lunis tried, there were no resolutions.

Thleath had everything to offer a disparaging Reerca, and the impoverished nation had nothing. Thleath simply had no reason to compromise. If anything, at the end of the long dispute resolution attempt, they were more against any solutions than before.

When it looked like Sophia and Lunis would fail, she felt her spirits bolstered by her dragon. She looked at him and wondered what he had in mind. Deciding against questioning it, she stepped in between the two leaders. "Give us one week. We will meet here at this time. If we don't have a solution that both countries are happy with, then we will help to build the wall on the border and offer aid directly to Reerca."

"Without question?" the leader for Thleath questioned tersely.

"Yes," Sophia said. "We will be in charge of drawing up the treaty, and there will be no question when you refuse passage to Reerca citizens to your lands."

The leader nodded. "You have yourself a deal." He turned at once, his entourage following him out.

Sophia turned to the leader for the country of Reerca, a tough expression on her face. "One week. That's all I ask for."

He shook his head, discouraged. "I hope you can fix things because although your being here is helpful, it will not save our nation. Only access to others will do that."

Sophia pulled in a breath, about to say something, but Lunis cut her off.

"You might think that's the only solution, but I believe you need to look deeper," the dragon said. "That will be our job. One week."

"One week," the leader of Reerca said, giving them a hopeful expression.

"So, I have absolutely no idea how to fix this," Sophia said as they soared through the skies, away from the disputing nations.

"Me either," Lunis said at once.

"Are you serious?" Sophia questioned, tensing.

"As a heart attack," he stated.

"Have you been watching episodes of *Full House?*"

"No," he answered at once, then said, "Yeah, maybe."

"How come you urged me to get them to reconvene for a solution when you didn't have one?" she asked.

"Because we need time to find the solution," he remarked. "They weren't going to come to an agreement, because Reerca simply has nothing to offer Thleath."

"So what's the plan?" she asked.

"I don't know," he said. "But we have a whole week to figure it out."

"Yes, we have a whole week to solve two nations problems that if it gets out of hand will result in the deaths of thousands."

"No pressure, right?" Lunis swerved toward a plot of land.

"Where are we going?" she asked, not used to him taking over navigation.

"I think your face is looking like it needs some extra attention."

"What?" she asked, offended. "How rude!"

"I didn't mean it that way," he stated. "It's just that your toenails are atrocious."

"Oh, please! What exactly is going on here?"

"I'm telling you that you should pay a visit to Mae Ling," Lunis said simply.

Sophia nodded, getting what Lunis was hinting at before. "You think my fairy godmother from another creature might have some insight on this?"

The dragon nodded as he descended. "It's worth a shot."

"Since you got us into a predicament and we have a problem to solve in under a week," she said, sounding overly dramatic.

"Oh, cut it out," he said, impersonating Uncle Joey from *Full House*.

Sophia laughed. "You got it, dude!"

CHAPTER SEVENTY-THREE

The entrance to Mae Ling's nail shop was blocked by construction barriers. Sophia's spirit sank, thinking the salon was closed. She peeked through the glass and tried to figure out what she'd do if Mae Ling wasn't available.

It was bizarre to Sophia that she'd come to rely on the little old Asian lady who did her nails. So far, her advice had been reliable, although delivered in the most confusing way.

It was hard to see through the glare of the window. When Sophia did make out what was on the other side of it, she nearly jumped back.

Mae Ling's face was right up against the glass, her large brown eyes staring at Sophia.

"Are you open?" Sophia mouthed, pointing at the door.

The woman shook her head.

"Oh, okay," Sophia said, backing away and forcing a smile.

She caught movement behind the glass as Mae Ling made for the door. A moment later, she pulled it back, sticking her head through. "Where are you, child?"

"Well, you're closed," Sophia explained.

Mae Ling rolled her eyes. "That is because Sophia Beaufont is coming to see me, and I didn't want others bothering us."

Sophia blinked. "You closed down the shop for me?"

"Of course." Mae Ling held the door open. "You're my current assignment."

"Assignment?" Sophia asked.

The woman sighed. "Yes, although I get that it's a bit strange for you to think of yourself that way."

"You mean that you're assigned to me as my fairy godmother?"

Mae Ling waved her into the shop. "Yes, dear."

"Does everyone have a fairy godmother?" Sophia asked, sliding by the little woman and entering the salon.

"Angels no," Mae Ling said, pulling the door closed and locking it.

The inside of the shop appeared to be under construction as well, plastic tarping covering many of the workstations.

"So who gets a fairy godmother?" Sophia asked.

"Those who need one," Mae Ling said simply, ushering her to the only open seat.

"And who makes the assignments?" she continued her questioning.

"Mama Jamba, of course." The woman snapped at Sophia. "Now, let's see those nails."

"Oh, you don't have to do them. It looks like you've got enough going on here." She swept her arm around at the shop.

"Don't be silly, child. Of course, I need to do your nails. That's why you are here."

"Actually," Sophia began, "I'm here for advice."

"Naturally," Mae Ling said, taking a seat on the other side of the table. "Famil. Rapoo. Bermuda Laurens. Now that I've told you what you need to know, give me your hands. It's time to get your nails done."

"Umm, I don't know what those first two things you said are. And what does the giantess have to do with anything?"

Mae Ling snapped again. "She's how you're going to find the rapoo."

Reluctantly, Sophia slid her hands across the table. "Why do I need to find a rapoo?"

"Because that's how you're going to mine the famil. Are you even paying attention, dear?" She went straight to work, trimming Sophia's nails, which were in a sorry state. "You're getting pink today."

"Actually, I was thinking—"

"Pink," Mae Ling said forcefully.

"It's just that the guys—"

"Pink," she repeated. "And you tell Evan he should get that wart on his face checked."

"What?" Sophia asked. "He doesn't have a wart on his face."

"He does now," Mae Ling said proudly.

"Oh, no. Please don't do that. Evan is annoying, but I like him."

Mae Ling pursed her lips. "Even after he stole half your stash of gummy bears?"

"What? He didn't do that," Sophia argued.

"And you know that because you're at the Castle right now?"

Sophia ground her teeth together. "Just give him a small wart."

"Of course, dear," Mae Ling sang. "And the Castle will clear it up the next time he sleeps. That place never lets me get away with anything for long. So intent on protecting its riders."

Sophia smiled proudly. "Okay, so I need to ask Bermuda Laurens where to find a rapoo, and that is…"

"A creature that mines famil," Mae Ling said, filing Sophia's nails.

"And famil is?"

"A rare gem with many protective and practical purposes," she answered.

"And I find that where?" Sophia continued to question.

The old woman's eyes darted up to Sophia, impatience heavy in them. "In the only place on Earth where it can be found, of course."

"Which is…"

Mae Ling sighed. "The country of Reerca."

"Of course," Sophia said, looking around the shop but not really seeing as she began to put it all together. "Do the leaders know that Reerca has this natural resource?"

"Absolutely, they do. But they have no way to mine it and refuse to contract with other countries. More importantly, they know that traditional methods of mining would pollute their lands, making their people sick and ruining their air quality."

Sophia nodded. "Which is where the rapoo comes in?"

"Yes, dear," Mae Ling said, sounding bored by the conversation, as if she were explaining basic math to Sophia.

"And Bermuda Laurens will know how to find the creatures," Sophia said to herself. "I give them to the government of Reerca and they mine these gems, bolstering their economy and erasing border tensions with Thleath."

"Maybe," Mae Ling sang. "Or they could become so incredibly rich that they lose sight of the values that kept them from mining in the first place, losing their souls to greed."

Sophia pulled her hands back. "Are you serious? That could happen?"

"Anything is possible," Mae Ling warned. "It's all about how you set it up. That's the key here."

Sophia nodded, looking down at her nails. Glittery pink winked back at her. It made her feel dainty, not the state usually associated with dragonriders. "Okay, well, thank you."

"And you owe me nothing in return," Mae Ling said, standing but her height not really changing.

That had been Sophia's next question. "Well, thank you. And thanks for seeing me while you have construction going on here. What are you doing to the shop, anyway?"

"Demolishing it," Mae Ling answered.

"Wait! What?"

The old woman looked around fondly at the tiny nail salon. "It's been a good run, but it's time to tear this place down."

"B-b-but where will I find you?" Sophia asked.

"No stuttering, my dear," Mae Ling stated. "And you'll find me."

"Will you be here?"

"I'm not sure where I'll be, but one thing is true no matter what."

"And that is?" Sophia questioned.

"When you need to find me, the universe will lead you," Mae Ling said with a smile. "You've got less than a week to find a creature most don't know exists. And my Hot Pocket is getting cold in the microwave."

Sophia blinked at the strange woman and nodded slowly. "Okay, thank you."

CHAPTER SEVENTY-FOUR

Sophia had no idea where to find Bermuda Laurens. The explorer and author of *Mysterious Creatures* was constantly off on adventures. Sophia decided to pay her son a visit, knowing he'd be aware of her current travel plans.

When she arrived in front of the giant's modest house in Los Angeles, Sophia knew something was off. Music spilled from the open door of the usually quiet bungalow, and the smell of apple pie was strong.

Tentatively, she slid up next to the door and poked her head into the house.

"You came!" Rudolf exclaimed, nearly knocking his very pregnant wife over to sprint to Sophia.

"Of course, I did," Sophia said, her eyes bulging as he swept her into a hug. Liv spied her over Rudolf's shoulder and appeared to be restraining her laughter. "I wasn't going to miss your baby shower."

Rudolf released her, smiling wide. "Your mean sister said you probably weren't going to make it because of some dinosaur-riding business."

"Dragon-riding," Sophia corrected.

Rudolf waved her off. "Same thing. Oh, and just so you know, we aren't all showering together, so it's okay if you don't have your bathing suit."

"Good to know," Sophia said, hugging Liv when she came over.

Rudolf held his hand out to her sister. "Liv, you remember your sister Sophia, right?"

Liv batted her eyelashes at the fae. "Yeah, thanks, pal."

"No problem. She's grown a lot, so I figured you might not recognize her," Rudolf stated.

"I don't think there's anything my little sister could do to make me not recognize her," Liv said, giving Sophia a ridiculous fond expression that was making her feel soft inside.

"Rudolf!" Serena yelled on the other side of the room. "Captain is kicking me in the bladder again. Do something!"

"Oh, duty calls," Rudolf chirped. "I'll just leave you two to get to know each other. Liv, Sophia has this awful friend who has the worst name in history. Sophia, I love the nail color. Tell me who your person is. I must get an appointment."

"She doesn't take referrals," Sophia said, giving him a confused expression. "And what are you going to do to help Serena?"

He sighed. "Serena tells him that their father will hear about this when he gets home. It usually does the trick." Rudolf pivoted, his hands on his hips. "Captain, is what your mother says true? That's going to result in a time out."

The king of the fae marched away, his chin held high and a pursed expression on his face.

"You totally forgot about the baby shower, didn't you?" Liv muttered when Rudolf was gone.

"Yep."

"So why are you here?" Liv asked.

"Because I need to find Bermuda Laurens. Is she here?"

Liv shook her head. "I'm afraid not. She's on a research trip to London. I can message you her coordinates."

"Thanks," Sophia said, watching as Rudolf wagged his finger at Serena's belly, disciplining one of his unborn children. "What's going to happen when that man is in charge of three humans?"

"Total chaos," Liv answered. "However, he's in charge of an entire nation of fae, and Las Vegas hasn't gone to hell yet. Well, no more than usual. Somehow, I think he'll manage, and probably end up accidentally raising three prodigies who save the Earth."

"That sounds about right," Sophia said with a laugh.

"Speaking of saving the Earth," Liv began, "how are you doing?"

Sophia quickly filled her sister in on all the happenings in the Gullington with the dragonriders.

Liv's usually cheerful face turned serious. "It sounds like Thad Reinhart might have the upper hand."

"There's no might about it," Sophia stated. "He's had time to get us to a major disadvantage, but we have Mother Nature now."

Liv laughed. "How is it that we went on to work for Father Time and Mother Nature?"

"Why didn't you tell me that Soph was here," Clark complained, sliding through the crowd.

"Hey, Clark," Liv began. "Soph is here."

"Thanks," her brother said dryly, offering Sophia a hug before looking her over. "You look like you've lost weight."

"It's called muscle," Liv stated. "Warriors and dragonriders get it because we move around unlike you lazy Councilors."

He shook his head at her and returned his attention to Sophia. "Are you getting enough rest? Proper meals? I can pack you a care package if you like. And are you making friends?"

"She's a dragonrider, for heaven's sake," Liv complained. "It's not like she's at a boarding school for girls."

"Quite the opposite, actually," Sophia stated. "And I'm great, thanks for asking. How are you?"

Clark shook his head. "There's an evil growing. At first, we thought the Phantom had returned, but Mother and Father rid the world of that atrocity, and nothing could ever bring it back."

"Right…" Sophia said, trying to keep her face neutral.

"But now we suspect," Clark began, "that the evil is connected to this Thad Reinhart you told us about, and since what he's doing harms

333

the Earth, it technically falls under the dragonriders' jurisdiction. And since Thad Reinhart is a dragonrider—"

"What did you just say?" Sophia exclaimed, earning looks from many of the chatting fae in the room.

Clark leaned forward. "You knew that, right?"

"No, I think when she yelled, 'What did you just say,' it was because she didn't know that piece of information," Liv stated with a laugh.

"How did you learn that?" Sophia asked her brother.

"Well, I ran across something in the *Forgotten Archives*," he explained. "It wasn't much, just a list of dragonriders. His name stuck out because you'd just told us he was behind the spreading evil."

Sophia had been looking for that list, but it was missing from the *Incomplete History of Dragonriders*—unsurprisingly. It seemed like the most pertinent information was missing from that book, which was probably why Trinity, the librarian for the Great Library in Tanzania, wanted the *Complete History of Dragonriders* so badly.

"Are you sure?" Sophia asked.

Clark held out his hand, and a moment later, the large volume appeared. "Yeah, I can show you."

"Watch this. It's sort of sick and also impressive," Liv said, pointing at her brother.

He rolled his eyes. "It's not sick. I simply have reviewed this book many times, although I still have much to read."

"And shockingly, you don't have a girlfriend," Liv teased. "I wonder why?"

He ignored her, flipping the book open and turning a few pages. A moment later, he pointed to a list. "There." Clark turned the book around and showed it to Sophia.

It was what appeared to be an incomplete list of dragonriders. Mahkah, Wilder, Evan, and of course, Sophia weren't on it. She guessed it only included riders from before the curse made mortals unable to see magic. The *Forgotten Archives*, after all, told the history before the Great War.

Her eyes skimmed the list and found three names close together that she recognized:

Adam Rivalry

Thad Reinhart

Hiker Wallace.

She scratched her head, totally bewildered.

"Hiker didn't tell you Thad was a dragonrider?" Liv asked.

Sophia shook her head. "No, but he loves his secrets, so I guess I shouldn't be surprised."

"Oh, and something else that's cool," Clark began, pointing to the top of the list. "One of our relatives was a dragonrider."

Sophia didn't have to read the name to know who he was talking to. "Yes, I met Oscar Beaufont."

"You what?" Clark asked. "He died eons ago."

"Well, I meant his ghost, or I assumed that it was him," Sophia explained. "It could have been that the Castle led me on a scavenger hunt. It likes to do that."

Liv stretched her arm around Clark's shoulder, hugging him tightly and offering Sophia a smile. "I don't know about you, bro, but I feel totally better about our little sister living with the Dragon Elite at the Gullington now. She has the ghosts of our ancestors and a possessed castle and a leader who hides important information."

Clark shook his head at his sister. "You're one to talk. What did you face down last night?"

"It was nothing," Liv argued.

"Oh, really? Since when are aliens bent on stealing magic from Earth nothing?" Clark challenged.

Liv stuck out her tongue. "Since now. And they weren't successful. I just need to figure out how they got here, or I'll have to keep kicking alien butt every day, which is annoying since getting their slime out of my hair takes forever."

"Oh, they probably got into our orbit because Wilder didn't actually cover my shift at the Gullington," Sophia said with a laugh.

"Say what?" Liv asked, confused.

Sophia smiled. "Inside joke."

Liv laid her head on her brother's shoulder. "Aww, see, she's making friends. Sophia has inside jokes with old dragonriders with cool names."

"Well," Clark said, a serious expression on his face, "I'd feel better if you'd let me send you with some sandwiches. Maybe muffins."

"Thanks," Sophia stated, "but I'm off to London right now. Liv, will you send me the information?"

Her sister nodded. "Consider it done. And tell Bermuda that I said… On second thought, don't mention me to the giantess unless you want to put her in a bad mood."

"Noted," Sophia said, backing toward the door before Rudolf could notice she was leaving. "Tell the parents-to-be that I had to leave, but I'll send them something ridiculously expensive for the triplets."

"We will," Liv said, waving. "And remember, since they are having triplets, you need to send four presents."

Sophia winked. "Can't wait until they have their babies and realize they only have three."

Liv laughed. "Yes, the nursery is going to have to be completely redone."

CHAPTER SEVENTY-FIVE

According to the message Liv sent Sophia, Bermuda Laurens could be found in the British Museum, but not in any public galleries. Evidently, the giantess's research had her working in the lower level in a restricted area. That was why Liv sent someone to help Sophia find Bermuda. She'd told Sophia to keep an eye out for a little guy named Ticker.

The smell of museums was one of Sophia's favorites. Yes, they usually were full of chemicals that kept the artwork and artifacts clean. But underneath that were the unique smells of plaster, art materials, dust, and magic.

Sophia strode down to the lower level, sliding through the crowd of tourists. She had no idea how she was going to find the guide Liv had sent, given the hordes of people. And she didn't know who she was looking for. By "little guy," did Liv mean she'd sent a gnome? Or was it simply a shorter magician?

A small black and white cat she recognized popped up beside her. "Plato? What are you doing here? You're the guide Liv sent me to find Bermuda Laurens?"

The lynx shook his head, appearing amused, as usual. "No, I'm doing some research of my own here and just happened to run into you."

There was no one in the vicinity to see her interacting with a talking cat. That was pretty typical. The lynx only showed up when no one else was around and disappeared at the slightest hint of anyone.

"The coincidence is uncanny." Sophia eyed the cat, trying to figure out if there was a side agenda. There usually was with Liv's sidekick, who was definitely not all he appeared or seemed.

"What is this research you're doing?" she asked him.

"I can't say," he stated.

She nodded. "Figured." Sophia looked around, still trying to locate her guide. "Well, can you help me find this Ticker Liv sent to help me?"

"Nope," he said at once.

She rolled her eyes at him. "You're thoroughly unhelpful."

"It's true."

"And why is it that you told me that to bond to Inexorabilis, I had to redo the death of the Phantom?" she asked, remembering that he'd helped her but in his own weird lynx way.

"It worked, didn't it?" he challenged.

"Sort of, but not at first. And I almost was killed or turned evil. I wasn't sure which one was going to happen first."

A smirk crossed his face. "But you weren't. And now you're bonded to your sword."

"You work in mysterious ways."

He nodded. "If I would have told you that you needed to do something of great significance to prove your loyalty to the sword, you would have been wracking your brain for days. As it happened, you were able to kill one bird with many stones, or in this case, arrows."

"You know about Devon's bow?" she questioned.

"Of course."

Sophia shook her head. "Then I suppose you know about all the other strange things that came out of that single mission."

The lynx strolled beside her, his black tail with a white tip flickering. "Naturally, and it was all executed perfectly to set up future events."

"And by future events, you mean…" Sophia trailed away, used to playing this game with the cat.

"I can't say," he replied at once.

"Of course you can't." She sighed. "Well, thanks for orchestrating things and tampering with events for unknown reasons."

"You're very welcome," he stated proudly.

"Any other wisdom you want to pass along before I find the guide Liv sent to help me?" Sophia asked him.

"Invest in board games," he said plainly.

Sophia blinked at him, wondering if she'd heard him correctly. "Say what? Why would I do that?"

"Because winter is approaching, and you'll want a way to pass the time at the Gullington," he offered.

"I'm a rider for the Dragon Elite," she argued. "I don't think I have the luxury of sitting around and playing Clue or Battleship."

"I don't think that Quiet would like those games that much," Plato said. "Get something a bit edgier. You have to make time for the little things. It can't always be missions and battles. If it is, you'll lose the point of doing it all in the first place."

"The point is to help the world be a better place and save this planet," Sophia imparted.

Plato shook his head. "I get that, but you don't have to lose your world for that to happen. Take a break every now and then. Hang with the ones you share the Castle with."

Sophia narrowed her eyes at him. "How do you know about Quiet? And why does it sound like you know about the others? I haven't mentioned them to Liv and Clark."

"You mean, you haven't told them Evan teases you every chance he gets, and Wilder has a dashing look about him?" Plato asked.

Sophia stuck her hands on her hips. "You've been in the Gullington? How? Only Dragon Elite and those who serve them are allowed through the Barrier."

"Well," he began with a long yawn, "I'm not allowed in the House of Fourteen either, and that hasn't stopped me."

Sophia shook her head at him. "You're such a strange creature."

"So are you, Sophia Beaufont. That's what I like about you."

She was about to say something else, but at that instant, Plato disappeared, leaving her alone in the wing of the museum.

For a minute, she walked on, browsing the displays and not finding anyone she thought could be a guide sent by her sister.

Casually, Sophia strolled through the Sainsbury African galleries, appreciating the artwork, metalwork, textiles, and sculpture. She halted in front of a particularly interesting pottery display, enjoying the fine detail on the largest pot.

Strangely, Sophia could swear that she heard scratching coming from inside it.

She leaned forward, trying to peer into it. When she was less than a foot away, a little brown creature popped his head out the top, a wide grin taking up most of his face.

Sophia jumped back, as startled as if a snake had spilled from the pot. When she recovered, she saw that it was a brownie, one of the many house-elves who took care of mortals' homes while they slept. This one was particularly small, with huge ears and eyes to match. He was incredibly cute.

"Hey," Sophia said, checking around to see that no one was paying attention.

"Te Micker!" the little brownie stated.

"Do you mean you're Ticker?" she asked.

He nodded adamantly, climbing all the way out of the pot. "Siv lent."

"Liv sent you?" Sophia asked, trying to understand the creature's strange way of communicating.

He nodded again. "Yes. Yes."

"You're going to help me find Bermuda?"

The brownie slid down the side of the pot, landing gracefully on the floor next to Sophia. "Mollow fe!"

The little guy took off fast, zig-zagging around the pottery collection. Sophia was about to object that she'd get in trouble for entering the display when she noticed the guard stationed in that room was asleep.

She sped up, trying to keep up with Ticker, who thankfully was looping around the pottery. When Sophia realized what he was doing, she paused until he started in a new direction.

He halted, an annoyed expression on his face as he pointed at where he'd just come. "Fou yollow."

"Do you mean you want me to do exactly as you did?" she asked.

He placed his fist on his hips and nodded.

"Okay," Sophia said, realizing there must be something to the series of events. Maybe doing them a specific way unlocked a secret room. Magic was strange like that.

Trying to recall the exact path the brownie had taken, Sophia began circling the pottery. When she was about to go around part of the display again, Ticker exclaimed.

"Mo nore!'

Sophia paused. "Okay, then what's next?"

He answered by speeding from the room into one with beautiful furniture and cotton panels hanging on the wall.

Again, the security guard was asleep. Sophia suspected the clever little brownie was behind putting the mortals to sleep. It was a gift brownies had since they could could clean houses after the mortals had gone to bed.

Ticker hurried around a huge chair three times. Then he did the same with a set of masks on stands. Sophia found it much more difficult to negotiate around the masks due to her size, but she managed to slide between them.

Once she'd completed that part of the obstacle course, she realized she'd lost sight of Ticker.

"Hey, where are you?" she whispered, searching the large room.

The tapestry hanging on the wall lifted up at the corner and the little brownie's head popped out. "Whis tay!"

Sophia checked over her shoulder before peeling back the tapestry to reveal a small round portal. "Oh, and hence the obstacle course. It opened this."

Carefully she stepped through the portal, momentarily blinded until she was firmly on the other side. It took her a moment for her eyes to adjust. She knew Ticker had led her in the right direction because standing right in front of her was the infamous and very accomplished Bermuda Laurens.

CHAPTER SEVENTY-SIX

"Finally, Liv, you brushed your hair," the giantess said, briefly looking up. She returned her attention to a large book sitting on a workstation in front of her, hunching over to read the text.

It appeared that Ticker had led Sophia to a storage area of sorts. Shelves lined the room, crammed with strange objects and artifacts. The room was mostly dim, with the main light over the station where Bermuda resided.

Kneeling, Sophia offered Ticker a finger. "Thanks so much for your help. Let me know if I can return the favor."

"Wou yelcome," the brownie chirped before hurrying through the storage area and disappearing.

"Do you have Bellator with you?" Bermuda said, referring to Liv's trusty sword. She held out her hand to the side, her eyes still pinned on the book. "I need a sword for something."

"Actually, I'm not Liv," Sophia said, nearing the giantess, who was deep in concentration.

She glanced up, blinking at Sophia as she neared. "Well, that explains the hair. The Beaufont sister who owns a brush and knows how to use it. You should teach your older sister."

Sophia laughed, bowing slightly to the accomplished giantess. "It's good to see you again, Mrs. Laurens."

The always stoic giantess simply nodded. Her curly brown hair was reminiscent of her son Rory's. He also had her facial features, making her more of a handsome woman than a dainty female. She was wearing a long brown dress and an extravagant hat with a bird on top.

Bermuda nodded appreciatively to her. "The honor is all mine. Being in the presence of the newest dragonrider and the first female of the Dragon Elite is a true gift for someone such as myself."

"Am I in your book, *Mysterious Creatures*?"

"Since the moment you were born," Bermuda stated.

That confounded Sophia, but she smiled instead of asking the questions needling her brain. "I'm here because I need to find the location of the rapoo. Can you help me?"

Shock registered in Bermuda's eyes. "Where did you hear about those cleverly helpful creatures? I haven't written about them yet because I've yet to find one."

"Oh," Sophia said, disappointment welling to the surface. "Well, a friend told me about them."

Bermuda tilted her head to the side, narrowing her gaze. "Yes, you would be the type to get a fairy godmother."

Sophia blinked at the giantess. "How did you guess?"

"Well, besides the fact that you're shimmering with pixie dust?" Bermuda asked.

Sophia glanced down at her arms and just then realized that she was, in fact, sparkling like she'd been dipped in glitter. "Yes, I guess besides that."

"Well, I don't know many who are aware of the presence of the rapoo," Bermuda stated. "But a fairy godmother, well, she'd be in the know because of her connection to Mother Nature." Bermuda paused. "Have you met the One? I've heard rumors that she's back."

"You mean Mama Jamba?" Sophia asked.

Bermuda's eyes lit up and she grabbed a pen and began scratching words on a piece of paper. "Mama Jamba. Her real name. What a gift. I guess the answer is yes, then. I want to hear all about her. Is she as willowy as I imagine? Her hair full of green leaves and her clothes made of vines?"

Sophia hesitated. "Not exactly. In this current form, she's wearing velour tracksuits and looks like a retired Southern debutante. But she's amazing, maybe even more so because she isn't what you expect."

Bermuda smiled, a rare sight on the giantess's face. "I like it very much. One day, I hope to meet her and tell her how very much I enjoy her work."

Sophia nodded. "In the meantime, I'm working on a mission where I need to help a country to excavate natural resources, and I heard the rapoo could help."

"It's a genius solution," Bermuda stated. "You've got a good fairy godmother."

"Are there bad ones?"

Bermuda tilted her head back and forth, considering this question. "There are some who aren't as helpful. Maybe they are still training, and that's the reason for their gaps in knowledge."

Sophia laughed. "Wait, is there a fairy godmother college or something?"

When Bermuda didn't join in, Sophia stopped.

"Of course, there is," the giantess said quite seriously. "How else are they going to prepare for their role? I suspect you have training you have to complete before you can be a true dragonrider. Is that right?"

Sophia nodded, feeling disciplined.

"Well, why would it be any different for anyone else in a skilled position?" Bermuda questioned.

Sophia shrugged. "I guess I never thought about it." She made a mental note that she needed to find the fairy godmother college and take a peek. The possibilities of what she would see there were intriguing.

"Anyway, your fairy godmother is absolutely correct," Bermuda stated. "A rapoo would be ideal for mining gems. However, I've yet to actually find one."

"Oh, well..."

Bermuda turned her attention to the book beside her and flipped the page to a map. "But it's been on my list to study the creatures." She pointed to the center of the page where a particularly mountainous area was depicted. "If we go to this location, I think we might find the rapoo."

"Why was the map for that area on the next page?" Sophia asked.

Bermuda shook her head. "I was hoping you wouldn't have your sister's sense of humor. Oh, well, something to overlook, as long you don't suffer from an overuse of sarcasm."

Sophia nodded. "I'll keep the comments to myself when I can."

Bermuda took off her hat, looking around. "Well, then we'd better get off. The jungle will be getting dark soon, and this is the prime time to find a rapoo."

"You're going to go with me?" Sophia asked.

"Of course," Bermuda answered. "How else are you going to carry those creatures back on your own?"

"Right," Sophia said, feeling hopeful.

Bermuda's eyes fell on the book she'd been studying. "Oh, I almost forgot. Do you have a sword?"

Sophia pulled Inexorabilis from its sheath. "Will this work?"

The giantess took the sword, appraising it appreciatively. "Why, yes, I think it will. An elfin-made sword of the highest quality." She flicked her gaze to Sophia. "And you've already bonded with it. You make quick work of things that take old men much longer. I can already see that you'll be good for the Dragon Elite."

"Oh, well, thank you."

"And thank you for the sword. I'll be quick." Bermuda thrust the blade of the sword straight through the book, sending a bright light radiating around the room, followed by a crackling sound.

Sophia shielded her face as a cloud of dust shot from the pages, covering everything nearby. When it had cleared, Bermuda yanked the sword from the pages and shook her head.

"That should just about do it," the giantess said, handing the sword back.

"What was that about?" Sophia asked.

"Oh, isn't it obvious?" Bermuda asked.

"Not really…"

"The book had a contagious disease," Bermuda explained. "I extracted the information I could, and then it was time to end it before the plague spread to other books."

"Okay," Sophia said, her eyes large. It was odd when the bizarre world she'd known since birth surprised her.

With a keen eye on the sword, Bermuda said, "You'll probably want to keep that out. Where we are headed isn't a tame area and may be full of dangerous creatures."

CHAPTER SEVENTY-SEVEN

When Sophia stepped through the portal, she was surprised to find the giantess wearing khakis pants and top and a safari hat, although she didn't remember seeing her change before they left the British Museum.

The sounds of the jungle were deafening, full of the calls of the many creatures that resided there.

"Where are we?" Sophia asked, nearly having to yell to be heard over the birds squawking in the trees.

"China," Bermuda answered, looking around, her hands on her hips.

"China is sort of big," Sophia stated. "Anything specific?"

"The jungle portion," Bermuda stated matter-of-factly.

"Thanks." Sophia tightened her hand on the hilt of her sword, surveying the dense jungle around them. "What are we looking for?"

"Corns," Bermuda answered. "They densely populate the area around where the rapoo can be found according to my research."

"You mean corn? As in the vegetable?" Sophia asked.

Bermuda sighed. "No, corns. As in corns." She set off at once, trudging through the jungle, easily negotiating the large roots buckling out of the ground and the low-hanging branches.

Sophia had to hike herself up over the trees and duck to avoid hitting leaves. "I get that you think that explains what you're referring to, but I'm not following."

"You'll get it when you see them," Bermuda said, her voice distant as she stared around the jungle. It was streaked with shadows, different creatures lurking in the trees and foliage.

"I can't wait," Sophia said dryly.

"You're doing it," Bermuda warned. "That was one of those sarcastic comments."

"Sorry," Sophia said, looking around even though she had no idea what she was searching for.

"We are close," Bermuda said speculatively.

"To what?" Sophia asked. "The rapoo?"

"No, to the danger that protects their natural habitat," Bermuda said, sliding to the side and waving Sophia forward.

"You want me to go first?"

"I want you to go forward, period," Bermuda explained. "I'll hang back while you fight the beasts. Try not to injure them, though. I'll be here when you're done."

"Okay…" Sophia held her sword tentatively, wondering how she'd gotten herself into this predicament. She was grateful that Bermuda was leading her to the rapoo, but a little put off that she now had to fight mystery creatures.

She let out a deep breath, wondering if she should summon Lunis for help. Then a large pair of eyes peeked through the branches. They resembled the precious expression in a bunny rabbit's round eyes.

When the creature stepped forward, Sophia nearly doubled over from cuteness overload. It was a small panda with a unicorn horn on its head. A unicorn!

Before she could scoop up the creature and hug it to her, a dozen more pairs of eyes popped up, all with the distinctively cute quality of the panda-corn.

"Corns!" Sophia exclaimed, realizing what Bermuda had been referring to.

"Stay focused!" the giantess warned from several yards behind Sophia.

"Why, because I'm about to be smothered by cuteness?" Sophia asked, as the animals stepped forward one by one. There was a monkey-corn, a mouse-corn, a squirrel-corn, and many other hybrid creatures.

After having to face the evil unicorn known as the Phantom, Sophia welcomed this experience.

She squatted, smiling at the animals as they approached, seemingly curious about her, their little noses sniffing.

Sophia extended a hand. "It's okay, little ones. I won't hurt you."

"I wouldn't do that," Bermuda sang at Sophia's back.

She sighed. "Why? They are so sweet, with their shiny horns and eyes that make me melt."

The panda-corn was the closest. When it was inches from Sophia's fingers, its eyes flashed red, changing completely, and fangs shot out of its mouth, making it go from cute to incredibly dangerous in seconds.

CHAPTER SEVENTY-EIGHT

With a frantic jerk, Sophia launched herself back, holding Inexorabilis in front of her.

"Don't hurt them," Bermuda said casually from behind Sophia.

"Do you see the teeth on those furry demons?" Sophia scanned the jungle, watching as the cute hybrids bared their teeth, their eyes flashing red. "What if they tear into me? Then can I slaughter the monsters?"

"You can," Bermuda sang. "But then the rapoo won't cooperate. The corns protect them."

"And they do an excellent job." Sophia backed up as the creatures inched forward. "What's up with evil unicorns and hybrids lately? Did the Phantom infect these guys?"

"The Phantom?" Bermuda's voice rose an octave. "That's been dead since your mother killed it."

"I killed it again," Sophia muttered, considering her options as the creatures crowded her.

"Fascinating," Bermuda said, scribbling in her notebook. "I must spend more time with you, Sophia."

"Cool. Let's plan something when I don't die from vampire hybrid unicorns."

"And no, the Phantom didn't infect these creatures," Bermuda explained. "Like I said, their job is to protect the rapoo from danger."

"Why?" Sophia questioned, feeling like she was missing something.

"I'm not entirely certain, which is why I'm here observing. Remember that I haven't seen the rapoo yet, only heard rumors of them."

"And others who have tried to fight these creatures have failed to find the rapoo?" Sophia asked.

"Yes," Bermuda answered simply, continuing to scribble in her notebook. "From what I've read, they're near extinction, which is why the corns protect them."

"Weird partnership, but I like it."

"Legend has it that the rapoo mined most of the gems in this area, and when they did, they released the unicorn hybrids buried in the rock," Bermuda explained.

"So it's payback," Sophia mused.

"Yes, and now they protect the rapoo, who are nonaggressive, although they have very sharp teeth," Bermuda stated.

"What if I didn't fight the corns?" Sophia speculated, something working in her mind, although she was still uncertain.

When facing a dozen creatures with sharp fangs and evil red eyes, not being on the defensive felt wrong, but maybe that was the key.

She lowered her sword and all of the horned animals paused in their advance, eyeing her. Sticking Inexorabilis in the dirt, Sophia thrust her hands into the air.

All the creatures' gaze darted to the blade sticking out of the ground.

"I'm not here to hurt you or the rapoo." Sophia drew a breath as the animals blinked at her impassively. "The rapoo are dwindling because they are out of gems, aren't they?"

The creatures looked around at each other, their red eyes dimming.

Sophia heard Bermuda's pen scratch across the paper faster. "Oh, astute observation."

"They need to mine to prosper, don't they?" Sophia asked the animals, hoping this strategy paid off.

The creatures moved forward a few more inches, lining up to create a wall between Sophia and where she suspected the rapoo were located behind the dense brush.

"What if I had a safe place where they would be valued and could mine?" Sophia offered.

"Interesting…" Bermuda mused.

The corns' sharp fangs began to retract and their eyes returned to normal.

Sophia sucked in a breath, feeling like she needed to keep talking. "And once they've mined the area I have in mind, we can move them to a new location where they can excavate and thrive."

The creatures moved closer to one another, forming a solid line.

Sophia was missing something in this negotiation. The corns weren't menacing her, but they weren't relenting either.

"What if…" Sophia chewed on her lip, thinking. "What if you could accompany them?"

This created a stir among the animals. Sophia tensed, her eyes on her sword.

"You could protect them," Sophia offered. "And my friend here will be in charge of monitoring and moving you and them when their mines are empty."

"I don't believe I signed on for that," Bermuda said tersely.

"And I didn't know you were going to leave me to deal with dangerous unicorn hybrids while you took notes," Sophia said over her shoulder to the giantess.

"I'm a very busy woman and can't commit to this."

"Well, then I guess you can't accompany me on trips, and I won't be sharing the information I learned about the Phantom or other creatures…like dragons."

A long breath slipped from the giantess's mouth. "Well played, Sophia Beaufont. I think you might have gotten yourself a deal."

Sophia smiled. "I *am* an adjudicator. We are fantastic at making deals."

"The dragonriders I've known were fantastic at killing to make deals," Bermuda imparted. "This talking business is new to the Dragon Elite."

"Well, let's hope it works in this case," Sophia said, looking intently at the corns, who were peering at her tentatively. "Do we have a deal? We relocate you and the rapoo. You can protect them, and Bermuda will ensure you're safe."

Sophia wasn't sure what she expected. Maybe for a representative for the corns to step up and answer her formally. Instead, a cloud of gold dust circled over the heads of the animals. A small tendril reached out for Sophia. She tensed but remained frozen, wondering what was happening.

Behind her, Bermuda sucked in a startled breath as the wisp of golden dust reached around Sophia, tethering her to the animals. It was very similar to the experience when she had made her first deal between the villagers and the government in Brazil.

"The mark of a Dragon Elite deal," Bermuda said in a hushed voice, echoing Sophia's thoughts.

"So they agreed," Sophia realized as the giantess stepped even with her.

"Yes, and now it's time that we transport." She twirled her large hand and a huge crate materialized. "That will be for the rapoo."

"What about the corns?" Sophia asked.

"I think we both know they can't be caged," Bermuda answered. "But the rapoo prefer small compartments."

"Like caves," Sophia added.

"Exactly." The giantess snapped her fingers, and the door on the front of the crate opened.

Sophia ran her eyes over the corns, wondering what was supposed to happen next. On the heels of her thought, little creatures began to squirm across the jungle floor. They were the size of rats, but much cuter. The rapoo resembled honey badgers, with a long body and bear-like faces. They also had the badgers' coloring, white on the top and black on the bottom. It was hard for Sophia to think of these little guys as expert miners, but it made sense when she studied their long-clawed paws and rows of sharp teeth.

"Simply incredible," Bermuda whispered as the rapoo filed into the crate, making little squeaky noises, seemingly driven by an invisible force. When all of them were in the crate, Bermuda closed the door. There were only twenty, which was a low number. Hopefully, they would recover once they were in their new home in the country of Reerca.

Sophia created a portal, realizing that she'd be early for the meeting with the leaders of the two nations. Under-promise and over-deliver, she thought as she watched the corns jump through the portal, headed to their new home.

Bermuda shook her head, amazement on her face. "I've never seen anything quite like it."

Sophia smiled, allowing herself to feel proud at that moment. "I'm just glad this is all going to work out."

The giantess nodded. "You, as I suspected, will mark a new era of dragonriders. I have my worries about the future and this planet, but this gives me hope."

CHAPTER SEVENTY-NINE

"I don't think either Reerca or Thealth expected that resolution," Lunis said to Sophia as they entered the Barrier, fresh from their adventures.

"But how thrilled did the leaders of Reerca look when we unveiled the rapoo?" Sophia asked, proudly.

"I couldn't have considered a better solution," Lunis stated.

"I can't take credit, though," Sophia admitted, having missed the cold of the Gullington and the way the winds swept across the Expanse. "It was Mae Ling who gave me the information."

"Yes, but we should take credit for the partnerships that lead to our successes," Lunis instructed sagely. "Those in our lives directly reflect on us. You are the type of person who has a fairy godmother. Never discount the importance of that."

Sophia shrugged. "I'm not sure I understand the whole Mae Ling thing, but isn't it possible that I was given a fairy godmother because I'm such a mess and need so much help?"

"It's possible, but I suspect it's because you're destined for incredible things and are being given the resources to do them."

Sophia pulled her cloak tighter as she walked beside Lunis, headed for the Cave. She needed rest and food, but for the time being, she needed to be on the Expanse, staring at the Castle she'd missed. Any amount of time away from the Gullington was too much. Sophia knew that the Castle replenished and healed the riders, as did the Cave for the dragons, but there was more to it. The Gullington filled up Sophia's spirit, making her feel connected to the world in a way she'd never known before.

Letting out a breath, Sophia suddenly felt lighter. "I'm just grateful we found a solution that benefited everyone and avoided violence."

"It won't always be that way," Lunis warned.

"I know," Sophia said softly. "But for this time, the people of Reerca have a future, with an economy that is sure to flourish with an incredible new export."

"And they've created a viable partnership with Thealth," Lunis stated.

"Yeah, instead of negotiating border controls, we made it so the citizens of Reerca didn't want to emigrate."

Lunis looked at the Pond, an eager expression in his eyes. "And two peaceful nations sit side by side, a new promising partnership about to bloom between them."

"Right. And the rapoo population will hopefully recover," Sophia said, remembering watching the strange creatures mine for the first time. It had amazed everyone in attendance. Well, not the corns. They simply watched protectively, eyeing the humans with skepticism. Bermuda's presence seemed to put them at ease, and now that she had accepted her role in helping the rapoo, she and Sophia had struck a deal. It was amazing to her that solutions worked out for so many as a result of adjudicating a single conflict. It was unexpected and entirely beautiful.

"That's what we were born for," Lunis said, having spied Sophia's thought.

"I'm starting to understand that," Sophia began. "I guess I expected being a dragonrider would involve more battles than discussions."

Lunis watched as a flock of birds crossed the Pond, a hungry expression in his eyes. "History supports your perception."

"You're ready to hunt," Sophia guessed.

"That I am, but I'll stay with you until you're ready to go up to the Castle."

She smiled at him. "Thank you, but I'm okay." Her gaze caught Quiet, hurrying back from the Pond, taking the same path he had the last time she'd seen him nervously glancing over his shoulder. Similar to that last time, the gnome seemed worried that he was being followed or something.

"What do you make of his suspicious behavior?" Sophia asked Lunis.

"I think that if anyone will figure it out, it will be you," her dragon stated. "Now, I'm going to take you up on your offer and take my leave."

Sophia's stomach rumbled. "Eat a bird for me."

He shook his head. "Eat your own bird." Lunis launched into the air soundlessly, his blue wings a brilliant contrast to the gray sky.

Sophia was surprised that Quiet hadn't noticed them on the other side of the hill, but it was probably because he kept looking between the Castle and the Pond, missing them tucked into the rolling landscape.

Using her enhanced speed and stealth, she hurried across the grounds, approaching the gnome from the side. He put his back to her when she was only five yards away. His gaze jumped to Lunis in the sky before he swung around, his beady eyes connecting with Sophia's.

She halted, trying to appear inconspicuous. "Hey, there—"

Her words were interrupted by the gnome snapping his fingers and making her disappear.

Sophia sucked in a breath, nearly choking on it as she teleported and landed with a thud in the entry of the Castle.

Disoriented, she swung around, trying to get her bearings and feeling like her insides had been hung up to dry before being shoved back inside her.

Suddenly she was breathless, her chest rising and falling dramatically. "Why?" she asked herself, considering bolting back out of the Castle since the groundskeeper was definitely up to something suspicious.

"Why what, darling?" Mama Jamba asked, her slipper-covered feet scooting across the stone floors. She had curlers in her hair and a perspiring glass of iced tea in her hand.

Sophia blinked at Mother Nature. "You always know what's in my head before I do. Why are you asking when I suspect you already know what I mean by why?"

Mama Jamba laughed. "Because it's more fun if we actually have a conversation. Otherwise, it would be quite boring around here. And I don't actually know *exactly* what's in your head. For instance, I know that you're wondering a why connected to Quiet, but I don't know any more than that. Similar to Father Time, I can see things, but not everything."

"Oh," Sophia said. "I guess that makes sense. I was wondering why Quiet keeps transporting me when I sneak up on him and what he's hiding."

"Well, who likes to be snuck up on?" Mama Jamba reasoned.

"I get that, but he's suspicious." Sophia covered her mouth, something suddenly occurring to her. "Maybe he's hiding the *Complete History of Dragonriders*."

Mama Jamba took a sip. "Or maybe he's got stomach issues and you're catching him hurrying to the loo."

Sophia narrowed her eyes. "I don't think that's it."

"It could be," Mama Jamba stated. "I mean, no one wants anyone around them when they've got gas, and you're trailing after him."

"No, I think he's hiding something," Sophia mused.

"And why do you think he's hiding the *Complete History of Dragonriders?*"

"Well, because it's missing," Sophia explained. "And it's supposedly in the Gullington, and it's the one book that the Great Library doesn't have."

Mama Jamba's fingers slipped on her glass. She covered up the blunder, grabbing it with her other hand. "Napkin, Castle."

A moment later, a napkin appeared in the air.

"Thank you," Mama Jamba said, taking the piece of cloth and

wrapping it around the glass. "Now, I think you've got enough to worry about. You shouldn't be worrying about this silly book."

"It's not a silly book," Sophia argued. "Much of the history isn't in the incomplete version."

"Naturally, darling," Mama Jamba chirped. "Hence the name."

Sophia's eyes flicked to Hiker's study at the top of the stairs. That was where she was headed next, and he'd have some tough questions to answer.

"I just feel like there's an important reason the *Complete History* is missing," Sophia stated.

Mama Jamba suddenly appeared conflicted. "I don't like to tell those I love to avoid their feelings. However, in this case, I'd like you to focus your attention somewhere else. Not forever, but until the time is right."

"Why?" Sophia asked at once.

Mama Jamba smiled. "It is a child's prerogative to ask that incessant question, but it is a mother's right to say, 'because I said so.'"

"When will the time be right to look for the book?" Sophia asked.

Mother Nature held out her free hand and touched Sophia's chin, her fingertips warm even though they had just been wrapped around the cold glass. "You will know. Just as your body knows when to wake from sleep or eat from hunger, you will know. Simply listen."

CHAPTER EIGHTY

Hiker Wallace was peering out the tiny window in his office when Sophia approached. The office was still cramped, having shrunk recently, all the furniture crammed together. The bookshelves were still bare, the books having been removed by the Castle and not found, even after Ainsley's attempts to locate them.

For a moment, Sophia sympathized with the man before her. He wasn't from this era, and entering the modern world obviously wasn't easy for him. He'd lost so many in the five-hundred years he'd been on the planet. And she knew that he desperately wished the Dragon Elite was the way it had been, but there was no looking back.

And worse for the leader of the Dragon Elite was the newest realization that the last of the dragon eggs and the total of the dragon population mostly resided within the Gullington. Ten dragons. That's all that they knew they had.

However, for as much sympathy that Sophia had for Hiker, she also knew that he wasn't always trying hard enough. It was always one step forward and two back with him. He wanted to embrace the modern world but refused technology. He wanted the Dragon Elite to take back their roles as adjudicators but dragged his feet when it came to missions. And he was definitely hiding something, but what she didn't know was why.

Clearing her throat, Sophia stepped into Hiker Wallace's office. "I think I know why the Castle is punishing you," she said, striding into this study and halting just in front of the Viking.

He turned, a tired expression on his face. "Because it's a deranged old building whose only pleasure is to annoy me?"

She shook her head. "Because you're keeping secrets."

Hiker visibly stiffened. "Maybe. I have a lot of secrets. That's the role of a leader."

"Important secrets," Sophia added. "Things that we should know about. Things that affect the dragonriders and what we're out there facing."

"Look, Missy." Hiker strode to his desk, picked up a piece of paper, and then dropped it. "I'm responsible for the lives of many. It may not be as many as the Dragon Elite once had, but I'm still responsible for you and the men. And now that our role as adjudicators has returned, I can't allow you to be privy to everything. You may not like it, but that isn't my concern. It's keeping you alive, which means guarding knowledge."

"Good speech. However, I disagree," Sophia argued.

"Of course, you do," he growled.

"Yes, guarding information is important, but I think telling us Thad Reinhart was a dragonrider is pretty important too. Furthermore, I think hiding that knowledge could get us killed."

Hiker's gaze fell to the floor for a moment. "How did you hear about that?"

"So it's true," she stated, her eyes narrowing with defiance.

"Answer my question."

"It's in the *Forgotten Archives*," she answered. "There is a list of riders from before the Great War. You are on it, and Adam. Imagine my surprise when I saw Thad's name."

"I don't really want to." Hiker nodded, running his hands through his blond hair. "You have access to that text through the House of Fourteen, I suspect."

"I suspect it's in the Great Library too now, but that is irrelevant. Why didn't you tell us?" Sophia asked. "Do the other guys know?"

He shook his head. "And that is what is *not* relevant."

"Not relevant?" Sophia exclaimed. "Mahkah is still recovering from near-death after going to one of Thad's facilities. One of his magical tech jets killed Adam. Evan and I were nearly killed recovering those dragon eggs. We are looking at a war with Thad Reinhart. He's the reason this planet is in flux. I think pertinent details like the fact that he was a dragonrider should be shared."

"But you're not the leader of the Dragon Elite, are you?" Hiker questioned.

"No, I'm just a young, inexperienced woman who knows nothing about this world, except that you're covering something up."

He narrowed his light eyes at her. "What happened with your adjudication case? Why are you back so soon?" Hiker asked, obviously wanting to change the subject.

"I finished it," she stated, folding her arms over her chest.

"Finished it?" he questioned. "How?"

Sophia sighed dramatically. "The impoverished nation will soon be wealthy. The other nation will be partners with them. A species of animal is now looking at avoiding extinction. And the unicorn hybrids didn't kill me."

For a long moment, he studied her before letting out a long breath, relaxing slightly. "I'll need a full report on that. I want every single detail."

"I'll email it over," Sophia shot back defiantly. "What's your email address again?"

He picked up a piece of blank parchment and thrust it at her.

"What do you want me to do with that? Make you a paper airplane?"

He growled. "Write down your report. You know full well that I don't have email, nor will I ever."

Sophia sighed, taking the piece of parchment. "Fine, but you could at least try to embrace technology."

"Because some pain in my ass says so?" he fired back. "That's not how it works."

"Seriously," Sophia began, "Thad Reinhart was a dragonrider. We should be addressing that."

Hiker stormed to the other side of the room, his boots clomping on the floor. "There's nothing to address. He had a dragon. Thad was one of the corrupt ones. There's one or two in every batch. He got out of control. Something happened to his dragon and we thought that we killed the man himself, but obviously we didn't. And he's adapted."

"Adapted?" Sophia asked. "He owns several major corporations. He has magical tech. He's—"

"I'm aware that he weathered the storm better than most dragonriders during our blackout," Hiker interrupted.

"What happened to his dragon?" Sophia asked, realizing he kept talking about it in the past tense. It made sense to her that if this global leader was running corporations, it was because he didn't have a dragon, something that would keep him grounded to the Earth rather than sitting high in a skyscraper, as she pictured Thad Reinhart doing.

"She was killed," Hiker said, a new bitterness surfacing on his face. "It was an accident, but irreversible. After that, Thad went on a rampage."

"Oh," Sophia said, her heart suddenly aching at the thought. She couldn't imagine living without Lunis. And actually, she didn't think it was possible. "I thought that our lives were tied to our dragons'. How can he still be alive if his dragon is dead? In the *Incomplete History of Dragonriders*, it says that when one dies, the other quickly follows for one reason or another."

Hiker nodded. "That's the way it has always gone. I don't know how he's lived all this time without her. Thad must have figured out a way around it. He is obviously a master with magical tech. I'm guessing he found a workaround."

"And you're certain the dragon is dead?" Sophia asked.

Hiker bit his lip, his eyes distant. "I'm certain of it."

"Because you were there," she guessed.

"It's not important," he said, shadows of ghosts dancing in his eyes.

"Are there other relevant details you're keeping to yourself?" she dared to ask.

"You don't know what's relevant," he argued. "That's my job."

"I just want to be able to trust you."

He studied her for a long moment. "In my day, leaders didn't have to earn trust. Riders followed them simply because they'd earned that title. But you seem to be from this generation, which thinks I have to prove something to you."

"What's wrong with that?" she asked.

"It's against everything I've ever known," he boomed.

"But the world is different from what you've ever known," she argued.

Hiker shook his head. "We aren't discussing this anymore. And you won't tell the others about this Thad business."

"Why?" Sophia questioned.

"Because I said so," he fired back.

She shook her head. "You and Mama Jamba…"

"We know what's best, kiddo."

Anger rose up in Sophia, making her want to stomp her feet and yell, but that would only reinforce Hiker's point, so she tried to breathe through the fury.

Hiker thundered back over to his desk, picking up a folder. "You finished your case, and as promised, I'll allow you to go after the only dragonrider I can locate."

"What? You will?" she asked, shocked. Was Hiker trying to get her to forget about this Thad Reinhart business? Was he bribing her? Or was he simply a man of his word?

"Well," he said, drawing out the word. "I'll have to review the case you just finished, but it sounds like, despite my concerns, you solved it effectively enough, finding solutions for more than just the two related parties."

"And no one got hurt," she added.

He cut his eyes at her. "Sometimes, someone needs to get hurt."

"Maybe," she fired back.

"There's a lot that I don't understand about you, Sophia Beaufont. But the way you work your cases isn't one of them. I'll give you that. You're a good adjudicator, but you have much to learn."

"So do I have to complete my training before going after this lone rider?" she asked, taking the file.

He shook his head. "No, we don't have that kind of time."

Sophia rolled her eyes. "Hey, I'm back before the others from my case."

"My point," Hiker began, "is that I don't think you need to complete your training for this particular case. As far as I can tell, this lone rider is simply that. He's a loner, living away from society and of course, other dragonriders. He might be a bit inept with social cues, but we may be able to fix that over time. I don't remember much about him, but I'm willing to give him another shot if you convince him to return to the Gullington."

"So, you want me to persuade him to come back and give us another chance?" Sophia asked, thinking that sounded fairly easy.

"I want you to use your instincts," Hiker corrected. "If he doesn't seem stable, then you are to leave him. If he does, he can follow you back to the Gullington. Without you to guide him, he won't be able to find it since it is lost to those not welcomed by the Dragon Elite. But firstly, you must assess the situation. If he isn't right, we will cut our losses and figure things out on our own."

"What does that mean, sir?" Sophia asked, sensing a new tension in the Viking.

Hiker let out a long breath. "As far as I can tell, this is the only rider left."

"Besides Thad Reinhart?" Sophia clarified.

He nodded. "Yes, but Thad doesn't show up on the Elite Globe, which might mean others don't either. This is the only one I've been able to locate. His name is Gordon Burgress."

Sophia thought for a moment. "Why do you think that there's only one rider we can locate?"

"I don't know," Hiker mused. "I believe Thad killed most of them.

He hates every dragonrider. But more importantly, Thad hates the Dragon Elite with a vengeance."

"You're not going to tell me why, right?" she asked.

"He was a bad seed, that's all," Hiker answered. "But I don't know what happened to the other riders—whether they are out there, and I can't find them, or they are all dead. That's why you have to go and learn as much about Gordon as possible. I think he'll offer us answers one way or another."

Sophia pressed the folder with the information on the lone rider to her chest, grateful for the opportunity.

"Thank you, sir. I'll do my best."

Hiker nodded. "I have no doubt about that. It's just that your best and my way of doing things are different."

CHAPTER EIGHTY-ONE

The Rocky Mountains with winter approaching was about as unforgiving as the Gullington. Snow crunched under Sophia's boots when she and Lunis stepped through the portal.

Her dragon's face stretched with delight.

"Is this your first experience with snow?" she asked him, watching his eyes dazzle with curiosity as he dragged his claws through the untouched snow.

"In this lifetime," he stated, sounding like a typical dragon with his mysterious talk.

"It's cold, isn't it?" Sophia asked, looking at the stony mountains in the distance, heavy with snow. Where they were located, at the edge of a slushy lake, there was little precipitation on the ground, just a few patches of snow like where they were currently standing.

Evergreens created a barrier between them and the peaks. Sophia suspected that many woodland creatures hid in the forest around them, although it felt like they were a million miles from any living creature.

Sophia had gotten so used to the remote stillness of the Gullington, she realized right then how much she enjoyed it. For a girl who was born and raised in a city with four million people, it was strange to find solace in such a place.

She always thought she'd miss the hum of the highway, the background music of her life. She'd suspected that she'd miss the buzz and amenities of the city, but in actuality, she never even thought about it anymore.

Her heart was so full when she looked at the Expanse, knowing that the Castle was attempting to give her everything she desired, even if she was a thousand miles from modern society.

There was something very enchanting about that, she thought as she studied the Rocky Mountains before her.

"Saying snow is cold is like saying that sunlight is warm," Lunis said. "It's implied in the word."

"Well, I guess I'm not in the business of words, now am I?" she bantered.

Lunis stretched out his wings, the shimmering blue catching the waning sunlight. He was somehow more beautiful in this location, but Sophia couldn't pinpoint why.

"How do you suspect we are going to find this Gordon Burgress?" Sophia asked. "Do you have a dragon radar that leads you to other dragons?"

"If I did, it would be called drag-dar, but no, we don't have that," he replied. "The only one I can find no matter what is you."

"I guess that makes sense," Sophia offered.

"We're going to find the lone rider through tracking," Lunis explained. "Although the Rocky Mountains are vast, a dragon leaves behind many signs I should be able to find and follow."

"Yeah, that makes sense," Sophia muttered, scanning the area and feeling like they were being watched.

"We're not," Lunis stated, sensing her thoughts. "But there is something off about this area."

"Yeah, it's like there's electricity in the air," Sophia said, hearing a buzzing in her ears.

"You're right," Lunis agreed. "Something isn't right about this place. I feel it too."

"Maybe it's the lone rider," she offered.

He shook his head. "I don't think so, but he might be a part of it."

"Well, we will figure it out. Where do we start this tracking business?" Sophia asked.

"Look for a cave or broken trees or—"

"Or a dragon," Sophia interrupted, performing a quick tracking spell. As before, it created a trail of gold dust that snaked ahead of them, weaving through the trees and heading up the mountain in front of them.

Feeling proud of herself, Sophia smiled at her dragon.

"That's not going to work," Lunis said dryly, not as impressed as she thought he should be.

She scoffed. "Why not?"

At that moment, the trail disappeared.

"Because," he began, "those who don't want to be found will banish a tracking spell as soon as they notice it. And a lone rider and dragon who live far from society seem like the perfect candidates for that."

Sophia growled. "Case in point."

Lunis nodded. "And now they know we're here, so we've lost the element of surprise."

"Sorry, rookie mistake," Sophia grumbled.

"Your instincts are good," Lunis consoled. "I think you'll be excellent at tracking dragons once I teach you what to look for."

"Thanks, but I'm obviously no mother of dragons," Sophia said with a laugh.

Steam spilled from Lunis' nostrils as he shook his head. "You didn't just go there."

"I did," Sophia stated. "I think comparing our dragons to those in *Game of Thrones* is a way to really muddy things up in our present situation. I have many more references to keep you entertained as we trek through the forest."

"I beg you not to," Lunis said dryly. "For one, I still haven't seen the final season. And for two, it's highly offensive comparing real dragons to a fantasy series."

"I don't know," Sophia teased. "You totally ruined the end of *How to Train Your Dragon* for me."

"That's your fault for falling asleep during the movie."

"I was tired from training all day," Sophia argued.

"Also, I don't think Hiker appreciates that your studying involves watching cartoon movies about dragons," Lunis said.

"No, I'm certain he doesn't." Sophia giggled. "But that seething look he gets when I reference scenes from the movie gives my life purpose."

"You will probably be the death of that man," Lunis stated.

"Probably," Sophia said plainly. "But my hope is to get him to use an iPhone before that happens."

"And that will be what sends him over the edge," Lunis said with a laugh.

"Well, sooner or later, he's going to have to pick up that Kindle if he wants his books," Sophia related. "We will progress from there."

Lunis' intuitive gaze followed the trail that Sophia had illuminated before. "At least we know which direction to head."

"Yes, but do you think it's a problem that they know we are here?" Sophia asked, wishing she hadn't made that mistake right off the bat.

Lunis shook his head. "There's no way to know for sure, but from what Hiker said, this Gordon Burgress is a loner. He probably just wants to be left alone. But maybe he doesn't and is waiting to be found. It's hard to tell."

Sophia held out her arm. "Okay, well, lead the way, and show me about this tracking."

"Yes, you will need it to pass our training." The dragon started forward, leaving behind footprints in the snow.

CHAPTER EIGHTY-TWO

The forest quickly grew denser, the snow on the ground thicker. Still, Sophia and Lunis were enlivened by trekking across the Rockies, springing over fallen trees and trudging through the brush.

"Could that fallen tree be from a dragon?" Sophia asked Lunis.

He shook his head. "No, it's from a large drop of snow last year." He pointed out the way she could tell, and suddenly Sophia could see the cause and effect of different weather patterns around the mountain. The way the branches drooped told a story. The way the stream they hiked beside trickled down the mountain told her what lay ahead. Somehow, she understood her environment much more clearly after a small explanation from Lunis.

"That's how we work," her dragon said. "It only takes a small tidbit from me to illuminate a great deal for you. And of course, vice versa."

"Why is that?" Sophia asked, having to take five strides to each of his.

"Because what took me time to learn, is transferred to you instantly," he explained.

"And the same from me to you," she guessed.

"That's right."

Sophia turned when they reached a rare stretch of flat ground.

"Should we cover our tracks?" she asked, staring at the path they'd made. There were her footprints on one side and less distinct prints from Lunis, confused by his tail dragging behind him.

"I don't see why at this point," he imparted. "Gordon Burgress and his dragon already know we are here."

"Okay," she consented, turning back around and enjoying the fresh air on her cheeks, although it was growing colder as they progressed up the mountain.

"Now, there is your first evidence of our dragon and rider." He nodded in the direction of broken branches. "Notice how they are fresh, no snow covering them. And the distance between the two trees with broken branches is the right size for a dragon."

"Do you think they were through here since I used the tracking spell?" Sophia asked, running her hands over the broken twigs on one of the trees. A shock of electricity made her recoil.

Lunis gave her a cautious expression. "I don't think so. But that's not right."

She pulled back her hand, giving the tree an offended expression. "What's that about?"

"Maybe just an electrical storm," Lunis said, but he didn't sound confident.

"Could it be..." Sophia paused, not even wanting to say it aloud.

"How could they have magical tech?" Lunis asked boldly, saying what she was avoiding. "Gordon Burgress and his dragon have secluded themselves from society. I suspect he's far less progressive than Hiker, to be honest. I'm sure it's just static electricity."

Sophia nodded, but neither Lunis nor she believed that. Something wasn't right about this place, but there was nothing to do about it but stay observant and on guard. She consoled herself with the fact that of any of the dragonriders, she and Lunis knew best how to deal with magical tech.

They continued to follow a path up the mountain, encouraged forward by small clues that showed a dragon had progressed that way. It had to have been before the last snowfall since there were no footprints, just broken branches and trees pushed to the side.

"I haven't seen any caves," Sophia said through heavy breaths.

"Me either," Lunis stated. "But my assumption is that's where they are staying."

"Gordon and his dragon could have built something," Sophia offered. "And it could be shielded so we can't see it. A cave could be, for that matter."

"That's a good point," Lunis said. "We just have to pay attention to the clues. They will lead to them."

Sophia hoped he was right. She didn't want to return to the Gullington having failed. Yes, she'd been successful with her last mission, but that only put more pressure on her to be successful once more. She knew it was mostly self-imposed, but she felt a need to prove herself, not just to Hiker, but to everyone. It would probably take another century or two before that went away.

After nearly half an hour of hiking in silence, Lunis said, "Prints."

Sophia's attention snapped to large footprints in the snow that skirted around a copse of trees. She narrowed her eyes, wondering why they didn't seem quite right. "Those don't belong to a man."

"Nor to a dragon," Lunis offered.

"But they are fresh," Sophia said, using the information her dragon had given her to dissect what she was seeing.

Lunis swung around suddenly, his wings splaying, knocking snow at Sophia.

"Hey there!" she exclaimed, her voice echoing.

Having checked that their backs were okay, Lunis swung back around and laughed. His rider was covered in a thin dusting of snow, having been ambushed when he unfolded his wings.

"Are you laughing at me?" she asked, kneeling.

"No, I'm laughing at the other human woman beside you who's covered in snow," he said, continuing to laugh.

Sophia was quick to form a snowball, firing at him before he knew what she was doing. He pulled up his wing as a shield when she threw the ball at him.

"That's so immature, Sophia," he complained, but when he lowered his wing, he launched a dozen snowballs at her he'd formed while shielding.

Sophia dove behind the base of a tree, avoiding the brunt of the attack. "Are you serious, you little juvenile dragon?"

"I know you are, but what am I?" Lunis asked, a hint of mischief in his voice.

"Do you have another dozen snowballs ready to shoot at me?" Sophia asked, her back pressed into the tree trunk and a smile plastered across her face.

"More like a hundred, give or take," he answered.

Sophia looked at the single snowball she'd packed while standing there. "I vote we make a truce."

"Because you're about to be buried by snowballs?" Lunis teased.

"Because we are on a mission, Lunis," she stated.

"Fine," he acquiesced. "Go ahead and pretend to make the truce and then fire that snowball at my face like you were planning. Then we will progress as we should."

Sophia stuck her head out from behind the tree. "It's not any fun when you spoil it like that."

He shrugged. "Well, it's all spoiled by sharing headspace with me, so deal."

Sophia threw the single snowball at Lunis' head but he ducked in time, avoiding being hit.

Laughing, he looked over his shoulder to where the snowball landed and stiffened, seeing what had made the tracks they'd found.

Standing only fifteen yards away and looking hungry and angry was a large black bear.

CHAPTER EIGHTY-THREE

Sophia marveled at the sight of the huge black bear, having never seen one in person. She was grateful that between her and the massive creature stood an even bigger animal.

However, the black bear wasn't as deterred by the sight of the dragon as she thought he should be. Instead, the sight of the dragon seemed to enrage the bear, putting it on the defensive.

It rocked back on its hind legs, opening its mouth wide. A ferocious roar spilled out, echoing through the valley where they stood.

The ground shook under Sophia's feet when the bear dropped back onto its front feet, its body quaking from the movement. It was half the size of Lunis but had a menace she didn't think should be underestimated.

Lunis protectively turned his back to Sophia, facing off with the bear.

"Lun..." she said, a warning in her tone.

"He started it," Lunis remarked.

"He's a bear," Sophia argued.

"As long as he's challenging me and my rider, he's an enemy," the dragon said, lowering his head and taking a step forward.

The black bear didn't appear intimidated. It immediately shot forward, swiping its large paw through the air at Lunis.

The dragon darted to the side, throwing his wing up to hit the bear.

The beast jumped onto Lunis' back.

Sophia screamed and drew her sword, but she didn't know what to do. It was hard to differentiate the furry creature from her dragon as Lunis swung around, teeth chomping as he tried to grab the monster on his back.

The dragon's tail flew through the air, nearly hitting Sophia in the face. She dropped to avoid a collision, her face in the snow.

Lunis slung the bear off his back, sending the six-hundred-pound beast into a snowdrift nearby. An eruption of white shot into the air, blanketing everything in sight.

Lunis shook like a dog after a bath and shot a neat stream of fire at the bear, causing it to retreat up the mountain. The snow around them melted at once and a stream of water rushed toward Sophia.

She was still reeling from the strange sequence of events when she noticed something just above on the nearest ridge. For a moment, she thought the bear had stopped retreating and was spying on them from up high. Then she made out the distinct figure of a man with wide shoulders and squinted to get a better look.

It has to be Gordon, Sophia thought.

Lunis was checking himself, having received a few puncture wounds from the altercation. He wasn't looking when the man, covered in animal pelts and a long red beard, brought up a strange-looking device. Sophia at first thought it was a gun. She tensed, ready to dive out of its way, but saw it wasn't a normal gun. It was large and strangely shaped, and the thing that shot from it wasn't a bullet. It was a streak of electric blue, followed by a thundering sound.

"Lunis!" Sophia yelled, throwing herself on the dragon, which did little good since her body barely covered his.

He swung around as she slid off him, catching sight of the lone dragonrider headed east up the mountain. Lunis picked up his foot, about to start forward, when something sprang from the trees where Gordon Burgress had been stationed.

A yellow dragon, bigger than Lunis but not by much, rose into the air, a murderous sound spilling from its mouth. It focused its green eyes on Sophia and Lunis before flying off to the west, the opposite direction its rider had gone in.

Sophia and Lunis turned to each other.

"What just happened?" Lunis asked, still disoriented from the attack with the bear, his wounds fresh on his back.

"I don't know," Sophia answered. "Gordon shot us with something. Magical tech, I think."

"That doesn't make any sense," Lunis said. "And I didn't feel anything."

Sophia nodded roughly. "Yeah, me either, but we need to follow them."

"I agree," Lunis stated as he backed away, a careful expression in his eyes. "I'll follow the dragon. You go after the rider."

"Okay," Sophia said. "I'll find you. Stay in contact."

"Of course," he answered. "Always."

CHAPTER EIGHTY-FOUR

The sun was starting to set at Sophia's back as she followed Gordon Burgress' tracks. Being that they were fresh made, it was incredibly easy to follow him.

She moved quickly, keeping up easily with the lone rider, growing closer with each passing minute. Soon she'd be confronting him, and Lunis his dragon. She didn't know what he had hit them with, or even that he had, but that would be one of her first questions. How did a lone rider who lived off the grid have magical tech? Something wasn't right about the whole situation, but she'd figure it out once she had Gordon's attention.

He wasn't far, she realized, hearing his heartbeat as she drew closer. The lone rider was crouched behind a set of rocks, his breath shallow from running. He wasn't retreating any longer, which hopefully meant he knew it was time to surrender and talk.

Sophia let out a long breath. *I think I have him*, she telepathically told Lunis.

As usual, she expected him to answer right away.

He didn't.

She shook her head, wondering if the cold was starting to get to her. *Lun, have you closed in on the dragon?*

Again, nothing.

Her heart began to pound in her chest, and she wondered if something had happened to her dragon. She would know, though, she thought. She would feel it, wouldn't she?

Lunis, are you okay?

When the dragon still didn't answer, Sophia nearly turned back. However, she had tracked the lone rider and could hear the small noises echoing from him just ahead.

She slid behind a tree trunk, gifting herself a moment with her eyes shut. Taking that brief opportunity, she tried to scry her dragon, hoping to see what he saw and know what he was experiencing.

There was nothing. Just blackness.

Sophia's eyes popped open. It didn't make any sense.

And even worse was that now that she was paying attention, the pulse that had beat within her since the moment she'd magnetized to Lunis' egg, was gone. She didn't feel like a dragonrider. Instead, she felt the way she had for all her life up until the moment she met Lunis.

She felt normal.

Deep in Sophia's heart, she knew something very powerful had disconnected her from her dragon.

That was the worst possible scenario.

CHAPTER EIGHTY-FIVE

Whatever Gordon Burgress had hit Sophia and Lunis with had somehow severed their connection. No matter how hard she tried, she couldn't communicate with him. No matter how much magic she used, she couldn't scry his visions.

It was a waking nightmare, and worst of all, Sophia didn't know how to find her way to Lunis. He had taken off after Gordon's dragon in the opposite direction, while she'd followed the lone dragonrider for maybe a mile. After the chaos of the bear attack and appearance of the other rider, Sophia wasn't sure she could track her dragon. Worse, if something had severed the connection, could it ever be reinstated? She didn't know, and that almost broke her heart.

However, Sophia shook off the pain and focused on the present. Gordon Burgress would have answers. He'd have to. He was the one who'd hit them with something. What, Sophia didn't know, but the dragonrider wasn't backing down until she knew more.

Tearing forward, she felt a relentless force propelling her toward the man she'd thought she was recruiting but might be murdering before the night was over.

Few things made Sophia this angry, but the idea that someone had severed her connection with her soulmate made her extraordinarily dangerous.

Although she couldn't feel her dragon like she had before, she still had the gifts loaned to her based on their connection. She tore through the forest, streaking between the trees, sensing a presence just ahead.

The sound of Gordon's breathing echoed in her ears like he was right beside her. Each step reminded her of what had been stolen from her soul. Lunis was hers, and she was his. Somehow, something had torn them apart.

Magical tech, Sophia assumed, thinking of the strange gun Gordon had been holding.

But how had he gotten it? There were more questions for her now than ever.

As Sophia jumped over rocks and branches covered in snow, she ignored the fear in her heart and focused. She had to find Lunis. Reconnect with him, if that was even possible. And find out where Gordon Burgress had gotten such advanced magical tech.

CHAPTER EIGHTY-SIX

The yellow dragon, which Lunis knew to be Sulfur, streaked over the mountains, flying low.

It wasn't until the blue dragon realized he'd been led in a circle that he started to suspect something.

What's going on down there? Lunis asked Sophia.

No reply came back.

His gaze shot to the ground below, but he was too far from where he'd left his rider.

Sophia, Lunis called again, nearing the large yellow dragon.

She didn't reply.

Sophia always replied, he reasoned. Well, ever since they'd improved their connection to each other. Telepathic communication was effortless.

Lunis reasoned that it could be because of the terrain. Or she could be busy in battle, magic overwhelming her senses.

Following the other dragon, which wasn't moving fast but rather seeming to trail Lunis along, he tried to scry Sophia, seeing where she was and what was happening to her.

His vision remained his own.

That didn't make any sense.

SARAH NOFFKE & MICHAEL ANDERLE

Even if she was overwhelmed, he should be able to see through her eyes.

At that moment, Lunis knew one of the worst possible things had happened to him and his rider.

They'd been disconnected.

CHAPTER EIGHTY-SEVEN

Sophia leaped over a large boulder, spinning to the right and pulling Inexorabilis out and to the side.

Gordon Burgress didn't have a chance to react before she was on him, her sword inches from his neck.

He tensed, pressing into the large rock at his back. The whites of his eyes were large as his gaze darted to the side, his neck not turning, fearful any movement would get his throat slit.

"What have you done?" Sophia asked through clenched teeth, her arm extended straight, each muscle in her body ready for the fight she was sure would come.

The lone dragonrider narrowed his eyes at her. "I don't know."

She blinked with confusion. "How can you not know?"

His face constricted.

Sophia pulled her sword back, offering him some room, but still keeping proximity.

"I don't know," he repeated. "I awoke the other day, and I haven't been the same. Who are you? Why have you come after me?"

The hint of crazy in the man's voice was palpable. Maybe he hadn't been right in the head for a while, or maybe whatever had happened to him recently was responsible. Sophia had never seen the deranged look that bounced around in his eyes before. Gordon Burgress had his own unique brand of crazy.

"Where's the weapon that you used on us?" Sophia asked, running her gaze over the man's clothes. He had a short knife strapped to his belt. His clothes were dirty and worn, and his hands were covered in scratches. His eyes were sunken, and his lips cracked. This wasn't a man who'd had an easy life.

He shook his head. "I threw it. I don't know where it is."

Sophia's hands tensed on her sword, brandishing it closer to him, making him straighten. "What did you hit us with?"

"I-I-I don't know," he stuttered.

"How can you not know!" she yelled, her voice echoing all around, making a flock of birds lift from the trees, sending snow down to the forest floor.

"I don't know!" Gordon answered. "I awoke the other day, and I knew that if I saw anyone, I was to shoot them with that weapon. I don't know where it came from or even how I knew how to use it. Sulfur and I have been in a daze for days. Something happened to us..."

Sophia carefully considered what the lone rider was saying. "Do you want help?"

It was hard for her to consider this since this man had done the most detestable thing to her, but her instincts told her he was innocent, although he still had that deranged expression in his dark eyes.

"You can't help me," he moaned.

"I'm with the Dragon Elite," she stated, lowering her sword slightly. "I think your mind has been poisoned. I think someone has pitted you against us."

"Maybe," Gordon answered, his eyes following her sword before rising back up to look at Sophia. "How do I know it wasn't you? I've been alone up here all this time, and now this is happening."

"It wasn't us," Sophia argued. "We are here to help. I came for the express purpose of asking if you wanted to join us. There's a war brewing, and we can use every dragonrider out there."

"I never wanted to be a Dragon Elite," Gordon answered. "Sulfur and I are better off alone. We always have been."

"Why?" Sophia asked, perplexed by this and wishing Lunis was in her head, offering insights. It made her ache all over not to feel her dragon. "We are stronger when we stand together."

A cold laugh issued from the man's mouth. "That's what Hiker Wallace would have you believe, but he's wrong. He was then, and if he still lives, he is now. He gave me that speech once, and it fell on deaf ears."

"I don't understand," Sophia said. "How can you not want to be a Dragon Elite?"

Gordon shook his head, his shifty eyes roaming over her sword and then her body. "I was not born to serve humanity. Neither was Sulfur. We both know that to be true. We were born to serve each other."

Right then, Sophia understood Hiker Wallace better than she ever had. He had been right to disqualify Gordon Burgress. This man wasn't a team player, as adjudicators needed to be. He only cared about himself and his dragon.

For some reason, Sophia had thought all dragonriders were good, born with the express intention of solving the world's problems, but now she knew that wasn't the case. There were some like her and Wilder and Mahkah, and even Evan, who wanted what was best for the world at the expense of their own safety. And then there was Gordon Burgress. There was Thad Reinhart. There were those who, as Hiker had stated, were born bad.

It hurt Sophia's heart that she'd pushed this mission. Asked for it. Gone for it. And now she'd lost the most important thing to her and learned a devastating truth.

Gordon Burgress couldn't come back to the Gullington with Sophia. He was best suited as a lone rider, as he had been. She was ready to back away and search for her dragon, repairing whatever had been done to them.

Sophia would have left Gordon there, even after what he'd done.

She truly didn't believe he was responsible for it. She figured he was a pawn, and Thad Reinhart was somehow behind him.

She was not given the choice to leave because while her thoughts roamed over all the details she'd learned, Gordon made his move.

CHAPTER EIGHTY-EIGHT

Lunis' mind screamed with panic. He was about to turn back in the direction of Sophia, knowing that he needed to find her.

However, Sulfur, the yellow dragon with an overwhelming spark of evil in her eyes, turned and shot fire at Lunis.

It was a quick movement, so fluid he almost didn't have time to react and avoid the attack.

She was fast. He had to give her that.

Rolling to the side, Lunis sped out of the path of the fire.

The last thing he wanted to do right then was battle another dragon. He wanted to find Sophia. Reconnect with her.

Sulfur had another agenda, though, and there was no getting away from it as she flew toward him, her neck craned to the side and pure craziness in her eyes.

She, like her rider, had been born bad.

Lunis knew that instinctively. Those two were better off alone.

But something had found them before Lunis and Sophia.

And now they were paying the price for it.

CHAPTER EIGHTY-NINE

The lone rider knocked into Sophia so hard that her vision went black momentarily. When she shoved up from the hard, cold ground, Gordon was bearing down on her with his knife, murder in his eyes.

Regret filled her at the thought that she'd sympathized with the man. He was deranged, that much was clear. He had been since Hiker had rejected him, and whatever had infected him recently had made matters worse. Regardless, there was no saving this man, and he might have just ruined everything for Sophia and Lunis.

She tensed on the ground, the weight of the man atop her making it hard to breathe. Her hand was still on Inexorabilis but with the huge man pressing into her, she couldn't maneuver her sword into place.

Gordon rammed his knee hard into Sophia's gut and her breath spilled out of her. She coughed, trying to struggle free.

Magic escaped her, outrun by her fear. That was always the easiest solution. Just summon the magic and fix problems. The caveats were always that magic couldn't be used when fear was too high, stress was overwhelming, or the body was at a total disadvantage.

Gordon bore down on Sophia, bringing the blade of his knife to her throat, similar to what she'd done to him upon their meeting. "How do you like it now?" he asked, spitting in her face.

She shook her head, reaching out for Lunis and not finding him. Sophia had nothing. Her sword was in her hand, unable to help her. Her dragon was somewhere close, unable to find her. And her magic was pulsing in her veins, unable to surface.

Sophia had everything, and also, she was completely screwed.

CHAPTER NINETY

The yellow dragon slammed into Lunis, knocking him into the side of the mountain. That sent a barrage of snow down, covering him and making his wings ineffective.

He tried to press up, but Sulfur sent a huge wave of fire at him.

Thankfully, it melted the snow pinning him, but it also scorched his skin, burning him and sending him back down to the ground.

He had to fight, but finding the advantage when he was simply a dragon was difficult.

It was at that moment that Lunis recognized how fortunate he'd been from the beginning.

Many dragons lived centuries before electing to choose a rider. He'd found Sophia early on because he believed that if soulmates existed, she was his and he was hers.

But they hadn't known life as dragon and magician separate from each other. Not really. Dragons elected to have riders because the bond made them both stronger. And when dragons magnetized to a magician, it was purely a gift for the human, lengthening their life-span, enhancing their senses, and increasing their skills.

The partnership was mutually beneficial. Dragons understood so much more when connected to a rider. They lost the savage part of their being and sank deep into the roots of humanity, connecting to the planet in a new way. Making them better. More conscious. More fulfilled.

Lunis and Sophia had had that from the beginning. To not have that now felt like a curse. Lunis was nothing without Sophia. He might have power and strength, but she was his heart, and that was everything.

He closed his eyes for a moment, trying yet again to reach out to her. Feeling nothing. Feeling hopeless.

Sulfur sent another attack his way, and Lunis knew he had to fight or lose the love of his life forever.

The blue dragon shook off the snow and launched into the air, even though he already felt defeated.

We aren't out until the end. I will never give up as long as my Sophia is out there.

CHAPTER NINETY-ONE

There were no options for Sophia. She was close to death. One more inch and Gordon would cut her throat. She knew it. He knew it. And if Lunis was there...well, he would have saved her. But that option was gone, maybe forever.

Gordon leaned down, his breath cascading into her face. "You want death, but that's too easy."

Sophia looked into his eyes and noticed the tiniest difference. He was him and slightly different. Was it possible that whatever had taken him over before was back, summoned for some reason?

"Don't kill me," she found herself begging.

He laughed. "I have no plans to kill you. My orders are to allow you to live, losing everything you hold dear."

With that, Gordon Burgress released Sophia and stood over her, evil heavy in his eyes.

"You are now as cursed as anyone else who has loved and lost," he said, and then the lone dragonrider disappeared.

CHAPTER NINETY-TWO

Just when Lunis expected Sulfur to attack him again, the yellow dragon disappeared. He didn't know where she went or if he'd blacked out. He was having a hard time trying to assimilate time.

And then the worst possible reality occurred to him. Without his rider, Lunis would perish. Even if Sophia was alive, their connection was what held them to this Earth. Without that, they'd lose their hold on reality. They would black out. They'd hallucinate. They'd forget each other until they were nothing.

That was the new reality he was presented with, and it was the worst he could ever consider.

It startled Lunis when he realized why Sulfur had abandoned their fight. She wasn't bowing out. She simply knew the damage had already been done, and she'd left him with his broken heart to suffer alone.

The blue dragon tried to stand, and although nothing was wrong with his legs, he found the task incredibly difficult.

Without her, he was powerless. He was weak. Sophia was his life force, and he hers.

But how would they ever find their way back to each other?

Someone had split them in two when they should be one. Lunis had to fix it. He had to figure out a way to put them back together.

Lunis would destroy the world if that was what it took. He hoped it didn't because the irony was, destroying the world would cut Sophia away. That's how good she was. But Lunis would do anything for her.

There was no world without Sophia Beaufont.

CHAPTER NINETY-THREE

S ophia stumbled through the snow as if she were drunk, trying to find her way home. But she wasn't drunk, and there was no home to return to—not without Lunis.

She staggered, trying to clear her vision and see the path ahead. There had to be a way to find her dragon.

He'd taught her to track just recently. She knew his tracks better than anyone, but there was so much that muddied the way she'd come.

Gordon had run through there. She had. And then there were deer and bears and whatnot.

Sophia shook her head, willing herself to stay lucid, although that seemed to be waning by the moment.

She didn't know why, but she was losing her hold on the Earth. She felt like she was dying. Gordon hadn't cut her. There were no lethal wounds on her body, and yet she felt minutes from death.

Stumbling around a copse of trees, Sophia found the place where the bear attack had happened. That was enough to fill her with hope, although she quickly realized Lunis had long ago left that spot.

He'd flown, she believed, because there were no other tracks leading away from the incident.

Her heart slumped in her chest. Since Lunis had flown, tracking him would be impossible. Her magic was failing her, and her spirit was close to zero. Portaling wasn't even an option, not that she'd choose it and leave Lunis. Even if they couldn't find one another, she wouldn't abandon him. She'd stumble around in the snow until she found him or died.

For Sophia, the idea that she was alone scared her more than anything else in her life. It was worse than the idea of starvation, freezing to death, or being murdered by Gordon. Being separated from Lunis was worse than losing her parents, her siblings, or her desire to be a part of the Dragon Elite.

Sophia had never been so low, but she had no idea that things were quickly about to change.

CHAPTER NINETY-FOUR

Lunis wasn't connected to Sophia anymore. He knew that. He'd tried incessantly to feel her. To talk to her. To do anything, and it hadn't worked.

But when he rose into the air and saw the most beautiful person in the world stumbling around in the snow, he knew it was his Sophia.

With fervent desire, he dove in her direction, hoping the connection would return as he neared her. When it didn't, Lunis worried that whatever magical tech had robbed them of their bond had erased it for good. He hadn't even thought something like that was possible, but technology changed everything. Maybe that was why the other dragons were so much against it? But how could you fight and negotiate in the modern world without technology?

Heartbroken, Lunis slid into the snow, sending a wave of it over Sophia, blanketing her in a sheet of white.

He halted, ready to be punished.

The woman before him was covered from head to toe in white snow, only her eyes and pink lips visible.

She blinked at him, and Lunis held his breath.

With an angry shake, Sophia threw the snow off her, returning to her normal appearance, although her hair was damp and her body shaking with cold.

"Soph…" Lunis said, feeling the desire for their connection, and yet not feeling the actual thing.

CHAPTER NINETY-FIVE

Sophia tried to blink. Tried to breathe.

She could see the blue dragon before her, but she couldn't feel the waves of emotions that had always been tied to him.

Looking at Lunis, she felt nothing.

It wasn't like she was staring at someone else's dragon. It was more like she cared little for the magical creature. She was completely ambivalent toward him and his species.

How could she not feel something her head told her she should? How could she make herself feel that connection again? Was it possible to force love, or had dragon and rider simply fallen out of love, with no way for redemption?

Night had fallen over the Rocky Mountains, and stars were starting to wink in the dark blue sky.

Sophia didn't dare say a word to the ancient creature staring at her. She could feel his grief, but not in her heart like before. Instead, it was her intellect that told her of his pain. She could see it in his eyes, and she felt that it was mirrored in her own.

So badly she wanted to make herself love him like she used to. So badly she wanted to hear his voice in her head, but the more she tried to force it, the farther the feeling seemed to slip from her.

Then, quite suddenly, a passage she'd read in one of her mother's books came back to her, written by Sham of Tabrizi. The words flowed to her as if she'd read them moments prior.

Intellect and love are made of different materials. Intellect ties people in knots and risks nothing, but love dissolves all tangles and risks everything. Intellect is always cautious and advises, "Beware too much ecstasy," whereas love says, "Oh, never mind! Take the plunge!" Intellect does not easily break down, whereas love can effortlessly reduce itself to rubble. But treasures are hidden among ruins. A broken heart hides treasures.

She sucked in a breath, allowing her heart to feel broken. It truly was. She gave way to reason and dropped to her knees, looking up at the dragon before her.

Bowing her head, Sophia allowed her heart to ache for the grief she was feeling. She saw herself standing on a cliff, ready to jump regardless of the repercussions. That was love. It was taking the plunge with no care for the pain one might endure.

With her eyes closed, she saw a light spray across her vision. Thinking she was hallucinating, she opened her eyes to find a crescent moon rising over the mountains.

Somehow the small glowing moon was more beautiful than she'd ever seen. It seemed to outshine even the fullest moons she'd observed. Even though the moon was incomplete, it was strangely perfect.

Deep in her heart, she felt waves connecting her to the cycles of the moon. And she felt the moon as if it were her, rising on a clear night. She was brand new, and dictating the seasons and the tides. She was a crescent moon, consciously growing larger each night.

Rising to her feet, Sophia stepped forward, feeling possessed by the moon.

So badly had she wanted to become one with Lunis, but he wasn't her, and she wasn't him. Sophia had been wrong all along. She'd always thought Lunis was tied to the moon, but that wasn't the case entirely. It was Sophia who was tied to the moon, and Lunis was tied to her.

They were two halves. She was the crescent moon and him the night sky, and together they formed a whole.

With a force she didn't control, Sophia stuck her hands out, grabbed the giant dragon's head, and pulled it closer.

It was like touching Lunis for the first time, but she knew it wasn't. When they touched, something changed.

At first, Sophia thought she was wishing it into existence, a part of her imagination. Yet the more she held the dragon's face in her hands, the more it intensified, until something encircled them, making her connect with the dragon she'd known most of her life without knowing him entirely.

Her heart was instantly full, her mind crammed with knowledge she thought she'd lost. And her being raced with impulses she knew weren't her own.

"Lunis," she said aloud.

In her head, she heard the most beautiful reply.

I'm here, Sophia.

How? she asked, perplexed.

He simply blinked at her, his eyes like her soul staring back at her.

They erased us, she argued. *How did you come back to me?*

Lunis nuzzled his face into her hands. *There are some things that can't be erased. I think they tried, but it didn't take because what we have is stronger than any magical tech on this Earth.*

CHAPTER NINETY-SIX

"They are still out there," Sophia said to Lunis, knowing she didn't need to expand. He knew who she was referring to.

"We have to let them go," he answered. "Gordon and Sulfur are no good for the Dragon Elite."

"I agree," she stated, leaning against her dragon, needing to be close to him. "However, we have to find the magical tech they used and destroy it. We can't allow what they did to us to happen to the others. What if the moon hadn't come out when it did? What if you'd never found me again?"

He rotated his head, pressing it into hers. "We didn't need the moon to reconnect, Sophia. We are connected in our souls. That magical tech was never going to work entirely on us. I suspect it won't work on the others either, but I agree with destroying it."

"Gordon didn't make it," Sophia imparted.

"No, of course not," Lunis stated. "This whole thing reeks of Thad Reinhart."

"We can discuss that more when we return to the Gullington," Sophia said, climbing onto her dragon's back. "For now, I want to find Gordon and Sulfur. They aren't right, although it may not be their fault, we can't allow them to spread this evil. It's our civic duty to stop them and recover that magical tech."

Lunis didn't have to agree for her to know he was on board. Instead, he rose into the air, willed by Sophia's intentions.

The cold mountain air was refreshing as they flew around the lake, looking for signs of the other rider and dragon. Their enhanced vision made it easy to see the battles that had happened in the snow on the ground.

Thoughtfully, Sophia touched one of the wounds on Lunis' back from either his fight with the bear or with Sulfur. She wanted to erase his pain but knew that it was important. What had happened to them in the Rocky Mountains had brought them closer. It had made them stronger, and one day, it would save their lives. That was how pain worked.

The Cave will fix me, Lunis assured her, knowing she was worried about his wounds.

She nodded, looking forward to returning to the Gullington.

There was where we were shot, Lunis stated, directing Sophia's attention toward the clearing where the bear attack had happened.

The dragon landed easily in the thick pile of snow, sinking deep.

"Gordon was stationed over there." Sophia pointed to the area where the rider had been when he shot them. She hurried, her boots plunging through the snow. Compared to how she'd felt when severed from Lunis, she was completely different. Energy pulsed through her, pushing her forward.

Sophia was almost to the trees where Gordon had been hiding when the lone rider stepped out again, once more aiming the magical tech at her and Lunis.

She froze, her hand instinctively darting to her sword.

"Don't do it, or I'll shoot you again," he said with a growl.

"It didn't work," Sophia exclaimed. "Hand it over, and you won't be harmed."

A loud laugh echoed across the valley. "What are you, two decades old? Some brand-new rider is going to beat me? I let you go before, but—"

"You thought you'd done the worst thing ever to us by severing our connection," Sophia interrupted. "You didn't let me go. You wanted me to go on, feeling punished."

Gordon shook his head, confusion in his gaze. It was like he knew what he was doing one moment and then forgot again.

"Yes, sever your connection." He looked at the device in his hands. "That's what this does. And it will again."

"It won't work," she argued. "No one has to get hurt." Even as she said the words, she knew they weren't true. Something had corrupted Gordon, and it was taking possession of him. She could see it as his eyes shifted and grew darker.

"You, little girl, can't hurt me." He fired just as a dark shadow crossed overhead, blanketing them in partial blackness.

Sulfur dove from overhead, hovering just beside her rider. He grabbed her reins and threw himself onto her back, all the while staring at Sophia with a murderous expression.

"I am no little girl!" she yelled. "But I'm proud to say I am a woman. And I'm about to kick your ass!"

CHAPTER NINETY-SEVEN

Sophia and Lunis didn't say a word to each other. Intuitively, they knew what would happen next. Sophia hadn't yet been successful at the running take off, but that was the best and fastest option right then.

It was similar to how Gordon had just gotten onto his dragon, but it would require that Lunis didn't stop.

Sophia felt her dragon running at her back. She didn't turn to look at him. Instead, she sprinted forward, picking up speed. When he was beside her and about to pass, Sophia dove for him, her hands clenching on the saddle.

Lunis lifted into the air, and for a moment, Sophia dangled from him as he rose, his wings beating below her.

With brute strength, and in one movement, Sophia hiked herself up, pulling her leg around and sliding over the back of the saddle and into place.

She leaned forward, grabbing the reins in one hand and pulling her sword with the other.

Well done, Lunis commented as he rose higher, gaining on Gordon and Sulfur.

Sophia's heart was beating so loud in her chest that it vibrated her

417

teeth. *Thanks,* she said, wondering what their next move would be. They had to get the magical tech, and something told her that they had to do something they both would rather not—but that was part of being a dragonrider. There weren't always peaceful solutions to problems. Sometimes ending those who would only further corrupt was the only option.

Sensing her thoughts, Lunis said in her mind, *I bet you wished you'd practiced more flight combat now.*

Great timing, she replied. *Thanks.*

No problem, he said with a bit of mischief. *But don't worry. They may be stronger, bigger and more experienced—*

If you're trying to make me feel better, it's not working, she cut in.

I was going to say, they will be all brute force, Lunis finished. *We can find the advantage, and when we do, we'll use it.*

Okay, sounds good. Sophia steered her dragon over the glistening mountain peaks reflecting the glow of the crescent moon hanging in the sky.

Gordon and Sulfur weren't far. The rider kept looking over his shoulder, fear growing in his eyes as they closed the distance between them.

What's the plan? Sophia asked Lunis.

Attack, he said simply.

Sophia sighed. *Wow, thanks for that. I was thinking more about that whole strategy thing.*

Oh, right, Lunis said. *Hold onto your butts.*

Seriously, you're not allowed to watch that movie anymore, Sophia said, tired of hearing about how sad it was when the T-Rex died in *Jurassic Park.*

They are one of our distant relatives, Lunis argued. *It makes me sad.*

Sophia leaned down, bracing herself, feeling the shift in Lunis just before he made his first move.

CHAPTER NINETY-EIGHT

Fire burst out of Lunis' mouth, stretching across the sky and nearly hitting Sulfur's tail. The dragon darted to the side to avoid it. Simultaneously she turned, launching her own attack on Lunis and Sophia.

He dove to miss the assault, but still the heat and flames grazed them.

I didn't need both eyebrows, Sophia related as they regained their speed.

I don't have eyebrows, Lunis commented. *Why do you?*

Because I'm a human with hair, Sophia said, silently encouraging her dragon to gain on the pair in front of them.

I think you'd look better with horns, Lunis commented.

You would, Sophia replied as Gordon turned and shot the magical tech device at them.

Lunis dropped suddenly, diving toward the ground to avoid the collision.

They might have proven they could restore their connection to one another, but now wasn't the time to get disconnected. Sophia never wanted to experience that loss again. She was sure the scars were etched on her heart.

Twice more, Gordon fired at them, making Lunis lose the distance he'd gained on Sulfur.

We need to get that device from him, Sophia told him, trying to think. *Can you get on top of them?*

You don't think it can shoot upward? Lunis questioned.

Not from what I've seen, she said tentatively. *Those pulses seem to drop, almost like it's weighted.*

Lunis carried them high into the clouds and Sophia was instantly drenched in cold wetness. Her vision was partially obscured as they passed through a particularly large cloud. When they came out on the other side, she was grateful to find that they had made up the space and were now overhead of the pair.

Gordon and Sulfur had lost sight of them and they looked around madly. Their searching was slowing them down, which gave Lunis an advantage. When another thick cloud passed overhead, Lunis shot up like a missile, hoping the dense haze would obscure them if Gordon and his dragon were to look up.

The blue dragon opened his mouth, shooting fire just before they were about to be close enough to attack.

The blast hit the dragon and rider straight on, making them tumble to the side. Gordon dropped the magical tech as he sought to hold on while Sulfur rolled to extinguish the flames.

Sophia held out her hand, summoning the strange device to her, and it flew to her. She hated the way it felt in her grasp, but she ignored it and slipped the magical tech into her wa. There was no way she was releasing it and allowing it to get into the wrong hands.

She would have considered portaling home, but Gordon and Sulfur had recovered and were angrier than hell, barreling after them. The yellow dragon shot fire at them many times, but their vantage point above them was working to their advantage.

Each time a dragon shot fire, it slowed them down slightly. The last time Sulfur attempted to attack, Lunis dove for her, his claws aiming for one of her wings.

The ripping sound and the scream of the dragon echoed in Sophia's head as they darted to the side. She stood on the back of her dragon, bringing her sword around as Gordon reached for her. The dragons were flying side by side, snapping at each other, their claws trying to find a place to attack, their wings flapping and tangling with one another.

The riders were jostled around until the dragons leveled out, Sulfur suffering from her damaged wing and burns.

Gordon stood with his chin down and eyes evilly pinned on Sophia. She faced him, her gaze unrelenting.

With her sword in both hands, she let out a long breath, knowing exactly what was coming next. It was a risky move, but battles were about doing the unexpected to hopefully take the advantage.

CHAPTER NINETY-NINE

Lunis threw his weight to the side, getting Sophia close to Gordon. The other rider hadn't expected that, and he faltered backward as Sophia swung Inexorabilis. His chest collapsed to avoid the assault.

He recovered quickly and jabbed his knife at her gut. Sophia's connection with her sword seemed to take over and she lifted it at precisely the right moment, knocking her elbow down on Gordon's forearm and making him drop the knife. It passed Lunis and fell to the ground below.

The blue dragon then grabbed Sulfur with his claws, pinning her legs to her body, making it hard for her to fly, especially with her injuries. The motion sent Gordon stumbling back. He probably would have caught himself if Sophia hadn't spun and launched a kick at his chest. When her boot was almost there, she added a magical boost to the combat move, sending him flying off his dragon and fifteen yards through the air, at which point he fell toward the ground.

Sulfur jerked, realizing what had happened, and tried to dive for her rider. However, Lunis still had one of her legs pinned. She snapped at him, trying to free herself, but he didn't release her until

Gordon had reached the ground. Only then did Lunis push her away, flying in the opposite direction.

The yellow dragon wasn't coming after them for retaliation. She could have, but her only focus was on her rider, who had fallen to his death. That meant that Sulfur would soon die too.

When Sophia and Lunis were a safe distance away, she opened a portal.

It's time to go home, she said to her dragon.

I've been wanting to return to the Gullington, he replied.

Me too, she said, settling back down and resting her face against his neck.

True love felt like home, and for the rest of her life, Sophia would always have that, as long as she and Lunis had one another.

CHAPTER ONE HUNDRED

Sophia trudged up to Hiker's office, storming straight in and interrupting a meeting he appeared to be having with Mama Jamba. The rider dropped the magical tech on his desk, making a clattering sound.

Mother Nature sat back in her armchair, giving Sophia a pleased smile. "Good to see you made it back."

"Barely," Sophia stated.

Hiker shot the device a repugnant expression, pushing it away with the tip of his pen. "What's that?"

"It's magical tech," she explained, taking a seat, exhaustion starting to overwhelm her. Lunis had gone directly to the Cave upon returning since his wounds needed to be looked after. Sophia had come straight to Hiker's office, ignoring Ainsley, who'd asked if she'd order from UberEATS since she was too tired to cook.

"I get that it's magical tech," Hiker said, pushing away from his desk. "It reeks of the stuff. Why did you bring it back here? You know how I feel about it."

"Because knowledge resides in investigation," Sophia stated. "We need to know what we're up against, and the only way we can do that is by dissecting what's out there, meant to destroy dragons and riders."

Mama Jamba arched a manicured eyebrow at her, looking impressed.

"How do you know this is aimed at destroying us?" Hiker asked.

"Because," Sophia began, "that device severs the connection between a rider and a dragon."

"Oh, dear me," Mama Jamba said, cupping her hand over her mouth.

"Seriously?" Hiker exclaimed, backing even further from his desk. "How dare you bring this in here! What were you thinking?"

Sophia wanted to laugh at Hiker's reaction, but that might also be due to the exhaustion. "It won't work unless Bell is with you. Lunis and I were hit at the same time, which is why I suppose it worked. However, I want to do more research. I think my sister can help."

"You and Lunis were hit?" Mama Jamba asked, looking Sophia over. "Are you okay?"

Hiker gestured at Sophia. "Obviously she is, or she wouldn't be here right now, putting poison on my desk."

"I'm fine, thank you," Sophia said to Mama Jamba before returning her attention to Hiker. "Thanks for the sympathy. We are fine now, but we almost didn't make it. Gordon Burgress hit us with this device, and it instantly severed our connection. I couldn't communicate with Lunis or scry or do anything that we hold so dear as dragonriders. I was completely cut off. However, by the grace of the angels, he found me, and our bond came back. I won't ever take that for granted, and I will never chance losing it again."

"That's because what you and Lunis have is special," Mama Jamba said proudly.

"What every dragon and rider has is special," Hiker stated, still sounding pissed off. "How did Gordon Burgress get hold of this? I thought he was living off the grid."

"I believe Thad Reinhart found him somehow," Sophia stated. "You said he'd been taking out dragonriders. Well, what if he killed all the lone riders but left one, knowing we'd try to recruit?"

Hiker seemed to be considering this. "Go on, then."

"Gordon Burgress was really confused," Sophia explained. "He seemed himself at one moment and then disoriented, like he was suffering from some sort of brainwashing. He said he and his dragon Sulfur lost memories and were told to use that device on anyone they came in contact with." She pointed to the magical tech still sitting menacingly on the desk. "He said things that didn't seem in line with his character."

"Like implanted ideas?" Hiker asked.

"Yeah, he said something about being severed from the one thing you love," Sophia imparted. "Then he left me when he could have easily killed me. His dragon did the same to Lunis."

"Because the one thing Thad would want more than anything is to rob a dragon and their rider of their connection," Hiker said almost to himself. "That makes sense. He's always felt that if he couldn't have his dragon, then others shouldn't have theirs. Well, ever since what happened to Ember, anyway."

"This actually puts recent events into focus," Mama Jamba said, crossing her legs and bouncing her foot casually.

"What?" Sophia asked, looking at Hiker and Mama Jamba. "What do you mean?"

Hiker let out a breath. "We still don't know what happened to Mahkah and Tala. They are fine, but they both describe being hit by something that seemed to try to separate them mentally. They resisted, and I think the only reason it didn't work was because of the longevity of the connection they have with one another."

"The technology could have also been untested," Sophia offered, indicating the magical tech. "This one worked, but not entirely, although I'm not sure what effect it would have on other dragons and riders."

"This is why I keep stressing her training," Mama Jamba sang. "That's the key here."

"Are you sure?" Hiker asked her.

She shrugged, her lips pursed. "There's no way to know for sure, but Mahkah and Tala were able to resist the attack, whereas it severed

Sophia's and Lunis' connection. It makes sense that Thad hasn't perfected it, and therefore, it only works on riders who haven't earned their wings yet."

Hiker nodded, chewing on his lip. "Go on, Sophia. What else happened?"

"Well," she said, not particularly excited to relate the next bit, "you were right about Gordon Burgress."

Hiker leaned over and pushed a piece of parchment in her direction. "Go ahead and write that down. Those words about me being right. I want proof you said that."

She sighed. "My point is that he wasn't a team player. He wasn't Dragon Elite material. Even before whatever it was infected him and Sulfur, they appeared to be only about themselves, not caring about the world's problems."

"That's right," Hiker stated proudly. "Not every dragonrider is born for us. Who knows why? Oh wait, that woman does." He pointed decisively at Mama Jamba.

She smiled. "I do, in fact, but no one wants a spoiler. Some seeds become trees that shade the forest, while others become weeds. You never know what you're going to get."

"Well, *you* do," Hiker fired back. "So, what happened to Gordon and his dragon?'

Sophia's gaze dropped. "Lunis and I did what we had to do. He was infected. We were certain that if we didn't stop them, they would do something to society or to us. They were working for Thad Reinhart."

Hiker put both his hands in his hair, disbelief heavy in his eyes. "You killed a dragonrider and his dragon who were easily several hundred years older than you?"

Sophia threw up her hands. "When is this stuff going to stop surprising you?"

"You haven't finished your training," Hiker argued. "Actually, you're quite new to life."

"Age and gender should have nothing to do with this." Sophia stuck her hands on her hips.

"I don't believe I said anything about you being female," Hiker stated.

"But you were thinking it," Mama Jamba chimed in.

He cast her a frustrated expression. "Not really appreciated at this point."

"But yes, we ended Gordon Burgress." Sophia pointed to the Elite Globe. "I'd like you to confirm that, though."

Hiker strode over, rotating the globe around until it was centered on the Rocky Mountains. A moment later, he turned back to them, a heavy expression on his face. "You did. Well done."

Sophia shook her head. "My first kill was one of our own. I don't feel good about that."

Hiker nodded, appreciation in his eyes for her statement. "I get that, but you did what you had to. And I agree, it was the right thing to do. Gordon and his dragon were poisoned. They might have tried to come after more of us. Who knows?"

"But he was the last lone rider," Sophia said, realization welling up in her being. "And he was ruined."

Mama Jamba waved this off. "Well, I sort of figured it was a long shot, recruiting the other dragonriders."

Hiker's eyes appeared ready to bulge out of his face. "What? Why did you insist we go after them, then?"

Again, she shrugged innocently. "Just thought it would be good to cross that one off the list. Now you know that who you've got is all you have."

"There are those eggs in the Cave," Hiker argued.

"Yes, but your efforts should be focused on what you have rather than what you might get." Mama Jamba held her hand out to Sophia. "I mean, you've got the first female dragonrider in history and the first one in over a hundred years. There's great magic in that."

"Are you telling me there's a chance to save the Dragon Elite?" Hiker asked, his face deadly serious.

"Hiker," Mama Jamba said, standing, the Southern accent making her sound very smooth. "You're never done until the last candle has been blown out." She leaned in and whispered loudly in the direction

429

of his ear, although she was still a couple of feet away. "Make Sophia your last candle. She's your chance."

Hiker seemed more than perplexed when the robust woman turned and strode for the door.

"Mama?" he said, a question in his voice.

"It's time for my bath, dear Hiker. I'll see you later for your bedtime story," Mama Jamba called over her shoulder.

"Mama," he said again, this time threateningly.

She laughed. "I'm only kidding." Then the woman who was the best of all of them looked at Sophia and winked. "Get that training, dear, would you? I don't like putting pressure on you, but you completing your training is pivotal."

"You've said that before," Sophia stated.

"That's because it's true," Mama Jamba replied. "You completing it isn't guaranteed in any future I've seen, nor anything Papa Creola has, but I know one thing for certain. If and when you finish your training, you might be able to save us all."

"How?" Sophia had to ask.

Mama Jamba smiled. "Oh, no. Like I said before, no spoilers, dear. Just keep that head down and that body moving. Completing your training is crucial. You did well to bond to your sword, but that's only the beginning."

"Mama, we both know that completing training takes time," Hiker stated, annoyance in his voice. "Time I don't believe we have. It's wrong to put so much pressure on her."

Mama Jamba bounced her curls with her hand like a young girl flirting with a boy on the playground. "Oh, I know, but we're talking about Sophia Beaufont. You underestimate her, and that will only make her do better. I encourage you to do so. Tell her she can't. Tell her she won't. Better yet, remind her that she's a girl, and young."

"Mama…" Hiker said, a warning in his voice.

"Don't you 'Mama' me," she interrupted, authority in her tone. "Sophia killed a dragonrider four times her age. She's done a lot you never thought she could do with her lack of experience and whatnot. Keep underestimating her, son. You're just fueling my fire."

Mama Jamba's face turned pleasant once more, her eyes finding Sophia. "Your training, dear. Nothing is more important."

"Okay," Sophia stated. "I'll do my best."

Mama Jamba shook her head. "Oh, no. That won't do, my dear. Do it like your life depends on it. Like all of ours do, because that's absolutely the case."

CHAPTER ONE HUNDRED ONE

I t was hard to get Mama Jamba's ominous words out of her head. However, she did her best as she showered off the battle in the Rocky Mountains. Tomorrow she'd do as she was ordered and start training with a vengeance.

If everything centered on her and Lunis completing training, then she'd give it her all. She'd find the *Complete History of Dragonriders* and learn all the secrets buried somewhere in the Gullington. She'd learn what Quiet was up to, and other secrets that Hiker was keeping. But that would wait for tomorrow when the sun rose and her dragon had recovered.

For now, what Sophia Beaufont needed was very simple. She cast her eyes at the bed against the wall, the covers rolled down and ready for her. But she wasn't ready for it just yet.

"Just one game, Castle?" Sophia asked aloud to the Castle. She didn't have to wait for more than a few seconds before her question was answered and the boxed game *Cards Against Humanity* appeared on the end table next to the sitting area.

It seemed the lynx's advice had come into play. She wasn't sure why, but he had orchestrated things once again.

Sophia snatched up the game, smiling. "Thank you. I promise I won't be long."

A clock appeared beside the door as Sophia strode for it. She paused, reading the time, which wasn't the present one. It read midnight.

Sophia nodded. "I'll be in bed by midnight, Castle. That's a promise."

It was no longer strange to Sophia that she talked to an ancient Castle. It was more of a sentient being than even the House of Fourteen where she had grown up. She never thought anyplace could replace that home in her heart, but there was no comparison to the Castle.

It was her home, her friend, and her guardian. Sophia knew little about the structure, which was more magical than anything she'd ever experienced, but she hoped to one day find out why it was the way it was and how. More riddles to unlock over time.

With the game in her arms, Sophia hurried down the stairs to the dining hall, where she could hear the men arguing and Ainsley cackling with delight.

She was in her pajamas and her hair still wet when she slid into the dining hall as everyone was finishing up their meal.

"Well," Ainsley said in a disapproving tone. "It's about time, S. Beaufont. Because of you, I had to cook."

"Sorry," Sophia said unapologetically. "I was sort of beat after that whole death-defying mission where I lost my dragon and killed a man."

"You've always got an excuse," Ainsley stated, shaking her head of red hair disapprovingly.

"Well, you know I could help you get a phone so you can order your own UberEATS," Sophia offered. "And then you wouldn't have to borrow mine to watch YouTube."

Ainsley lowered her chin. "You know Hiker won't allow that. He says none of us can have phones and technology, but you're grandfathered in because you grew up with it."

"That seems about right," Sophia muttered.

"Well, now that you've shown up late, I bet you want me to go and get you something to eat that isn't cold, don't you?" Ainsley put her hands on her hips, looking annoyed.

"Thank you. That would be lovely," Sophia said, sliding into the chair next to Quiet and smiling at him. "I can't remember the last time I ate."

Ainsley sighed dramatically. "Fine." She held out her hand, and a plate of steaming hot roast beef with roasted vegetables appeared in it. "This really put me out, but I'll let it slide since you were strolling around the Expanse all day."

"Recovering magical tech that could wipe us all out, actually," Sophia corrected, laying the game down between Wilder and Evan.

"Whatever," Ainsley said, striding toward the kitchen. "Same thing, really."

"What's this?" Wilder asked, picking up the game.

"It's a card game I thought we could play," Sophia explained. "I mean, I know you've been asking about video games, but I think it's better if we start with something less technical."

"You mean, something Hiker won't have your head for," Evan said with a laugh.

"Yeah. Again, I don't think he wants you all on electronics, even if you're borrowing them from me," Sophia stated. "I'll work on him, but it might be difficult now that magical tech has turned evil."

Quiet grumbled.

"I agree," Ainsley said to the gnome before turning her attention to Sophia. "And S. Beaufont, can you manage to wear formal clothes at my dinner table? This is Dragon Elite Castle, and you weren't raised in a barn. There are certain customs we must observe."

Sophia looked at Quiet, who she was pretty certain had sheep poop on him, and then at Evan and Wilder, who were both fairly dirty. "I'm clean. Does that count?"

Ainsley sighed. "It absolutely does." She glanced at the men. "Soap. You have heard of it, right? S. Beaufont washes her hair every single day."

"I don't want to know how you know that," Sophia muttered.

"Soap, you say?" Wilder asked. "I haven't heard of this substance."

"Obviously," Ainsley replied, giving her attention back to Sophia. "And I'm simply jealous. I want to wear my pajamas too."

"Well, then, why don't you?" Sophia offered.

The housekeeper's face lit with delight. "Fantastic idea! I do have free will, and can do as I please." She leaned forward, whispering, "Tell Hiker that. And if he finds out about this pajama thing, I'm blaming it on you."

Sophia nodded proudly. "I think he will pretty much always assume that I'm behind any changes he doesn't approve of."

The shapeshifter snapped her fingers, suddenly wearing a long nightgown and a stocking cap. She smiled. "Oh, much better."

"I vote we make it a pajama party," Wilder said, and he also changed into something loose and comfortable. The others joined in.

"So, how do we play this game?" Evan asked, picking up the box.

"Well, the idea," Sophia began to explain, pointing to the game, "is to be as offensive as possible."

"I've already won," Evan said victoriously.

"By matching up cards," Sophia continued, taking the box back. "It isn't a game for the faint of heart, and the worse your answers are, the better."

Quiet leaned over, eyeing the box and muttering.

"I agree," Ainsley said, pulling up a seat. "This will be your game, Quiet."

"What are you all doing?" a voice that Sophia had sorely missed asked from the entry hall. She looked up to see Mahkah, wearing a dressing gown. He was pale but appeared to have recovered.

She stood and went over to him. Without his permission, she threw her arms around him, hugging him to her. "How are you? I've missed you so."

Her dragon trainer blushed, pushing his long black hair behind one ear. "I'm much better. Thank you. I figured it was time I came down and joined you all. When I heard the noise, I couldn't resist."

"And you're dressed for the occasion," Ainsley said, gesturing at the table, where everyone was wearing their pajamas. "Now, I think we just need one more thing to do this up right." She tapped the side of her head, where the scar was always present, even when she shapeshifted. "Where does that man keep his stash? Oh, that's right."

She snapped her fingers, and two bottles of whiskey appeared on the table, surrounded by small tumblers.

"Where did you get that?" Wilder asked curiously.

"From Hiker's room," Ainsley said with a laugh.

"I won't tell if you all don't," Evan called, pouring everyone a glass.

Mahkah and Sophia settled down with everyone at the table as the Scotch was passed around. She handed out the cards as they all lifted their glasses, celebrating that Mahkah was almost back to normal, that everyone was home at the Gullington, and that hopefully, tomorrow brought answers to old questions and new problems.

Sophia took her first sip of whiskey. She was certain it would not be her last, just as she hoped to have many more adventures with the people surrounding her right then in the Gullington.

The Dragon Elite might be small in numbers, but these were the best people in the world, and she had no doubt they would save it one day.

SARAH'S AUTHOR NOTES

NOVEMBER 2019

Thank you so much for reading. Your support of the Liv Beaufont series and this one has been life changing. Thank you! Seriously! Thank you.

Recently, Michael and I met in Vegas shortly after the first book hit. We were there for a conference that was simply the best ever and super exhausting. I dressed up as a ninja one day because Malorie Cooper convinced me it was a good idea. I almost bailed at the last moment, but decided to put on the costume because disclaimer, I've always wanted to be a freaking ninja. And the result was: best day ever!

One of the best parts of the day was when I came downstairs in the hotel to find Steve Campbell (Operations guru for LMBPN) innocently walking across the casino. I pulled up my mask and very un-ninja-like pranced between the slot machines making him double over from laughter. I was simply the worst ninja ever and that made it all the better.

Then I went to lunch with Ramy Vance where every time he'd ask me a question, I'd reply with, "Yeah, I'm a mother-freaking ninja." I'm not sure it was as productive of a meeting as Ramy hoped. I don't get out much, what can I say. Anyway, now I've got a reputation as a photo bombing ninja. I'm mostly proud of this, but ask me again in a few months.

Okay, back to Michael and Vegas. You see how I derail so effortlessly. It's a gift. Anyway, I stalked Michael for a meeting because the man was in high demand, as you'd expect. When we finally sat down, it was great. I shared many things I hadn't told him this year, like how I was so close to quitting this author business. And then Liv hit and everything absolutely changed. I changed. And Michael was very much a catalyst to that. I really value that I can confide these things in him, although sometimes it takes me a bit because I want to pretend I've got it all together and he can count on me for the books. But at the end of the day, Michael knows I'm human and not actually a badass ninja.

After our heart to heart, Michael and I outlined the major arcs for the rest of the series. We had originally planned three books for Sophia. It was impossible to know if the series would be a hit or not. Well, thanks to you all, it is. And now you can look forward to 12 giant books! That means next year I plan to write 19 books. I better go put back on my ninja suit. I couldn't be happier that the series inspired by the fierceness of my little girl, Lydia, is a success. And I'm so grateful to still be doing this author business. Thank you to you and to Michael.

I write these author notes after marathon writing the second book. It always hits me when I finish and I feel like I've been knocked down by a truck. While writing, I'm high as a kite (figuratively) and hardly sleep or eat. And then I write, "the end" and totally crash. It will pass. It always does and tomorrow I'll start book 3. But the most exciting part of this for me, is that I'll be writing book 3 in Scotland, the location of the Gullington.

I've been wanting to go to Scotland ever since the 20Booksto50K conference in July that was in Edinburgh. Due to circumstances, I had to cancel that trip. And then I started writing this series and set it in Scotland and I *really* wanted to go. JL Hendricks kept trying to entice me and she's quite persuasive. The opportunity arose and the timing worked out perfectly, as happens when the universe is conspiring.

And so, this week I head to Scotland. I'll be staying in Old Town Edinburgh, next to the Castle. I plan to write book three in pubs that are from the 1700s and get lost in the city and find new ideas.

I've written 15 books this year and I've loved every minute of it. But something in my soul told me that if I was going to write 10 more Sophia books that I needed to refill the creative tank. I don't just want to describe the hills in Scotland as green. Or talk about the Castle and call it old. I want to catalogue smells, feel the cold winds and meet the people who are an inspiration for the setting of the Exceptional S. Beaufont series.

I don't think I'll actually meet a Viking named Hiker Wallace, but I plan to chat with a lot of Scotsmen in kilts and learn as much about the culture as possible. And hopefully that makes the series that much richer.

A couple of things about the cover. In the first one, we obstructed MA's name but I forgot to mention it in the author's notes. We tried to do it on this one but it didn't work when we resized the dragon. The idea was to block out his name on each cover and say that it was because he pissed off Lunis. Also, this cover was in the bag when I realized something of great importance. We had Sophia as a brunette. She's a Beaufont and modeled after Lydia—a very blonde little girl. So I felt sort of ditzy when I went back to the designer and was like, "Oh, yeah, I forgot that my character is blonde. Quick change, please." Anyway, thankful for the awesome team of people I work with who are understanding when my brain stops working.

And you all can thank Crystal, a wonderful reader, for the Linus joke. She asked for that specifically. I love suggestions and try to include them when I can.

I've also enjoyed dropping in pop culture references that keep this more urban fantasy. It's fun including all the TV references. Martin, another awesome reader, and I have fun talking about Father Ted and other BBC shows that inspire many of the references in this book.

Again, I'm feeling so grateful that the series is doing well and you're enjoying it. I'm feeling grateful for Michael and LMBPN. And more than anything, I'm glad I know the real Sophia. She's my muse, always and forever.

Okay, I'm turning this over to Mike and I'm not even going to call him a name this time. See, being a ninja has really matured me.

MICHAEL'S AUTHOR NOTES

DECEMBER 14, 2019

Thank you so much for reading our tales of adventure and our author notes here in the back of the books.

I'm presently in Cabo San Lucas, typing this from a small restaurant area overlooking the very southern tip of the Sea of Cortez. If I turned around and strained my eyes, I could see the Pacific.

I'm feeling very old and creaky, and really do NOT desire to turn around and pull a muscle at the moment, so will console myself with only the sea.

Four years ago (2015) I was just releasing book 04 of The Kurtherian Gambit. I had written book 03 right here at the resort I'm staying at (The Pacifica at Quivera.) I had no idea where my life was going and how it would change.

I certainly did NOT know a short bad-ass ninja named Sarah Noffke at the time, but I do now. It is amazing (to me) how life can take forty-nine years to become an overnight success and how much work is involved.

Same as with Sarah.

A year ago, Sarah was considering leaving the authoring business and getting a job to make sure she took care of her daughter. I had already told her that if she worked with LMBPN, I'd do my best for her (but would it be enough?)

Enter the discussion that changed it for both of us, the Liv Beaufont series and now the S. Beaufont series.

I bring this up only to highlight that you NEVER know what small effort is going to change your future. For an artist, it could be the next painting. For a songwriter, it could be a star picking up your song or it touches a nerve on Youtube.

For a writer, it could be a series patterned after yourself and the people that are in your life.

I personally believe that some of the best stories are those with great characters we want to spend time with as readers. Add fun, some snark, action and friendship and I'm usually right there reading along.

It's odd, though. When I create characters my mind can become very 'ho-hum' and be horrible about giving me ideas. Let me talk with another author, and I can always pull out three items of interest from their own life to help create a compelling character I'd like to know more about.

I probably need to do more talking with people.

If you ever see Sarah Noffke in person, ask her about her friend which became the character Rory.

I wonder if she ever mentioned to him that he's a giant in her books?

I look forward to a great 2020 and hope you all have a fantastic new year!

Ad Aeternitatem,

Michael

ACKNOWLEDGMENTS

SARAH NOFFKE

I feel like I'm on the stage at the Oscars, accepting an award when I write my acknowledgments. I stand there, holding this award, my hands shaking and my words racing around in my mind. I'm not an actress for a reason. I'm a writer and talking to people in "real life" is hard. Not to mention a ton of people all at once.

I picture looking out at the audience and being blinded by spotlights and forgetting every word of the speech I memorized just in case I won. The speech would go like this and it's meant for all of you, not the guild. For the fans. The supporters. The people who are the reason I would ever stand on any stage, ever.

Okay, here we go. I clear my throat and smile, looking up at the camera, holding the little golden man. And then I begin:

This was never supposed to happen. I was never meant to publish a book and then another one. And then another. I was supposed to write in private and live a life that Henry David Thoreau called a life of "quiet desperation." I would always hope to share my books, but never bring myself to do it. And you would never read my words. But then, in a crazed moment of brashness, I did share my books and you all liked them. And because of that, I've never been the same. And here I am feeling grateful all just because...

That's why I'm here. Because of you. Thank you to my first readers. The ones who picked up those books that I didn't even outline and you still liked them. You messaged me and maybe you thought it was no big deal, but when your ego is new to the publishing world, it's a big deal.

I can't thank you readers enough. I've found that reading your reviews helps me to start a chapter when I'm stuck or lazy.

I really need to thank someone who has made this all possible and that's my father. I was going to quit. I can't tell you how many times I quit. But when I wasn't making it, he was the one who told me to not throw in the towel. "Give yourself a timeline," he suggested. If I didn't get to my goal by then, I'd quit. And apparently there was magic in that advice, because I'm still doing this. Dad, you're the pragmatic one, but when you believed in me enough to tell me to not quit, I knew I had to follow your advice.

And I thank all my friends who are constantly supporting me with thoughts of love and encouragement. Most don't read my books. I'm sort of self-deprecating, although I'm working on it and will be the first to tell my friends, "My books probably aren't for you." However, every now and then a friend surprises me and says, "I was up all night reading your books." It's always a total shock. But my point is, that even if they didn't read, I still have the best friends ever. Diane, you're my rock. And I love you, even though you will probably not read this.

Thank you to everyone at LMBPN. Those people are like family to me, although I'm not sure if they'll let me sleep on their couch. Well, who am I kidding? They totally will. Big thanks to Steve, Lynne, Mihaela, Kelly, Jen and the entire team. The JIT members are the best.

Huge thank you to the LMBPN Ladies group on Facebook. Micky, you're the best. And that group keeps me sane.

And a giant thank you to the betas for this series. Juergen you are my first reader and friend. Thanks for all the help. And thanks to Martin and Crystal for being some of the best people I know. What would I do without you? A huge thanks to the ARC team. Seriously, if it weren't for you all I might pass out before release day, wondering if anyone will like the book.

And with all my books, my final thank you goes to my lovely muse, Lydia. Oh sweet darling, I write these books for you, but ironically, I couldn't write them without you. You are my inspiration. My sounding board. And the reason that I want to succeed. I love you.

Thank you all! I'm sorry if I forgot anyone. Blame Michael. For no other reason than just because.

BOOKS BY SARAH NOFFKE

Sarah Noffke writes YA and NA science fiction, fantasy, paranormal and urban fantasy. In addition to being an author, she is a mother, podcaster and professor. Noffke holds a Masters of Management and teaches college business/writing courses. Most of her students have no idea that she toils away her hours crafting fictional characters. www.sarahnoffke.com

Check out other work by Sarah author here.

Ghost Squadron:

Formation #1:
   Kill the bad guys. Save the Galaxy. All in a hard day's work.
   After ten years of wandering the outer rim of the galaxy, Eddie Teach is a man without a purpose. He was one of the toughest pilots in the Federation, but now he's just a regular guy, getting into bar fights and making a difference wherever he can. It's not the same as flying a ship and saving colonies, but it'll have to do.
   That is, until General Lance Reynolds tracks Eddie down and offers him a job. There are bad people out there, plotting terrible

things, killing innocent people, and destroying entire colonies. **Someone has to stop them.**

Eddie, along with the genetically-enhanced combat pilot Julianna Fregin and her trusty E.I. named Pip, must recruit a diverse team of specialists, both human and alien. They'll need to master their new Q-Ship, one of the most powerful strike ships ever constructed. And finally, they'll have to stop a faceless enemy so powerful, it threatens to destroy the entire Federation.

All in a day's work, right?

Experience this exciting military sci-fi saga and the latest addition to the expanded Kurtherian Gambit Universe. If you're a fan of Mass Effect, Firefly, or Star Wars, you'll love this riveting new space opera.

NOTE: If cursing is a problem, then this might not be for you.

Check out the entire series <u>here</u>.

The Precious Galaxy Series:

Corruption #1

A new evil lurks in the darkness.

After an explosion, the crew of a battlecruiser mysteriously disappears.

Bailey and Lewis, complete strangers, find themselves suddenly onboard the damaged ship. Lewis hasn't worked a case in years, not since the final one broke his spirit and his bank account. The last thing Bailey remembers is preparing to take down a fugitive on Onyx Station.

Mysteries are harder to solve when there's no evidence left behind.

Bailey and Lewis don't know how they got onboard *Ricky Bobby* or why. However, they quickly learn that whatever was responsible for the explosion and disappearance of the crew is still on the ship.

Monsters are real and what this one can do changes everything.

The new team bands together to discover what happened and how to fight the monster lurking in the bottom of the battlecruiser.

Will they find the missing crew? Or will the monster end them all?

The Soul Stone Mage Series:

House of Enchanted #1:

The Kingdom of Virgo has lived in peace for thousands of years...until now.

The humans from Terran have always been real assholes to the witches of Virgo. Now a silent war is brewing, and the timing couldn't be worse. Princess Azure will soon be crowned queen of the Kingdom of Virgo.

In the Dark Forest a powerful potion-maker has been murdered.

Charmsgood was the only wizard who could stop a deadly virus plaguing Virgo. He also knew about the devastation the people from Terran had done to the forest.

Azure must protect her people. Mend the Dark Forest. Create alliances with savage beasts. No biggie, right?

But on coronation day everything changes. Princess Azure isn't who she thought she was and that's a big freaking problem.

Welcome to The Revelations of Oriceran. Check out the entire series here.

The Lucidites Series:

Awoken, #1:

Around the world humans are hallucinating after sleepless nights.

In a sterile, underground institute the forecasters keep reporting the same events.

And in the backwoods of Texas, a sixteen-year-old girl is about to be caught up in a fierce, ethereal battle.

Meet Roya Stark. She drowns every night in her dreams, spends her hours reading classic literature to avoid her family's ridicule, and is prone to premonitions—which are becoming more frequent. And now her dreams are filled with strangers offering to reveal what she has always wanted to know: Who is she? That's the question that haunts her, and she's about to find out. But will Roya live to regret learning the truth?

Stunned, #2

Revived, #3

The Reverians Series:

Defects, #1:

In the happy, clean community of Austin Valley, everything appears to be perfect. Seventeen-year-old Em Fuller, however, fears something is askew. Em is one of the new generation of Dream Travelers. For some reason, the gods have not seen fit to gift all of them with their expected special abilities. Em is a Defect—one of the unfortunate Dream Travelers not gifted with a psychic power. Desperate to do whatever it takes to earn her gift, she endures painful daily injections along with commands from her overbearing, loveless father. One of the few bright spots in her life is the return of a friend she had thought dead—but with his return comes the knowledge of a shocking, unforgivable truth. The society Em thought was protecting her has actually been betraying her, but she has no idea how to break away from its authority without hurting everyone she loves.

Rebels, #2

Warriors, #3

Vagabond Circus Series:

Suspended, #1:

When a stranger joins the cast of Vagabond Circus—a circus that is run by Dream Travelers and features real magic—mysterious events start happening. The once orderly grounds of the circus become riddled with hidden threats. And the ringmaster realizes not only are his circus and its magic at risk, but also his very life.

Vagabond Circus caters to the skeptics. Without skeptics, it would close its doors. This is because Vagabond Circus runs for two reasons and only two reasons: first and foremost to provide the lost and lonely Dream Travelers a place to be illustrious. And secondly, to show the nonbelievers that there's still magic in the world. If they believe, then they care, and if they care, then they don't destroy. They stop the small abuse that day-by-day breaks down humanity's spirit. If Vagabond Circus makes one skeptic believe in magic, then they halt the cycle, just a little bit. They allow a little more love into this world. That's Dr. Dave Raydon's mission. And that's why this ringmaster recruits. That's why he directs. That's why he puts on a show that makes people question their beliefs. He wants the world to believe in magic once again.

Paralyzed, #2
Released, #3

Ren Series:

Ren: The Man Behind the Monster, #1:
Born with the power to control minds, hypnotize others, and read thoughts, Ren Lewis, is certain of one thing: God made a mistake. No one should be born with so much power. A monster awoke in him the same year he received his gifts. At ten years old. A prepubescent boy with the ability to control others might merely abuse his powers, but Ren allowed it to corrupt him. And since he can have and do anything he wants, Ren should be happy. However, his journey teaches him that harboring so much power doesn't bring happiness, it steals it. Once this realization sets in, Ren makes up his mind to do the one thing that can bring his tortured soul some peace. He must kill the monster.

Note This book is NA and has strong language, violence and sexual references.

Ren: God's Little Monster, #2
Ren: The Monster Inside the Monster, #3
Ren: The Monster's Adventure, #3.5
Ren: The Monster's Death

Olento Research Series:

Alpha Wolf, #1:
Twelve men went missing.

Six months later they awake from drug-induced stupors to find themselves locked in a lab.

And on the night of a new moon, eleven of those men, possessed by new—and inhuman—powers, break out of their prison and race through the streets of Los Angeles until they disappear one by one into the night.

Olento Research wants its experiments back. Its CEO, Mika Lenna, will tear every city apart until he has his werewolves imprisoned once again. He didn't undertake a huge risk just to lose his would-be assassins.

However, the Lucidite Institute's main mission is to save the world from injustices. Now, it's Adelaide's job to find these mutated men and protect them and society, and fast. Already around the nation, wolflike men are being spotted. Attacks on innocent women are happening. And then, Adelaide realizes what her next step must be: She has to find the alpha wolf first. Only once she's located him can she stop whoever is behind this experiment to create wild beasts out of human beings.

Lone Wolf, #2
Rabid Wolf, #3
Bad Wolf, #4

BOOKS BY MICHAEL ANDERLE

For a complete list of books by Michael Anderle, please visit:

www.lmbpn.com/ma-books/

All LMBPN Audiobooks are Available at Audible.com and iTunes

To see all LMBPN audiobooks, including those written by Michael Anderle
please visit:

www.lmbpn.com/audible

CONNECT WITH THE AUTHORS

Connect with Sarah and sign up for her email list here:

http://www.sarahnoffke.com/connect/

You can catch her podcast, LA Chicks, here:

http://lachicks.libsyn.com/

Connect with Michael Anderle and sign up for his email list here:

Website: http://lmbpn.com

Email List: http://lmbpn.com/email/

Facebook:
www.facebook.com/TheKurtherianGambitBooks

CPSIA information can be obtained
at www.ICGtesting.com
Printed in the USA
FSHW020546160620
71240FS